Truth Revealed

A NOVEL

EBONY ESSENCE

outskirts
press

This book is dedicated to my children, Elijah and Nia. Always stay true to yourself; never let anyone tell you that your imagination is too wild. Let your imagination run free and see where it takes you, because you never know where it will lead. I Love You, Mommy.

And to my other half, Maurice, thank you my love for your patience, friendship, humor, unconditional support and catching all my typos. (I guess you can say you're a "reader" now).

To my strong and beautiful mother. Thank you for blazing the trail of success. Your Life lessons and unconditional love has helped mold me into becoming the woman I am today. Thank you for teaching me that Diva's NEVER settle. With Love Always.

Dad, thank you for ALWAYS loving and protecting me. Thank you for helping me to discover: every little girl should know what it feels like to be treated like a princess, for when she grows up, she'll REMEMBER that she is a QUEEN. I wear my crown with confidence... I love you more than words can say.

You May Not Understand today or tomorrow, but eventually God will reveal why you went through everything you did
-unknown

Chapter One

"Devin, Devin, I know you hear me talking to you, answer me." I was beyond pissed.

This was really happening. I felt like I was outside myself, watching my life spiral out of control and there wasn't shit I could do about it.

I didn't understand it. I mean… I AM La'Dai Roswell, yes that's right "La'Dai" pronounce La-Day, with an "I" not a "Y". With that being said, allow me to reintroduce myself. La'Dai Roswell…alumni Grambling State University, happily married to Devin Roswell, entrepreneurs of five businesses, which includes our very own commercial real estate company, Roswell, LLC.

My slender petite body stood five feet five inches tall, with my size four waist mapping into my curvy hips that met a pair of sexy thick thighs and let's not forget about my Georgia peach ass to match. Baby was bad, not to mention a smile that could make a grown man blush. Modeling was never my thing, but I could have put all of those magazine cover models to shame. I had it all together. Was I sure of myself? Damn straight I was.

It took me years to become the woman I am. So, to downplay myself would be an injustice. Let's just say growing up in high society and having your best attribute be intelligence didn't necessarily put me with the "in crowd." It was rough. Once I got rid of the acne, the braces and put some meat on my bones that fell into all the right places, it was on from there. It wasn't until my freshman year in college that this diamond in the rough started to shine. That's when I met Devin. He came along and rocked my world.

Everything was perfect, until it wasn't.

There I stood in front of Devin, wearing a red pencil skirt and a black very sexy Victoria Secret push up bra that my cleavage was spilling out of. My curly black hair draped over my bare shoulders falling past my bra strap.

"Devin," I said as my voice caught in my throat; I was trying not to cry. "We've been through some things but choosing our god-daughters seventh birthday party as a platform to announce your desire for a divorce, really? In this moment I'm still your wife and you owe me an explanation."

I couldn't believe what I was saying. Didn't I say I was happily married? I thought he was too. I mean I know things had gotten a bit off course but that's marriage. Better or worse. Thick or thin. Did he not get the memo?

"I mean what's going on, Dee?" I demanded Devin to give me an answer.

Devin was my rock. He was young, ambitious, tolerant and easygoing. He had an adventurous personality and treated me like a queen. I was never into athletes while I was in high school but once I got to college and saw that college guys had much more to offer physically, I stopped limiting myself to the below average male species. I wanted to explore. Devin was six feet tall; basketball had done his body well. His trim build was maintained in the gym five days a week, and it wasn't overly muscular. He wore a neatly cut fade and a shiny goatee that curved around his smooth–as-butter full lips.

He looked up at me with his almond-shaped eyes as he sat at

the edge of our Cal-king bed taking off his shoes.

"Look LD, my intention wasn't to put us on blast." His voice was deep but calming. "This isn't easy for me either. I love you and we've had a beautiful life together but it's time for me to turn the page onto something else. I'm not the man I was when we graduated college, eleven years ago and got married. Things have changed and I think it would be in the best interest of both of us if we got a divorce. It's time for me to live a different way; being married is not what's best for me right now or you."

I couldn't believe my ears. I was still holding back tears of disbelief.

Before I knew it, I yelled, "Who is she or he?" As the words came rolling off my tongue, I knew better. Devin had always held me in the highest regard. He never even so much as glanced at another woman.

An angry look flashed across his face and he replied, "You know damn well I would never disrespect you and cheat on you with another woman and I'm going to ignore the "he" part of that question."

"Then what is it? Are you going through some type of midlife crisis, this is not us. We communicate better than this, Devin. And now you're wanting a divorce with little to no explanation."

Devin stood up, grabbed my left hand as he came closer and said, "I've always had the utmost respect for you and our marriage." He was right. "I'm being honest with you; it's time that I live a life that's more about me. LD, you're going to be alright, I've set you up real nice."

"You selfish bas…"

"Watch yourself." He quickly corrected me, my emotions were starting to rise high, and I was on the brink of letting him have it and rightfully so.

"What the hell does that mean, Devin?"

He pulled out a stack of documents from the top drawer of his side of the dresser. It listed all of our assets and accounts. From our six-bedroom home, to rental properties, all five businesses, cars, stocks, and bonds. Everything was detailed regarding who would take ownership of what and, from what I could see, I was getting the majority.

This wasn't making any damn sense. My head was spinning.

He continued, "You deserve a great life, with kids and a husband who can give you forever, someone you can continue to build with. Just so we're clear, as far as the businesses go, you can keep all of our commercial real estate and we will split the rental properties. I'm going to keep and run the barber shop. Danny Lanes has always been close to me."

Danny Lanes Barbershop was one of our startup businesses. We named it after Devin's late father, Danny Lane Roswell, who passed away while we were in college.

I wanted so bad to slap some sense into his ass. Mad was not the word to describe how upset I was, hotter than fish grease on Friday. I calmly gathered myself, "We're not doing this. I'm not losing my husband, my best friend or the only life I know and have worked so hard to build." I was serious and he knew it.

I walked into the kitchen and poured a full glass of Dom Perignon I was saving for our eleven-year anniversary.

"I guess I won't need this," I said to myself as I drank straight out the bottle. Wait. Was I accepting this? Hell no. In that moment, the truth was: the longer I stood there in my beautifully designed kitchen, the more I was reminded of how my life was about to change. Who was I kidding? Our connection had been off for months, but I will admit I still didn't see this coming.

I decided to get into my car and drive to my parents' house. My parents modeled the life I wanted to live. They were a respectable black couple who successfully owned many businesses and made marriage look easy. So, I had no choice but to go and talk to one of the wisest women I knew, my momma. I knew her advice would be solid.

The drive from Sherman Oaks to View Park was going to be brutal at this hour. LA traffic was no joke, but the time I spent in traffic was what I needed to pull myself together anyway before I saw Ma. I knew she would not want to be invited to my pity party.

As I pulled onto the 405 freeway, I let the top down on my ruby red 2020 Lexus LC 500 convertible. The top was down, and I could feel the sun beaming down on the back of my neck, reminding me that it was summertime in June.

"Google...play Tamar Braxton's Love and War." I said aloud. I turned the music up and began having my own self's concert. Hell, I even thought about saying to hell with it, I'd throw myself a divorce party. If he wasn't going to fight for us, why should I?

Music gave me life. It expressed my feelings when I wasn't able to put them into words. It touched my soul. I turned the volume up even louder and entered into music therapy.

We'll just be chillin and laughin, I'm lying on your chest. Don't know what happened cause things just went left... The lyrics to Tamar's song pierced my soul, I felt such heartbreak, it was like someone had just ripped my heart completely out of my chest. It hurt like hell. I sang the song to the top of my lungs. Traffic was moving at 15 miles per hour, and I didn't care who heard me. I wanted someone to hear me because Devin sure as hell didn't. The thought of the divorce sent tears rushing down my face, along with my mascara.

The drive was long, and I went through a range of emotions. From Tamar Braxton's Love and War, to Beyoncé's Irreplaceable, and Big Sean's I Don't Fuck with you, music was blaring from my sound system. I was on an emotional roller coaster to say the least.

Finally, I was five minutes away from my parents' house. I pulled over, let the top up on the convertible and played Mary J. Blige's Just Fine as I reapplied my makeup.

Turning into my parents' driveway I could see that my sister, Sasha, was there. Sasha always parked sideways in the driveway, claiming she didn't want to be blocked in. My mood changed instantly, she brought out the best in me. Sasha wasn't my blood sister, my parents adopted her when she was about two years old, but you would have thought she came screaming out of Ma's punani just like I did; we were inseparable.

I rushed in, arms open wide, "Sash, hey boo." She greeted me back with a big smile on her face.

"Hey Sis."

"I'm so happy you're here," I said.

"Not for long, I was just heading out, going to get my hair done. Got a hot date tonight. I think I found my next ex-boyfriend," she said jokingly.

Little did she know, we were both soon to be a part of the "men" search party.

"Well, call me later."

"Six o' clock on the dot just like any other day."

"Okay baby, be safe."

"Always," she shouted, rushing out the door. "Oh, Ma's out back on the patio. Love you."

"Bye." I waved and went to find Ma.

Although my parents had other properties, View Park is where home was. View Park was crowned as the "Black Beverly Hills." View Park was rich with style and elegance. From tree-lined sidewalks to beautifully manicured lawns; and exclusively designed houses and mansions. With surrounding cities: Ladera Heights and Baldwin Hills, getting where you needed to go was within arm's reach. I mean View Park was once a place to call home for

Ike and Tina Turner.

Mom and Dad were determined to make the memories last forever in that house. Ma made me and Sasha promise to keep it in the family. Which I could understand. Unlike Sasha and me, my parents didn't grow up with money and opportunities like we did. Dad grew up in the tough streets of Watts and Ma in the city of Compton. But Dad had the mindset that anything was possible, all you needed was the right opportunity with the right attitude to match, and skies were the limit. In their younger days, Ma had friends not too far from where Dad lived, they met, and Dad fell in love with Ma. He didn't waste any time marrying her. Dad was left with a small inheritance from his grandmother not a heck of a lot of money, but Dad was wise. He made some really smart investments, enough to start a new life with Ma. And the rest is black history.

"Hi Ma," I greeted her with a kiss on the cheek.

"Oh, hi baby girl, you just missed your sister, she ran out of here so fast."

"Oh no, I saw her."

"Well, what brings you over on this beautiful summer afternoon?"

I moved from the outdoor lounge chaise I was sitting in onto the sofa seat next to Ma.

"Oh Mommy," I said as I laid on her shoulder, my voice starting to crack.

"Uh-oh, let me brace myself. When you call me Mommy either you did something wrong, or someone hurt my baby."

Me and Ma always had a great relationship. She had a way of being open and judgment free while still being motherly. She was my heart.

"Mommy, Devin wants a divorce."

"Oh, LD honey, I'm sorry. Did he say why?"

"Ma, he says it's time for him to live a different life, but I don't understand it. I can't stomach living without my husband; this is a hard pill to swallow. I just don't know what to do," I was rambling on and sobbing like a two-year-old child. My words were starting to become unclear behind all the crying.

"LD, we are going to talk about this, but you need to cut out all that crying. Stop being at the mercy of your emotions. Sometimes in life, it takes a good fall to really know where you stand. Now I know it's easier said than done but you're not the first woman to get a divorce nor will you be the last, you will survive. And another thing: if you know you've been a good wife and you've done nothing wrong then let things unfold naturally."

"So… don't fight for my marriage?"

"Baby, sometimes it takes two to fight. And sometimes God has something else planned for our lives far beyond what we can see."

Ma handed me a Kleenex, and in two seconds it was covered with all of my MAC makeup.

"La'Dai, nothing in life is promised. Nor is anything in life forever, people either break up or someone dies. This means you count your blessings, remember the good times, and move on when the time comes. Now I'm not saying this is going to be easy, but I promise you one day you'll look back and everything will make sense. Proverbs three verses five to six, tells us to trust in the Lord, and to lean not on our own understanding. Trust me, baby girl, this too shall pass. In the meantime, I'll be here every step of the way."

Ma was right. She always had a way of helping situations make sense when she added the scripture into the mix. Ma went to church faithfully, raised me and Sasha as Christians. It just seemed like the older I became the busier I got and did not have time to make it to church. But the foundation was laid and every now and again I'd watch Joel Osteen on YouTube.

She continued on to say, "Now what you need to do is go home, meditate, clear your head and get a good night's rest. That's my recipe for stress and it works every time."

Dad came outside in a panic. I guess he could hear me crying from inside.

"What's going on out here? La'Dai, honey, are you okay?" Dad asked.

"No," I replied and before I could say another word Ma interrupted me.

"But she will be."

"What's going on?"

"Dad, Devin and I are getting a divorce. And I don't understand what's happening and why. This is not the life I know, Dad. The life I know is being married for 30 plus years like you and Ma. Where did I go wrong?"

"A lot of times LD things don't make sense to us. There's this wise saying, 'believe none of what you hear and half of what you see.' What I mean by that is, situations aren't always what they seem. I know Devin loves you but it's his life and his decision."

"How can you say that Dad? Are you taking his side?"

"No, honey, I'm not. But Devin came to me man to man and told me what he was going to do. He didn't go into much detail as to why, but he was respectful and logical in a sense; he promised me he would not hurt you in any of this. He told me that when the time is right, he would explain more. We had a long serious conversation. And I respect the things he had to say."

"Dad, why didn't you tell me that this was coming?"

"LD, I don't get into married couple's business, they're forbidden areas. When you two said I do, I adopted Devin as my son and until he does something that crosses the line. I've opted to stay in my lane."

"Daddy, this is crossing the line."

"No, honey, he's ending the marriage because he thinks it's best. From what he says, there's no malicious intent involved. Now I've always had to tread lightly when it came to the beautiful women in my life. I respect your feelings and they're valid. But the best advice I can give you honey is accept things for what they are and move forward the best way you can. I know there's a lot more life for you to live."

"Dad, I really don't want to hear that right now."

"Just be happy that you have a good support system to help you through this. And be happy knowing that the man was honest with you and isn't trying to take you for everything you have, like in divorces that other people have gone through. I'm just trying to give you some perspective, honey."

Dad gave me a hug and went back into the house.

I tried having dinner with my parents but was in a daze the entire time. The more I saw how happy my parents were, the sadder I got. I decided to end dinner early and head home.

Once I got home and noticed that Devin hadn't made it in yet, my first thought was to fall into Bernadine mode and Waiting to Exhale his ass. Burn all his shit. Armani suits, red bottoms, Gucci belts, Versace, Louis Vuitton, everything. Except I wasn't going to stop at burning up one car. Nah, I was going to put a spin on it and drive one car into the other, Yeah, his pretty little BMW that was parked in the garage was going to have to go too. But I thought about how my garage would burn up right along with his shit and I couldn't have that. I looked up and saw our wedding picture in the entryway, and it brought me back to reality. The conversation I had with my parents resonated with me and I decided to take a hot bath and calm down instead.

I thought I had the black card to Devin's heart. In my eyes our love had no limits. We were forever.

The bath water started to get cold, and I was getting sleepy. I could hear Devin downstairs coming in from the garage, then dishes rattling in the kitchen.

I started to blow out the candles around the bathtub and dry myself off.

"LD, you still awake?" He yelled up from downstairs.

"Yes, I am," I responded with an irritated tone.

"Oh, you're taking a bath?" he asked as he walked into the bathroom and stopped in the doorway.

I didn't respond, I mean it was obvious and I was in no mood for small talk. I noticed Devin had two wine glasses in his hands. I grew curious.

"What's up, Devin?"

"Look LD, we need to talk."

"No, no we don't. Not tonight at least. I'm tired and mentally drained. I responded getting out the bathtub. "Plus, we have a meeting tomorrow to talk about the vacant lot we just purchased. BUT...I will take the glass of wine. Thanks," I said arrogantly as I grabbed the glass out of his hand and walked past him naked.

I took a big gulp of the Merlot, sat it onto my nightstand and started to lotion my body.

As he pulled out his pajamas from the dresser drawer and took off his pants, I could see his manhood starting to rise.

"I think it would be best if you slept in one of the guest bedrooms, Devin."

"Nope, that's not happening."

"What do you want from me? Huh? One minute you're asking me for a divorce, now you want to talk things out and sleep together? I'm not to be played with."

He said, "Look, all I want to do is talk. But since you're not in the mood for that maybe you're in the mood for this."

He pulled me close to him, put both of my breasts in his

hands then his mouth. I could feel my body starting to get hot and my kitty cat starting to purr. I was tingling, wanting badly to jump right on top of him and let him have his way with me while holding me up against the wall, but I knew I couldn't let this go any further.

I pushed him away, "What the hell are you doing? This isn't some movie fairy tale BS, where we kiss and make up. Go into the other room, Devin."

He calmly responded, "I'm not asking for your forgiveness, nor do I need permission to want to make love to my wife."

Again, I was confused.

He grabbed me again and this time he pulled me even closer, I could feel the tip of his penis pressing against the top of my inner thigh, as he placed his hands on the small of my back. Devin moved my hair to one side of my neck and started to kiss me from the side of my neck down to my navel. He knew damn well that was my soft spot. His lips moved from my navel, around to my back and up to my neck again, and he slightly turned my chin, where his lips met mine. He kissed me hard and passionately, I gently bit his lower lip and stuck my tongue right into his mouth and he took it in like it like there was no tomorrow. Still trying to play hard to get, I moaned, "Devin, I'm seri…"

It felt so good to know that he still wanted me. To know that I was still desirable to him. I guess being naked played a part too.

I began to moan louder as he slipped his fingers inside of me. My nipples were hard, and I was wet. Devin always knew exactly what to do. What to touch and when to touch it. I was always satisfied and wanting more of him.

He grabbed my left hand and put it into his boxers. He hardened as I touched him, I could feel his thick veins on both sides of his penis. He was rock hard. Standing at full attention. I used my other hand to pull his boxers down and off, when that was done, I used that same hand to massage his sack. One hand was stroking him up and down and the other was in full around and about motion. I could tell by the way he was panting that he was ready to go all in.

He turned me around, bent me over the bed and entered me from behind. He pulled it back out and put it back again. There was no turning back for me once he teased me like that. I moaned louder and louder as he went deeper inside of me. He pulled my hair; each thrust was hard and strong. My back was arched, and I was loving every minute. At this point, I didn't want him to stop. I could feel his warm body against mine.

"Don't stop, please don't stop." I moaned over and over again until my legs began to shake, and I had one of the best orgasms I'd had in a long time.

My legs stopped shaking and the moans became faint. Devin kissed me on my right cheek and whispered in my ear, "I love you." Still bent over the bed, I rested on the bed with my head in my hands. I was back to reality and left to face our ugly truth.

I woke up the next morning feeling more confused than I did the night before. I was satisfied sexually yet in mental anguish. Satisfied because Devin always had a way of doing my body right. Truth be told we hadn't made love like that in months. My body missed him, hell, it yearned for him. He fit right like a glove, it was his and he knew it. He owned it with every stroke, and I wanted more. Of course, I was still angry for all the obvious reasons, he still wanted a divorce. I knew that if I continued having sex with him, I would overlook our harsh reality and not deal with the issue at hand. I thought about the fact that I was going back to being La'Dai Bell, no longer Roswell. I mean yes, I was going to keep my last name, but I was no longer going to be a married woman. Something almost every woman sets out to be.

I put my robe over my naked body and walked into the living

room where Devin was. He was sitting on the couch checking out the stocks on his laptop. He looked up over his shoulder at me as I entered the room.

"Oh, you're up, good morning, beautiful."

"Good morning," I said as I sat on the couch next to him.

"Couldn't sleep?" Devin asked. "Usually, you sleep until at least nine on Saturdays." He turned back to the paper, not at all fazed by the awkwardness of the divorce that was still on the table.

"Yeah, I couldn't sleep. I have a lot on my mind."

"Do you need help going back to sleep?" he asked as he leaned in to kiss me and put one hand inside my robe onto my left breast.

"No Devin, stop, I don't need help. In fact, you're the reason why I can't sleep."

He stopped, drew back his hand and said, "Okay, let's talk. I wanted to talk last night to clear the air, but you didn't. Are you ready now?"

"Yes, I am. Tell me how this is okay, how is any of this okay?" I was so angry that I couldn't express myself the way I wanted to. I could not express how I wanted this to work, nor could I say "please, let's just talk this through and reevaluate what the real issue is." The rage was taking over my chance to be honest and vulnerable.

He responded with, "How is what okay, LD? Me trying to have sex with my wife?"

"You trying to have sex with your soon-to-be ex-wife. How about the mere fact that you're making me your soon-to-be ex-wife by asking for a divorce. Or the other fact that you're trying to turn our perfect world upside down just like that." I snapped my fingers somewhat close to his face and realized I had become beyond angry and frustrated.

"La'Dai, I love you. I love you more than life itself. But life has other plans for us. Our marriage has been a top priority to me for the last eleven years, and you have been a priority for the last fifteen. But now it's time for me to take a different approach to how I do things and how I'm living my life. I will always have love and respect for you no matter what. And just because we won't be married anymore doesn't mean we can't continue to be best friends; we'll remain business partners and most importantly we will always have our unbreakable bond."

"A bond, Devin, seriously? And how in the hell are you so calm about all of this?"

"Well, of course I thought this all the way through before I made my decision. And don't think I haven't been dreading this day because I have. But my mind is made up and this is what it has to be."

"Fuck you, Devin."

"I know you're upset but we've never talked to each other that way before and we aren't about to start now. This does not have to be a messy divorce."

"It was messy when you decided to pull wanting a divorce out of your ass."

"Calm down, La'Dai."

"Calm down?!, I'm just supposed to accept this, I'm just supposed to lay down and take it."

"Well, you did that last night." Devin started laughing and I grew furious. "Oh, c'mon LD, I'm just joking. I'm trying to lighten up the mood."

"Well, here's something I'm not joking about. I want you moved out in two weeks. All your shit."

I got up off the couch and stormed upstairs. I could feel my eyes filling with tears and my heart growing heavy with pain. I was completely heartbroken.

Chapter Two

"Sash, I have to call you back. It looks like the moving truck is here to help Devin move his things."

"You guys decided to part ways before the divorce is finalized, huh?"

"I mean yeah, after we had sex two weeks ago, I decided that it was not a good idea to stay under the same roof. Right now, I'm messed up mentally and emotionally and he has no problem being 'Mr. Chill as a damn cucumber'. Something doesn't feel right about this whole thing. I mean, it's out of left field. Plus, I'm still madly in love with him, Sasha. You mix that with sex, and I'm bound to have some type of residual of regret for begging 'Please don't leave me' and I'll be damned if I become that pathetic."

"What do you mean by something doesn't feel right, La'Dai."

"Sis, we have a perfect life. Right after he asked for a divorce, we made love like we were newlyweds again. The passion is still there so why is he still continuing on with his plans to be a divorcee. Do you understand what I mean?"

"Were you guys having any problems that you haven't told anyone about? I mean all couples have problems; I'm talking about deeply rooted issues that can't be fixed."

"NO! I tell you everything."

"Hey, I'm just asking. Out of shame and embarrassment,

sometimes we as women don't let others completely in on what's really going on with us. And hey I'm not here to judge you, they call it privacy for a reason. You know, La' Dai, you are allowed to keep some things to yourself."

"No, I've been completely transparent. But hey I didn't call you to have a pity party. Hold on, pause, you want to tell me why you're going on dates? What happened to Sean?"

It had been two weeks since I really had a chance to talk to Sasha. All of our conversations before this one was quick. We tried to make it a point to talk every day. It was our way of making sure we stayed grounded and didn't lose our sister ship or ourselves in the whirlwind of everyday life.

"Girl, please, your little choirboy Sean was not it. He made it a point to tell me my sexy ass was getting too fat. The nerve of him to call me and say... 'Hey Babe, I was thinking that we should get a gym membership.' You know that irritated me."

I chuckled and Sasha continued, "I asked him why the sudden need to get a gym membership, and his response was, "Well, I just remember when you were fifteen pounds lighter and used to wear those sexy tights I like." Sasha mocked Sean in a man's voice. So, I told him, 'Yeah, and I remember when I wasn't with your ass.' I hung up on him, pressed call block, and never looked back. And I've been eating happily ever after since that moment."

I spit out the water I was drinking and laughed hysterically. "Well Sis, I was going to tell you, you are looking a little fluffy nowadays."

"Don't make me hang up on your ass too. Besides, shouldn't you be in the house begging Devin not to leave."

"Oh, that was dirty," I said continuing to laugh.

"Yeah, and so was you calling me fluffy."

We both laughed and said goodbye. I had thick skin when it came to my sister. She had no filter and was very direct. When she dealt with me, I knew it was coming from a place of love. And although her little joke was too soon, it wouldn't have been Sasha if she didn't take the opportunity to get back at me with a little taste of my own medicine. Just a little sisterly love is what she always called it.

I continued laughing as we hung up the phone. Talking to Sasha always put me in a good mood.

Hearing Sasha say she kicked Sean to the curb for not accepting her for who she was, was no surprise to me. Sasha knew that her life had a purpose. Sasha didn't take anything for granted. She had a blasé approach to life, and if something were unimportant to her, you could forget about it; she didn't pay it any mind at all. It's like she didn't waste her time worrying about the little things, and men were on the category of her list as "little things."

I walked up the driveway to our house. When I stepped up to the front door, Devin was in the entryway with his back turned to the door, he was talking on the phone, and with who I wondered. Devin was so engaged in conversation that he hadn't noticed I was there. I lightened up my footsteps and got a little closer to try and hear what he was saying. His tone was low, and he spoke with passion. My first thought was Oh so he's going to talk to another woman while he's still in our house. The nerve of him. My heart dropped in my stomach.

I could hear Devin saying, "No, I'm not going to tell her, I can't. Listen bro I hear you, but I'm taking this to my grave literally."

I took a deep breath and suddenly felt my body loosen up, I was at ease knowing that he was talking to a man and not a woman. I made a mental note that he was intending to withhold some information from me. My mind was starting to race, and I became convinced that he was talking about something related to our marriage or what was soon to be the lack thereof.

My mind kept going…What was he talking about? What wasn't he going to tell me? I thought to myself, Mmmm hmmm, I knew it was something; feeding me that life-is-taking-a-different-turn bullshit. I was sure Devin was up to no good.

One thing was for sure about my husband; the man was pretty consistent. Once his mind was made up, it stayed that way. I knew if I asked him what he was talking about, one: he would know I was eavesdropping and two: at that point he really wouldn't spill the beans. Now I was determined to find out the truth and get to the bottom of his rationale behind divorcing me. I needed a game plan. I took a few steps back and pretended that I was just then approaching. Trying to make my presence known, I yelled to one of the movers, "Hey, be careful with that."

My fake attempt to make my presence known made me feel foolish as the mover glanced at me strangely, looked down at the small box he was carrying labeled "miscellaneous", shook his head and continued on.

I smiled in embarrassment and went into the house. Devin turned around, motioned hello with a wave and ended his phone call saying, "Alright, we'll link up tomorrow at four, don't be late, bye."

I looked around and the spaces where his belongings once were, were now empty. He embraced me with a hug, and said, "Hey LD, we're almost finished, then I'll—."

I stopped him and with a jealous tone, asked, "Who was that on the phone? Your little girlfriend?" Yes, I was acting completely oblivious to the other information I heard, but I wanted to see what he had to say. And although I knew it wasn't a woman on the phone, I needed to know who he was talking to if I was going to try and find out the truth.

"Girlfriend? Funny. No, that was Tony. We are meeting up

to go over the blueprints for the vacant lot so plan to meet at four p.m. tomorrow alright."

I nodded my head yes.

"LD, we make great business partners and I intend for it to stay that way. Our divorce doesn't have to get in the way of things. Let's just take our emotions out of it, there's no love lost, right?", Devin said hugging me.

I can be honest and say, as much as I wanted to be angry and bitter, Devin made that hard. In my mind being angry and bitter came with the territory, so I was well within my rights. He was still handling me in a loving and respectful way. The way he always had, from day one.

Words were still coming out of his mouth but my ears fell deaf as I reminisced. The look in his eyes took me back to our Grambling days. The days when he would pick me up from campus and take me to the house he was renting. He lived with two roommates and for college bachelors they kept it pretty clean. We'd go back to his place; he would somehow manage to get his roommates to leave so we could be alone. Staying up all night and talking for hours was something we enjoyed doing. When he talked, he would look me straight in the eyes. It was as if he was making love to me one blink at a time. His eyes pierced straight through to my soul. When he spoke, he was so passionate, his voice sent chills down my spine.

Three hours had gone by since Devin and the movers left. I decided to get up and organize my bedroom. With Devin moving out, getting organized was a priority in order for me to stay on track and sane. My phone rang, it was Sasha.

"Hello."

"Hey it's me. Tammy and I are going to Jazzy's tonight and I want you to tag along so get dressed."

"On a Thursday?" I asked.

"Ummm yeah, last time I checked, you were single and ready to mingle. And Jazzy's the perfect Jazz club full of sexy eligible bachelors. Plus, tonight is also hip-hop night, it'll be fun."

"Sash, I'm not technically divorced yet."

"Yeah, but court is not that far away and who said you needed to be divorced to have fun? There's nothing wrong with celebrating early. Get dressed La'Dai. I'll see you in an hour."

I let out a long sigh and hung up the phone. I poured another glass of wine and walked into my closet. I decided to wear a black strapless dress with a pair of Christian Dior heels. I laid the dress across my bed and went to take a shower.

When we got to the bar, there was a table waiting for us. Sasha and Tammy were regulars there, so the bouncers always looked out for them. Sasha stood up, glanced around the room and said, "Alright y'all got minutes to sit down so get it in while I go get the drinks. La'Dai, you're on dirty martinis tonight and Tammy you're on Hennessy neat." Sasha always quarterbacked the drinks when she wanted to make sure everyone would have a good time. I responded, "That's alright with me; just make sure they use belvie." Belvedere allowed me to remain standing at the end of the night no matter how much I drank.

Sasha walked away sashing across the room; she owned every inch of those four walls. My sister was looking good, fluffy or not. She sure did know how to attract attention and stand out in a room full of people.

I was bobbing my head to the music and scanning the atmosphere just to see what the crowd was like. I was really in no mood to meet anyone new. I wasn't ready. But I noticed this brotha who was the epitome of Morris Chestnut. He seemed to be the real deal. I could tell by his demeanor that his ego was on high. I could tell that he was straight up about his business. For a moment, I forgot about everything I was going through, hell I even forgot about Devin.

He caught me staring, I tried to look away but there was something about his aura that wouldn't let me turn my head. His vibe was captivating. Our eyes locked and I used the best thing I was wearing. My smile. I put my shoulders back crossed my legs and sat up super straight. In that moment I felt like Audrey Hepburn having breakfast at Tiffany's. I was giving him the serious, mysterious, but sexy vibe. I looked away as though I'd lost interest and he was on his way to our table.

He walked over, said hello to Tammy, then approached me. As he got closer, my heart raced faster. It had been years since I'd talked to another man on a level other than business. I mean what would I say? Hi, I'm La'Dai soon-to-be-divorced, and you are? As I was trying to get my game plan together, his was already in action. He walked up to me, put his hand around my upper back, leaned into me, brushed past my cheek and whispered into my ear, "You're absolutely gorgeous." I wanted to melt; I could smell his cologne. Savage smelled good on him, and the aroma made me quiver. I couldn't believe this stranger was having such an effect on me. He took me by surprise, I didn't know to check him for thinking he could touch me off back or to be flattered because his demeanor was of a perfect gentleman. He knew exactly what he wanted and was not willing to let anyone or anything dictate how he got it. I mean I could respect that, so I went with the flow.

I was trying to stay calm, cool, and collected but he smelled so good, was smooth and not to mention I was vulnerable. Hell, he might as well have been Morris Chestnut himself as debonair as he was.

"Thank you," I said flirtatiously still not taking my eyes off of him.

"I know you're here with your girls, but I have to know who you are."

I stuck out my hand, "Hi, I'm La'Dai."

"Ms. La'Dai, I'm Jason, and hopefully the guy you'll allow to know you better."

I hesitated to answer, "Ummm, I ugh—".

"I'm sorry are you married or here with someone? I didn't see a ring on your finger, so I assumed…."

"It's complicated but if you give me your number, maybe I can call you when it's a better time." I didn't want to say that but hell I had to keep it real.

"Fair enough. I respect your honesty; can I at least buy you a drink?"

"That's nice but my sister is on her way back from the bar now with our drinks."

"Okay well, if you're still thirsty later, come find me and I'll be happy to be at your service."

As corny as his line was, I smirked and nodded as I responded, "Will do."

As he was getting ready to walk away, he suddenly turned around and said, "But let me ask you a question before I go, may I ask, what do you do for a living?"

I was thrown off by his question, but I noticed Sasha was walking back, and I knew she would have insisted he stay so I answered quickly, hoping that they would not cross paths, "I sell commercial real estate."

"Okay, he said, "have a good night. I look forward to you calling me and if you don't. I'll call you." He winked at me and walked away."

Somehow, I believe that his last statement was said with intent as if he had some type of ulterior motive behind his line of questioning.

Sasha walked up as he walked away. She looked him up and down, then turned to me and said, "Damn, who was that and why is he walking away? Tell me he's coming back, or you'll be seeing him again."

"No sis, I have to get my affairs in order first. It's too soon."

"Too soon? We all know the way to get over a man is to find another one."

The bar was all the way live, and I needed to get up and dance. I downed my dirty martini and headed to the dance floor. Sasha and Tammy followed.

I was having the time of my life. The sound of the music bounced off the walls and into my ears making love to my soul with every melody. My hips started to sway side to side, and I began to gyrate my hips as if there was a man standing behind me. My arms were straight up in the air, with my wrist twirling round and round, my body beginning to follow. I danced slowly with my eyes closed, you would have thought I was a world class showgirl getting ready to perform. I realized that I was giving the entire club a private show. I opened my eyes and snapped back into reality. I didn't realize how much time had gone by.

I looked at the table, Sasha was engaged in conversation with some guy and Tammy had left an hour before, something about her babysitter having diarrhea. If you asked me, she was on a mission to a booty call. I mean who hangs up the phone at one a.m. with a smile on her face because the babysitter has diarrhea. But, hey, girlfriend was living her best life. I looked at my phone; it was one-forty-five a.m. I had two missed calls from Devin and a text that read: Hey, remember our meeting in the morning, and remember to bring the blueprints for our other meeting at 4:00 with Tony. I rolled my eyes and walked over to our table where Sasha was, took one last sip of my drink.

"Hey sis, you ready to head out?"

"I'm ready when you are."

"Well, then let me get us an Uber."

Sasha looked at the man she was talking to and said, "It's been great talking to you, you have my number; let's finish this conversation over dinner. Call me." She gave him a kiss on the cheek, and we left.

Lying in my bed alone made me miss Devin. If this is what being single was like, I didn't want it. I felt so lonely, so deprived. The thought of calling Devin crossed my mind. But what was I going to say? Please just come home. Yeah, no that wasn't going to work. Besides, it was two-thirty in the morning. My TV was on but there was no sound. The rerun show of the Golden Girls reminded me of how late it was. I grabbed the pillow next to me to see if it still had Devin's scent and it did.

I got out of bed and took what was supposed to be a five -minute shower and reacquainted myself with the shower head. The water was warm, and it clung to my body like milk to honey. Before I knew it my leg was up on the wall, and I was breathing heavily. I was all in as if it were the real thing. Twenty minutes later I was out of the shower and laid out across my bed. The adrenaline rush from the orgasm must have made me sleepy, two minutes later I was in what felt like stage 3 of REM sleep. The sound of myself snoring woke me up out of my sleep. I stood up, looked down at my naked body, then glanced at my silhouette on the wall for a moment, I was pleased that I was able to maintain my body after all these years. I turned off the TV and climbed back into bed.

I woke at 6:00 a.m. to my alarm screaming in my ears. Deciding to start my day off right, I put on some music and started to get dressed.

By the time I made it downstairs to try and eat breakfast, time had gotten away from me. I grabbed a protein shake and ran out the door. Five minutes up the road, "Oh shoot, the blueprints!" I yelled.

I made an illegal U-turn and accelerated; I felt a big bump, the front of my car hit a giant pothole, I could tell I'd done some damage. When I reached the house and got out of my car, I saw the damage to my bumper. "Shit!" The neighbor across the street was startled as I yelled out. I ran into the house, grabbed the blueprints and rushed back out the door.

When I got to the lot, Devin and Tony had already started.

Devin turned around and said, "LD, I tried calling you, we started twenty minutes ago."

"Hi Tony," I said as I walked over and stood alongside Devin.

"Hi LD, how are you?"

"I've had better days, here are the blueprints." I said handing them to Tony.

"Oh good, you're right on time. I'll take those." Tony responded smiling, and giving me a look of reassurance, as if not to worry about being late.

Tony was our contractor; he was going to be in charge of building on the lot. We decided to build four buildings, which would include office suites and store fronts to a growing community. One of the buildings was specifically designed to be an after-school program.

As soon as we were done meeting, I headed to my car. We had several hours before our next meeting and I needed a breather.

"LD, wait," Devin said, trying to catch up to me as I speed walked to my car.

"Yes, Devin, what is it?"

"Let me walk you to your car, I want to talk to you."

"I'm listening," I said, slightly turning back, glancing at him nonchalantly.

"Whoa, what happened to your bumper?"

"I hit a pothole on the way here."

"Alright, take my car, and I'll take yours to the dealer to get fixed."

"No Devin, I can handle it."

"Stop being stubborn and give me your keys."

"No, I can't allow you to be there for me as if we aren't going through a divorce. That's why I asked you to move out. You want to act as if this isn't happening and we're just going to continue on like normal."

"That's not true, LD. Before we were husband and wife, we were friends and I'm always going to have your back. We can still be amicable through this. Don't shut me out."

"I'll let you in, Devin, when you let me in and be honest about this whole thing."

"What does that mean?"

"Never mind; I'll see you at four."

I got in my car and headed to the dealership.

I didn't know where to begin because Devin had always taken care of these types of things, but it was time that I figured it out. I called Sasha, hoping she could give me some guidance.

The phone rang three times before she picked up.

"Sasha, hey, I need your help," I said with a sense of urgency in my voice.

"With what? I'm not up yet. I think I may be a little hung over."

"This should only take a minute. My bumper is all jacked up from hitting a pothole; I'm on my way to the dealer now but need to know how the process works. Devin offered to do it, but..."

"But what, why didn't you let the man help you?"

"Because, Sasha, he trying to act all nice and shit probably just in time for court."

"Or maybe his gestures are genuine, La'Dai. You guys have history. Not to mention the talk Dad and Uncle Allen gave him when y'all first got married, letting him know what would happen to him if ever disrespected you."

"Ha-ha, oh please. Uncle Allen is not a defensive back for

the Raiders anymore. Now he's just a big six-three, two-hundred-and-fifty-pound teddy bear, living life retired from the NFL and raising his family."

"Yeah well, I wouldn't want to take my chances with his big ass if I were a man."

"Girl, you're crazy."

"Call me when you get to the dealer, and I'll walk you through it. I need ten more minutes of sleep; my head is pounding."

We hung up. I turned up the music and got my roll on.

I was determined to get my mind right and stop depending on Devin.

Chapter Three

"You know, Devin, I was going to try and rise above this divorce, but I can't believe that you would even try to hide the fact that you purchased another property without me knowing and not only that, but you're trying to keep it all to yourself. The audacity!"

I tried to keep my composure once we stepped out of the courtroom in efforts to settle our divorce. But being blindsided by the fact that Devin purchased property that I didn't know about made it hard. This was just another insult to injury, and I was over the man with whom I once shared every little detail of life with keeping secrets from me. It started with the fact that for a month and Sundays he hid wanting a divorce from me.

"Listen, LD...."

"Don't waste your time trying to explain. I've been courteous and amicable during this entire time. But this is some bullshit. Oh, but you better believe payback is a bitch. Move out of my way." I pushed past him and instantly called Sasha.

I got her voicemail, "Hey it's Sasha, leave me a message or, better yet, shoot me a text." I always hated leaving her voice messages because I knew she would not check them.

"Sasha, it's your sister. Girl, call me back. We just got out of court, and you won't believe this shit. Matter of fact I'm on my way over to your place; I'll be there in fifteen, bye."

Frustrated I threw my phone into my purse, then threw the purse into the passenger seat and floored it, I went from 40 mph to 80 in 2.5 seconds, all gas and no brakes.

I pulled up to Sasha's, her car was in the driveway, and I could hear music playing.

I rang the doorbell a couple of times, but she did not answer. I went back to the car and got my copy of the key to her house.

I walked in and yelled from the door, "Sasha, turn this music down; I've been calling you."

As I walked into the kitchen, I could see a trail of blood leading from the kitchen to the guest bathroom. The shower was running, Sasha was slumped over in the bathtub, fully clothed. Water and blood were everywhere.

"Sasha!" I yelled her name. She didn't respond. My heart was beating so fast I thought it was going to jump outside my chest. I yelled her name again, "Sasha!"

I turned her over and started shaking her. Sasha was unresponsive, and blood was coming from her head.

I quickly scanned her to see if there were any other injuries. I felt my back pocket for my phone, it wasn't there. I panicked some more. I turned off the water and rushed into the kitchen. I grabbed my phone off the counter and tried to catch my balance as I almost slipped on Sasha's blood. My hands were shaking, and I was in complete panic mode.

"Nine-one-one what's your emergency?"

"I need an ambulance, my sister needs help. There's blood everywhere."

"Ma'am, can you tell me where she's bleeding from?" the 911 dispatcher asked sounding calm. "Yeah, her head. It's gushing with blood, please hurry."

"Help is on the way, what's your address."

"Nineteen fifty-six Lane port Circle."

"Can you tell me if she's alert?"

"No."

"Is she breathing?"

"Barely."

"Is she conscious?"

"No. Please just hurry up," I yelled.

"Paramedics should be arriving momentarily, just try and remain calm."

"Okay, Okay. Dear God, help her!"

I was holding Sasha in my arms; all kind of thoughts were going through my mind.

As the paramedics came swooshing in and working on Sasha, I gathered enough calm. I thought to call Ma but paused when the EMT stretched out Sasha's arm to check her blood pressure. I noticed needle marks. Sasha hadn't mentioned going to any doctor's appointments. I glanced over the bathroom floor hoping not to look suspicious and there it was. The needle had fallen behind the toilet.

I knew I couldn't let the paramedics see the needle nor could I bend down to pick it up without them noticing. I had to get them to work a little faster so I could try to keep Sasha's secret from coming to the surface.

"Please hurry up and just get her to the hospital, please."

"Ma'am, we're working as fast as we can."

Two minutes later Sasha was in the back of the ambulance and on her way to Cedar Sinai Hospital.

I called Ma, told her Sasha almost OD'ed again and headed out to trail behind the ambulance.

Sasha was no addict. Her biological mother was. In fact, Sasha was born with drugs in her system and at the very young age of two years old; she got a hold of her mother's drugs and almost overdosed and died. Both her parents were sentenced to prison, where her mother died from an overdose six months after being there. Her father landed a life sentence for attempted murder against another inmate; two years after being in prison. Ma and Sasha's biological mother were best friends. Ma felt like she failed Sasha's mother by not getting her away from the toxic relationship with Sasha's father. Once Sasha's parents went to prison, Ma adopted Sasha and vowed to raise her as her own and not to ever let anyone harm a hair on her head. Not even Sasha's own father.

Because of Sasha's early history with drugs, even with the treatment she received, she still had triggers. It took something really close to home to trigger her. In high school it was her mother's sister, she saw Sasha for the first time in years and reminded Sasha of everything about her mother, it was as though she was reliving her past. So now my wheels were spinning wondering what it took this time, nearly seventeen years later.

Once I got to the hospital, they led me to where Sasha was. By this time, she had come to and had gauze wrapped around the entire top part of her head. I could see blood seeping through.

"Sasha, are you okay? You almost gave me a heart attack."

"Yeah, I'll be okay. I must have slipped when I went to take a shower and hit my head."

Not wanting to upset her, I calmly brought up the needle.

"Did your falling have anything to do with you using again?"

Sasha put her head in her hands and started crying hysterically. "La'Dai, he called me again. And this time something made me listen to his evil ass instead of hanging up."

"Who, Sash?"

"My biological father. Somehow, he got a hold of a cellphone. He started calling often. Usually, I would threaten to call the prison and let the Warden know that he had a cell phone and hang up on him but this time I didn't, and I should have. He started going on about my mother and how I was just like her, a disloyal drug head. He told me just because your parents took me in doesn't mean I'm any better. He said his blood still runs through my veins and I am who I am."

"Oh my God, Sasha. We have to tell Mom and Dad about this."

"I know."

"You know what, La'Dai? After his phone call my reality sunk in. The real reason why I don't give guys a winning chance has nothing to do with them and it's not because I haven't found the right one. I haven't given them a real chance because I don't want to end up like my mother, so in love with a man that when he says jump, I say how high or lose myself because I'm so busy trying to get him to validate me and when he doesn't validate me I lose my self-worth and turn to drugs to numb the pain of rejection and turn selfish enough to almost kill my two-year-old child because I was too high to keep my drugs out of her reach." Sasha was rambling.

Sasha started crying again, her hatred for her parents was real. It ran deep. I could hear the resentment in her voice. My sister was at her weakest point, vulnerable, and wide open. I knew I had to be there for her no matter what, so I disregarded the drugs and became empathetic.

"Sasha, you have to let that go. During that time of her life your mom was weak but that's not who you are. Ma didn't raise us to be weak women. Hell, you stood up to your ex, Fabian, when he tried to control you and ever since then you've been putting these men in their places."

"Nah LD, the story I told you about me and Fabian's break up was a lie. The truth is he was married. I found out when he stood me up one night and his assistant told me he had just left to meet me at the W hotel. Problem was he told me he had a last-minute out-of-town business meeting. So, I went to the W hotel, said I was Mrs. Mitchell and had forgotten my key."

"And they let you in just like that?"

"Nope. I pretended to be drunk, told them I was too wasted, and I'd caught my husband cheating on me, I lost my mind and my purse, so I had no ID. I mixed that story with a little flirting and in less than five minutes, I had the key and the room number."

"So, what did you do?"

"I went upstairs, they were about to have sex. I yelled, 'son of a bitch!' She screamed, he looked like he saw a ghost and I looked at her and politely said, 'I hope he's wearing a condom because he's been sleeping with me too.' And I walked out."

"My gosh, how come you never told me?"

"I was embarrassed, LaDai. He tried for months to get me back, but I can't stand a cheater. I wasn't about to end up being one of his side pieces, that spends endless nights daydreaming about him leaving his wife and us starting a life of our own. We all know how those stories end. But, girl, he couldn't let go; his wife became desperate and tried to friend me on Facebook and when I didn't accept, she called me."

"What?"

"Yes, she called me crying asking for advice on how to get him to come home. She said, 'You seem to be all he wants, and all he can think about, what should I do? I've tried everything. I told him to bring you home and we'll add you to the equation'."

"So, what did you tell her?"

"LaDai, I'm a woman first, so I told her to leave him. But judging from her cry out for help, she wasn't about to do that, so I did everything in my power to keep him away from me so he could focus his attention back on her or elsewhere. Bottom line was, I couldn't become her, karma is a bitch that likes to come around two times, sometimes three."

"Poor woman."

"Yeah well, that's my point, when you love someone more than you love yourself, all bets are off."

I could tell Sasha was feeling better; by this time Ma and Dad showed up. The look in their eyes was of pure love they just wanted to make sure Sasha was okay. Ma knew when she adopted Sasha that she may have trouble with drugs because of what she had been through, and because of that Ma showed Sasha grace and helped her in any way that she could. Ma knew all odds were against her before she was even born, so she was determined to help Sasha overcome.

Having the heart to heart with Sasha made me think about Devin, court earlier that day, and our divorce. Hearing her story about Fabian only made me grow more suspicious of Devin and what else he may be hiding from me. So, I went out on a limb and decided that I was going to call Tony. I still wanted answers.

Standing in my kitchen I looked around contemplating cleaning it. I walked to the refrigerator and pulled out the bottle of Pinot Gorgio instead. I remembered the housekeeper was coming the next morning. I poured myself a glass of wine and decided to call Tony to try to find out whatever I could. Just the mere thought of what information Tony might have, gave me goosebumps. Was I really ready for whatever truth he had? Suddenly I felt my stomach muscles tighten up. I put the glass of wine in the refrigerator and took out the bottle of tequila; I needed something strong if I was going to stomach the truth. In the cabinet were the many shot glasses Devin and I collected over the years from the places we'd traveled to. I took out the one from Costa Rica and took two shots, back-to-back. I went upstairs, changed my clothes; the sight of Sasha's blood on them had my mind completely bent out of shape.

"Google, play my Kenny G playlist."

The sound of jazz came through the Bose speakers in my ceiling. Jazz always had a way of calming me all the way down.

I sat down in the loveseat at the foot of my bed and called Tony.

"Hello."

"Hey Tony, it's me LD."

"Hey LD, what's going on? Are you okay? You usually don't call me after seven p.m. during the week, not that it's late but your call caught me by surprise."

"Yeah, I know, I just need to talk to you, do you have a few minutes."

"What's on your mind?"

"Tony, I'm having a hard time coming to terms with the reason why Devin wants this divorce. You know I would never want to put you in the middle of our marital issues, but I need some type of closure or advice. We still have businesses to run, and my mind is off thinking about what he may be hiding from me."

"You and Devin are family to me, hell you're the kids' godparents for Christ's sake. And you know Devin is my boy. I know for sure that he would never keep anything from you unless it was in your best interest. No point intended by that; I'm just saying. I mean of course I don't like the fact of you two splitting up and I've always admired the way you guys work together on the business end of things, but Devin is a very smart man, almost everything he does has a reason."

"I hear you, Tony, but this whole 'it's time to live life in a different direction and I'm not the man I used to be' is bull. Not to mention him trying to be there for me like he's still my husband."

"You know he has the utmost respect for you. That's why I wouldn't even be concerned with the new girl he's seeing."

"What girl?"

"What do you mean what girl, LD? You just said you knew that he was living the single life."

"The single life…? What I said was: he told me he wanted to live life in a different direction but getting involved with someone else doesn't exactly make him single now does it? See what I mean. What the hell is going on?"

"I appreciate you coming to me and I'm here for you in any other way except for discussing things about Devin and his personal life. It doesn't feel right talking to you about things that you really should be talking to him about. It's hard for me to remain neutral but it's for the best."

"I can't even fault you for that." I could feel my heart beating fast, still trying to digest Tony's claim that Devin was seeing someone.

"Well, Tony, thank you and do me a favor; don't tell Devin I called."

"Your secret is safe with me and hey Devin still loves you; I should know, I was right there when he proposed, and he still has that same spark in his eyes when he sees you now that he had in his eyes then."

"Thank you, Tony, kiss the babies for me."

"You got it, good night."

"Night."

I hung up the phone and went to the kitchen to pour me another shot of Tequila. I just wanted to drink myself into oblivion. Sitting on the couch, I took out our wedding photo album and started to reminisce.

Thinking back to the day Devin proposed, I remembered it like it was yesterday. Summer 2007, it was the Bayou Classic and everybody that was somebody was there. The streets were jamming, glasses were full, and the ladies were definitely walking around collecting their beads. While girls were walking up and down the streets lifting up their shirts for beads and the guys happy to throw them, I was in my own world. The game between Grambling and Southern was on but Devin was in the other room, he had reserved us a room at the Bourbon Orleans Hotel. I remember feeling so special knowing that he put us up in such a fancy hotel, even back then I knew Devin wanted the best for me. I walked onto the balcony. Two minutes later I heard Devin call my name and when I turned around, he was on one knee and there was Tony off to the side catching the entire thing on video with his phone. I felt so loved, so wanted, and so lucky. I was becoming Mrs. Devin Roswell.

It would have been naïve of me to think that Devin could not be seeing someone but that wasn't the issue. Did he think that he was going to just up and let another woman take my place, let her reap the benefits of everything we built together? He had another thing coming. No woman was going to take everything I worked so hard for and claim it as her own, not even my husband, just because he had lost his mind and filed for divorce. If Tony wasn't going to help me find out the truth, I was going to help my damn self.

I called Ma to check on Sasha. She planned to stay the night at the hospital with her.

"Hey Ma, how's she doing?"

"She's doing okay, she's sleeping right now. The nurse just came in to give her some pain meds and that was a mess."

"Why?"

"Well, with her almost overdosing, they are skeptical about giving her the medication."

"Yeah, well in the meantime, Ma, she has a gash on her head the size of my fist. Do you need me to come back there?"

"No honey, I worked it out, right before she fell asleep, she said the medicine was working and the pain was letting up."

"Okay Ma, and where's Dad?"

"He's headed home; he has to meet with the adjusters tomorrow so that we can get ready to sell the Sunland Property. I'm probably going to be here all day tomorrow and I could tell he was really worried about your sister so see if he'll let you take him to lunch."

"No problem, that's just like Dad keeping himself busy so he doesn't have time to worry. I'll be sure to take him, plus I need some father-daughter time anyhow."

"Thank you, baby. I'm going to try and rest while Sasha is asleep. Call me tomorrow, good night."

"Good night Ma, I love you."

In the Essence of truth lies deceit.
-Dejan Stojanovic

Chapter Four

It had been a month since the incident with Sasha, she was off to rehab, the builders were building on the lot, and I spent the last four weeks avoiding Devin face to face, trying to ignore the fact that he might have a girlfriend. Everything in my life seemed to be moving forward except for me. The weekend was coming, and I promised my parents that I would go to church with them on Sunday. After looking at myself in the mirror and realizing that I was letting myself go with all the heavy drinking, I decided to make myself a hair appointment. As a matter of fact, I was going to make it an all-day event and get myself a manicure and pedicure along with a massage. I wanted to be rejuvenated. Not to mention Devin and I were scheduled to meet with the builders and check on the progress at the lot. I knew for sure he would notice the extra ten pounds I put on, so my plan was to keep him focused on my face.

"Hair and All beauty salon, how can I help you?" The girl on the other end of the phone answered, sounding young and full of life.

"Hi, may I speak with Lisa please."

"She's currently with a client at the shampoo bowl. Can I take a message?"

"Yes, I was recommended by a friend, and I would like to

make an appointment."

"Oh, I can help you with that, what are you getting done and when would you like to come in?"

"Umm, just the basic wash, blow dry, press and curl. Does she have an open spot for Saturday?" I glanced at myself in the mirror looking at the ponytail I'd been wearing for about three weeks.

"Okay, how's Saturday at nine a.m. sound?"

"That will work."

"And what is your name."

"L…" The girl cut me off mid-sentence.

"Can you please hold?" I could hear her trying to muffle the phone as she talked to someone in the background.

"Ma'am, Stacy is ready for you, please go to the back." The background noise got louder, and she returned to the phone with a sense of urgency in her voice.

"I'm sorry about that, we're so busy. Okay Ms. Elle, I have you down for Saturday at nine a.m., Lisa will see you then. Bye-bye."

I was going to correct her on my name and get the address, but I thought what the hell, I'll google the address and give her my correct name on Saturday. I was a little hesitant to go to a new beautician but my old one was out on maternity leave and Lord knows I needed a hair miracle. Besides, this beautician came highly recommended by a client of mine.

Saturday came fast when I got there the place was packed. Women and little girls all trying to get beautified. The shop was gorgeous and clean. It was dressed with lively plants and the atmosphere felt warm. The booths were all privately secluded but were uniformly in a row on both sides of the shop. Looking towards the back of the shop, I could see the area where the shampoo bowls and hair dryers were. There was also an extension of the salon that seemed to be a mini nail salon. This was the place to be if you wanted to get glamorous. I walked up to the front desk.

"Hi, I have a nine o'clock with Lisa."

"She's ready for you; come on back." Once the girl standing at the front desk spoke, I could tell she was the one who made my appointment.

She led me to the third station on the right of the salon where a beautiful middle aged black woman greeted me.

"Hi, you must be Elle. Nice to meet you, I'm Lisa."

"Actually, my name is- "

"Umm, hold on a minute honey", she said. Gesturing for me to wait, while holding up her index finger she turned around and stopped the young girl as she was walking off. "Jessica, can you check and see if there's a shampoo bowl open and let my nine-thirty client know she's early and I'll be with her shortly."

Judging from the tone of Lisa's voice, she was a boss and did not mess around. This led me to think she might be used to doing hair her way and not the way the client wanted, but I remained open minded.

"I'm sorry what were you saying?"

"Oh, I said it's nice to meet you." I decided to stick with the name Elle just in case she did my hair, and I didn't like it. I was definitely going to yelp about it.

"You too, honey, have a seat. Now who referred you?"

"A friend of mine named Sheila."

"Yes… little Sheila, how is she doing? I haven't seen her in a while."

"That's because she and her husband moved up North. She got a new job."

"Well, good for her, I remember her saying she was looking. I guess she'll call me when things settle down. Okay, well come on back to the shampoo bowl and tell me what we're doing today."

When we got to the shampoo bowl there was another beautician with her client, I smiled as I walked by and the beautician smiled back but seemed to be deeply engaged in conversation with her client. We sat right next to them. Lisa laid me back and started to wash my hair.

"Let me know if the water is too warm."

I closed my eyes and started to enjoy the warmth of the water on my scalp.

I could hear the other beautician and her client talking.

"So where did you guys end up going to dinner the other week?" the beautician asked her client.

I couldn't see the woman in the shampoo bowl, but she sounded very excited when she answered.

"We went downtown to Flemings and then we went to some lounge that had a rooftop. Girl, it was perfect. And he was such a gentleman. He opened my doors, held my hand, made sure I was comfortable every step of the way. He planned everything to the tee. You can't find men like that anymore. Who said chivalry is dead?"

I could hear them both laughing. I smiled to myself and thought about Devin--with him chivalry wasn't dead. I continued listening to their conversation.

"I heard that. Does he have any kids?"

"No, and you know since I don't either that gives us a whole lot of free time together. As a matter of fact, we're going out tonight."

"Oh okay, where to?"

"I don't know, Devin is full of surprises. We just met but it's like he knows my taste already."

Hold on, did this bitch just say Devin…. I suddenly sat up and water went flying everywhere.

"Girl, are you okay?" Lisa looked at me strangely.

"Um, yeah, I just got a sharp pain in my side; where's your bathroom."

"It's over there but let me put a plastic cap on your head."

I could see out the corner of my eye the other beautician

staring at me too. Their conversation paused and I rushed to the bathroom.

When I got to the bathroom, I started to hyperventilate. My hands were shaking, and I could not breathe. I splashed water on my face and moved to the corner of the restroom. I took several deep breaths trying to calm myself down. Was this some kind of sick joke? Maybe she didn't say Devin. Maybe she said Kevin and I've been so suspicious that I heard Devin. I took one last deep breath, put my shoulders back and pulled myself together. I was convinced that she couldn't have been talking about Devin.

I walked back to the shampoo bowl where Lisa was standing waiting for me. Still sitting in the seat next to me, I could see that little miss "deep in love" was now waiting for the brown cellophane in her hair to take. She had her phone in her hand and I had to admit she was beautiful.

Her cocoa complexion had a glow to it. A pair of arched eyebrows looked down on her long eyelashes. She did not hide her emotions; she was happy, and she wanted the world to see. Her pearl-white teeth gleamed through the smile she wore as she texted on her phone with her perfectly manicured pastel-pink fingernails. I guess she could sense me staring at her because her hazel eyes gazed up at me. Whatever she was texting made her fingers move a mile a minute and everything about her personality seemed bouncy.

Her beautician called over to her, "Sage, come to my station for a moment."

As she stood up, her all black tanked maxi dress clung to her shapely figure and her five-foot five frame moved in the direction of her beautician.

During the entire hour and a half that Lisa was finishing up on my hair I was restless, I could hear little miss "deep in love" laughing two hair stations down but I could not make out their conversation. I wanted Lisa to hurry the hell up so I could get a better look at her before she left.

I took my cellphone out of my purse and texted Devin; if he was going on a date I was going to find out.

Hey, I was thinking that we should get together tonight and go over some of the things I missed last week. I won't be able to do it tomorrow and I want to be prepared for Monday's meeting. Let's meet up at 7.

I pressed send and waited for his response.

One minute later the text alert went off on my phone. It was Devin. *"Sorry honey, I can't tonight I already have something set up but call me tomorrow and we can discuss it over the phone."* I was floored. I didn't misunderstand her. She was seeing my husband. I wanted to call his ass and ask him what or who the hell was more important than me. I always came first. This was not happening. My leg started shaking in anticipation for Lisa to finish with my hair.

"Okay, take a look and tell me what you think." Lisa said with a big smile on her face, I could tell she was happy with her work.

She handed me a mirror and I pretended to look at my hair with detail.

"Looks good to me."

"You sure? Let me know if you want me to change anything, even though I agree with you." Lisa took her hands and started fluffing my curls.

"No, it looks good girl, thank you. How much do I owe you?"

"It's going to be one-hundred and twenty dollars."

I took one-hundred and forty dollars out of my purse and handed it to Lisa.

"Thank you and umm if you're satisfied come back in two weeks, so I can give you a deep condition and trim those ends."

"Okay, sure thing."

Across the room I heard: "Okay, thanks Rhonda. I'll see you

in two weeks. Oh, and I'll let you know how my night went." I heard little miss "deep in love" wrapping up her hair appointment.

If she was coming back in two weeks so was I. We needed to be formally introduced.

She made it to the front counter right before me.

"Hey, Jessica can you schedule me an appointment with Rhonda two weeks from now. Same time, nine a.m."

"Sure, and I like this aura that you're giving off. Somebody is making you happy."

"Well, ya know," Little miss "deep in love" said as she did a hair flip.

I felt myself cringe. I wanted to snatch her up by her newly done flat ironed hair and rag tag her all over that salon, then slap Jessica and Rhonda for egging her on. Devin was my husband, and he should have been making me happy by stopping the stupid divorce, not playing nice, leading women on as if they had a chance. I was the only woman for him, why wasn't he getting that?

"Okay, see you in two weeks, Sage." Jessica handed her an appointment card.

She dropped it and I bent down to pick it up. When I stood up to hand it to her, I paused.

I was staring my threat right in the face. "Oh, here you go." I handed her the card and gave her a fake, forced smile.

"Thank you."

As she moved passed me, I walked up to the counter to make an appointment.

"Sooo how was your experience, do you like your hair?" Jessica asked.

"I love my hair and I'm so happy that I decided to come here from now on."

She had no idea my happiness was because I found out some new information on my soon-to-be ex-husband.

"Well, I'm happy you're satisfied."

Oh, I wasn't satisfied just yet. I thought to myself.

"Yes, I am, and actually I would like to schedule an appointment for two weeks from now."

"Okay, same time?"

"Let's do nine a.m."

I wanted to arrive at the same time as little miss "deep in love." I needed to know what type of car she drove, where she worked, everything. And since she likes to run her mouth to her beautician, I'm sure I was going to be able to find it all out.

"Let me see if she's available, yup she is."

"Okay, I'll be here."

"Here's your appointment card. See you in two weeks Ms. Elle."

"Huh?" I asked confused as she called me Elle.

"I said see you in two weeks Ms. Elle."

I remembered that I decided to keep the alias.

I wanted so bad to call Sasha, but she was in rehab and couldn't have phone calls. I needed a drink, a stiff one.

The past couple of weeks had flown by. I spent a lot of time going to meeting after meeting with Devin and our contractors. The lot was still under construction, and we had to meet with the lessees and their lawyers. I was drained. Somehow, I managed to keep my composure while working with Devin. But that got pretty pricy. When we were done with our meetings I left with a major headache or bad attitude, the intent to focus on business and not let our drama put so much pressure on me called for some retail therapy. In my mind it was much needed anyway. I had to somehow fill the empty space in the closet where Devin once hung his clothes. I even went as far as to have it redesigned. Between the meetings and the construction at my house, I stayed busy and out of trouble. Well, at least until I figured out my next plan of action.

Sasha was coming home the next day and I knew I was going

to have to fill her in. I got onto my laptop and scheduled us a spa day at Glen Ivy and dinner. I knew she would want to go out for drinks, so I didn't make dinner reservations anywhere too fancy.

It was the Thursday before my next hair appointment and my schedule was free and clear. I thought to go for a jog but poured me a mimosa instead. I climbed back into my bed and binge watched previous episodes of reality shows I set to record during the past weeks. There was something about the shows that drew me to them other than the entertaining drama.

It was like I was able to relate to some of the drama happening on the show. Suddenly I didn't feel all alone in my madness. I wanted so bad to let go and move on with my life. I no longer wanted to feel connected to my past. I just wanted to feel happy, like I used to. I wanted to feel in love again. I longed for my life to get back to what it used to be. But at this point I was feeling hopeless and alone. I tried hard to mask my pain and heartache with as much MAC makeup and Gucci clothing as I could. Ma taught us growing up: just because you feel like a mess, doesn't mean you have to look it. And when you look good, you feel good. So, this was a concept I stuck by.

I was watching my show when two of the cast mates got into a fight, it's like I was right there. I started yelling at the television, coaching one of the girls.

"Don't let her talk to you like that. Who the hell does she think she is?" My yelling got louder as the fight on the television became physical.

"Oh, hell no, she done went too damn far. Whoop her ass." I mean I was all into it, so much that I spilled my mimosa on my all white five-hundred-dollar duvet comforter.

"Damn," I said out loud.

I paused the show I was watching and started taking the comforter off of my bed so that I could wash it. I heard the text alert on my phone go off. To my surprise it was Devin. We didn't have any meetings, what could he possibly want?

The text read: *Hey LD, I need you to meet me at the office. I just got a message from one of the lessees for the new building and they may be backing out.*

This wasn't good. We met all week to go over and sign the contracts. The deals were signed, sealed, and delivered.

I responded: *Okay, I'll get a hold of Paul and have him meet us at the office. I'll be there in about an hour.*

Paul was our attorney and a good one; if anyone could sort this mess out it would be him.

As I put the comforter into the washer, I thought, good thing my drink spilled because I couldn't imagine showing up to the meeting smelling like liquor had I drank the entire glass.

I was dressed in forty-five minutes and at the office in twenty.

Devin pulled up right after me. He was texting on his phone as he walked up to the double glass doors of the office, and I couldn't help but wonder if he was texting her.

Devin greeted me with a hug and a kiss on the cheek like he always had done and started filling me in.

"So, here's what's going on, apparently their business has done exceptionally well over the last week and the premises they were planning on leasing from us, will be too small. They will need to expand to keep up with customers' demands."

"What? Yeah, right. There's no way."

"That's what I said, but they did offer for us to sublease to another company they are associated with on a different business."

"We don't really know these other people. We would have to research them. Say we do decide to go with them—we would need to rewrite the contracts, pushing back the grand opening of the entire lot. The other businesses will be affected."

"I know, I know."

"The reason for having an all-inclusive business grand opening was to market the entire lot so that it would jump start revenue for everyone. Having an empty building during the grand opening is not a good look."

"That's why I called this emergency meeting LD. Relax, honey."

Hearing him call me honey felt good especially since I found out about his little plaything, for a moment I no longer felt threatened.

"Paul isn't here yet; can you reach out to him and see what his ETA is?" Devin asked.

"I left my phone in the car, let me use yours," I responded.

"Here." He handed me his phone and walked into another part of the office.

Just then I got the idea to go into his text messages, and sure enough he had messages from a "Sage Nickels." I quickly wrote down her name and number. I decided not to read his text messages; I wanted to at least respect his privacy in that manner. I went to Paul's contact and called him. He was five minutes out.

Devin came back into our office, and I handed him his cellphone before going to set up the conference room. Devin and I always had a trusting relationship; going through his phone on the other hand didn't feel so wrong since I felt like it was one of the keys to saving our marriage. I needed to be in the know. I mean how else was I going to find out everything about this woman? I needed him to break up with her and come to his senses.

The meeting with the lessees ended and we were at a point where we were probably going to have to take them to court. I was fine with that as long as I could hurry up and get home to look this girl up on Facebook.

The moment I got home, I poured a tall glass of wine and took out my laptop. I was like a kid in a candy store. For a moment,

I thought to call her phone and hang up just to hear her voice to make sure she was the same girl from the salon, but Facebook was about to tell all.

I spent hours going through her pictures, searching to see if there were any of her and Devin. Anything to indicate if he had been cheating on me. But Devin was no man for social media, nor would he be so sloppy as to advertise an affair on it. I looked through her list of friends and realized we had a mutual friend. Some girl named Stephanie that I went to high school with. They even had a picture together, looked like they were out at some club. The picture seemed to be old because 'ole girl didn't look like that now. Sage had grown up. The club hoppin hoe had upgraded her appearance. But she was going to need to upgrade it more if she expected to keep up with me.

As I scrolled through her page, I could see she graduated from Spellman University with a master's degree in finance. I thought to myself good because there's no money for her ass over here. I don't care what Devin has in mind. I'm about to shut all this down.

I sat there for a couple more hours, scrolling through her pictures, reading the posts she had written, going onto her friends' pages to see what she had written to them. I just wanted to get a fill of who she really was. Before I knew it one a.m. had rolled around, and I was tired. Lying there trying to get some sleep, my mind was racing. I replayed everything back in my mind, her conversation with her beautician about Devin, the Facebook pictures, everything. I couldn't help but wonder how she and Devin met and when they met. It was killing me not to have the answers to these questions.

The next morning, I woke up with her still on my mind. I went back onto Facebook just to see what else I could try and find out about her. And I could see that she had just posted. Her post read:

"Morning Loves, Happy Friday. Just got to Target and let me

just say I'm NOT ready for the crowd. Hope everyone enjoys their day."

Right underneath her post was a casual picture of her with a big smile on her face.

And just like that my morning was made when I saw her location. She was at the Target ten minutes from my house.

When I got there, I pretended that I was shopping, but in reality, I was looking for Sage. I was putting any and everything in my basket, racing down the aisle like I was on one of those game shows where they gave away free groceries if you filled your basket up in a minute or less.

I went down every aisle but could not find her. I was anxious and getting impatient. I pulled out my phone to look at the screen shot of her picture I'd taken to help me remember exactly what she was wearing. A few minutes later there she was, on the aisle with all the home décors.

Suddenly my sense of urgency subsided. What was I going to say to her? Do I walk up and tell her Devin's my husband and to stay away from him? Do I walk up to her and slap fire from her? And then it came to me. I walked past her, casually roaming the aisle. Then conveniently hit her basket with mine.

"Oops, I'm sorry, excuse me."

"Oh no worries." She moved her basket over and continued looking at the bath towels.

"Wait, do I know you from somewhere?" I asked as she walked past me.

"I don't think we've met before," she replied with an odd look on her face.

"You look so familiar; are you a nurse at Cedar Sinai?" I thought that was so farfetched but worth a try.

"No, I'm in commercial banking, specifically finance."

What were the freaking odds?

"That's what it must be; I work in commercial real estate. Maybe we've crossed paths at some point."

"Yeah, maybe. Which company do you work for?"

I for sure couldn't tell her about Roswell Realty. So, I lied.

"Oh, I'm a broker with MGR Real Estate."

"Aren't they mainly in the Inland Empire?"

I could tell I was losing her, so I did what I do best. I did what every woman takes heed to, flattery.

"Yes, and by the way girl I love the color of your hair. Where do you get your hair done?"

"Hair and All beauty salon."

"Shit, so do I, that's where I know you from. Weren't you there two weeks ago?"

She eased up and smiled.

"Yeah, yes I was."

"Okay, well now I don't feel so confused. I forget names but I don't forget faces."

"Well, since you go there, I'll see you around. Nice meeting you." She started to leave.

"You too and hey I love networking; do you have a business card? You never know–I might want to change professions."

"Oh yeah, as a matter of fact I do. I always tell people finance is where it's at."

"I hear you, how is it working in finance?"

"Awesome, I'm the VP loan officer at Premier Commercial Banking in Santa Monica. There's a banking mixer coming up, you should go. Email me for the details, I have to go. Again, nice meeting you. But I didn't catch your name."

"I'm Elle," I continued with the alias.

"L as in the letter? Is that short for something?"

"That's how it's pronounced but its spelled Elle, like the magazine."

She nonchalantly shrugged her shoulders, "Okay, well email me." She pushed her basket past me and headed down another aisle.

"Will do, bye girl."

I had her right where I wanted her. I had her exactly where I wanted her. Now where we went from there, I just needed to figure that part out.

I felt the vibration from my phone going off in my back pocket.

"Hello, hey Sasha."

"Hi Sisssyyyy. Where are you?"

"I'm at Target, are you home yet? I've been waiting for you, there's so much for us to talk about."

"Target? What are you buying at Target?"

"Nothing." I said as I pushed my half full basket to the side and started walking out. "I already got what I came for."

"Okay well, I feel like eating somewhere casual; meet me at the Olive Garden."

"Okay, give me an hour, you know I scheduled us a date at Glen Ivy and dinner afterwards, but the reservations are for to-morrow, I thought you were coming home tomorrow."

"I'll explain everything when I see you."

The parking lot for Olive Garden was packed for some odd reason. As I walked in, I got a text from Sasha letting me know she had gotten us a table in the back next to the window.

Sasha got up out of her seat and gave me a tight hug.

"Oh my gosh, I missed you."

"So, did I, how are you? How are you feeling?"

"I'm good and I feel good."

"You look good, Sash."

"Thank you, I lost fifteen pounds. They had us working out hard core and eating kale and carrots and crap; talking about the right nutrition helps with mental clarity. That's why I wanted to come here for the endless pasta. I need some carbs."

"What's new La'Dai? You already know what my time away was like. A bunch of therapists and self-help groups and everyone hugging, singing kumbaya."

I was eager to tell Sasha everything, but I was going to start with the most important detail.

"Wait, before you catch me up let me order a drink, do you want one?" Sasha asked.

"Right now? It's barely twelve o clock."

"Hey it's five o' clock somewhere."

"What the hell, why not? Anything for you, sis."

Sasha motioned the waiter over and said, "What's up, fill me in."

"Well, Devin has a little girlfriend."

"Devin has a what?"

"Yup, you heard me."

"How do you know?"

"I have my ways."

"Have you seen her, what does she look like."

"Yes, I've seen her, this morning as a matter of fact."

"Was she at his house."

"Nope, I followed her to Target."

"You did what? You know I'm going to tell you how wrong you are, but first girl give me ALL the tea. Who is this little chicken head?"

Sash was excited, like a dog waiting for a bone.

"She's far from a chicken head. She has a master's degree in finance, she's the VP at her company and she's gorgeous, Sasha."

"Don't tell me you're intimidated by her."

I guess the look on my face gave it away.

"Hell no," I said trying to save face.

The truth is, I was. I was afraid their relationship would become a marriage of convenience and Devin would be gone forever.

"C'mon LD, I was only gone for a month. Don't tell me you got soft. Besides, I don't know why they kept me for so long this time anyway. It's not like I have a real problem."

"Sasha, you overdosed and almost died."

"Yeah, I'm fine as long as people learn how to leave me the hell alone. First my mom's sister, Brenda, and now this sperm donating low life thinks he can mind fuck me like there's no tomorrow. But I got news for him."

"Sash, calm down, are you good?"

"Yes, but I have to put some closure to what happened. He almost had me and that can never happen again. He cannot get the upper hand."

"What do you mean?"

"I'm going to simply write him a letter that says, 'Dear Daddy Dearest. Fuck you and Fuck that. I'm not weak like my mom. As a matter of fact, you are right about something, your blood does run through my veins which means don't underestimate me because I just might be crazy like you. You're lucky that I don't have my homies on the C yard make their way over to the D yard and lay you on your back. Keep fucking with me and you will wish that you lived on the sensitive needs yard where no one could get to your trifling ass.' That's it."

"Where did you learn how to talk like that?"

"Girl, you know we're from the hood."

"No Mom and Dad are, we were born and raised in View Park."

"Ha, I watch a lot of those "Locked Up" shows." One of us has to be tough. We both can't walk around stuck up and bougie. All jokes aside, sis, I AM my mother/father's child. I mean I have my vices and fight every day to overcome them. But sometimes I think that it's going to take a miracle to help me. But enough of that, so are you okay with this whole Devin thing?"

"No, not even close."

"LD please, Devin loves your dirty drawers. If he is messing with her it ain't deep. Now I don't know what's up with Devin wanting a divorce, but something tells me there's more to his story. Whatever it is, it isn't about you. You were a good wife and partner."

"Which is why I have to find out through this girl he's seeing."

"By stalking her?"

"I'm not stalking her; I'm just doing my research."

"LD, curiosity killed the cat. Stop now. It will all come out sooner or later, let it go."

"I can't."

"Yeah, you did luck out with Devin. He's the best brother-in-law a girl could ask for. He treats you phenomenally; he's humble and loves your family. You don't find them like that anymore. Trust me."

"Can you stop rubbing it in? Do you know Dad had a conversation with him?"

"Yeah, he told me."

"Well, Dad doesn't seem the least bit bothered by all this."

"Why should he be? Dad knows he raised a beautiful, talented, and successful woman who can have any man she wants. He knows you won't be single for long. We all know this, but you have to see it. Get your confidence back."

I could not for the life of me figure out why everyone was suggesting for me to move on effortlessly as if this divorce between Devin and me was anticipated. It came as a surprise, during what was supposed to be one of the most joyous times of our lives, just before our eleventh-year wedding anniversary. I don't think anyone ever says, "Oh divorce, piece of cake, let me just move on and pick up where I left off before I got married." It doesn't work like that. Besides, Dad was also another person who had pieces to my missing puzzle, but I knew there was no use trying to get him to talk.

Chapter Five

*I*f I was going to go to the mixer and try to get to know who this girl was, I had to make sure Devin was not going to be there. I walked into the office about a quarter past ten. Walking past the receptionist in the lobby I was trying not to drop the Starbucks I brought for Devin and me.

"Good morning, Roxanne."

"Good morning, Mrs. Roswell."

"Mr. Roswell is in the conference room and Tony called to say he's running late."

"Okay, thank you. Oh, and cancel my two o' clock. I believe Devin and I are going to go out in the field to see the lot and the rental properties."

"Okay."

I put my things down in the office and noticed Devin had picked up the post cards for the grand opening. I quickly got on-line and looked up some prospective properties in San Diego; my plan was to send Devin out of town. My mood was light, and I had put the divorce behind me for now. I was on a mission. And if I wanted Devin to cooperate with me then I was going to have to play nice.

Devin walked into the office and smiled when he saw me.

"Good morning, La'Dai."

"There you are. Good morning." I stood up to give him a hug.

"I see you picked up the announcements for the grand opening." I continued.

"Actually, Roxanne did on her way in this morning. La'Dai, I appreciate you putting our personal life aside and still focusing on our businesses."

"Yeah, well Devin, it hasn't been easy. But we've worked hard to build our brand and I won't let anything jeopardize that."

"I know this hasn't been easy."

"No, it hasn't, Devin, you're my husband and when I said our vows, I meant them. And to be honest, I still don't understand why we're getting a divorce. BUT for argument's sake let me say this, I had to dig deep inside myself and make peace with our situation for now. I'm mature enough to respect what you want, and I'm unselfish enough to put my own feelings aside and respect yours."

Clearly, I was lying. I wasn't at peace with the divorce. But the truth was for the first time since this entire thing unfolded, pretending to be at peace was actually helping me to gain some perspective.

"I want you to know that I meant it when I said I still love you and that I still want us to hold on to the friendship that we have. Brian and Erica are still friends even though they aren't married anymore."

"Devin, you know I hate it when you try to compare us to other couples."

"That's not what I'm doing; I was giving you an example."

"Well, I hear you."

"So, do you think we can connect on another level other than husband and wife?"

"Let's just take it one day at a time."

"Okay, I can live with that."

"But listen, Devin, I wanted to run something by you. I was thinking that we should expand to San Diego. Hear me out. We go up there every other month to check on the vacation home, anyway, so why not open a small business there?"

Devin was an open-minded man and never shot down any of my ideas. He was about his money so if there was an opportunity to capitalize, he was going to take it.

"Okay, what do you have in mind?"

"Well, there's a few properties for sale. I will have a better idea of what to do with the space once I see it. So, let's go up there this Saturday; we can leave Friday afternoon."

Devin thought for a moment. "Okay, we'll stay at the vacation spot, but call Imelda and have her go over there to clean it up and pick up a few groceries so it's ready when we get there."

Our housekeeper Imelda was phenomenal. She kept an eye on the property and made sure to keep squatters away. Since it was a beach house, it caught the eye of many, especially now since it was summer.

I knew damn well I wasn't going to go with Devin. I just needed to get him out of town so that I could make sure he wasn't going to go to the mixer, that's if she invited him. And if I knew my husband, which I did, he was not going to turn down a business opportunity for some mixer.

Friday had come and I spent the entire afternoon at the Beverly Center shopping to find something to wear. I went from Fendi, Giuseppe, Prada and finally Saint Laurent. That's when I found this stunning black dress that gave me the body of a goddess.

It was four p.m. and Devin was set to pick me up in twenty minutes. I went into the backyard and sprinted back and forth, working up a sweat. I still had on my pajamas and my hair was all over my head. When I was done, I went inside and grabbed two bottles of water and put them on my nightstand. I got into bed and texted Devin to use his key to come in.

"La'Dai, where you at, girl? Let's go." Devin said, walking into the house.

Devin walked into the bedroom and saw me lying in bed. "My gosh La'Dai, are you okay. Have you been throwing up?" He noticed the trash can next to the bed and the sweat on my face.

"Yeah, I have, and I can't stop."

Devin walked over to the bed and put his hand against my head.

"You're burning up and sweating like a pig."

"I know, can you hand me one of those water bottles?" I pointed to the water on the nightstand.

"Get up, I'm taking you to the hospital."

Little did he know I was so damn hot because I'd just run my ass off outside, but my plan was working so I ran with it.

"No Devin, I'll be fine. I just need some rest." I started to dry heave as if I were going to throw up. I should have been nominated for a Grammy award.

"La'Dai, we can't go to San Diego with you like this." He was so concerned.

"No, we can't, but you can. Take Tony, I already called him and he's packing now. I really want us to check out the space, when you get there, you can just facetime me, plus I had Imelda clean and go grocery shopping and the rental property needs to be checked on anyway." I was ranting.

"Okay, okay, okay. I'll go but first I'm taking you to the hospital."

"No, it's okay; I'll have Sasha come over. I don't want you guys on the road all night."

"Okay fine but I'm calling Sasha right now," Devin said as he pulled out his cellphone.

Sasha came over two hours later and I was up and getting

ready for the mixer.

"Okay, so help me to understand why Devin called me to rush over here and your ass is in the mirror puckering your lips with red matte lipstick."

"Because I'm going out."

"Out? La'Dai, I thought you were sick."

"That was just a cover up so that I can stay home and get Devin off to San Diego without me."

"Girl, you aren't making any sense."

"Devin's girlfriend invited me to a mixer and I'm going so that I can get to know her better. And I needed to make sure Devin was not going to be there, so I sent him to San Diego to check out some prospective properties."

"Who does this girl think you are?"

"She thinks I'm a woman named Elle who works for MGR Real Estate and I'm going to this mixer to network."

"You have lost your mind. I thought you were going to be okay but going through this divorce has got you all messed up and desperate. We are going to meet with Devin when he gets back and you're going to see a therapist, you need help."

"No, Sasha, I don't, and you aren't going to say a thing to Devin. Look, I know he's not being honest with me and I just want to find out why. If he's not being honest with me maybe he has been honest with her, and I will get her to tell me at some point."

"And how are you going to do that? She will figure you out eventually." Sasha said sarcastically.

"Maybe, maybe not."

"Oh my gosh, La'Dai; this is a bad idea."

"Okay, now tell me which shoe looks better," I said modeling two different pair of Giuseppe heels in front of her, ignoring her last comment.

"The one on your left foot," Sasha replied nonchalantly.

"I'm going to stay here while you go to this thing because I want to make sure you don't do nothing stupid; I mean other than going to this thing under false pretenses. In the meantime, you're driving me to drink. I 'm going to the kitchen."

"Okay, there's a new bottle of bubbles down there; feel free to open it."

When I got to the mixer, I valeted and suddenly it dawned on me. What if anyone I knew was there? I mean Devin and I had been in the real estate business for quite some time and had built up a decent clientele.

I walked in and scanned the room, so far, I was off the hook. I noticed Sage was at a table mingling with a group of people. I went into the ladies' room to check my frame and to make sure that I didn't have lipstick on my teeth.

When I came out, I suddenly got butterflies in my stomach. I thought to myself, "Damn, I know that guy, and he's walking over here."

"Well, hello gorgeous. You never called so I'm assuming things are still complicated." It was Mister Morris Chestnut from the club.

"Yes, yes they are," I responded not trying to seem uninterested.

"I was hoping you would be here; I remember you telling me that you were in commercial real estate. And to be honest, I haven't been able to stop thinking about you since I met you at the club."

"So, you came here solely for me?" I was starting to get creeped out. The nerve of me.

"Actually no. I own a restaurant and I'm hoping to open up a sister location."

"Oh okay."

"Yeah, usually I don't have time to come to stuff like this, being a doctor comes with a very busy schedule, but my agent is out of town and I thought it would be good for me to get my feet wet. So here I am."

I went from being creeped out to impressed. But I still had a lot going on and could not lead this man on.

"Doctor, what type?"

"I'm an oncologist."

"Okay, well Mister…"

"You forgot my name."

"Guilty."

"It's Jason, Ms. La'Dai."

"And you remembered mine."

"Yes, I did."

"Well, it's nice to see you again. I still have your number and I'll use it when the time is right."

"Please just let me take you out to dinner."

"It's really not a good time."

Jason waited for a moment before responding, as if he wanted to give one last plea but chose to be respectful instead.

"Okay, I see a friend of mine so have yourself a good night, just so you know, I'm not giving up," he replied.

"Okay. I won't try and stop you. You have a good night as well."

I glanced around the room a second time just to make sure there weren't any more familiar faces. That's when Sage noticed me and gestured for me to come over to her. By this time, she was by herself.

"Hi, I thought that was you, but I wasn't too sure until you turned around. I was thinking to myself; I hope I remember what she looks like." She laughed to herself.

"I definitely would have remembered what you look like; remember I told you that I never forget a face."

"Well, let's get a couple of drinks and mingle, girl."

We went to the bar and ordered two dirty martinis, and to my surprise we liked the same drink. I noticed Sage had been to the bar a couple of times. When we stepped up to order, the bartender asked her if it was going to be another dirty martini.

As the night went on, I could tell Sage was starting to have too much to drink. She didn't seem like the type to use a business event as a platform to let loose and get drunk but who was I to judge?

"So, Elle, how long have you been in real estate?" she asked with her words slurring.

"For a while, I've been…"

"Hold that thought; I have to pee. I'll be right back."

Sage sat her drink down almost missing the table. She stumbled as she walked away and looked down at the ground as if someone had just put it there. I thought to myself this girl is about to make a fool out of herself. As much as I would have loved to watch her do it, I couldn't be that cruel. Besides karma is a bitch that likes to come around twice, at least that's how I understand it.

I waited a moment before I went into the restroom to check on her. When I walked into the restroom, I could hear the toilet flushing and Sage singing Beyoncé's Drunk in Love.

"Drrruuunnk in looove, we be all night, aye." She sang and two stepped by herself.

She was singing in a tone that only dogs could understand. She stumbled out of the bathroom stall and over to the sink.

"Hey girl, ohhh hot," she said pulling her hands out from underneath the water. "What do you say we leave here and go to the club? It's not like I have anyone to go home to anyway. My man is out of town and you seem like a fun person to hang out with."

"I think you've had too much to drink and should get home."

She took a glance at herself in the mirror, reapplied some lipstick and said, "I think you're right, but I look so good tonight and I'm not tired."

"Why don't I call you an uber?"

"Hell no, I'm not riding with some stranger. Can you give me a ride?"

I paused and thought for a moment… a chance to see where this girl lives and try to understand why Devin would be mildly interested in her, HELL YES! From what I could tell she didn't seem like his type. And I wondered why she was so trusting; I get it that sometimes alcohol throws off your better judgment, but she was acting as if we had been friends for years.

"Sure, I'll make sure you get home safe."

"Good, let's go."

Sage made a stop at one of the tables before she headed out to my car. I went ahead to the valet and waited for her there.

Getting into my car, she turned the music up loudly and started singing again.

"Sage, girl relax, give me your address so that I can put it into the GPS." I was starting to get annoyed.

"Okay, I just love that song."

I put her address into my GPS. This girl lived twenty -five minutes in the opposite direction of the freeway, which was completely out of my way but like I said I was on a mission.

"Are you sure you don't want to go to the club?"

"Yes, I'm pretty sure."

"I just don't want to go home to an empty house plus it's only nine-thirty, not even close to my bedtime."

"You said you were married?" I asked playing dumb and trying to spark conversation about her and Devin. I couldn't even believe I was inquiring about Devin with another woman.

"No, I'm seeing this guy and he's so amazing. I mean Devin

is heaven sent, he charming, a gentleman and he's successful. You know it's funny the way we met."

She loved any moment she got to gloat about Devin.

"Yeah, how so girl?"

"I was just helping him get a loan for some commercial property he wanted to buy."

So that's how he went behind my back and bought that property.

She continued, "And everything was casual, I mean he never really flirted with me, and I was flattered by that, so I asked him to dinner which I've never done. We went out and I've been seeing him ever since. I mean we haven't been seeing each other that long but I think we're getting somewhere."

"Oh yeah, how can you be so sure?" I asked not trying to sound jealous.

"As a matter of fact, let me call him." She pulled out her cellphone and turned the music even lower.

"Okay, shh it's ringing." She began her conversation. "Hey Dev."

Dev, what was he, twelve? I continued listening.

"What are you doing, babe?" Before letting him answer, she continued talking. "Well, I'm on my way home from that business thing I was telling you about and I could really use your warm body next to mine. If you leave now, you'll get back to LA a little after midnight. C'mon baby."

His ass better not leave; I started to get sick to my stomach hearing her talk to my husband.

"Have I been drinking? Umm I had a couple of drinks," she said. Still talking to Devin, she answered, "No, I'm not drunk, and my words are not slurring. How am I getting home?" She glanced over at me with a huge smile on her face before replying, "My new friend Elle is taking me."

Unless the word "drunk" had a different meaning now a days, this girl was in denial...

"Elle say hi to Dev." Sage held the phone up to my ear and I pushed it away trying not to say a word and risk getting exposed, clearly her ass was drunk.

"Well, baby since you aren't going to come, I guess I'll just go home take a hot shower and go to bed. Do you want me to face time you while I'm in the shower? Ha, ha," she laughed out loud. Her drunken laugh was getting on my nerves. "Okay Dev, I'll talk to you in the morning then," she said as she hung up the phone.

"You know, Elle, I don't get it, don't get me wrong. Devin is a good man, but I just offered to show him my naked body and he dismissed it, saying he has to get up early in the morning. Any other man would have killed just at the thought of seeing me naked."

"Maybe he's not like any other guy."

The streets were quiet as we drove down Torrance Boulevard, it was a full moon, and I could tell we were getting closer to the beach as the air grew misty and cooler.

"I guess that's the price you pay when dealing with a successful man, focus. You compete for their mind and their time. Or do you think it has something to do with him going through a divorce? Oh my gosh Elle, what if he's with her right now? What if they decided to get back together? I'm going to call him back."

Little did she know she was with "her" right now and I had the same thoughts she had one time or another since this started.

"He's going through a divorce?" I asked trying to sound surprised.

"Yeah."

"Well, did he say why?"

"Does it matter?" she snapped at me.

Oh no, this bitch did not.

"Look Sage, you're a little drunk and I don't want you to do anything you'd regret; don't call him back." Even though I really did want her to do something stupid so Devin could see her true colors.

"Plus, it looks like we're pulling up at your house." I said putting the car in park.

My phone rang and Sasha's name came up on the screen of my car's radio. I pressed the decline button. "We're here," I said as we pulled up to a newly built house in Redondo Beach.

My phone went off again, and it was a text from Sasha. *"Hey, I'm checking on you, how's it going?" Her text read.*

I'm at her house, I'll call you in a minute.

We texted back and forth, and I could sense that Sasha was upset.

You're what?! La'Dai, call me right NOW! her text read.

Sasha, hold on. I texted back.

Now La'Dai. She replied.

I pulled into the driveway to get her as close as possible to her doorstep.

"Well girl, thank you so much for the ride. I'll get my car tomorrow."

"You're welcome, have a good night."

"Yeah, some night, it's ending too early."

I watched her stumble into her house, and I drove off.

My phone rang again. "Damn you, Sasha." I said out loud. But this time it wasn't Sasha it was Devin.

I hurried and rolled up all the windows and quickly pulled over at the shopping center that was well lit from all the shops.

"Hello," I said trying to sound sleepy.

"Hey, how are you feeling? I tried to call you a couple of times and when you didn't answer I called Sasha. She told me you were asleep."

"Yeah, I've just been trying to get some rest ya know."

My other line rang, Sasha was blowing me up. I quickly rushed Devin off the phone.

"Hey, this Nyquil really has me drowsy; I'll call you in the morning, okay?"

"Okay sweetheart, get some rest."

I thought I'd better stop playing and get home before Sasha sends out an APB on me. Knowing my sister, she would. Sasha truly was her sister's keeper. Although she was six months younger than I she had crowned herself the older sister, saying that it was for the best. Ha. And truly acted like it.

I put my address in the GPS before calling Sasha back and sped off, it felt like I was catching every green light.

"Sash."

"La'Dai, what the hell?"

"I know, I know—my bad, sis. I didn't mean to leave you hanging."

"Where are you? Don't tell me you're still at her house."

"No, I'm not. I was just dropping her off because she was too drunk to drive. Home girl was a mess."

"I don't like where this is going."

"Sasha, I'll be home in a minute, we can talk then."

"Can we go get some food? I'm starving and you have nothing good to eat here."

"Yes, only if you drive. This girl lives way in Redondo Beach."

"Alright."

An hour later I arrived at home. Sasha and I spent the next three hours talking about my night and how wrong I was. We never left the house, I found us something to cook instead. After about three shots and wine, I was feeling good. With the night I'd had, drinking three bottles of wine was called for. Living a lie was not easy, I don't know how Devin was doing it so well. I'm pretty sure I drank one bottle by myself. It was extremely late, and the wine was making me sleepy. But my mind was still racing from all the shenanigans and Sasha was in my living room trying to teach herself how to salsa. Apparently, she was dating this Hispanic guy who wanted to take her dancing.

Lying on my couch I asked, "When's the last time we had a sleepover?"

"I don't know," then she paused, "yes I do, how about that time I thought I was pregnant."

"Oh yeah, I remember that, and you swore you were having cravings. So, we stayed up all night eating ice cream and honey buns. I think you even ate an entire pepperoni pizza by yourself."

"I gained five pounds that weekend."

Sasha fell out laughing on the all-white cashmere area rug covering my living room floor.

"Man, I was scared shitless, my career was taking off; and I know Ma and Dad would have had a fit if I was pregnant and not married."

"Probably, but our parents would have loved you the same."

"That's what I love about them, they never judge. They just want the best for us."

"Yeah, we are pretty blessed; that's why I'm going to count my blessings and try to move on. I'm done trying to find out what Devin is hiding. Truth is he does still love me, he proved that this weekend without even knowing it. And from what I saw tonight, his little plaything is not going to last."

"Good sis, so are we going on that trip?"

"Where to?"

"Jamaica, remember?" Sasha said as she started dancing like she was from the islands.

"Yes, I told you to count me in and set it up."

Chapter Six

"Okay everyone listen up, today is a big day and we have all been working very hard toward the grand opening here at this new lot for Roswell Gateway. Today will be one of the hottest days in August so stay hydrated. Sharon, I need you to make sure all five food trucks have the appropriate spacing, also make sure the tent is up in time for the clown and the snow cone machine." I was giving orders as if I were directing a movie. Clipboard in hand and ready to conquer the success Devin and I had been waiting for.

It was only ten a.m. and already the temperature was seventy-five degrees. We collaborated with each store to ensure they had complimentary water for their customers, their air conditioners were up and running and we made sure they were fully staffed.

"Tim, please go around to each store and see if there is anything they need. The lot will be open for business in an hour and it's important that each store is on point." I pointed my finger around like it was the long hand on the clock to demonstrate to Tim that I meant every store.

The live band was already set up and the sound of music filled the atmosphere. Balloons were flying in the air and cars were already lined up waiting to come in and shop. I couldn't have been prouder, but my feet were singing a different tune. The Prada wedges I wore had my feet begging for mercy.

"La'Dai, honey, the channel five news is here."

"Are they going to interview us now?"

"They want to capture the atmosphere first, get a couple of interviews with the storeowners and of course save the best for last, us."

"That works well because then we'll be up and running and they will be able to film business running successfully."

Devin, our crew, and the business owners were all standing near the big red ribbon that stretched across the front of the parking lot waiting to be cut, when out the corner of my eye this familiar face walked up. He walked straight over to Devin, and said, "Do you mind if I join you. This is another part of black history in the making."

Devin responded, "Hello Mayor Johnson, don't mind if you do."

I thought to myself, I didn't know Devin was on a first name basis with the mayor. Mayor Johnson Newman was good for the city of Los Angeles. We could have been doing business on another level had I known about this.

I cleared my throat as if to say, hello, aren't you going to introduce me? Devin turned around looked at me and back at the mayor and said, "This is my lovely, intelligent partner, La'Dai, she's the brains behind this entire operation."

The mayor shook my hand and said, "La'Dai is it?"

"Yes, La'Dai Roswell." I was sure to mention my last name as I noticed Devin referred to me as his business partner and not his wife. Yes, we were getting a divorce, but it wasn't final, and I'd be damned if he was going to cheat me out of the last name I worked hard to get and keep. But what happened next was odd and caught me by surprise.

"Roswell. Devin, you mean to tell me that this beautiful

woman is your wife?"

The mayor did not know that Devin was married. I felt myself getting hot; I was becoming upset. But I knew better than to show my horns at that moment.

Devin responded, "Umm Mayor Johnson the media is waiting to film the cutting of the bow, business first, shall we?"

"Well, of course." The mayor responded looking puzzled and confused.

As Devin walked over to stand alongside me, I whispered very low under my breath, "And how exactly do you know the mayor and why didn't you tell me that you knew him, oh, and business partner?"

"I met him through a friend LD, can we talk about this later, please. The media is waiting and need I remind you, watching too!"

"Oh yeah, we WILL talk later," I said putting on my fakest smile yet. When it came to money, my money and business, I was always quick to put my emotions last. I understood the concept of "money talks and bullshit walks" very well. You didn't have to tell me twice.

Once the bow was cut and the media cameras were rolling, everything was in full effect and so was I. I was in an entirely different realm of business mind. I was on cloud ten. I surpassed cloud nine three hours ago. Devin and I did it again. Business and success as usual. My smile was bright and so was our future.

Everything was going great, the stores were full of consumers, kids were enjoying the free snow cones, the food trucks had lines and food ready to be served. Then suddenly my heart fell into my stomach when I saw Sage walking in my direction. I knew damn well this was not her type of scene for leisure.

"Hey girl, I thought that was you," Sage said as she walked up to me wearing a pair of short jeans shorts, a tee shirt that clearly advertised her company, and a cute pair of wedges that I probably would have worn myself. I had to admit girlfriend had style.

"Umm Hi, what are you doing here?"

"Well, my uncle is Mayor Johnson and he's here to support my boo, remember the guy I told you I was seeing, well this is his lot and he's hosting the grand opening. I called my uncle to see how things were going and he said exceptionally well so I thought that I would drop by and surprise Devin."

"Wait, did you say your uncle is Mayor Johnson?"

"Yes, but besides that, can you believe I showed up to support this man and he kind of gave me the cold shoulder. I guess his soon-to-be ex-wife is running around here somewhere and he doesn't think it would be a good idea for me to stay. I mean I get that they're in business together but what am I supposed to do? Go into hiding? She's going to meet me someday, you know. The nerve of him. But anyway, I didn't expect to see you here. What a surprise."

"Yeah, well I heard about this place and decided to come and see what all the fuss was about, but I was getting ready to head out."

"Oh really, I literally just got here. Stay a while. Since Devin kicked me to the curb, I could use the company."

"Did you say he didn't want you here?"

"No, what I said was he said he didn't think it was a good idea for me to be here, but I think he's just under a lot of pressure and doesn't want any drama. And rightfully so, so I intend on getting something to eat, maybe shop around to help sales, chat with my uncle, and then leave. Stay in my own lane you know, and if I do that there can be no traffic."

I thought to myself *if you know like I know you would get yourself out of here.* But clearly, I was smarter than she was and knew when to leave, even if it was my own event. And like I mentioned earlier, I didn't play with my money. Since things were coming to a close soon and everything went as planned, I decided to let Devin finish up, and let the cleaning crew we hired do their job. They worked for us before, so they knew my expectations.

"Sorry, I can't stay. I have plans with my sister tonight. But I'm sure we'll chat later."

"Okay, talk to you soon girl."

I left Sage standing there as I hurried to our office, hoping Sage didn't see me enter. And she didn't, she was too busy eyeing my husband. I was a little hesitant about leaving but I knew I couldn't risk everything. I sent Devin a text telling him to meet me in the office that it was urgent, and I came up with a lie about Sasha's car breaking down on her way home. Of course, he offered to help but I told him that he needed to give a thank you speech to everyone still at the Grand Opening. No time was better than the present because it would create the perfect diversion for me to get the hell out of there.

As soon as I got home, I was all set to take a shower. Just as I was getting in, from the bathroom window, I could see headlights from a car coming up my driveway, but I couldn't tell who it was. I wondered who could be coming to my house at this time of night and without calling. Could it be Sasha?

Heading downstairs wrapped in a towel, I went to investigate. I could hear keys being put into the lock and for a moment I panicked. Two seconds later I was calmed down by Devin's smiling face.

"Hey LD. I was going to call but I was already almost here."

"Devin, what are you doing here?"

We weren't officially divorced, and it was technically still his house, so I didn't bother taking Devin's key away. It's not like I had anything to hide, unlike his ass anyway.

"Look, today's event made me realize that you and I need to

talk. I want to talk to you about something." He sat down on the couch.

"What do you want to talk to me about? Huh? The fact that you invited the mayor to our event, he had no prior knowledge of me or of our marriage. In that moment you showed no regard for me at all. That's what we're doing now, Devin?"

"LD, there's an explanation."

"Devin, you introduced me as your business partner, not as your wife. That tells me a lot."

"If you're willing to listen, I'm willing to explain," Devin replied with the utmost sincerity.

Truth be told I was not trying to hear him at that moment, his behavior was inexcusable.

"You know what, there's no need for you to explain. I get it, I get the fact that you've already mentally checked out of this marriage with the intention of recreating your entire existence as a single man."

"La'Dai, you are overacting and overthinking this entire situation."

"No, no I'm not. Trust me, I know I'm not."

Just then I realized that maybe I was overacting but I didn't care. My feelings were hurt, and this was the exact outlet I needed, so I just went ahead and let it all out.

"Devin, you know this is hard for me and it's going to take some getting used to. I've been worked hard to build this life with you and now I'm supposed to praise you and be happy because you're giving me the majority of everything? Rightfully so, don't you think?"

"Well, I'll be honest; it was a poor decision on my part to not tell you that I knew the mayor."

"You know I appreciate you owning up to that but tell me why you introduced me the way you did. Why was he so shocked to know that there is a 'Mrs. Roswell'?"

"I mean the status of our relationship hasn't necessarily been the topic of discussion and with the direction that our marriage is headed in, I didn't want it to be. So, I tried to avoid it at all costs. Plus, it isn't anyone's business."

"Devin, what the hell are you talking about? I know better than that, so please don't play on my intelligence. Why do I have a gut feeling that you're not wanting the mayor in our business has something to do with you dating another woman?"

"You have some real serious trust issues, and I don't know where they stem from. Why are you adamant that I'm dating someone, it's like you get these ideas in your head and you run with them. I may have not been forthcoming with the mayor, but I've been honest with you. I've been truthful where it matters."

"Truth? You want to talk about truth? Let's start with the reason why we're in this mess to begin with."

"Here we go again."

"I mean did you really think that I was going to buy the excuse that you just woke up one day and decided that you wanted to be single. Sorry, try again. I don't know what's going on with you, Devin, but I'm definitely starting to notice a change."

"You're reading too much into things, LD. Your imagination is running wild, and you sound crazy. Listen, I think it's time that I clear the air about everything."

I began to walk to the kitchen as Devin made himself more comfortable on the couch.

"Hold that thought, I need a drink," I said as I turned around to face him and gave him a look of try me if you want to.

As I walked back into the living room, I heard the text alert go off on my phone. I set my drink down on the living room end table and went upstairs to get it. It was a message from Sage. She said something to the effect that she could really use some girls talk and asked if I was free. I was in the middle of texting her back as I walked down the stairs. Devin could see me engaged in my phone. He got up off the couch and met me at the end of the stairs. In that moment I had forgotten that he was there.

"Right now, is not a good time to talk I take it. It looks like whatever you're texting about has your attention and you're upset anyway so we can try this again some other time. Good night." Devin kissed me on the forehead and headed to the door.

"That sounds like a good idea, I don't want to argue anymore."

As Devin walked out the door, I went to sit on the couch to finish texting Sage. I took two large gulps of my wine and tried to gather my thoughts. I guess it wouldn't have killed me to give Devin a minute to explain but hell I was seeing things with my own two eyes. And I mean what could he possibly have told me that I didn't already know? I thought for a moment about sending the text but thought twice since I promised Sasha that I was done being in contact with this girl. But she was making it too easy, and how foolish would I be to pass up a free meal and some girl time anyway.

A week went by, and I had not talked to Devin since he came by my house. I mean we had very limited casual conversation about business but nothing serious. I was trying to avoid addressing the elephant in the room for now. Besides, for the first time in Roswell history, I think Devin was genuinely upset with me.

As I pulled up to dinner with Sage, I could see her a few cars ahead valet parking her black Mercedes Benz, CLK400.

It was three o clock in the afternoon, and Saturdays at Rodeo Drive were usually filled with shoppers who walked the streets without a care in the world just ready to spend, spend and spend...

"Oh girl, I told you it wasn't a problem, we girls have to look out for each other," I said to Sage as we walked down Rodeo drive, passing by Louis Vuitton.

"I understand what you're saying but I really wanted to thank you. I don't deal with a lot of females. I'm not bragging but I'm doing well for myself, and it's been hard finding down-to-earth females who won't get jealous or think I'm trying to one up them because I'm constantly challenging myself to level up, you know?"

I thought to myself, "Bitch, you're sleeping with my husband, who would be jealous of being a homewrecker?" But then it wasn't her fault, she didn't know the details of my pending divorce but still we weren't friends, so she wasn't about to get a pass.

"I hear you," I responded.

I didn't want to tell her anything about myself. I figured if I made the conversations about her, she would open up more and I would soon find out what the hell she was doing with my husband in the first place.

"Speaking of which," I continued to say, "did you ever meet up with the guy you were seeing after that event?"

"Actually, I did. The next day him, my uncle, Mayor Johnson, and I went to brunch. It was mainly business talk, but he and I had a heart-to-heart afterwards. He basically tried to explain to me why I should not have popped up at the event. And let me tell you, Devin is so reserved that he stayed calm, cool, and collected the entire time. Do you know how hard it was for me not to lose my cool, because in my mind I was like what's the big deal, you know?"

"What do you mean?"

"Well, Devin thinks it would be bad for business if my uncle knew that we are seeing each other so when my uncle is around, in my opinion, Devin puts up this façade. But I'm like we're grownups—who cares?"

Little did she know that this was how Devin conducted business--business first pleasure later. I was his wife and business partner but when we were in the field, it's all work and no play, and rightfully so. This girl had a lot of growing up to do, especially if she was going to compete with the "Mrs." Roswell.

"Yeah, I get it. If you don't mind me asking, what kind of business does he do?"

"Well, I remember I told you that I helped him purchase commercial property and that's how we met. The reason why he purchased the property is so that he could--."

Sage paused and looked down at her phone, when she read the text message a big smile came over her face.

"Speaking of the devil, that's him texting me now. We're supposed to go to dinner tonight but since you and I are having a late lunch, I told him to meet us here," she said excitedly, nudging my shoulder. "This way you can meet him, and hey since you're in real estate too he may have some insight or business endeavors for you. See I got you, girl."

I began to panic. I was trying not to lose my cool, but did Sage just say that she invited Devin to lunch with us. Oh, hell no, I needed to get out of here. This was about to get ugly and fast. Damn, and just when she was about to spill the beans and tell me about this new property that he purchased. I had to go, but what was I going to say? I needed to get my lie straight.

"Thank you for having my back but I have a few projects I'm working on right now and I've just been given a new one so work is pretty busy."

"Okay, well I still would like for you to meet him; he's a great guy and this way you can put a face to the name. It's so funny how you and I just clicked."

I was trying to think, and she just kept talking, I wanted her to be quiet for a second.

"I need to go to the restroom really quick; I'll be right back." I scurried away and didn't think twice about how silly I looked walking away in a panic.

I did an about-face and went into the first store front that I could step foot into.

The young woman inside of the Gucci store greeted me with such style and sophistication. It just so happened that she was the same woman who helped me purchase a purse a few weeks prior.

She said in excitement, "Oh hello, you're back. What can I help you find today?"

I replied, "I'm sorry, I actually did not come to shop today but may I use your ladies' room please."

"Absolutely, you're one of our valued customers; the answer is always yes to you."

"Okay, thank you."

"Right this way, Miss."

As she guided me to the restroom, I turned around to see where Sage was, and of course she was not far behind me, browsing.

I went into the restroom, looked myself in the mirror and said, "Okay, LD, think, think. You are too close to getting the info you need, you cannot let her mess this whole thing up because she got the bright idea that you and Devin should meet. Think, think."

Then I came up with the simplest dumbest excuse that every woman uses but it does the job every time.

Coming out the restroom, Sage was at the counter buying a new purse. Of course, she would. I rolled my eyes at her frivolous spending, thinking to myself Devin better not be fronting the bill.

I walked over to her and whispered in her ear, "Hey girl, Aunt Flo' just came to visit can you check my pants and make sure that I'm all good."

I turned around trying not to be obvious.

"Oh, you're good, nothing to worry about."

"Phew, always at the worst time. I checked in the restroom,

but I wanted to be sure. This was so unexpected; this is the second time that it has come this month."

"Really, are you good or do you need to go to the nearest store?"

"Actually girl, I'm going to have to take a rain check on lunch. I need to clean myself up and change. I don't know how I didn't feel it coming down."

"Oh, it's that bad."

"Yeah, I need to head out and get myself together. I hate to leave like this, but you have your boo coming anyway so the day isn't completely wasted. Who knows? Maybe you'll be able to continue to shop, and on his dime." I couldn't believe the words that were coming out of my mouth. But the words made me sound genuine.

"That's not such a bad idea."

I chuckled, said my last 'see you later' and darted out the door.

Walking down Rodeo Drive and over to where I valeted my car, I mumbled to myself, "That was too damn close."

Chapter Seven

"Guess who made district attorney," Sasha said giddy as all outdoors.

"My intelligent sister did," I replied.

"That's right. I did yup, I did that," Sasha responded pointing into her chest.

It was no surprise to me that Sasha made DA. I mean, she spent all of her twenties and a lot of Mom and Dad's money trying to find her way. She graduated college, set out to be a social worker, but after ten months on the job Sasha said she was heartbroken from all the case files she read.

After that it was law enforcement, she was hell bent on putting away some of the people she read about in the case files while being a social worker. Sasha graduated the academy but couldn't get used to having a partner and working the structured long hours patrolling the streets. So, still wanting to pursue law enforcement, she went down the road of becoming a correctional officer. Then her excuse became, all she could think about was her parents being in prison and how working for the Department of Corrections only made her envision her mother dying in that hell hole. Sad and alone in her cell and the prison walls being the last thing her eyes saw before she took her last breath. Finally, it was law school and that's where Sasha found her niche. She was not going to give up being a woman of power, being right and sticking it to people who she thought needed to be off the streets. She wanted to become the district attorney. Let's not forget the money she would be bringing in. Things moved fast over the years for Sasha, opportunities presenting themselves and doors opening wide. Getting the jobs, she wanted was not hard for her at all. Once she put her mind to something, she did it, determination was her best friend. Let's not forget that she was beautiful, wise and could charm the pants off of anyone, literally, women included. But women weren't her cup of tea, she was just that good. Sasha wasn't afraid to use what she had to get what she wanted, and since she was good at it, why not, I suppose.

"I'm so proud of you, but you know that this means you have to stop going on dates with Judge Carney, right?"

"Oh, you mean Judge Corny; yeah, I stopped seeing him weeks ago," Sasha said sitting down on the sofa.

We were at her house, where smooth jazz played softly in the background and our two glasses of Chardonnay sat chilled on top of the marble table coaster, Sasha made sure I used.

"Good, because that's a real conflict of interest."

"What? Him calling me into his chambers to personally swear me in himself while I straddled him on top of his desk or us role playing in court room number ten."

"Sasha!"

"What! I went easy on him, I didn't handcuff both of his hands, plus he was under arrest for something very bad." She said as she bit her bottom lip.

"Ew, you're disgusting. Anyway, all of that is a conflict of interest."

"I know, that's why I cut it off when I found out I was going to become DA. I just needed his help to put in a good word for me, plus he was fine. I had to."

"Sash, when are you going to settle down?"

"We've been over this. I need a man like I need a hole in my head."

"I don't get you. You're young, beautiful, intelligent and can cook better than Martha Stewart herself. You would make any man very happy."

"See that's it right there. I'm not going to spend my life waiting hand and foot trying to make someone else happy. I'm spending my time making Sasha happy. And right now, Sasha would be happy with dinner reservations so we can go out and celebrate."

"Yes, we can, but for the record; relationships aren't about independence or dependence. They are about interdependence."

"Okay Dr. Phil. Can we go now?"

We got to the restaurant and the atmosphere was familiar, I couldn't figure out what it was until I looked over at the live band and remembered they were the same band playing the last time Devin and I had eaten at this restaurant. We sat down and Sasha ordered two glasses of Dom Perignon.

"So, what's going on? What's new?" Sasha said being inquisitive.

"Nothing is new; I'm hoping we finalize the divorce soon."

"What's the holdup now?"

"This new property Devin decided to buy and not tell me about, and then he has the nerve not to want to split it down the middle, remember I told you that?"

"Okay sis, you know I love you but..." Sasha said as she took a drink from her water before she continued. "I have to be real with you. Devin has been very generous during this entire divorce, when we think about how he divided everything he been more than just generous. So why won't you let this go?"

"Sasha, whose side are you on?"

"The right side and right now I'm starting to believe that this may be your way of trying to prolong the divorce so you can stay with Devin."

"That wouldn't be such a bad idea, and then he wouldn't be able to move forward with his little girlfriend so fast. Do you know that I went out with her last week and while we were out together with plans to have lunch, her ass gets the bright idea to invite Devin to join us for lunch so that he and I could meet?"

"What?!"

"Sasha yes, I had to get out of there so fast. She almost blew my cover."

"You sound crazy and deranged."

"I beg to differ; I'm just a woman going through a divorce. Trying to get the answers that my husband won't give me."

"Please for Christ's sake let this go. He wished you well and is still looking out for your well-being. Speaking of well-being I see he's lost some weight."

"Yeah, probably because her ass can't cook. Anyway, so now that we have even more reason to go to Jamaica, when are we leaving, Ms. DA?"

"I emailed you our itinerary. Hold on, I believe it's on the 8th, two weeks from now." Sasha replied, picking up her iPhone.

"Two weeks? Shoot, I haven't went shopping for anything. Guess I better get on my master cleanse and shed some of this weight."

"Girl, please you don't need no master cleanse, those Jamaican men are going to love you just the way you are. They are nothing like American men, they aren't shallow. Jamaican men see the beauty in everything and are always so damn positive. They're charming and their energy is infectious. A Jamaican man will make you laugh until your cheeks hurt. And did I mention that they are foodies. You'll never have to cook again a day in your life; food is just a part of their culture. They are full of confidence and would dance circles around Michael Jackson if he were still alive. So, you know what that means in the bedroom department, right?"

"Damn Sasha, who died and made you their advocate? If I didn't know any better, I would think you were speaking from experience."

"I am," Sasha replied sitting back in her chair like Mack of the year himself.

"What, who haven't you dated?"

"You know I don't discriminate. If he has the qualities, I'm looking for then I'm going to reel him right on in."

"So, when did you date a Jamaican?"

"Since you're all in my business, I met him online and I flew out there for two weeks to meet him."

"Sasha, what if something had happened to you?"

"La'Dai, I mean I'm single, right? Last time I checked I don't have any kids tying me down either. So yes, I did. Life is too short to be hanging on to the 'What ifs."

"So, then what happened?"

"Ummm, Jamaica isn't just around the corner and the distance doesn't make for your ideal relationship. Plus, it's a tourist spot; I'm sure he sees all types of women all the time, with their exotic fantasies. Why would he pass that up for someone he barely met? No time for games."

"But what if it could have possibly become something?"

"Well, maybe I'll give him a call when we get out there and see. But besides that, I just love the Jamaican culture. It's so vibrant and unique. Shit, let's leave now."

An hour and half later, Sasha and I ended up at our parent's house. Dad was in the family room; I could hear the commentators on the TV talking about Derek Carr and how they suspect the Raiders might conceivably have a decent season this year. Although I'd been a Raiders fan all my life, I thought to myself yeah, we'll see.

Dad was snoring loudly and his Raiders jersey displaying the number twenty-four on it had a small cheese stain from the nachos he had been eating. Judging from the stain and his snoring I could tell he had fallen asleep watching the game and eating Mom's famous chicken nachos he loved so much. Hell, we all did. I took the tray of nachos out of his hand. Trying not to wake him, I gently kissed him on the cheek. Dad rarely made it through an entire game nowadays. A couple of beers, a shot of Patron, and a full belly did it every time. Dad worked hard and watching sports was his favorite way to relax.

I found Mom and Sasha outside in the backyard, Mom was lying poolside and Sasha had her feet in the water. Sasha handed me a dirty martini, and from what I could see, she made her and Ma one too. She stood up, taking her feet out the pool and raised her glass. Ma and I followed her lead and raised our glasses too.

Sasha started talking, standing proud and sounding so enthusiastic, "I just want to thank my two best friends, my mother and my sister. Thank you, you two beautiful souls, for standing by me even though I changed careers twenty million times. Ma, thank you for supporting me and always believing in me. La'Dai, thank you for taking all my phone calls no matter what time of the night it was. I would call you crying about how hard law school was and you'd talk me off the ledge. I love you both and I just want to say, 'All for one and Justice for all'." Sasha started laughing and downed her drink. Ma took a sip of hers and I downed mine as well.

I let out a long sigh and Ma asked what was wrong.

"I'm sitting here, Ma, and don't take this the wrong way but I envy you."

"What do you mean, honey?" Ma sounded confused.

"I mean Dad's in the house, sleeping peacefully and content right where he is, and you're outside lying poolside, secure in knowing your husband is by your side no matter what. Your Sunday routine is in full effect and you have no worries. Straight up stress free. I wish I could be just like you."

Ma took a deep breath. "Okay, I think it's time to let you girls in on a little secret. I vowed that I would only tell it when it was needed. But I can see desperate times call for desperate measures. You know I'll never place your father in a negative light, so what I'm about to tell you requires a mature and open mind."

Sasha started walking into the house, "Oh shoot, hold on Ma, let me refill mine's and LD's drink. Sounds like we may need it."

I sat up straight, my feet still in the water and I'm sure I had a very peculiar look on my face. Five minutes later, Sasha walked back outside with two more dirty martinis in her hand. She handed me my drink and sat back down next to me poolside as she said, "Okay, Ma, you were saying."

Ma began talking, picked up her glass of wine and looked down at the ground and smiled as she reminisced: "You girls had to be about four years old. Your dad's and my businesses were starting to take off and we had just purchased this home. At the time, your dad was going to the gym four days a week with your Uncle Allen. Since Uncle Allen was trying to make it pro, they made sure they were faithfully there, you know before he got signed by the Raiders. I guess there was this young lady at the gym who had grown quite fond of your father."

I was in shock as Ma continued on with her story.

"What raised my suspicion was the fact that, one day I got dressed and told them I wanted to go to the gym too. I mean there I was looking cute in my spandex Adidas outfit, and your Uncle Allen gave your dad this look, and your dad responded, let me mention he was stuttering, 'Umm honey it's just going to be us guys and you won't like this gym anyway, it's always crowded, and treadmills are always broken. We lift weights so we're able to get our workout done regardless.' Ma continued. "Now when he said that my woman's intuition kicked in. Your father would have never intervened with me joining him anywhere. He was over-explaining himself and as nervous as a hooker in church."

Sasha and I looked at each other and then again at Ma as she continued her story.

"So, I politely said, 'Oh, okay honey. Thank you for looking out for me. I'll go change and let my mother know I'm not going to bring the girls over after all, see you when you get back'."

Sasha exclaimed, "Ma, you should have demanded to go."

Ma calmly responded, "Sasha dear, you never let your right hand know what your left hand is doing. I let them leave and ten minutes after they left, I dropped you girls off with grandma anyway and went to the gym."

"My momma is a G," Sasha said excited and slightly drunk.

Ma ignored Sasha and continued telling her story. "I got to the gym, I told the front desk representative that I was there earlier and left my wedding ring in the locker. He let me in, and I spotted your Uncle Allen lifting weights with some guys, but your father was nowhere in sight."

By this time, Ma had me and Sash's full attention and nothing could break it. "I walked around the gym, trying not to be seen and when I looked in the pool area, there your dad was, in the pool with some woman."

"Ma, Nooooooo," I said in shock.

Ma put her finger up, telling me to wait a minute and said, "I stood there for a minute, my eyes started to fill with tears. I grabbed the door to the pool and was ready to whip him and her. But I remembered that I had two babies at home, and I also remembered that at some point he had to come home, and I would let him have it then. So, I went back to my car instead, cried and drove home. I got home, I started talking to God. In deep prayer,

I prayed, 'I know you didn't bring me this far just to let me down; this is my husband, what is he thinking?' I got on my knees and did what I do best, I prayed even harder. You see, girls, temptation comes in many different ways, shapes, and forms. And let me also say that success and money have a way of changing people if they let it. At the time the only person who could turn that situation around was God. I was smart enough to know that what God blessed me with no man or woman could take away. And I always felt like your father was a gift from God. So anyway, I prayed, I left it at the feet of Jesus, and I waited."

"You waited?" Sasha questioned.

"Yes, I waited. Your father isn't a stupid man and after one look at that heffa I could tell that she was trouble, so I left him to see for himself. Self-discover if you will. Three weeks later, your dad came home, with a look of defeat on his face. He sat me down at the table and confessed everything. He said he had been seeing this woman and turns out she was just using him for his money and when he caught on to her and tried to end it, she had her brother follow your dad home with a gun and demand more money. Turns out this tramp was just that, a tramp. Your dad was crying like an infant fresh out the womb. I stood up from the table and I told his cheating behind, 'You put this family in jeopardy, your own life and you were cheated out of God knows how much money. And for what? Some tired ass tramp who smiled at you and made you feel good for five minutes every now and again. You risked everything we built for meaningless sex.' I looked him dead in the eyes and said, 'I hope you learned your lesson because if you haven't, we won't be having this conversation again, you'll just be signing everything over to me along with divorce papers.' I left him in the kitchen, picking his face up off the ground and I walked away. Needless to say, we never had that conversation again."

I had never heard Ma cuss like that before but then Ma said something that made me rethink everything.

"I mean sure I could have acted a fool that day I seen him and that tramp together. But I would have risked my dignity, self-respect and risked being embarrassed by being put out the gym. So, I prayed, and let the situation work itself out. See men get caught in the trap all the time, and we as women see things coming from a mile away, that's why they call it a woman's intuition. I knew that nothing good was going to come from that situation so did I let your father hang himself? Yes, I did. He was feeling himself and I knew I wasn't ready to leave him. Life and experience teach the hardest lessons. That evening your father came home he was completely defeated. He lost his pride, almost lost his life, his family, and his livelihood all in one day, you know that bitch named karma, she showed up and showed out, so I didn't need to do anything more. What I want you girls to learn from this is one, take everything to God. He will always guide the footsteps of those who seek him and two, don't be in these streets acting a fool, everything always works itself out--EVERYTHING."

Ma paused and turned my way. "Which brings me to you, La'Dai. You need to stop stalking Devin by way of this girl he's seeing."

I quickly turned my head to Sasha and before I said anything she started to confess.

"What? I had to tell her because if things get out of control, someone has to be there to bail you out of jail. You and I both know that Ma and Mr. Benjamin Franklin will be right there, ready to welcome you home with open arms. And if you call me, I'm going to let you sit there and rethink all the 'I told you so's' that I've said to you."

I thought about what Sasha said for a moment and she was right. I took my foot and kicked water over in Sasha's direction.

She let out a playful scream. "You know I'm right, LD." We all laughed.

Ma interjected saying, "Oh, I'm on to you too."

Sasha looked in my direction and I threw my hands in the air suggesting that I was innocent.

"I know my girls. Sasha, La'Dai didn't tell me anything. I know that you're running through men like they're going out of style. Mmm Hmmm. You just better be careful."

"Oh Ma, you know I can handle myself." Sasha replied. She took her feet out of the water and walked over to Ma. She leaned down and gave her a kiss on the cheek.

"Hold on, Sasha," I said scurrying out of the water, "hold that pose right there." I met them on the side of Ma's other cheek and suggested we take a selfie. Our wonderful mother and daughters' heart to heart memory was caught right there in three seconds. The picture was beautiful, Ma's smile was radiant and for a moment I forgot about everything that was happening.

Dad had finally awakened. He came out back with a fresh tray of chicken nachos. Stuffing his face, he yelled out the sliding door, "The Raiders won, looks like we're off to a good start."

"Dad don't speak too soon; you know how they do," I said.

"LD, if I didn't know any better, I would think you weren't a Raider fan at all talking like that, but I'm going to ignore that comment. It's probably all those dirty martinis y'all out here slurping down. Got your head all messed up." Dad laughed to himself and went back inside.

And just then I smiled to myself. For the first time, it felt like everything was going to be alright. I was basking in all the love and support of my family.

It was two days before we were set to leave for Jamaica, and I was feeling some really good energy. I was happy and well prepared for our trip. Wanting to keep the momentum going, I took it upon myself to be productive and go see my sister in action in court, Sasha inspired me. Sasha told me she picked up a really big case and the defendant was being indicted that morning.

There I was, heading to court and for once it had nothing to do with the divorce. Some might think, what's the excitement in that? Well, here my sister was, Ms. Prosecutor; accomplished and ready to take charge. She finally decided on a career. Motivated, educated, and elevated to the next level of her life, she was on her way.

When I walked into the courtroom Sasha was standing there shuffling through some files. She wore a tan pantsuit with a navy-blue button up underneath. From what I could see she had on a pair of nude red bottoms. She had the words "Let's Get Down to Business" written all over her. I sat down two rows behind the prosecutor's desk. Sasha finally took a moment to scan the room before she noticed me. She turned in my direction, gave me a smile and winked. I smiled back and nodded. Given the circumstance, Sasha wanted the punishment on this case to be the death penalty, so we probably shouldn't have been smiling. But I couldn't help it; my sister was working on a high-profile case, and I was proud of her. In all seriousness, according to her, this man was a monster.

The room grew quiet as the judge walked in.

"All rise for the Honorable Judge Christopher Malkiin." The bailiff called out and we all stood.

When I looked over to the defendant, I couldn't figure out why he looked so familiar. He was a middle-aged Hispanic man. Standing about five inches over his lawyer, he looked down at him then up at the judge. He wore an orange jumpsuit, with the words CDCR PRISONER on the back of it. Metal restraints were handcuffed onto both his wrists, down and around his waist and ending at his ankles. This guy was going nowhere. His piercing green eyes glanced around the room as he stared into the jury section. He had a bald head, a tattoo on the side of his neck, with block numbers that read "323." Judging from the wrinkles that made his tattoo almost hard to read, he was aging, and it was not gracefully.

The judge sat down and told us all to be seated. The courtroom was quiet, and the judge began with, "Nicolas Nunez, you are being charged with murder in the first degree, aggravated assault and obstruction of a peace officer, how do you plea?"

My heart dropped in my stomach; did he just say Nicolas Nunez? Was Sasha out of her rabbit ass mind? She was prosecuting her own father. I don't know if Sasha could sense my energy or if she was just looking to see my reaction because she turned around to me with an evil smirk on her face and then looked at him. He was looking at her, their eyes met, and Sasha turned back to the judge. The smile she wore was of confidence and assurance. What the hell was going on? What had my sister gotten herself into? I could not believe what I was hearing or seeing.

Sasha's father responded, "Not guilty." And all pandemonium broke out.

A black lady from the other side of the court room yelled out, "Not guilty, you son of a bitch, you killed my husband. I want you to rot in hell."

The judge began to bang his gavel, yelling, "Order in the court, order in the courtroom right now." But the mayhem continued. Sasha's father turned around to the woman shamelessly and said, "If I were you, I would get either my money or my drugs or your ass will be next."

The jury looked so shocked and terrified that I don't think they heard Nicolas at all. I looked at Sasha with my hand over my mouth. With a smirk on her face and no sound she just mouthed the words: "Told you so."

"Bailiff, remove this woman, order in the court." Judge Malkiin was still banging his gavel as the woman with the loud outburst, crying hysterically, was escorted out the courtroom.

"Court will reconvene tomorrow at nine a.m., court is dismissed." The judge quickly rose and angrily walked out.

Sasha came walking into the aisle of the courtroom where I joined her.

"Sasha, what the hell was that what are you doing?"

"What are you talking about? I told you that he's a monster and now you got a chance to see it for yourself. So, do you really want to fix your lips to ask me what I'm doing? Because the answer will be my damn job, La'Dai."

I stood there for a moment and shook my head. My sister was red with revenge and rage. But the troubling part is she found room to giggle about this.

We went back to Sasha's office and my hands were still shaking from my adrenaline rush. She sat down at her desk and said, "This case is going to be a piece of cake. Who knows? I might make judge someday."

"You are prosecuting your father. It's not just unethical, it's psychotic. They're going to have your job for this."

"La'Dai, stop being so damn naïve. Look at his file and then tell me how you feel."

"Sasha, isn't this information privileged? I mean I really don't feel comfortable reading all of this confidential information," I said as I still curiously scanned through the large file with his mug shot on the left side of the file folder staring straight at me. I was definitely creeped out.

"Just look at all of the charges he's caught while being in custody, LD," Sasha snatched the folder from me and began thumbing through the files as she paced back and forth, "battery on a peace officer-resulting in use of physical force, possession of a controlled substance (methamphetamine), serious injury to an inmate resulting in serious bodily injury, threatening the life of a peace officer, introduction of a controlled substance again- this time heroin, this list goes on… escape, willfully inciting a riot, and last but not least, death in custody-homicide. The man is a menace and does not deserve to live. Prison walls can't even tame him. He's a danger to society and threatens the safety and security of the public and whatever institution he steps foot onto."

Sasha finally sat down and threw the file folder across her desk.

"Sasha, 'the man' is your father and not only that, but he's also tied to the Mexican Mafia. Do you have a death wish?" I was bewildered and in utter disbelief that she didn't consider that major factor before deciding to take this case and adjudicating this man.

Yes, you heard me right; Sasha's father was a part of the Mexican Mafia. Always had been. He was full blown Hispanic, spoke Spanish but did not have an accent. When we were younger, out of guilt Ma would allow him to call Sasha from prison and talk to her. That's until he started asking Ma for money and demanding that she bring her to see him. Ma would refer to him as our uncle. Sasha's dad being part of the Mexican mafia was another reason why her mother could never get away and even more reason why she became strung out on drugs, easy access.

Sasha was crossing the line and I was in fear for her. The more I tried to talk her out of it, the more my words fell on deaf ears.

"The bottom line, La'Dai, is this. I'm a prosecutor. Crime doesn't discriminate, why should I? And I'm damn sure not going to give him a pass because he's my father. Did you even read the file on the homicide he committed?

This man lured another inmate into his cell, used his bed sheets as a noose to hang him and as he was hanging, he took a man-made shank, gutted him like a fish and sliced his face up like he was Edward Scissor Hands or some shit. And if that's not enough, as the guards were approaching his cell, he jammed the shank into the side of this inmate's neck and said with laughter 'Stick a fork in this motherfucker, he's done--I mean dead' then he laughed hysterically. I'm not done LD, hold on. Then he sat down on his bunk covered in blood and told the C/Os, 'I'm not coming out until I finish my sandwich, I'm hungry got damn it.' This man was bleeding out dying and my dad sat on his bed, leisurely eating a sandwich. A sandwich. There was blood everywhere; it took them an hour to extract him out of his cell. Here, look at the crime scene photos."

Sasha got up to hand me the file folder, but my jaw was still on the floor. I was shaking.

"And you know what's even worse, this inmate he killed, was due to parole and go home in two weeks, apparently he was threatened and coerced to smuggle in some drugs during his visit. Problem was, he got caught. So, when he couldn't produce the drugs or the money," Sasha paused for a second before continuing, "well, you know the rest. This inmate was only in prison for repeated offenses of DUIs, no heinous crimes of any sort. So, tell me, how is it that he dies and my father lives? Where's the justice in that? I'm asking for the death penalty and that's final!"

"Sasha, aren't you the least bit worried that you might tap into his rage?"

"Hell, he's the one who should be worried because he's already tapped into mine."

I walked out of her office, leaving her with her head buried in the case files of the mess she was about to create. The look on Sasha's face was of pure hate. I had never seen her that angry or determined to take someone's life. I was worried and contemplated if I should tell Ma or not. I needed help calming Sasha down, I needed someone to try and get through to her so I called the one person who I knew would remain calm and could possibly be the voice of reason, Devin.

The phone rang for what seemed like forever before Devin picked up. I couldn't help but think that maybe he was with her. My insecurities had me on an emotional rollercoaster. Here I was thinking about who Devin was laying up under, when my main focus should have been bringing Sasha back down to reality.

"Hello?" Devin answered in a lazy tone.

"Hey, are you sleeping?" I asked.

"Yeah, I must have dozed off. I'm not feeling too well today."

"Late night?" I asked sarcastically.

"What's up, LD? I don't feel like going there with you today. What do you need?"

I could tell Devin was getting frustrated and annoyed to say the least. Maybe he really didn't feel good.

"I don't need anything. It's Sasha. Devin, she's getting herself caught up."

"What do you mean?"

"She's trying to vindicate herself by putting her dad on death row."

"What, what do you mean? That sounds crazy. She's the district attorney, does she know she could lose her job if they find out that he's her father and realize what her motives are?"

"I know, I know. But it's deeper than that, D. You know that he's still tied up with the Mexican mafia. But she doesn't care. I've never seen her so determined. She's serious about prosecuting him."

"The Mexican Mafia--LD I need to get all the details about this. But in the meantime, I want you to stay away from that courthouse and I'll deal with Sasha."

"Okay," I said, my eyes starting to water. It was just like Devin to take over the situation and make me feel safe and like everything was going to be okay. But his words weren't enough, I needed to see him, feel him, so I made myself vulnerable.

"Devin, I could really use a shoulder to lean on right now, can you please come over?"

"LD now is not a good time. I told you I'm not feeling well, honey." Devin started coughing and, in my mind, he was trying to play on my intelligence.

"You know what, Devin? Forget I asked. I can't believe that you're sitting up here trying to put on a show. I get it, you're probably over there with some hootchie. But it's all good. Let me know when you're going to meet with Sasha. Bye."

I hung up the phone and began crying. I opened myself up and was shot down. Up until now I had perfected everything in my life. And it was killing me that I couldn't figure Devin out these days. This was my husband. The man I thought I knew like the back of my own hand. The man that I had spent the last thirteen years getting to know and love more than life itself, and now this man no longer looked at me as someone special. I felt like I was being tolerated more than anything else.

Chapter Eight

Clear skies, sun shining and a rum punch in hand, Jamaica was giving me life! Walking through the airport wearing a bright yellow sundress, I felt like America's Next Top Model. My faux locks ran down the middle of my back with blonde highlights complementing my eyes. Bob Marley's *Three Little Birds* was playing on the airport's sound system, and I had no problem dancing to it singing out loud, "Don't worry 'bout a thing, every little is going to be alright," as we exited. As soon as we hit the sidewalk, I was sun kissed in what seemed to be eighty-five-degree weather. The breeze was just right, and it felt like heaven.

Standing curbside waiting for our car service, I threw my head back and yelled, "Jamaica, where have you been all my life?"

Sasha glanced at me and then down at her watch, "LD, you're crazy. The question is what took you so long to get here. C'mon, our car is here. This way."

I followed her slightly intoxicated and ready to let loose completely. Sasha was in a pair of very short white shorts that barely went past her butt cheeks and an aqua blue top. It took us sixteen hours to get to Jamaica but as soon as we hit the ground, I forgot all about that. I also forgot all about Sasha and her shenanigans.

After the court room escapade, she returned to court that next morning and I stayed away just like Devin suggested. Sasha met me at the airport and had the nerve to snore the entire flight. I thought for sure she would have us put out of first class. Sasha mentioned not getting much rest lately, which served her right, she was in over her head, and everyone knew it BUT her.

Talking the entire drive to the hotel and asking twenty-one questions I could tell Sasha was getting slightly annoyed.

"I told you, Sis, I'm going to tell you our entire get down as soon as we get settled in. Right now, I want you to take it all in, enjoy that rum punch high you got and chill."

"Okay."

I directed my attention to the driver and started talking to him instead. He looked into the rearview mirror at me and said, "I take it it's your first time here in Jamaica?" His accent almost made me melt. He wasn't much of a sight to see but when he spoke, damn.

"Yes, it's my first time here, but not hers so you can imagine how excited I am."

"LD, leave the man alone and let him drive." Sasha said tapping me on my knee.

"It iz okay ma'am, no problem," the driver said with a smile on his face.

"Yeah, Sasha, no problem. No worry, no cry," I said, trying to sound Jamaican. We all started laughing.

By the time we made it to the resort, the alcohol had sunk in, and I was completely intoxicated. Walking past the pool on the way to check into our rooms, I thought to myself, damn that pool looks inviting. The water glistened like liquid diamonds that was calling my name.

With a daring look on my face, I turned around to Sasha and said, "Hey Sis, we're on vacation, right?"

"Yes, LD, it started seventeen hours ago."

"Well good, I don't need permission to do this."

I threw my bag down and jumped into the water fully clothed. I wanted to wash away all life's recent drama and let my hair down. Jumping into the pool was not only refreshing but it came with a sense of freedom.

Sasha stood there looking at me for a moment before shrugging her shoulders and shouting, "Oh what the hell." She jumped in right behind me.

We laughed out loud and so did the other guests who were witness to our footloose and fancy-free acts of child's play.

"Sasha, I love you sis," I said soaking wet as we both struggled to get out of the water. The staff walked over and handed us towels to dry off.

"Welcome to Ocho Rios, we've been waiting for you." The man said with a huge smile on his face.

"Please continue to have fun, drink up as much rum punch as you would like and let me know if you need anyting."

"Thank you," Sasha responded, drying her hair. Her curly locks bounced right back to a beautiful curly fro' after about ten minutes. The humidity had no effect on her. Sasha being biracial of black and Hispanic descent showed in her beautiful complexion. She always wore her hair was always long and curly. Ma never did cut it.

Jamaica was everything I imagined and some. Taking it all in, I inhaled and exhaled wanting the breathes of fresh air to last forever. Our first couple of days there we spent sight-seeing, basking in the ambience of waterfalls, reaching for the sky while parasailing and eating some of the best jerk chicken and oxtails I had ever tasted while dancing under the sun, moon, and stars. We partied day and night, that was for sure. I was having the time of my life. I wondered why I had not visited Jamaica sooner. It's not like we didn't have the money or could not have made the time.

It was our third day in Ochos Rios, and a mouth-watering,

looking good enough to eat, masculine Adonis stood six feet two inches tall at the bar. Baby caught my attention, causing me to have a wet daydream. I could tell he was familiar with the bartender. Leaning over the bar, talking, and laughing with all thirty-two of his pearly whites shining in the sun. He wore dreads that stopped just past his shoulders, neatly platted as if they had just been done. This man was clean. The interesting part is he was a light skinned brotha', I surprised myself being interested in him at all. I won't say I have a type, but I usually went for the caramel, milk choco-late, or even dark chocolate types. I've just always been attracted to the darker shades of brown. Anyway, we locked eyes. And before I knew it, he threw his drink back and was headed in my direction.

"Hello, beautiful."

"Hi, handsome."

"I've been watching you ever since you jumped into the pool on your first day here."

I was taken by surprise. I had no recollection of seeing him at all, not even a glance. I wish this had been one of those mo-ments where I could have responded with, "Yeah, I was watching you watch me." But that would have been far from the truth, the truth was I was busy in my own world of escapades. Divorce what? And Devin who?

So, I simply responded, "Watching me?"

"Yes, you are definitely a sight to see, and I haven't been able to take my eyes off of you."

Giving him a look of seduction, I stepped out of my comfort zone, taking my index finger, and running it over his right triceps as I said flirtatiously, "Yeah, well you aren't so hard on the eyes yourself."

"Let me get you a drink, is that alright?" he asked, being the perfect gentleman.

"Of course, I'm on vacation, turning down a drink while

sitting poolside is not something I came to do."

"Have a seat right here and I'll be right back."

Judging by his harmless command for me to sit down and based on the fact that he didn't ask me what I wanted to drink, I could tell he was a take charge type guy.

"There you are, I've been looking for you," Sasha said, walking up on me with her hands in the air.

"What happened to meeting in the lobby?"

Walking back over to me, sexy and strong with two drinks in his hand, Sasha took one glance at the man I was getting acquainted with and said, "Oh, he's what happened."

"Hello, yellow. I'm her sister, Sasha," she continued to say holding her hand out, "It is very nice to mee you."

"Hi, I'm Desmond. Are you going to sit down and join us?" he asked, gesturing with the palm of his hand out for her to sit down next to me.

"Ummmm ..." Sasha danced around the question.

"Yes, you should. Here, take my drink and I'll go and order another one. I promise you I haven't drank from it yet."

Standing speechless, Sasha took the drink and sat down next to me as Desmond walked back to the bar. Trying to compose her excitement, she gently pinched me on my side, before saying, "Girl, him taking a sip from the drink is the least of my worries. Hell, a man that fine, I would drink his bathwater."

"Sasha, eeww, not the man's bathwater."

"Yes, his bathwater. And please tell me that I've had some type of an influence on you, that you'll take a page out of my book and make him a focus of your attention tonight."

"Girl, the man is fine, but I didn't come to Jamaica to get acquainted with the first King Dong that I ran into. I didn't come here to be a hoe."

"Who said you had to be a hoe? Besides having him "dicktate" your night doesn't have to be a bad thing. Be responsible, have some fun and be an adult, LD. You only live once girl, stop being a stick in the mud."

"Easy for you to say," I snapped back.

"I never said you had to sleep with the man. Although I would, but then again you are not me. Besides even if you did, don't worry I won't tell."

"I know you won't because I'll kick your butt." I replied jokingly.

"Live a little. Hell, you've had the same King Dong for the last ten years ruling your world, maybe this will help you start to get over Devin."

"Sasha, there isn't enough meaningless sex in the world that can erase all the memories a wife has had with her husband. All it is, is a temporary fix of distraction. I mean I know the way Devin went about things is messed up but what if my thought process about the whole thing has been wrong."

"We are not having this conversation right now. You're going to sip these drinks now, so you can take advantage of his fine ass later."

Desmond and I danced all night at the Reggae Club. Sasha had gotten in contact with her Jamaican fling and was back in her room getting reacquainted. The Jamaican vernacular of the reggae music had me feeling relaxed, my heart was thumping to the beat of the drums. The confluence of chaos and calm came together making the perfect music to my ears. The music was an extension–an example of my current life status. Calm to my realistic storm.

Drinks were pouring and joints were firing. I had never been into getting blazed, but I did like the rum punch. Dancing with Desmond, and the way he moved his body left my imagination running wild. I mean it should have been a crime for a man this fine to move that way.

We danced for forty-five more minutes before Desmond hinted to me that he was ready for us to be alone.

I took one last drink and followed behind him as he took my hand and led us out of the club.

We touched down in my room, and we couldn't keep our hands off each other. Going on vacation and having sex with a man I barely knew was not my get down, so I tried to hide behind the guilt and shame by masking it with champagne and pre-sex pillow talk. I pretended that I was wildly excited and interested in who he was, what he thought about, and what his dreams were.

What came next was only natural, if pillow talk happens in bed, sex was sure to follow. I could feel the liquor getting to me. Kissing on my neck, he had me going. He picked me up and laid me down in the position he wanted me. I reached down and grabbed all of his manhood in my hand, and he was not lackin'. He exceeded my expectations. Fully erect, he climbed on top of me and placed my legs straight up in the air where he took my toes into his mouth. He kissed me from the bottom of my foot up to my inner thighs, where he spread them apart. He was ready to go to work, right before I came to my senses and thought to myself, I could not let this go on any further.

Why in the hell did I listen to Sasha? This wasn't who I was. I could tell he sensed my resistance; he began to slow down.

I mean did not want the first man I slept with aside from my husband to be some guy I was never going to see again. I wanted to hold onto the little self-respect and dignity I had left, the rest of it went out the door with Devin when he left.

I was not about to stoop so low as to lose my moral compass between the legs of a complete stranger. I was still La'Dai, and La'Dai didn't get down like that.

"Please stop." I said, pushing him away. "Look, I'm sorry. You being inside of me would feel so good right now, but it's going to feel even better waking up tomorrow with no regrets. We can't do this." I hoped I was not coming off as a tease.

"You're going to leave me like this?"

He stood up and I could tell his blood was pumping in the right direction.

"I'm sorry. What can I say? Blame it on the alcohol."

"You're so damn gorgeous, I can't do nothing but respect how you feel. I should have known a woman like you was not the one-night stand type," he said with all sincerity."

"What can I say?" I replied.

"Well, I'm not going to let you completely off the hook. I'm going to stay and at least get to know more about you. You're interesting and I love looking at you."

"I guess there's no harm in talking. But you're going to have to put your pants back on because that right there is a very big distraction."

He was still hard as a rock.

"Are you sure you don't want to go for a test drive? You might want to ride all night long. I promise I aim to please," Desmond said trying to entice me.

"I usually don't deny myself guilty pleasures but this time I'm going to pass."

"Can I kiss you one last time?" He pulled me close and slipped his tongue into my mouth. We spent the rest of the night talking about his childhood and how he hoped to one day travel the world.

Jamaica was fun but short lived. I received a phone call the next morning from Devin telling me that my house was broken into and vandalized. Sasha and I were on the first thing smokin back to the states. Needless to say, I was uneasy the entire flight.

Chapter Nine

"Devin, I can't believe this, I mean who would do something like this?"

I looked around my living room, shocked and in disbelief. The front window was completely broken. My white leather sectional was torn and ripped apart; material was hanging out of every angle. The word "BITCH" was spray painted black, big, and bold across the living room wall onto my DaVinci painting. Everything was turned upside down.

"I don't know, La'Dai, but I promise you, I'll find out."

"How?" I questioned. "The guy walked straight up to the video camera and was bold enough to give me a "Big F You." He held his finger right in the camera. I don't know why he just didn't take off his ski mask if he was going to be that daring. He made sure I got the message. None of this made any sense.

"Look, I know you're upset, and I know this situation seems hopeless but let me fix it. Trust me; I'm going to figure this out."

"Devin, I'm not just upset, I'm scared. What if he comes back and what if this time, I'm home? This was personal, someone wants me to know that they mean business."

"I know, I know...hear me out: I have the cleaning crew on their way, along with the painter. In a few hours, a contractor will be here to fix the window."

"What about the furniture?"

"I ordered new furniture, but it won't be delivered until to-morrow, along with the TV. So, let's go grab something to eat, get you a massage and then we'll come back. By that time the house should be almost put back together."

Emotions were running high, hell and low. My adrenaline was flowing but I felt drained at the same time. I felt like total damsel in distress. Still and yet with Devin right there as my helping hand, I couldn't figure out how things took a turn between us, again nothing was making sense.

Devin tried his best to uplift my spirits by taking me to my favorite restaurant and engaging me in conversation about my trip but that only stirred up an entirely different range of emotions that I did not want to deal with.

When we got back to my place, I could smell fresh paint. The walls were freshly painted white, and when I stepped foot onto the carpeted area of the living room the bottom of my feet were slightly damped from the carpet being cleaned. My living room was bare, the damaged furniture and broken TV had been removed, along with the damaged white fur area rug.

It was starting to look like home again. While Devin made endless efforts to calm me down at the Beverly Center and at dinner, Tony stopped by the house to make sure the window was replaced correctly and everything else was done to par.

By the time we got back he was gone. I thought to text him thank you but that seemed a little impersonal, so I decided to call him later instead.

"I'm going to stay here for the next couple of nights at least until the new security system is installed and until they're finished putting up the new security gates."

I nodded my head in agreeance and just then tears began running down my face.

"LD, what's wrong?" Devin asked as I hit the floor bawling like a two-year-old child.

Devin sat down on the floor next to me and pulled me into him.

Lifting my head off his shoulders I responded, "Life has been on a downward spiral ever since this entire thing with us has unfolded. I don't know how to feel anymore or what to think."

"What do you mean by you don't know what to think?"

"You're here right now, you're acting in the capacity of my husband but yet you're one signature away from being my ex-husband."

"LD let's not continue to beat a dead horse. I've told you that I'm always going to be here for you no matter what. Our divorce isn't going to change that, I'll be here for whatever you need."

"I do need you; I need you as my husband. Please don't do this to us."

"I love you and I always will, but the decision has been made, you're going to be okay, I promise."

"Why do you keep saying that? How can you be so damn sure?"

"LD, why aren't you listening?" Devin exclaimed. "I said I'm always going to be here for you. That's how I'm so sure, so trust that. Just because the situation isn't going in the direction that you think it should, doesn't mean that things are headed the wrong way. Let this go!"

Devin became noticeably irritated. "I'm going to sleep in the guest room. Good night."

Devin kissed me on my forehead, and I could sense that he was slightly frustrated.

As I stepped into the kitchen to pour me a drink, I decided that now would be good as time as any to start hanging and putting up the new décor I bought while we were out.

After what just happened, along with everything else, the house could use a new feel to it. I turned some music on and got busy.

By the time I sat down to take a break, it was midnight. I headed upstairs to shower and unwind a little bit more.

The water was warm and the three drinks I had made me feel like I was on top of the world.

Lathering my body with body wash, my mind started running wild. Thoughts of the last time Devin and I made love came to mind. I thought about how good my husband felt inside of me.

I turned off the shower and walked dripping wet and naked to the guest room where Devin was sleeping. My next move had to be my best move.

I leaned down and gently kissed Devin on his cheek, then on his neck. The warmth of my tongue, clung to his neck, as I whispered in his ear, "Baby, wake up."

"LD, what are you doing? And why are you wet?"

"Because Daddy, it's slippery when wet, and I want you right here, right now." I took his hand and put his fingers deep inside of me. Moving them inside and out, deeper and deeper each time, he pulled me into bed with him and climbed on top of me.

I pulled off his shirt, and before I could get to his boxers, he stopped me dead in my tracks.

"WAIT! LD, I don't know if we should do this."

"What?!"

"Today was an emotional day for you, I know you're vulnerable right now and I don't want this to lead you into getting the wrong idea."

"The wrong idea? Devin, I can handle this."

"I don't want you waking up tomorrow feeling confused or thinking I took advantage of you."

"Please take advantage of me, all of me."

I hopped up and assumed the position, face down and I'm sure you can guess what was up. Doggy-style was my favorite position, especially if he pulled my hair just right.

There I was ready to take every inch of him and he was still talking and being concerned with not hurting my feelings. Everything he was saying was going in one ear and out the other. I was hot and definitely starting to be bothered.

I took matters even more into my own hands and gained control over the situation.

I reached into his boxers putting him in between my lips then into my mouth. This type of foreplay had never been my thing, but I needed to do something out of the ordinary if I was going to get him to just shut up and go with the flow. I want MY husband, MY way.

With a mouth full of him, I said, "Come on, Devin don't you miss me?" right before I laid on my back and put my legs over his shoulders.

"Yes, I do," he replied, rubbing my legs, and kissing my feet. "But I want it to be clear that if we do this, nothing changes; I'm still moving forward with our divorce."

"Okay," I said, pulling him into me.

After ten minutes of foreplay Devin couldn't get hard. Was he not attracted to me anymore? I was naked and touching all the right things in all the right places, we should have been at least ten minutes in by now.

"I'm sorry; just give me a minute," Devin said getting up and walking toward the bathroom.

I couldn't believe what was happening. Just then a bright light went off on the nightstand. It was Devin's phone. I thought for a minute before picking it up. I called out to him making sure he was still occupied before I started snooping.

"Devin?" I yelled down the hall.

"Give me a minute, I'll be right out."

I reached over and grabbed his phone.

"Hello," I said trying to answer before they hung up.

"Hey, you never called me when you made it home," the woman's voice on the other end of the phone said.

"That's because he is busy, who is this?" I challenged her.

"I'm sorry, I think I have the wrong number."

"I know you have the wrong number," I snapped back at her.

The girl on the other end hung up. I looked at the name on the phone and it read "Ms. S".

I sat up in the bed, staring at the wall in front of me, trying to piece the situation together. I was pissed off. If smoke could come out of my ears, it would have. My mind started jumping to conclusions. Is this why he can't get it up? I asked myself because he's too busy giving it to someone else. And who the hell was Ms. S?

A text came through from "Ms. S". I opened it and it was a picture of her nasty ass in lingerie and message that read: I didn't have the wrong number. Tell Devin when he's done playing with you, a real woman is waiting for him.

Devin wasn't dealing with "All these women" just this bitch. Sage. I was furious. Devin was my husband and not even I had sent him pictures like that through text. I had no idea he was into this type of thing, sexting, really? This trifling heffa was starting to get on my last nerve. She was barking up the wrong tree.

I heard Devin coming down the hall. I hurried up and put his phone back, then got up from the bed.

Devin grabbed me and tried to finish what we started.

"Let's try this again," he said kissing me.

I pulled away and replied, "Nope. I'm good, we're done. Find someone else to play with."

I left Devin with a view of naked body walking down the hall and away from him.

"What? LD?" Devin yelled out.

I ignored him and kept walking to my room and slammed the door. Right before I yelled down to him, "Don't play with me, Devin, I don't come with dice."

My bedroom door was slightly shut but I could still hear Devin yell back at me, "I knew this would happen."

Morning came and when I woke up, he was gone. Even though I went to bed furious, I slept like a baby. The day before had been long and full of circumstances that had me in a tailspin. From my house being vandalized to trying to rekindle the flame between my husband then having my efforts sabotaged by this new chick sexting him; I needed to clear my mind. I knew exactly what would get the job done.

When I arrived at the beach, the wind was still, and birds made their stride in the air carelessly. I stood in the shallow waters letting the end of the waves hit my feet, taking in the view. The water was cold but warmed by the morning sun. I got a sudden urge to jog. I left my blanket and shoes waiting for me as I took off running with no destination in mind.

Malibu was the absolute go-to, the sandstone cliffs at Paradise Cove was great for my mental. My feet were hitting the warm-golden sand with every step I took. The beach vibes were paradisiacal, and the sun was fierce.

During my entire jog I kept repeating to myself "you're going to get through this, you're going to get through this. You still love Devin but it's time to move on. You're going to get through this."

Momentum was flowing, and I ran faster and faster. In this moment, the only B.S. I needed was my bikini and sun. Adrenaline pumping and the ocean breeze hitting my face was the perfect equation for my algorithms.

Anyone who has ever loved before and experienced a breakup, especially one that comes out of left field, knows the struggle. The struggle of trying to make sense of it all. The battle with yourself, trying to figure out whose fault it was anyway. Only for the fault-finding to lead to even more confusion. It's an emotional roller-coaster all in a theme park of its own.

I got back to the spot where I left my things. Breathing heavily, I sat down and tried to catch my breath. I felt my phone vibrating in my yoga pants pocket. Sasha was calling.

"Hello," I answered.

"LD, why aren't you answering? I've been trying to call you for the last twenty minutes."

"My bad, sis, I went for a jog, I guess I didn't feel my phone vibrating. What's up?"

"Okay, so listen, what I'm about to tell you, I need you to try and stay calm…"

"Oh my gosh, what happened to Ma?"

"Girl, nothing happened to Ma…or Dad. I said stay calm and you already done jumped off in the deep end."

"Well, Sash, damn, spit it out."

"Okay, but like I said, be calm!"

"Ugh. Hold on, it's Daniel from the barbershop on the other line."

I clicked over and I could hear Danie talking to someone in the background, the tone of his voice was in a panic.

"Hey, Daniel," I answered.

"Hi, La'Dai. I'm sorry to bother you with this, I would have much rather talked to Devin but he's not answering and it's an emergency."

"Don't apologize, what's wrong? Why are you talking so fast?"

"The cops are already on their way but I…"

"Cops?" I asked, interrupting him.

"Yes, some guy walked into the shop right after I opened, everything happened so fast. He walked into the shop with a baseball bat. Next thing I knew he was swinging it everywhere, hitting everything in sight. All the mirrors on the stations are completely shattered and the walls, well, the drywall is completely damaged."

"What!?" I yelled.

"When I tried to stop him, he turned the baseball bat onto me. I think my kneecap is broken. There was nothing I could do, he pulled out a gun and said, 'Tell La'Dai to have her bitch of a sister drop the case or her house and shop won't be the only things we come after. Next time there'll be bloodshed'."

"Damn?!, Daniel, are you okay?"

"Yeah, but my knee is busted up pretty bad. I guess my adrenaline was pumping so much I didn't realize how hard he hit me with the bat. The cops and ambulance just got here."

"Daniel, leave and go to the hospital right now, the police can take your statement from there. I want to make sure that your kneecap isn't broken. Don't worry about the shop. I'm on my way, and I'll get a hold of Devin. Please go to the hospital right now."

"Okay," he responded.

"Devin and I will take care of your medical bills. I'm so sorry for this. Was anyone else hurt?"

"No, luckily I was barely opening up and no customers or other barbers had arrived yet. Oh, and I'm telling you homeboy looked straight up Mexican Mafia."

I stood there for a moment in shock. I could not believe we were being targeted. This was serious. As if I needed another life-altering event to take place. Frantic and now paranoid, I needed to get a hold of Devin like not now but right now. Then my mind grew curious as to why the hell Devin wasn't answering his phone.

I got into my car completely out of my mind. I almost drove onto the freeway headed in the wrong direction. When I did get onto the right on ramp, I floored it doing ninety miles per hour.

Finally, my phone rang, it was Devin calling me back after I'd called his phone five times with no answer.

"Devin, Daniel has been trying to get a hold of you. And so, have I. Where are you? Why weren't you answering?"

"I had a doctor's appointment."

"On a Saturday?"

"Yes LD, but never mind that, what's wrong? I have several missed calls from Daniel and now you're calling me in a state of panic. Tell me what's wrong."

Just as I was getting ready to tell him, Sasha called, I forgot that I left her on hold.

"My God," I yelled out in frustration, it was too much going on and I was starting to feel overwhelmed. My hands were shaking, and beads of sweat were starting to run down the side of my face.

I clicked over, "Sasha, sorry I forgot you were on hold but let me call you back; I have a 911 situation at the shop."

"LD, that's what I was calling about."

Letting out a long sign, I replied, "Okay give me a minute, don't hang up, I have Devin on the other line."

"Okay."

"Hello, Devin, you still there?"

"Yes."

"We need to meet at Danny Lane's. Some guy vandalized the shop, beat up Daniel, and pulled a gun on him. I'll explain more when we get there."

"Okay, say no more, I'm on my way."

I clicked back over to Sasha.

"LD, the Mexican Mafia is behind the break-in at your house and at Danny Lane's."

"Sasha, what the hell is going on?"

"They want me to drop the case against Psycho-Michael."

"Who?"

"Psycho-Michael, you know my crazy and deranged sperm donor, the one I'm prosecuting."

"The fact that you just called him that is even more reason why you should drop the case."

"Hell no, they are not, and I repeat, are NOT going to scare me into dropping this case. Shit like this comes with the territory of being the DA."

"Shit like this? Sasha, you say that as if there's some type of normality to it. Your family is being terrorized by the Mexican Mafia, they are not just making idle threats, they are acting out on them. Earth to Sasha, pull your head out of your ass."

"Hey careful, LD, no need for all that."

"Sasha, my shop manager is on his way to the hospital; this guy had a gun. What if I had customers there? They know where I live, they've been to my house. Drop the case, they aren't playing around."

"Yeah well, neither am I. And stop talking to me as if I don't understand the magnitude of the situation. Hell, they vandalized my car this morning. I might bend but I for damn sure am not going to break."

"I can't believe you. While you are busy ego tripping, let's pray that I don't wind up in the hospital next or even worse, dead, behind all of this nonsense. I hope this case is worth it."

"LD calm down. No one is going to die. They are getting the exact results that they want. You being petrified enough to influence me into dropping the case. We will not fold, baby girl. I will pay for the damages at the shop. I called in a favor at the Sheriff's Department, they are going to put a protective detail on you until I straighten this mess out."

"Sasha, do you hear yourself? You are not Superwoman against the Mexican Mafia, one of the strongest gangs in LA. They are not to be played with."

"Again, neither am I. You're underestimating me. This is a part of the job. It gets hot and heavy sometimes and this seems to be one of those times."

"I can't with you right now. I'm headed to the shop, so I have to go. Good-bye."

I had never been so upset with my sister. Never. What was she thinking?

I looked up to the sky and yelled out, "God, what did I do, what did I do? Please put my life back together!"

I couldn't believe Sasha was willing to put her life and the life of people close to her in jeopardy. My sister was changing, and I didn't like it one bit. I mean she already wasn't in touch with her emotions as it was, but I thought she still had some heart left. It's as if she was becoming desensitized.

After Devin and I finished cleaning up the mess at the shop, we headed over to my parents' house. At this point, I had no words for Sasha. Devin called her and told her to meet us there. He was adamant about holding a family meeting, he felt strongly that Sasha needed some type of intervention, and I couldn't have agreed more. He was convinced that Mom and Dad could talk some sense into her. And I was convinced that she had lost her mind and was way past reasoning with.

Sitting across the living room from me on the beige love seat in our parents' living room, Sasha sat with her legs and arms folded. She appeared to have some type of attitude as if I had done something to her, the nerve! Dad sat on the arm of the couch rubbing her back. I knew exactly why dad was catering to her. It was important to my parents to help Sasha maintain a stable mental state, whether she was wrong or not. I mean none of us wanted her to relapse, but I was running out of patience this time. She was making her own bed, and maybe she needed to lie in it, ALONE. It's as if my parents were excusing her behavior. If you ask me Devin was wrong. My parents were not going to be able to talk sense into Sasha.

Ma walked into the living room from the kitchen carrying a tray of drinks, I only wished they had liquor in them.

"So, I wanted us to get together and talk about what's been going on lately," Devin started, trying to tread lightly.

I blurted out, "What's going on could have been avoided, completely preventable. I'm sure before these thugs started busting down doors and terrorizing us, they gave some type of warning first. Right or wrong, Sasha?" I looked in her direction with piercing eyes.

"Well damn, LD, if looks could kill, I'd be dead right now."

"Answer the question, Sasha."

"LD, I know you're upset but watch your tone, you've been borderline disrespectful since I called you this morning."

"Yeah well, you've been borderline stupid since you decided to prosecute your own father."

"Excuse me?"

"LD, calm down," Devin said, trying to comfort me. "I didn't call this meeting just so you could be at each other's throat. We're here so we can figure this out together."

"No, Devin. She acts like she doesn't get it."

"She has a name," Sasha said.

"Sasha, enough," Ma interjected. "Devin, I got it from here," Ma said, hijacking the conversation. "Now I know that there's a lot going on. Emotions are running high, and the chain of events has caught us all off guard but you two will not disrespect my house nor will you disrespect each other. This entire thing is a mess and pointing fingers won't help none. Get it together, girls, both of you."

I sat there, thinking to myself, what's next? Why is everyone always calming me down lately when I have every right to be upset, every right to be pissed off. I was the one losing here.

"Okay," I said calmly. "I have a solution. Sasha, it's in everyone's best interest that you pass this case onto one of your colleagues."

"No, that's not an option," she said with all seriousness. "I've been working relentlessly on this case for weeks on end, hours upon hours, I'm not just going to turn my hard work over to someone else. Doing so could change the entire trajectory of what happens to this SOB."

"How haven't they caught on to you yet?" I asked in utter annoyance. "I know your boss can't possibly be on board with this."

"Don't you worry your pretty little head about that."

"I wouldn't have to worry about none of this if you were thinking on the capacity of someone who gave a damn."

"La'Dai, enough!" Mom yelled.

"Well, I'm not dropping the case. I can protect you guys during this entire trial," Sasha said, trying to reassure us.

"Oh, because you've done such a good job at protecting us already," I responded rolling my eyes. Sasha wasn't only delusional, thinking this could end well. She was in denial; she knew doggone well that she was wrong.

"LD, what's wrong with you? Why are you being so nasty?" Mom asked sounding concerned.

"Because Ma, Sasha is being selfish. This situation is serious and she's not the only one that is being affected by her lapse in judgment. She's being stubborn and inconsiderate as if I don't have enough going on already. Now I have to deal with the residual of her stuff too."

"LD just be quiet," Sasha said walking into the kitchen.

"See Ma she's a lost cause, always has…." I stopped myself, hardly believing the words that had just come out of my mouth.

"I'm going to pretend you didn't say that", Sasha said looking over her shoulder at me as she continued into the kitchen.

She grabbed her car keys and headed toward the door. Stopping mid-stride, she turned around toward me.

"But you know what? Now I see why Devin is leaving you. Grow up LD, there's a real thing called life. And in life everything doesn't always go your way or as planned. I didn't plan for any of this to happen. But what would you know about reality anyway? You're too busy walking around with your head up your butt, oblivious to everything going on around you except for what Devin is doing. Get a clue, sister, it's over for the Roswell's." Sasha turned to Ma and said, "I'm sorry Ma but I'm leaving before she says something else, she will regret."

Sasha walked out the door.

I looked over at Ma and Dad and they had the look of what the hell just happened on their faces. They were completely speechless.

Devin grabbed my hand and said, "LD, it's going to be okay."

"I really wish everyone would stop telling me that. I really wish everyone would realize that my entire life is in an uproar right now. Nothing is okay. I'm caught in the middle of everyone else's B.S."

Although I was still mad at Devin, and wanted no parts of him right now, I sat there with him for another twenty minutes. At this point bringing up the text message from "Ms. S." was ir-relevant. We had much bigger fish to fry.

"La'Dai, come onto the patio, I want to have a word with you," Ma said, walking outside, suggesting that I had no choice but to follow her.

Sitting out near the pool, Ma patted her palm on the seat next to her, gesturing for me to sit down.

"Now I'm not pointing any fingers nor am I taking sides, but from what I saw in there, honey, you aren't yourself. What's going on with you? I've never heard you talk to your sister like that."

"I know Ma, and I feel terrible for what I said to her. I didn't mean that at all. You know, lately everything feels like it's crashing down all at once."

"What do you mean?"

"I mean come on, Ma, let's not forget that I am going through a divorce and still don't understand why, adjusting to the ups and downs of that. If that's not enough, here comes Sasha and this situation. Ma, they vandalized my house and now my business, and the shop manager was hurt. Not only that, I didn't come this far in life to live terrorized."

"No matter how far you get in life, I don't think anyone wants to live terrorized."

"That's just my point. I mean I don't understand why she is not willing to drop the case, even with things spiraling out of control like they are, putting us all in jeopardy."

"Your sister is passionate about this, I don't agree with how she's going about the whole situation and, trust me, she and I have had our own conversation, but the fact remains that Sasha is a responsible adult and I trust her judgment. I also believe her when she says she will handle it. Her new career and the dynamics of it are new to us all, her included. She may not get everything right; in fact, I know she won't because her new career is very complex. Despite that, we are going to stand firm as a family unit and support her: right, wrong, or otherwise. Trust me when I say, God has not given you the spirit of fear. I'm praying these devils away. Do know that my prayers are always answered."

"Thanks Ma, that helps," I responded, wiping the tears from my eyes.

"That's what mothers are for. I do have one question, LD."

"Yes Ma, what is it?"

"Are you still in touch with the girl that you think Devin has something going on with?"

"To be honest, I haven't had any interaction with her lately."

"Good! Let that go because nothing good could come out of it anyhow."

She was right. I needed to completely stop talking to this girl, before things really got out of hand. Leaving my parents' house, I decided to call Sage and have her meet me at Tyrone's Sport Bar and Grill downtown Santa Monica. Funny little story about Tyrone's. It's owned by a white guy whose best friend's name is Tyrone. Apparently, the owner of the bar came second place in fantasy basketball against his friend Tyrone and when he couldn't pay his wager, it came down to, 'forget the money, name your bar after me.' He had to have the final standings, enlarged and framed, making its home right behind the bar. That little fun fact always makes me laugh, especially since it all started with a sport anyhow.

I knew Tyrone's would give me the right atmosphere, calm and chill. Which is what might have been my saving grace once I dropped this bomb in her lap—the truth about who I was. I decided that I was going to tell her everything. Who I really was, the entire story about Devin and me, and what my ulterior motives were? Besides, I was ready to put my life back together and holding onto Devin and following this chick around was going to hinder me from doing just that.

I texted Sage telling her to meet me, and she agreed. As I was pulling up to the bar, I noticed her getting ready to park. She got out of her car, looking dainty and cute. Wearing a jean jump suit and a pair of black pumps. I could tell she had just got her hair done. The curls were flawless and blowing in the wind. Just then Devin called. My adrenaline started pumping, I looked at my phone then back at her ass walking into the bar and then back at my phone. Declining Devin's phone call, I sat there thinking about her text to him the other night and I thought if he had not filed for divorce in the first place, maybe I wouldn't have been under so much stress and could have probably handled this whole thing with Sasha better and I never would have gone off on her to begin with, so technically my range of negative emotions and the horrible outburst to Sasha was Devin and this girl's fault. They were to blame.

I pulled into a parking spot a few spaces from hers. I could tell the restaurant was packed by how full the parking lot was. Tires screeching and trying to channel my mind on how I was about to let his broad have it, I was ready. But just then something clicked, and I was reminded that I still didn't have all the answers I needed and wanted. Not only that, what if I let the cat out the bag and this girl loses her mind. I mean there's no doubt in my mind that I would tap that ass. But was the risk greater than the reward? On second thought, my sister is the DA and I know she could pull some strings to get me out. Then again, we're talking about Sasha. The same Sasha who was still mad at me for crossing the line earlier. The same Sasha who would probably leave me in jail just to prove a point: "I told you so." It was apparent that my thoughts were not in check. I thought of doing something else instead. Something I knew would satisfy my anger, even if just for a moment.

I got out of my car and walked over to Sage's car, looking around and over my shoulder, making sure no one was watching me, I pulled out red lipstick from my purse, headed to Sage's car, checked my back one more time. Call me petty but the words, "TRIFLING BITCH" decorated her driver side window. Big and bold.

Trying to hurry up and put the evidence back in my purse, I was startled by a childlike voice. I looked up and noticed this young boy standing there, holding a box of chocolates. He seemed to be about twelve years old.

"Lady, you are too old to be out here sneaking around like this, why don't you tell the "TRIFLING BITCH" to her face that she's a trifling bitch?"

"Little boy, you're too young not to be minding your own business."

"Yeah well, stop putting your business out in the street in broad daylight. Out here acting a fool." He snapped back shaking his head as he walked away.

The nerve of this damn kid. I hurried up, fast walking to my car, trying to make sure that no one else saw me. The little smart mouth kid was right. I was acting a damn fool. But did I give a damn? Nope. Not at all.

I sent Sage a text that read:

I'M SORRY BUT I HAVE TO CANCEL OUR PLANS, MY REALITY JUST SUNK IN.

Thirty minutes later I was home, by that time Sage texted back saying:

Hey girl, sorry for the delayed response. I got your text, but when I got out to my car to leave, one of these drunk females at that damn bar wrote on my car window with cheap ass lipstick. But it's okay, some cute guy helped me get it off (smiley face)

I thought to myself: cheap? That was Chanel. But what would she know anyway?

I texted back:

Oh no, well it's a good thing you left.

I had no choice but to go along with it. I threw my phone down on the bed and yelled out loud, "Ugh! What does Devin see in her?"

Chapter Ten

"Hey girl, how's it going?" she embraced me with a hug, and I thought to myself, okay, this is getting too close for comfort. Not wanting to seem rude, I hugged Sage back but not tight.

A couple of weeks later Sage called me asking if we could meet up, she emphasized that she really needed to talk to me about something. Out of curiosity I agreed and went to meet her.

"Hey," I responded trying not to sound dry.

Because I still wanted to maintain my summer body, I told her to meet me at the Culver City stairs–the hike came with breathtaking views. The air was crisp, and the sun was shining but it wasn't too hot. We started off walking at a slow pace with other hikers passing us by.

Sage complimented me. "I like your Nike get-up, that's really cute and purple looks good on you too."

"Thank you," I responded, feeling myself as I repositioned my shirt. "So, what was so important that you couldn't text me or discuss it over the phone?"

"Okay, look I know I haven't been knowing you for a very long time but during this short time you've become a listening ear and someone I can trust. You know I don't have a sister and I'm not that close with my mother. The girlfriends I do have are judgmental and busy with their own life issues."

I thought to myself, and what am I? Your personal freaking therapist with nothing better to do? We aren't friends. You're some bimbo seeing my husband and you haven't given me any real information, so I don't know why I'm even still dealing with your ass. I was ranting in my head, for a moment I zoned out.

"Elle, did you hear me?"

"Sorry, girl repeat what you said."

"I saaaiiid that what I'm about to tell you is strictly confidential and is going to require a judgment free zone."

"Okay, I've heard your disclosure loud and clear, now what's up?"

"So, a couple of weeks ago I noticed that I wasn't feeling like myself. I was moody and my period came but lasted only two days, so I went to the doctor and they had me take a pregnancy test."

"Wait a minute; stop right there…I need to sit down."

I sat down right where I was standing, right in the dirt. My heart was beating fast, I began to feel hot and began hyperventilating a little bit. I know she was not about to tell me that she is pregnant. But why, how could this be happening? I started to think about my own little secret I had that drove me over the wall every time I thought about pregnancy and my breathing got heavier.

"Damn girl, are you okay?"

"Yeah, yeah umm, I'm fine. It's just I haven't worked out in a while, so this hike has me a little winded."

"Well, let's just take a moment because I don't need you passing out. But like I was saying, I took a pregnancy test, and it came back negative. So, I went home but-"

After the words negative rolled off her tongue I just laid back in the dirt. A sense of relief came over me and all I could do was lay there.

"Girl, do you realize that you are lying in dirt?"

"I do but you don't understand exactly how I'm feeling right now."

"No, I don't, but I'm confused because you're breathing heavy with a smile on your face. What did I say to make you smile?"

"Nothing girl, I'm just happy. I'm feeling better. I got a sudden burst of energy, let's jog." I got up brushed off as much dirt as I could off my pants, and we started jogging.

"Okay, well the test came back negative so what's the big deal?" I asked.

"Well, I haven't got to that part yet, you keep interrupting."

"Go on."

"So, after I took the test, I went home but I was still feeling like shit, so I went back to the doctor. They did some labs which included a blood pregnancy test. Turns out I'm pregnant."

When I opened my eyes, Sage was standing over me, and so were some strangers. Beyond their faces I could see the clouds in the sky. I was lying on the ground, flat on my back.

"Why am I on the ground?" I asked. Trying to get up, I could feel dirt stuck to the side of my face.

"You fainted and almost gave me a damn heart attack. Maybe you're out of shape more than you think," Sage said, pulling me up off the ground.

"Fainted?"

"Thank you, guys, for your help, I think she's going to be okay." Sage shook the strangers' hands and they walked away looking back as if to make sure that they weren't needed to offer any more assistance.

She sat down next to me.

"Girl, you scared me half to death, we were jogging and talking about my pregnancy, and you just collapsed. Let's get you out of here."

"No, just give me a minute. Ummm so you're pregnant?"

"Yes."

"Ummm, congrat…"

I couldn't get the words out. I was still processing what I was hearing. Was Devin about to be a father? One minute I was happily married, and now I'm sitting down with this woman who could possibly be the mother of Devin's first child. I felt like I was in a trance, none of it seemed real.

"Don't congratulate me just yet."

"Why not?"

"Because I'm confused and I ummm, well, I'm not really sure about this whole thing."

"I'm not sure I follow you, Sage."

"Well, I'm not quite ready to be a mother and besides I'm not particularly in the best of circumstances to raise a child. Kids should be raised in a two parent, stable household."

The words I thought about saying to her were of pure selfishness, but I didn't care. I did not care one bit. My husband was being stolen right from me and the woman responsible was in my face seeking me for counsel. I mean was Sasha, right? was this getting out of control? Maybe, but how was I going to stop now? I mean I couldn't, right? I would be selling myself short if I did. All interactions with her thus far would be in vain. And I couldn't let that be how this story ends. So, I fixed my lips to say it, the one word that even I dreaded, and thought was awful. I suggested something to her that I knew was dead ass wrong.

"Well Sage, I know you probably don't want to hear this, but if I were you, I would get an abortion."

"An abortion? Yeah ummm, well, that's not in my belief system."

"You said you weren't sure about this whole thing."

"I also said don't congratulate me yet but what I didn't say is I want to be a murderer. This is my child we're talking about here."

"I don't think it's considered a child just yet or murder."

"If the baby has a heartbeat, in my eyes its murder."

"Have you already had your first appointment?"

"No, but I'm just saying in general, if the fetus has a heartbeat, in my eyes it's a person so having an abortion would be an act of murder. But to be one hundred percent sure about the pregnancy, I have another appointment in two weeks."

I wanted to pick her little ass up and toss her over the scenic overlook. I'd done passed out and my heart almost stopped twice just to hear her say she wasn't one hundred percent sure. This tramp.

"Look, I understand that you have your morals and beliefs. But you are at the prime of your life, and I don't think you've come this far just to end up being someone's "Baby Mama." You're young, smart and have a lot going for yourself. Wait until things are more serious, wait until you can happily announce your pregnancy to the world without shame."

"You know up until now, I hadn't really considered the circumstances to the that degree," Sage said. "But I think you may have a point."

"I know I do, so I know a good clinic you can go to. They will take good care of you, and their follow up policy is phenomenal. Real good support system, ya know, the best."

"I don't know, girl, that just doesn't seem right."

"I'll do you a favor. I understand that you're probably overwhelmed and even tired. So, trust me to make all the arrangements for you. I'll even pick you up and take you to the procedure."

"You would do that for me?"

"Absolutely, girl."

What she didn't know was, I wasn't doing it for her. I was doing it for us. All three of us. I was doing it for her, to save her the heartache and pain of having a fatherless child. Over my dead body was Devin going to divorce me and live happily ever after with some woman who'd just been in his life for a hot minute.

Then there's Devin, I mean c'mon he left me because he said he wanted to live life for himself, clearly a new baby and dependent woman would mess that up. They both would require all of his time. In hindsight I was helping him out, helping him fulfil his dream if you will. And of course, there's me. I knew damn well with her and a new baby in Devin's life it would completely change the trajectory of how Devin and I interacted, even on a business level. And I've said it once, maybe even twice, so I'll say it again: I'm serious about my money.

I left the park feeling spun. Devin and I were not this type of couple, reality T.V. drama-like predicaments were not anywhere near our vortex. Five months ago, I was in love with who I thought was supposed to be my life partner. Fast forward to today and we were going through a divorce. And now he may have gotten some broad pregnant. Somehow, I'd convinced myself that being close to her would solve my problems of the unknown. Damn. I was in too deep now to turn back. When life takes you on a rollercoaster, I see why they say buckle up and enjoy the ride. I should have been going bat shit crazy.

Once I got home, I was pacing back and forth. I replayed the suggestion I made to Sage to get an abortion over and over again in my head. Yeah, I was misguiding this poor vulnerable woman, playing on her weaknesses, but, hell, love will make you do some crazy things. And the fact remained that I still didn't have all the details about why Devin wanted a divorce in the first place. So, I was going to continue to play every situation involving her to my advantage. I mean sure, he may have been seeing this woman, but something still wasn't adding up to me.

Finally, I sat down and made the call. I don't know why I was battling with myself over this. The girl was no friend of mine and plus I was referring her to one of the best doctors in Los Angeles. She was going to be in good hands.

"Hi, Sarah. It's Mrs. Roswell. I need to make an appointment for termination of pregnancy."

Sarah was Dr. Long's secretary. We'd built very good rapport over the years.

"Oh no, thank you but it's not for me. You know the situation I have with my uterus. It would take a miracle." I said to her as I could hear typing on the computer keyboard.

"Which date is that? Three weeks from now, perfect. Since it's not for me I will have the patient send you over all of her health insurance information. As always it was pleasure speaking with you, Sarah, bye."

As quick as I hung up, my business phone rang. The number was unfamiliar but that wasn't unusual.

"Roswell Reality, this is La'Dai."

The voice on the other end was not what I expected, going into what I thought to be a business matter.

"Hello beautiful, this is Jason."

"I'm sorry, who is this?" I said getting a little sassy. I was a little irritated at the fact that someone thought they could play on my business line.

"Jason, sweetheart. The oncologist from Jazzy's. I also saw you at the real estate mixer."

"Oh, hello." My tone changed from feisty to flirtatious.

"Is now a good time to talk?"

"Umm yeah, but how did you get my number?"

"I told you that night at Jazzy's if you don't call me, then I'll call you."

"I can't say that I'm mad at that but how did you find me?"

"You told me you sold commercial real estate and I went on the hunt after that."

"The hunt?"

"Don't take all my words literal. So, how are you? I would love to take you out."

"Wow, you don't waste no time, do you?"

"We've wasted enough time. It took me months to find your number and it was another waiting period trying to figure out when the right time was to call you."

"And how did you figure out that it was the right time?"

"I had this feeling that maybe you needed me right now at this exact moment."

"Go on…because I'm not impressed just yet."

He laughed and I could tell that he was moving around on his end.

"I would love to, hun. But truth be told, I saw your sister at Jazzy's, and she told me that I needed to call you. I already had your number, but she insisted on giving it to me again just to be sure that it was the correct one."

"Wait, how did you know that she was my sister?"

"I did not. She actually came up to me and said, "I remember you, you're MC." I laughed to myself because only Sasha would let him in on our little secret. That girl has no filter and loves to tell it like it is, good or bad.

"I didn't know what "Mr. MC" meant but we conversed for a moment before she insisted that I call you."

MC was a nickname that Sasha and I came up with the night after meeting Jason, we both agreed that he resembled Morris Chestnut.

"Well, let me just say that I'm happy you did."

"You are?"

"Yes, I am."

"I gave you my number, why didn't you use it?" he asked curiously.

"Life has been very busy lately and I too was waiting for the right time."

"Oh, you catch on fast."

We shared laughter and continued our conversation.

"So, Jason, tell me, how often do you go to Jazzy's and buy drinks, if you know what I mean."

"I know exactly what you mean, but I'm no schoolboy looking for just a good time."

"I don't go often, life as a doctor is busy, and I usually don't have the time. But I like that place because the drinks are good, the atmosphere is right, and the crowd is live. I usually stay for a couple of hours then head home. But the night you were there, I did not want to leave. You were beautiful eye candy, and I was on a sugar high."

"You better stop. Eye candy? You have to do better than that."

"Come on, you won't let me in far enough to get to know you better so I can only comment on what I've seen so far. And from what I see, you're a gorgeous woman with the potential of being someone I can connect with on an entirely different level. A level I've been looking and waiting to reach. So, may I take you out?"

I thought for a moment before responding. I mean here I was, had just made an abortion appointment for Devin's little fling and now I was contemplating on passing up dinner plans as if I had anything else interesting going on in my life. At this point there was no way that I was going to say no.

"Yes, you can take me out to Patina Restaurant, have you heard of it."

"I can't say that I have."

"It's at the Walt Disney Concert Hall, Downtown LA. The menu serves French-American food."

"If that's where you want to go, then that's where we'll be."

"I'll pick you up this Friday around 7:30?"

"No, I don't think so, Sir, that's not going to work."

"I'm sorry, is that too close to your bedtime?"

He thought he was so funny, laughing at his own jokes.

"Nice try but I will meet you at the restaurant."

"Really? You don't trust me?"

"No."

"Oh, that hurt, that hurt bad."

We laughed.

"You know what, I can respect that. I'm just happy you finally agreed to let me take you out. But not being able to pick you up puts a damper on my plans to be the perfect gentleman who wanted to chauffer you with a dozen long red stem roses but--."

"You seem like a smart man, I guess you'll have to execute plan b."

"Ms. La'Dai, you're keeping me on my toes already. I will see you at 7:30 on Friday. It's time for me to get ready to head into the hospital."

"Mr. Jason, you enjoy your shift, and I will see you Friday."

"Wait, do I need to call you on Thursday and make sure that you don't get cold feet."

"Oh, whatever."

"Okay, I was trying to find a way to talk to you again between now and our date."

"Then just call me. Let me give you my disclosure now, texting is not my choice of communicating, it's actually a turn off."

"I appreciate the heads up. We will talk later. Have a good one, okay?"

"Will do, thank you."

Hanging up the phone, I instantly began to jump up and down on my sofa. It had been a while since I'd been on a date and I was unable to maintain my composure. This man was fine.

I contemplated calling Sasha and telling her everything about

Devin and this whole baby ordeal, but I decided to call and let her have it for getting all in my business. Of course, I would wind up thanking her because, Lord knows, this date is exactly what the doctor ordered.

Wednesday snuck up on me fast. I was two days away from meeting up with Jason and being wined and dined. The plan was to go to Micela's Boutique and find me a nice dress to wear but I wasn't feeling it. I decided to go into my garden instead.

Zen City was no vegetable garden. Zen City was custom designed by yours truly. It was a Japanese inspired garden, a place that I liked to refer to as a piece of heaven on earth, right in my back yard. Peace of mind is something that I've always sought out. Not to mention I am a lover of all things beautiful: Words, sounds, people, music, nature; ALL THINGS.

Every detail of Zen City was well thought out and the intricacy of the garden took landscapers almost a year to finalize. I walked onto the bamboo entryway and suddenly felt a sense of peace settle over my body. Walking along the steppingstone path, I smiled at the outdoor elegance and sought to relax, rebalance, refresh, and meditate in the spiritual entrapment centered right in my backyard.

When I got to the end of the steppingstones, I walked over to the koi pond and closed my eyes as I listened to the soothing trickle of the waterfall. There was something about the waterfall that brought a sense of balance. All seven chakras became aligned. I took a sip of my stress relief tea that I brewed an hour before and began to rethink my entire interaction with Sage.

Again, I thought maybe I should just walk away from the entire ordeal and just sign the divorce papers so that I could finally start to heal and move forward. I continued to think that maybe in my mind this was my way of fighting for my marriage and then I realized that maybe I was going about the fight the wrong way. But in my defense, I never learned how to really fight. Not physically, or maybe what I mean is I never really learned how to be strong. How to take things as they come, forget how they were, and see things for what they are becoming.

Just then I snapped out of the mental trance I was in. Distracted by the sound of the birds chirping coming from the mini bird retreat in a corner of the garden, I walked over to find one of the birds stuck in the rock bird house.

I set the bird free, spent about twenty more minutes walking around the garden before I went back into the house.

My phone had three missed calls from Sage, and a text that read: Please call me back; it's urgent. I rolled my eyes, "Okay, she's becoming too dependent on me," I said aloud as I was calling her back.

"Hey Sage, its Elle. What's up?" I thought it would be a challenge keeping up with the alias after all this time, but I was handling it like a champ. I put the thoughts that I had while I was in Zen City to the back of my mind for the time being. All in all, she and I had some unfinished business to tend to, and I needed to stay focused.

"Hey girl, I've been over here nail biting and going crazy."

"Well, what's up?"

"I think it's better if we talk in person," Sage responded, sounding frantic.

"I was going to head over to Micela's Boutique, the one near the Beverly center, you can meet me there," I said, looking for my shoes.

"Umm yeah, that works. I just need to talk. Things have definitely changed since I saw you last."

"Okay well, give me about an hour to get ready and I'll text you when I'm headed out."

Sage and I arrived at the boutique at about the same time. She was dressed as if she had just thrown something on after getting out of bed. She wasn't well put together, her hair was in a messy bun, no makeup on, just lip gloss. She wore a pair of black tights, and a white tank top and a jean jacket, with a pair of all black thong Nike flip flops. Surprisingly, she was in a good mood.

Her energy reminded me of the mood she was in the day I discovered her in the hair salon. She gave off a child-like happy demeanor. I don't know if I expected her to be a little off due to morning sickness or maybe it was the sense of urgency in her voice when she called me that made me assume the worst.

Standing outside the boutique, I greeted Sage. "Hey, I take it you weren't planning on going anywhere after this," I said referencing her poor appearance.

"Oh, I do, I plan on celebrating tonight. I plan on enjoying a couple of glasses of bubbles. In fact, I'll be going wine tasting later."

"Oh good, so you've made up your mind on the abortion. I'm glad we don't have to go down that road of indecisiveness anymore because I made your appointment."

"Sshh, you're talking too loud," she said as she looked around, checking to see if anyone was listening. She continued, "And yeah, umm about that, that's why I needed to talk to you."

"Girl, no one is listening to us and let's get inside because you're one word away from getting on my nerves. No disrespect but I thought we were in agreeance that it would be in your best interest."

I know my horns were starting to show but this needed to happen, and I needed her to follow through.

"Oh girl, please, I'm not offended easily. My situation is a lot to deal with—I get it, but I'll explain everything."

We stepped into the boutique and there were two young ladies waiting to greet us as we walked in.

One of the young ladies offered to help. "Oh no I'm fine,"

Sage answered one of them. "I'm here with her."

"What are you doing here, anyway?" Sage turned to me and asked.

"I have a date on Friday, and I need something to wear. So, help me as you explain yourself."

She laughed and said, "A date, well, that's good because I was beginning to wonder. I mean you don't seem like the type to be into women, but you aren't married, and you've never mentioned dating or seeing anyone."

"I'm a pretty private person. But enough about me, what did you need to talk about?"

I was scanning through the racks, and she was following me around like a two-year old would her mother.

"So, I know you said that you scheduled the appointment for me to have you-know-what done, but you can cancel it."

Trying to maintain my composure, I asked why.

"Well, because the day after I saw you, I got a call from my doctor's office and apparently, they mixed up my test with another patient who has the same last name as I do. They were very apologetic, and I guess the nurse was a new grad still learning. I told them that it wasn't that big of a deal and…".

"Wait, so you're not pregnant?"

"Nope. As a matter of fact, my period started this morning, hence why I just threw something on and didn't feel like getting dressed. These cramps are a mother."

"Girl, I'm so happy for you. I could kiss you right now."

Sage looked at me with a strange look on her face, confused and puzzled.

"What I mean is, now you don't have to get the procedure done and you don't have to jeopardize your beliefs, ya know?"

I was trying my best to clean up my obvious display of being overjoyed.

"I know, right? Not to mention the fact that I don't have to embarrass myself and tell Devin everything."

"Yeah girl, I would keep that little secret to myself."

I didn't need Devin getting any emotional ties to this chick.

"C'mon, let's go to the dressing rooms, I need to try on these dresses."

I went into the dressing room and Sage sat on the couch; I could hear her still talking as I was trying on the dresses.

"Could you imagine? I would have had to tell this guy every-thing and I do mean everything?"

"What do you mean everything?" I responded, struggling to zip up my dress. I stepped out of the dressing room and in front of Sage, motioning for her to zip up my dress.

"Oh, this is cute. Turn around," she said spinning me around.

"Sage, what do you mean everything?" I asked, looking in the mirror then back at her.

She looked over her shoulder again, seeing who was around before answering.

With an embarrassed look on her face, she said, "I would have had to tell Devin that I was pregnant with another man's baby."

"What?" I exclaimed loudly.

She put her head down in shame.

"I know, remember when I initially told you about this whole thing while we were hiking, I told you that it would require a judgment free zone. I just never got around to giving you all the details."

"But why are you all worked up anyway?" she asked with one eyebrow raised.

I was trying not to show too much emotion. But this girl and her entire situation was working on my last nerve. Too many ups and downs, yes, no and maybes. Was she sure about anything?

"Well, because you've been talking about this guy and you

really seem into him. I just want to see things work out for you, that's all," I lied.

By this time, I was sitting next to Sage, curious as a cat.

"That's the thing, I'm into him but there isn't much reciprocity. We haven't slept together at all. I try to be intimate with him, but he isn't receptive."

"Wait, you guys haven't slept together?" I was itching to drag her through the boutique. What was her purpose in Devin's life? What was their relationship or lack thereof? I was getting more and more irritated the more she opened her mouth.

"No! And at first, I thought it was because he was trying to be a gentleman. And you know a girl has needs so then I thought that maybe I should let him know what time was by taking the initiative but doing that made it seem as if I was being too aggressive."

She looked at me with a sign of hopelessness, and I could have cared less. I couldn't be happier about being wrong about Devin sleeping with another woman. Yes, he was still seeing her but at least they hadn't slept together, and from what she was saying, it seemed like he had no desire to.

So then again back to the million-dollar question, what was he doing with her? And why on earth did she feel the need to defend her stance that night by sexting that picture along with making that sly ass comment? Was she looking for trouble because she was trouble all on her own? She didn't have to go far to look for it. Trying to seduce my man.

"Not only that," she continued. "I think he's seeing someone else."

"What makes you think that?"

"A little while back I called him, and some woman answered his phone and told me that I had the wrong number; then she said Devin didn't know a Sage. She laughed and hung up on me."

Oh, and she's a liar, I thought to myself, I don't remember it happening exactly like that but whatever.

She continued trying to make logical sense about Devin, saying, "He doesn't seem like the kind of guy to play games like that so, when she hung up, I didn't get upset I thought for sure he and I would talk about it later and there would be a reasonable explanation. Like I said, he's a standup guy. After she hung up, I got to thinking and I was like 'to hell with that, I can play too.' Yes, I was being petty but what can I say. So, I took a picture of me in my best lingerie and sent it to his phone, with a caption that said, *"When Devin is done playing with you, let him know that his real woman is waiting for him."*

I was trying so hard not to let her see how furious I was becoming, I remembered that text oh so well.

I commented, "Yeah, you were being very childish with that one. Honey, you won't get any man with those kinds of antics."

"Okay, slow your role. And be careful," she snapped.

"Sage, I'm sorry, that came out wrong." I knew I was starting to get on the defensive.

"It's cool. Like I said, I'm not easily offended but it's a respect thing."

"No, girl, I get it. Finish what you were saying."

"Anyway, the next time I saw him, he gave me grief about the picture and message, and that caught me off guard. Most men would have been apologetic and happy to have gotten a picture like that. But not Devin--homeboy was pissed."

"Well, did he say why and did he say who answered his phone."

"He said, 'I should be more respectful', and I quote, 'Please don't question me about my phone.' I was completely thrown off by his demeanor, but then he calmed down, gave me a foot massage, we watched a movie, and he fell asleep on the couch."

"Does he know that you're seeing someone else?"

"I'm not technically seeing anyone else."

"Sage, you thought you were pregnant, what are you, the modern-day Virgin Mary?"

She laughed. "Girl no, let me finish. An ex of mine was in town on business, and he invited me to his hotel for some drinks at the bar. I went and on this particular night, I called Devin a couple of times before leaving, to see if he wanted to come over. You know how it is after having a good time and a few drinks, you want to go home and finish the party. Long story short, Devin said he was tired, and we could hang out the next day. I guess my ex could sense that I was frustrated about something, so for old times' sake he suggested that we finish what we started and go up to his room. We did and one thing led to another. I can't say that I wasn't happy the next morning and to be honest I had no guilt. Devin won't let me in, and I don't know what the status of our relationship is."

"But haven't you been seeing this Devin guy for months?"

"Yes, but that's the thing, like I said we haven't slept together. Not even so much as foreplay. And maybe that's what attracts me to him so much because he's the perfect gentleman. But then I got to thinking, is this guy gay because I'm fine and the most intimate we've been is, hugging, massages and forehead kisses."

"I think this guy's sexual preference is the least of your worries. I mean I'm just saying, you're seeing him but sleeping with someone else. How are you going to explain that to him?"

"I'm not! Are you crazy?"

"Look, maybe you should have had this conversation with someone else. I'm not here to judge you but I'm also not here to sugar coat things either. You should be completely honest with him."

"I hear you girl, but listen," Sage said looking down at her watch. "I have to go; I have an important business meeting to get ready for. We can chat later."

"Okay," I said nodding my head.

"Oh, and Elle, thank you for listening and giving me advice. I really appreciate your help. Oh, and I think the black dress looks great on you." She smiled and headed for the door.

I stood there, totally blown away. I was happy about the information I just found out but still confused as to what Devin was doing with her. My next move was to try and get her to tell Devin just how much of a mess she really was. Yes, I was relentless. I needed her completely out of the picture and she was going to set her own self up.

I put both dresses back and headed to my car. Given this new information there was no way I was going on a date with Jason. I was going to get my man back. Sage was not it. Devin was not going to find another like me, and he needed to see that. Devin Roswell needed me.

Chapter Eleven

I knew I needed to come with my A-game. Lately I had been Negative Nancy and not going about the situation of my divorce the right way, but I must admit everything I knew about divorce was ugly and hopeless. I'm not talking from a point of having experienced it myself but more so from a point that I'd witnessed from people I knew or heard about—the horror stories of Ghosts from girlfriends' past. All my preconceived notions had me in a whirlwind of assumption, fear, and anxiety. But my divorce with Devin, although I still did not understand it to begin with, was far from fear and anxiety. Nonetheless, here I was ready to plead my case and win my husband's heart back.

Devin walked into the house, took one look around and I could tell he was taken back by the candles, soft music and my beautiful body standing there in six-inch heels, and lingerie that was slightly covered up by a black apron that read, "Will cook for shoes" across it. Devin knew cooking was not my forte'. If I was in the kitchen whipping up a meal, it meant one thing, a special occasion.

Handing Devin, a glass of wine, I began explaining to him why I invited him over, "I thought with everything that's been going on over the past months we could have a nice dinner and talk."

"Talk? What would you like to talk about?"

There was no way I was letting up this time. I'd spent the last two hours getting myself all dolled up; shaving, curling my hair, and perfecting my make-up. Time was of the essence and I was going to seize every moment.

"Devin, I know that I haven't been the easiest person to get along with lately. And I know that may have been the cause of us becoming distant but I'm ready to turn over a new leaf. Right now, in this moment, I'm still your wife, and to be honest, we need to keep it that way. Divorce is no longer an option, I'm here to stay."

"C'mon LD, not this again."

"Listen to me, Devin," I said trying to maintain my composure and wheel him in.

"Let's face facts, obviously we still have something between us, I can feel it when you're with me, I can tell by the way you still show up in my times of need, ready to be my knight in shining armor. And you already know where I stand; I've made it clear from the beginning. But to show you that I'm serious and willing to put the past behind us I went as far as to get you this."

I handed Devin a small black box. In amazement he opened it with wide eyes and in complete awe.

"You had my wedding ring upgraded?"

"Not just upgraded, but engraved too, read it," I said in excitement. I grabbed the ring out of Devin's hand and read it aloud.

"FOREVER YOURS, FOREVER MINE. OUR LOVE WILL WITHSTAND THE TEST OF TIME."

"LD, I don't know what to say about this."

"It's easy, say yes just like we both did ten years ago, in front of all of our family and friends. Remember the words, for better or for worse? We'll call our lawyers first thing in the morning and let them know that we decided against the divorce. You'll move back into our home and we can continue on like normal. Forgetting that any of this ever happened. Only this time it will be better." I was rambling but I didn't care. "C'mon, Devin, they say absence makes the heart grow fonder and your absence has definitely made me realize some things."

"LD, LD, slow down. I mean all of this is a great gesture; the ambiance, the dinner that smells amazing by the way, and getting my ring upgraded–that was truly unexpected but…"

"But Devin? No buts! Not this time."

"It's not that easy. We can't just pick up where we left off."

"Why not? I don't get it. You don't have a legit reason as to why you want a divorce. You say that you still love me but yet you're comfortable walking out of my life just like that. I mean NEVER in a million years did I think this could happen to me, to us. Where did we go wrong D? Please help me to understand."

"I wish I could help you understand." Devin paused for a moment before continuing. "Life is full of twist and turns. I've taken such good care of you all these years, you've never wanted or needed for anything. I honestly think you've lost touch with reality. But my job as your husband was to protect you and I may have sheltered you a little bit. I felt it was necessary to protect you at all cost: from heartbreak, from lack, from the pitfalls of life, just anything that tried to come against you in general. The truth is I still intended to protect you. That's why this divorce has to happen. I get it, it feels like the rug has been pulled from underneath you but please trust me when I say this is not where your story ends. Sometimes God will break your heart to save your soul."

Tears were streaming down my face. I wanted so badly to fall off the face of the earth. Why was he rejecting me? It was as if Devin was emotionally disconnected from me.

"God? Devin, you haven't mentioned God or spirituality for

that matter in a very long time."

"God has a way of getting our attention. This hasn't been an easy time for me either. I miss you a lot, but this is what has to be done. As long as I still have breath in my body, I'm always going to be here for you, circumstances don't change that. I know you're upset, know that I love you and what I'm doing is in your best interest."

"Devin, are you seeing anyone else?"

"On a romantic level, no. Do I have friends? Of course, but the majority of them you know, except for maybe a couple. Wait, I know where this question is coming from; you answered my phone the other night. You shouldn't have done that; you were out of line. But lucky for you I'm understanding."

"Lucky for me?"

"It was a joke, relax, LD."

"Well, explain that text message."

"No, I'm not. It's irrelevant, I answered your question and I've already taken care of it. So, let's drop it."

"I'm not going to drop it. Some broad texts you after midnight, sending you half naked pictures of her scrawny little ass and you want me to drop it. Nope, don't think so. Obviously, you have given her some indication that you guys are more than friends if she felt comfortable enough to send that to you."

Although I had gotten some facts from Sage, I still needed to press the issue to find out why Devin was hanging out with her in the first place.

"I'm not going there and opening up that can of worms. What happened to let's mend fences, the song you were singing when I first got here. I say something you don't want to hear, and you go back to being Cruella Deville?" Devin took a deep breath and said, "Tonight doesn't have to be a total waste of time. We can still have dinner and watch a movie. I don't see any harm in us enjoying each other's company. But in order for this to stay PG-13, I need you to go and change your clothes. Damn girl, you do a good job at getting my attention!" He was staring at me and shaking his head.

"Yeah, whatever Devin. I'm going to agree to that for two reasons: One, I slaved in the kitchen cooking us dinner for over two hours and you know I'm not one for the kitchen. Two, you could use a home-cooked meal, you're looking a little thin these days." I tried to give an amused giggle.

Just as I said that my phone started ringing and it was Jason. I completely forgot to cancel our plans. Declining his call, I immediately sent him a text apologizing with a lame ass excuse that my cat was sick. I didn't even like cats, let alone have one as a pet. I threw my phone back on the counter and thought to myself, I will deal with him later.

Devin didn't stay long; he fell asleep right in the middle of the movie. And rightfully so, I guess business was running him a little low nowadays. Everything was going well, and we were definitely prosperous.

Weeks had gone by, but they felt like months. Devin was wrapped up in the business, the little engagements we did have were business related. Sasha was still not speaking to me, and I was figuring out my next move with this Sage chick. I wouldn't say that I was depressed, but my days weren't so bright either. Although it was Friday night, I was not geeked up about my date with Jason. He reached out yet again, forgiving, and ready to give us and our date another shot.

Friday nights definitely had a different feel to them. Yes, I was newly single, but socializing was not at the front of my mind. I was used to date night with my husband or with family and friends. This was new and I was slightly nervous; it felt foreign. I mean what was I supposed to say, what would we talk about? I planned on taking it one step at a time and just letting the conversation flow.

Truth be told, I thought for sure after I'd cancelled on him that he was going to lose interest. But he called twice to set this date up and was not shy about letting me know he couldn't get me off his mind. It would have been wrong for me to cancel on him yet again. He made sure to let me know that he was not letting me off that easy.

The black tights I wore clung to my body, accentuating every curve. I lined my lips with a plum lipstick and was out the door. We met at Javier's Mexican Restaurant, the one in Newport Beach was my favorite. I loved the atmosphere; the ocean view was to die for, and the restaurant design was phenomenal. Pulling up to valet, I could tell it was packed. I got out and handed the valet attendant my keys. Walking to the front entrance, I hoped that I would recognize Jason in the crowd. Just then I heard a voice from behind, "Hello gorgeous." Jason greeted me with a smile and a dozen red stemmed roses in his hand. I had to admit, if he had not come up to me first, I may not have recognized him, he had done something different with his hair.

"Hello gorgeous, hello," he said again, this time embracing me with a hug and a kiss on the cheek. "My god, you look stunning."

"Thank you, and you clean up well yourself."

"Thank you," he replied, handing me the red roses. "These are for you."

"Thank you."

"You're welcome. Let's go inside, I have our table ready. I was going to order you a drink but was not sure what you wanted."

Halfway through our meal we had already discussed the awkward, annoying first date questions. Favorite color, hobbies, embarrassing moments, stuff like that. Needless to say, I was enjoying myself, our conversation was light and flowing. Full of good energy and positive vibes.

The first time I met Jason it was dark, and my mind was elsewhere. Sitting directly across from him now, in a well-lit room; I was focused in on his Colgate smile, his neatly cut fade and his manicured hands. This man took really good care of himself, and it showed. Jason was beyond statuesque; he was a male god. The word suave did him no justice. I can't believe newly single me almost passed him up.

As the night went on, he started telling me about his life as an oncologist and how it came to be. My heart felt for him as he elaborated on his wife, who lost her life at a very young age to breast cancer. Although it had been eleven years since her death, he spoke of her death as if it had just happened yesterday. He mentioned he didn't know which part hurt the most: the fact that she lost her battle to cancer or that she never got to experience life as she had always wanted. I agreed that twenty-four is a young age to die. Jason described her as full of life and ambition. He went on to say she had such high hopes and dreams, dreams of them one day owning their family business and building their legacy. I could feel my heart starting to flutter as I sensed the deepest sympathy for him. The way he described how the cancer took over her body was hard to hear.

He showed me a picture of what she looked like on their wedding day; she was absolutely stunning. The moments of sadness did not last too long once he expressed what he held as a happy lasting memory–the image of her smile that he envisions over and over again. He told me that he keeps a bottle of her favorite perfume because it helps him to keep her spirit alive. I could tell that he still loved and missed her dearly. He ended one conversation and started another with a comment that took me by surprise.

"The day my wife took her last breath is the day that I thought my life would never ever be the same, until I saw you."

To be held with that regard was breathtaking. He spoke about his late wife as if she was a goddess. He didn't know me yet and already he felt as if I was the one who could come into his life and fill those shoes. What did he see in me that I didn't?

I mean I couldn't have imagined ever experiencing the loss of my spouse, let alone watching him slowly but surely knock-on death's door. I thought how strong he must have been to endure such pain with nothing he could do about it. Yes, I wanted to reach out and touch him. I want to wrap him in my arms and tell him that everything was going to be okay. But how could he have possibly known that I was the missing piece to his puzzle. He barely knew me.

Not realizing it until I looked down, we were holding hands. I guess I had gotten caught up in the moment. Our eyes met, Jason leaned in, and our lips locked. I was confused about kissing him back but the moment he touched my lower jaw, confusion went out the door and fire and desire came in.

We shared the most passionate kiss. I could feel the hairs on the back of my neck starting to stand up. The kiss lasted about a minute. In that moment I felt connected to Jason, chills ran down my spine and I couldn't stop kissing him--plus he had it down to a science.

Jason and I spent the next couple of months getting to know each other. We were spending a lot of time together. I had finally opened up and allowed myself to think of all the possibilities of what a relationship with him could bring, and the thought of it had me feeling somewhat optimistic. I felt safe with Jason, there was something familiar about his spirit. I could tell he had a kind heart, but I could also tell that he was looking for something serious, someone to be serious with. Was I ready to dive into another serious relationship? Nope.

Our divorce was not final yet; Devin and I was still battling it out in court. We had one more court appearance, which was still surreal. Nonetheless, I was letting go. I was done fighting.

Trying to get my life back on track I stopped all contact with Sage. Interaction with her opened my eyes to the fact that I was fighting for something and someone that was no longer mine. Devin made it clear what he wanted, and I just needed to accept it, whether I understood it or not.

It dawned on me that the more I fought the more he resisted. At the end of the day, everyone was right. We had some very good years together and it was not like we had a messy divorce. I was okay holding on to the fact that we could still be friends and business partners. My new life was ahead of me, and I was not looking back.

Serious relationship or not, I was going to give Jason a chance. I needed the breath of fresh air.

Chapter Twelve

Jason was no stranger to romance. He loved showering me in the ambience of intimacy. He expressed romance in a way that I had never experienced before. Every word he spoke, every touch I felt, was gentle and particularly masculine. The way he touched me left me feeling like I was floating on cloud nine--never wanting to come down, leaving me with a keen sense of passion. Massaging the nape of my neck, down my spine, Jason was always sure to be respectful and not let his hands go past my waist. Whenever we kissed, he would gently caress my face and pull me in closer, making me feel so wanted, so alive, so appreciated.

Let's face it, I'm a one-man type of woman anyway. What Jason wanted is what I truly needed. Despite how I felt about wanting to take things slow, I realized that I was fighting temptation. Jason was fine, a true force to be reckoned with. And since Devin was unable to get it up the last time, we were together, that situation really put me in a compromising position. The position of wanting to be in any position, whether it be 69, missionary, or my personal favorite, doggy style, with the next man I felt was worthy of meeting me in my bedroom. What can I say? Every woman has a little promiscuity in her. Let me make it clear, my moral judgments weren't completely gone, I intended on taking every precautionary measure before I got down with the get down. I was horny not dick dumbfounded.

"Thank you for the bubble bath Jason, that was a nice touch. And Sade—man, her music never gets old."

"I'm happy you enjoyed it; I'll be in the kitchen waiting for you."

The bubble bath, with pink-colored rose petals and lavender scented candles to match set the mood off right. He had a cold glass of champagne waiting for me as I soaked the day's stress away. Sade's "soldier of love" played in his ceiling sound system. I relaxed as he cooked in the kitchen. Just before I got into the bathtub, he was sure to let me know that he was cooking my favorite and I was to put on the sexy lingerie number he single-handedly picked out at Victoria's Secret for me.

I dried myself off, moisturized my body in Nivea lotion and emerged as a beautiful black goddess walking down the stairs, my head held high and shoulders back. The smell of sweet perfume went before me in a tantalizing aroma. Jason damn near dropped the plates out of his hands as I hit the corner into the kitchen.

Hair pulled up into a sleek but messy bun. The black, strapless one-piece lingerie, fit just right, hugging every curve. I even went as far as to slip on my black, red bottoms. This beautiful black stallion had no problem strutting across the marble kitchen floor, with her shoulders back and head held high. I deserved this happiness. I was unapologetic and unbothered.

Jason stuttered over his words." Hey, hey gorgeous. Wow! How did I get so lucky?"

I played modest, "Lucky? I'm the lucky one, bubble baths, sexy lingerie, expensive champagne, and a home-cooked meal cooked by you!"

"Well, let's just say when you know you know. You don't take chances or anything for granted."

"Jason, I love the gesture, but don't you think we may be moving a little too fast?"

"Moving too fast? Baby, no. Where did this doubt come from all of a sudden? When opportunity knocks at your door, you don't shine it off with the what-ifs of life. You grab hold of it and keep moving forward. When you allow doubt to creep in, that's where opportunities are missed. You are heaven sent. The woman I've been praying for."

"Wait. Before you go getting all holy on me and having me feel guilty and like I'm going to hell with gasoline drawers on for being here with you, kiss me before I change my mind."

"Kiss you? Should I kiss you like this or like this." Jason said as he started kissing my lips and down the nape of my neck. Then from my neck to the top of my breasts.

"Oooh, like that and like that," I said breathing heavily.

I guided Jason to his couch, I laid down, with him kneeling over me, and I draped my legs over his shoulders. Suddenly I was unable to go any further, this same feeling came over me the last time Jason and I tried to make love. The feeling of guilt and shame. Guilt because I had not slept with another man but Devin in the last eleven years and the shame, hell I have no clue where that shit came from.

I knew Jason would soon get tired of me leading him on, only to let him down. Not that there was a timeline to follow but it had been months and we still had not had sex. I was very aware that he had needs but I still wanted to make sure that my emotions were in check, I didn't want to mess this up.

"Jason, I'm sorry. I'm still not ready yet," I said sitting up.

"It's okay, gorgeous, I understand that this is new to you. For you I'll wait a lifetime."

I looked at him and gave him a faint smile.

"Come here, let's just lie here and relax for a moment before dinner is ready."

Jason took my left foot in his hand and started giving it a massage. He was charming and sweet and gentle by nature, what every woman should experience in her life. But not with Jason, let me be clear: he was mine.

The more time I spent with Jason the closer we became. Like I've said before, there was something familiar about him. Not only that he was right on point with knowing me, but it's like we had also been together in another life. He knew me and knew me well. I couldn't figure out if he was just that good at being attentive and observant or if he was getting some insight from Ma or Sasha. Either way I was liking the way things were going.

But with all that I had been through I wanted to be sure that I wasn't grasping at false hope that this could really work. There was a little part of me that was hesitant to move forward. I was afraid of him waking up one day, just like Devin, after I'd invested time, effort, genuine emotion and out-of-nowhere deciding this was not what he wanted anymore. I typically didn't operate from a place of doubt, my entire life I was used to everything working itself out in my favor; but my marriage or what used to be my marriage changed all that. Challenged my entire belief system.

At times, I could tell Jason felt my resistance, but he still didn't let that stop him. He was relentless at wanting us to be on the same page. Jason knew what he wanted. He wanted to start his life all over again and with me. This was exactly what I wanted, but subconsciously, Devin was still on my mind. I thought to myself, poor Jason. All he wanted was to move forward in life and here I was blocking that with not being able to. The back and forth I experienced definitely had me up and down emotionally.

It's not every day that you meet a man who knows what he wants, who he wants to do it with and how. Jason had all the answers to all these circumstances. I was the main factor. Me.

He was so attentive, so loving, so into me. I only wished I could get over my marriage ending, even with an entirely new beginning staring me in the face. I was paralyzed from what no longer existed.

I wanted to fix it, fix me, so I went out on a limb, and decided to get insight from a neutral party. Call me crazy but I sensed that Sage would be able to help. I promised myself I wouldn't bait her and talk about Devin. I just needed some sound advice and for whatever reason I got a strong inkling that she could be the one to help me.

Hey Girl, I know it's been a while, but I could really use some girls talk and your advice. I texted.

Had I lost my mind? We weren't friends. Well, she thought we were. Regardless of the truth behind everything, my lies and deceit, Sage was under the impression that we could confide in each other, so I was going to take full advantage of that.

Although I considered her a threat at one point in time, since I was fully letting go of Devin, that thought went out the window and it was no longer how I felt about her. I was moving on; I mean we could never be "real friends" considering how I went about things but what I needed from her didn't require a true look into our future together as friends nor did it require me to come clean to her.

For the time being, I was going to continue as I had previously, depicting myself as someone she could trust. Only this time there was no malicious intent. So, no harm, no foul, right?

At daybreak I was up and, on my treadmill, getting my energy and vibes flowing. Immediately afterward, I juiced myself some carrots and celery. I caught wind of this new juice diet that was sure to bring about results. I could afford to shed a few extra pounds from all the eating out Jason and I were doing. I threw on a maxi dress and went to meet Sage.

"Hey girl, thanks for meeting me," I said sitting down in the spa chair next to her, eagerly awaiting my foot massage.

"No, thank *you* for the spa day and girl time," Sage responded. "Both have been much needed. I have so much to tell you."

I could tell that she was excited about the spa but even more excited meeting up with me.

"Tell me about it, but this time I want to get some advice from you on some things I'm dealing with."

"Of course, I'm flattered that you would consider me a reliable source. Usually, it's me bombarding you with my drama. So, I'm all ears, what's up?"

"So, I'm newly divorced. And-."

"My gosh, Elle, I had no idea. You hid that pretty well. Here I was, and forgive me for saying this, but here I was passing judgment on you thinking you were a lesbian because you never talked about having a man nor ever paid them attention while we were out, and this entire time you've been going through a divorce. Not only that but I've been giving you all the fabulous details of my newly developing love life. I hope you weren't triggered by any of that."

"Ummm, I'm okay, I appreciate your concern, but I would like to finish what I was saying so I don't lose focus and get off subject. Besides my emotions about the divorce is behind me now. And what I was about to say is, I've been seeing this new guy and…."

"Oh, is this why you went MIA on me?"

"Girl, can I finish?"

"Okay go, I'm sorry; I'm just excited."

"Thank you. Like I was saying, missy. I've been dating this guy and he's very interested. As a matter of fact, he's ready to start an entirely new life with me. I'm talking wedding and all."

"Okay, so what's the problem? Wait, in order for me to gain

the full scope of everything and understand what's going on, I have a few questions."

"Ugh, okay what?" I yelled jokingly, slightly bothered that she would not let me finish.

"Is he good-looking?"

"Yes."

"What does he do for a living?"

"He's a doctor."

"A doctor? Girl say no more. What are you waiting for?"

"Sage, unfortunately it's not that easy."

"Not that easy, Elle you're newly divorced. Most women are afraid of divorce, fearing they'll end up alone for the rest of their lives or unable to find an eligible bachelor. You don't have to fear either and you're second guessing yourself. Plus, he's a doctor--need I say more?"

"I'm not an opportunist, I have my own money and ambitions."

"It's not about being opportunistic. But when this type of gift presents itself, you have to take it, you can't waste it with thoughts of doubt."

"That's his exact motto. Where are you guys getting this from? Do you know him?"

"No, I doubt it. I don't know any fine doctors. If I did, he wouldn't be your problem, he would be mine," she said laughing. "But no, all jokes aside, I don't know, but it sounds like he and I both know what's up and you need to get on board. Girl, if he and I have said the same thing and we don't know each other, then there's only one explanation. The universe is talking to you. You better listen."

"The universe?"

"Yes, let me put it like this. You have favor right now, the opportunity that me and Dr. Fine are talking about is, the golden chance to start all over. Things are lining up for you. Who knows if this will ever happen again? Time waits for no man, not even the ones who want to waste it second guessing every miracle, sign, and wonder that presents itself."

"So, you think, this relationship could be a key to my happiness, a key to me moving forward?"

"Definitely."

"Mmm-hmmm." I sat there for a moment.

"Let me ask you this," Sage said. "Did he pursue you or you pursue him. What exactly led things into what they are now?"

"He's been pursuing me from the beginning; he's gone out of his way every step of the way. He's charming, romantic, and extremely passionate."

"I have to ask...how's the love-making?"

"I can't bring myself to have sex with him just yet, not that I'm not attracted to him, I'm very attracted to him. The problem is, I've only slept with one man in the last ten years, and I haven't got over that hump yet."

"And how is he dealing with it?"

"He's actually been very patient. But I know men have needs and I'm not sure how long he can hold out."

"You're right about men having needs. So, what you need to do is, take about three shots of tequila, get completely naked, and ride him like you're in the damn Kentucky Derby going for the win."

We both laughed hysterically.

"Sex is the least of my worries. How do I let go of controlling the situation and let things flow? I know he can feel my resistance. I don't want to keep sending him mixed signals nor do I want to keep beating a dead horse with the 'I just need time' speech."

"Okay so look, cliché or not. One day at a time. Divorces can be hard and take a toll on you, give you all types of confusion. A real emotional roller coaster ride."

"Are you speaking from experience?"

"No but remember the guy I'm seeing. He's going through a divorce, and I have the front row seat to the ups and downs that he faces. I can't say for certain if he's still in love with his ex-wife, he doesn't talk about her much, but I do know something is bothering him and that's the only reasonable explanation."

My gosh, this wasn't helping. Did she just say Devin could be affected by our divorce? Recently, during our interactions he seemed emotionless. Had he been putting up a facade of "This is what needs to happen, so deal with it." I shook my head, trying to distract my thoughts and stop thinking about Devin.

"Well, I guess I have a decision to make and soon. Thank you for your insight, girl. I really do appreciate it."

"Anytime. Especially if it comes with an all-expenses-paid spa day." She giggled.

On my way home from the spa, I got a surprising text from Sasha. It caught me off guard because we still hadn't really talked since that day at Ma and Dad's house. I missed her. Her text read:

I guess I'm going to let you buy me dinner and drinks so that you can apologize for running your mouth. Oh, and don't expect an apology from me either. I'm innocent in all of this.

I smiled at the phone and responded:

Martell's Italian Restaurant in Beverly tomorrow night at 8:00 pm.

She texted back: Don't be late either.

Sasha's text was her funny way of apologizing. The last time we had a falling out like this we were teenagers. And Sasha was out of line then. Instead of coming to me and apologizing like she should have, she left me a note in my gym locker at school that said, I know you're sorry. I heard a rumor that you wanted to apologize. Meet me after school and I'll let you walk home with me.

Even back then I knew what it was. I'm a pretty forgiving person, especially when it comes to my sister.

Just as I was pulling up at home, I got a call from Tony. What could he possibly want? It was well after our business hours.

"Hey Tony, what's going on?"

"Listen, I wanted to talk to you about you and Devin."

"What about?" I was confused and curious.

Tony had never inserted himself into our relationship.

"Devin needs you, LD, and…"

I was not getting ready to go down this road especially since I was experiencing the most stability I had had in months, not to mention I had my mind right and came to terms with everything. My new life with Jason was the direction I was going in, which means on a personal level Devin was no longer my concern.

"News flash, Tony. Our divorce was finalized three weeks ago, if Devin needed me, he hasn't been at all forthcoming about it."

"LD, I know the way things unfolded were hard and I promised Devin I wouldn't say anything to you about this but he seriously…."

I cut him off again, "Tony, I've seriously moved on. I've been seeing someone new and I'm happy. Now Devin and I are friends and business partners just like he wanted."

"LD, just hear me out for a second."

"No, Tony. And you're right, our divorce and not understanding everything was hard on me, very hard. I crossed some boundaries in areas that I would have never crossed had we not gotten divorced. But that's all behind me now and being there for Devin would be going backwards, putting me back into a place of vulnerability. I just don't care to enter that space again."

"LD, I really don't think you understand."

"I don't think you understand. I appreciate you calling but I really would rather not continue this conversation. You're like a brother to me, but I think you picked whose side you wanted to be on a long time ago. Good night, Tony."

I hung up the phone. Wanting to appease my fragile conscience, I was tempted to call Tony right back to apologize and hear him out. But emotions were running high, and I couldn't bring myself to do it.

I still loved and cared about Devin but if I was going to move on with my life and continue taking my relationship with Jason seriously, I couldn't take the walk back down memory lane. Besides, he still had Sage. Let him lean on her like he had been doing since this entire thing started.

I still kept in contact with her, but only for the benefit of getting her advice on helping me get the situation with me and Jason off the ground. Surprisingly, the tables had turned, and her advice turned out to be solid. At first, I was desperate. At the time Sasha wasn't talking to me and I hadn't dated another man besides Devin in over a decade, so I had to keep her around.

I continued to dominate the conversations when we met up, leaving very little room for her to bring up her and Devin's relationship or whatever it was. No longer my concern. But I will say, the little insight I did allow her to give was like therapy, it slowly but surely weaned me off of Devin. Instead of breaking up cold turkey like he wanted, I came up with my own method of how to move on. I mean it's not like there's some woman's guide to divorce. I know my actions with Sage were not only unorthodox but wrong as well. But hey, being used came with a lot of free incentives for her. From my perspective, she was benefiting from knowing me.

A couple of days later I met up with Sasha, she'd lost weight and was looking good.

"Hey sis, you look good," I said giving her a hug. I sat down at the table of the restaurant we met at as she handed me a glass of red wine.

"Hi baby girl and thank you. I've lost a total of twenty pounds so far."

"Wow, I'm impressed. You finally got the weight off like you've been wanting."

"Well, the first ten pounds were not by choice. The stress from us not talking and almost losing my career was a major contribution."

"Almost losing your career?"

"Yes, I'll tell you more about that later. But first I want to say, I'm happy you're here. There's no need for you to apologize, your presence here says it all. I wanted to reach out to you sooner, but I had to do some soul searching. I've been seeing a therapist again and he helped me to face some facts about myself that I was try-ing hard to deny."

"A therapist?" I said nodding my head.

"Yes, and I've come to realize that I needed you to say what you said that day. The words cut deep like a knife, but they caused me to take a step back and reexamine who I really was. And just know, LD, I've turned over a new leaf. I want my sister back; I want to reconnect with my best friend. I'm so blessed to have you, who gets to have their sister and best friend be one and the same?"

"I'm right here, I've never left. And let me say that I've missed you too. I know you said that I didn't need to apologize but I am truly sorry, and I didn't mean what I said. I was under a lot of stress and pressure at the time, I mean not that it's an excuse but--."

"No hey, I get it. Say no more. Speaking of stress, so it's finally final, huh? Your divorce."

"Yup. And you know my relationship with Jason is taking off. I have to admit, sis, it feels pretty good to be falling in love again. But the last couple of days Jason has been acting a little strange, like he has something on his mind and is keeping quiet about it."

"Well, does he usually keep his thoughts to himself?"

"No, that's the thing, he's a great communicator. But I'm going to remain patient with him and try to have the conversation to figure out what it is."

Sasha stayed quiet for a moment, processing what I was saying.

"That's a good idea, I was happy to learn that you were moving on. Yes, I used Ma to give me all the juicy details," Sasha told me, "Like I said, I missed you, sis."

"Well, the journey hasn't been easy. And let me tell you, before you judge me, let me say at the time I was desperate for guidance and clarity."

"Oh my, what sis?"

"I needed someone to talk to; Sage was my last resort. I reached out to her and believe it or not she has helped me get through this."

"Wait, you're talking about the girl that you were stalking, trying to get information out of her about Devin?"

"Yes."

"Oh sis, I'm definitely going to judge you. That's some soap opera shit. So, she still doesn't know who you really are?"

"Nope."

"Oh, damn you're good or she's just stupid."

"She isn't that stupid; she's been able to hold Devin's attention this long."

"Speaking of your ex-husband. He isn't looking like himself these days. I saw him at Ma and Dad's. He and Dad seemed to be having a deep conversation."

"Yeah well, from what I'm gathering he isn't okay. Apparently, he's having regrets about our marriage ending. Tony called me telling me that I needed to call and check on him."

"I might have to agree with Tony, LD. He didn't have the look of depression on his face, it seemed like something else. I tried to pry by asking Dad, but you know Devin is like a son to him and they have some kind of father and son code that Dad is not breaking."

"Yeah, tell me about it. I guess since you're bringing it up and since Sage mentioned something too, I'll reach out to him. Ugh. Things are going so good with Jason and me. I just want to hold on to this peace and mental clarity that I have, you know? I still love Devin, but this is what he wanted. Isn't that just like life? The moment you start looking to your future, your past shows up."

"Yup. Speaking of which. I have to tell you how my future almost ended. Not too long after our falling out, the favors I was calling in got back to my boss along with who my father was."

"What?!"

"Yup, I mean I knew it was a matter of time. I just hoped it would happen long after the case was over. I was almost disbarred and threatened to be arrested, if I didn't come completely clean and stand down. My sex appeal wasn't getting me out of this one."

"Serves you right, hootchie. The sex appeal part," I clarified.

"Well, I recused myself from the case. I still have my job and he was sent up to San Quentin State Prison awaiting a new trial, the death penalty is still on the table."

"Ma told me that they caught the guy who broke into my house and vandalized my shop."

"Yup, you know damn well I was going to make sure of that."

"I love you, Sasha. You always have had my back. And if you've ever felt like I've taken our sisterhood for granted, forgive me now."

"I love you too, lovely," Sasha said, giving me a tight hug.

When I got home, Jason arrived at my house thirty minutes later. I was torn about bringing up his sudden change in demeanor, but I knew the conversation had to be had.

"Hey, gorgeous, how was your day?"

"Not too bad, I met up with my sister earlier."

"I remember you telling me, how'd that go?"

"It went well but I want to talk to you about something else."

"Sure gorgeous, anything you want. What's on your brain?"

"Jason, call me crazy, but you seem a little distant lately. It's like you're here physically but your mind is elsewhere."

"Umm okay, that's fair. And you're right. I'm going to come straight out and say this, it may seem weird, but I think it's for the best."

"Jason, please, spit it out."

"When's the last time you talked to your ex-husband?"

"I'm sorry but I'm confused by that question, are you suspicious of something?"

"No, not at all. In fact, I think you should call and get some type of real closure."

"Where is this coming from?"

"Well, being that you and I have been together since you signed on the dotted line, I don't know if you've had a lot of time to process exactly what has happened. I mean you never talk about it and even that day after court, you were vague and seemed to be hiding some of your emotions."

"Mmmm, I see. Well, Jason you have to understand, before I met you, I had plenty of time to process what was going on. When things between us started to get serious, the ending of my relationship was starting to come to a head. Not only that, just because I don't talk to you about my divorce doesn't mean I don't talk about it. I'd rather not bring that negative energy into our atmosphere, so I find other shoulders to lean on. That's what girlfriends are for."

"I understand, I still think you should give him a call and get some closure."

"Why is everyone insinuating that I call this man? What is

going on? Why is he so popular all of a sudden? I really just want to move on and continue rebuilding my brand as a woman."

"Calm down, beautiful, it was just a suggestion. I won't bring it up again."

"Thank you. Now can we please go get something to eat and get back to enjoying us?"

"Whatever you want."

"That's more like it," I said giving Jason a kiss on the cheek.

After replaying the conversations with Tony, Sage, Sasha and Jason over in my head for several days. I decided that it was too much of a coincidence for everyone to be on one accord. I was going to have to reach out to Devin on a nonprofessional level. I'd not seen him since our final appearance in court. We both agreed that until things cooled down, I would take care of my responsibilities with our businesses in the office, and he would continue to work in the field with Tony and from home. All of our interactions were done remotely. Although Devin had given me complete ownership of almost everything, he still took ownership in handling the essential functions of the businesses. I just put him on payroll as management instead of co-owner. It's what he wanted, and he got no argument from me there.

"Hey Devin, it's me. Do you have a moment?" I asked from the other end of the phone.

"Yes, I was just about to go grab something to eat but I've also been waiting to hear from you."

"Yeah well, I've been busy trying to put my life back together."

"I sense that there's still some animosity between us."

"Animosity? Nope. I'm just a tad bit irritated. I mean why is it that now that I'm moving on you decided you want to hear from me? When I wanted to talk things out, you were a one answer type man and now we need to talk?"

"No, we don't. I really just wanted to make sure you're okay.

You left the courtroom that day like we never were. I need you to understand something. One day, when this is really all said and done, and as things continue to unfold, I hope you can find it in your heart to forgive me and truly understand that everything I did was for your best interest."

"See Devin, there you go again with the subliminal messages. What the hell does that mean?"

"What it means is, I never stopped caring for you, and I never will. I want you to have the happily-ever-after you've longed for since before, we got married."

"Devin, you were my happily-ever-after. This phone call was a waste of time, why are we doing this? Are you trying to wheel me back in?"

"No LD, I'm trying to tell you that I love you, stay strong and know that Jason is the right choice."

"Wait, who told you about Jason. Why are you referencing him? Oh yeah, you've been talking to my dad. I should have known that's what this was all about. Devin, please just let me move on, it's been hard enough."

"I'm not trying to stop you, honey."

"Okay, well now that I know that you're okay and in the land of the living, can we go back to being ex-lovers and friends." I said sarcastically. "Take care of yourself, Devin, I have to go."

I hung up the phone feeling awful. I cried and cried for a good forty-five minutes. Why did I have to take everyone's stupid advice and get myself emotionally involved again. Why? I had worked so hard and now I felt like I was back at step one. This shit was so unfair.

"By doubting we are led to question,
By questioning we arrive
at the Truth."
-Peter Abelard

Chapter Thirteen

ehind every great man is a strong woman so they say. Somehow, I convinced myself that this was not the case between Devin and me. Ever since our last phone call, I couldn't get him off my mind. I was starting to question my entire existence.

My mind was replaying my role in the madness of the divorce that had taken over my life, and it all became clear to me. Behind the big house, the successful businesses, the large amounts of money, expensive jewelry, clothes, and lastly with all the love I'd been given from my husband and family; I never stopped to truly love myself. I never stopped to figure out who I was, where I was truly going or what my purpose was.

That ugly duckling that grew into a beautiful swan had become obsessed with perfection, image, and the idea of having it all together. I was going through and, undoubtedly, not growing through life. I'd programmed myself to just go through the motions and whatever "seemed" to be right. The standards of society became my own.

I was comfortable with society viewing me as the model black woman; graduated college, married a handsome man with drive and ambition, a success magnet and business mogul, up until now. I had it all together, right? Nope. I wasn't at all fulfilled.

Oh, and let's not forget the icing on the cake, Beauty and brains. WRONG! I was dead wrong. I was still that insecure young girl who was rejected as a child, never learning how to deal with it. I thought that beating the status quo was dealing with it. WRONG AGAIN! As long as Devin was my everything, I had everything. Yet again, WRONG, WRONG, WRONG!

What pressure he must have felt over the years. He couldn't have possibly been my everything; it's not humanly possible. He wasn't responsible for my happiness, I was. I'm an individual and so was he. He was my husband, my lover, friend, support system, life partner. He was not intended to be my "EVERYTHING." My God, did I run my husband away with my spoiled unrealistic persona of what love looked like? I mean sure Disney was awesome at airbrushing love and making us young girls think that we could someday have the love that the movies portrayed and silly me, I thought that I was living a real live fairytale, but my reality was I never made a break with reality until now. Perfection did not exist.

How was I going to fix this? In my feelings again, I felt as if I had not fought hard enough, I felt like I'd spent too much time whining and giving my attention to the wrong things. All I could think now was, God, please help me fix this. I think I've really messed up. I got the idea that maybe Devin would be open to talking again.

I did something that I hadn't done in a very long time. I pulled over, turned the music off, put my hands together and started talking to the one person my momma said would always listen and understand exactly where I was coming from, judgment free and ready to help: GOD.

"Lord, I know it's been a while. But you've blessed me tremendously and I've been busy living in those blessings. I mean I'm never too busy for you, I mean…Lord, just see my heart. Right now, I come to you as

humble as I know how. Asking for your guidance and your mercy. As you know I'm newly divorced. I love my husband and realize that I may have messed up. Big time. Lord, I really want to make this right. Please give me the opportunity to talk to Devin and help us to reconcile our differences and reach a level in our communication that we've never reached before. Lord, please help me to make sense of all of this. I know and understand that we are not to lean on our own understanding, but I really need help with this one. In Jesus Mighty Name I pray. Amen."

As I said Amen, in that moment I felt slightly relieved. I felt an overwhelming presence that everything was going to be okay. I started the car and headed over to Sasha's.

Every year around the holiday season, we made it a point to make fifty holiday Christmas bags that were gender neutral, and we'd drive around giving them away to the homeless. We would drive around Hollywood, Downtown LA, Crenshaw, and even as far out as the Inland Empire and give away bags filled with toiletries, hats/scarfs, socks, a few food items and gift cards to Subway or Starbucks. It was our way of giving back and it allowed us to spend time together on another level. When we were done, we did good and felt good. Win, Win, you know.

When I got to Sasha's house, I could hear Mariah Carey's *All I want for Christmas is You* playing loudly. I could see Sasha dancing from the big living room window that faced the street. Her Christmas tree was dressed in a peacock theme, it was beautifully designed. Sasha never decorated the trees herself. She had this very talented interior decorator named Mildred help her every year, and every year Mildred delivered.

"Hey sis, finally. What have you been doing this entire time?" Sasha asked, still dancing to the music and sipping something out of her custom-made Christmas glass as she opened the door. I'm almost certain that it was liquor.

"I see Mildred has already made her way over here to bless

your living room with her creativity," I responded as I walked into her house referencing the Christmas tree.

The smell of pine dominated Sasha's living room, along with the cinnamon scented candle that was lit on the living room table. I walked over to the Christmas tree to see it more in detail. My admiration for it grew stronger as I noticed the peacock ribbons, shaped in the form of big bows, that coordinated with the royal blue and turquoise ornaments. Sasha's house was beautiful, and it fit her every need as a single woman. White and grey marble counter tops. White granite flooring in the kitchen. Top of the line wood floors throughout. And a living room with white furniture that made you not want to sit down because of how neatly and beautifully everything was arranged.

Sasha was not a slave to her possessions; in her mind she bought the house to live in and everything in it was set to be a part of the living experience. Her motto was, "If I bought it once I can buy it again. The moments we share and make in this house are priceless. Cherish people, not things," she always said.

"You know, I have her come in the first week of December. I love Christmas. Although neither one of us have kids, it feels good that we still find a way to give back and participate in the toy drives, volunteer at the women's shelter giving them holiday makeovers. The Holiday Christmas bags we give out every year puts a smile on my face, knowing that we are doing something that's greater than ourselves."

I was becoming slightly frustrated thinking about all the good I was doing; I had no choice but to feel entitled to good karma. But with the divorce it felt like all I was catching was bad karma instead, even with the eye-opening experience I just had.

"You know Sasha, I don't get it; I've spent my entire life "doing right" and still I feel like nothing is...." Sasha cut me off mid-sentence.

"N-No La'Dai, you don't get to make tonight about you and Devin and the circumstances that you believe to be your mishaps. What you're experiencing may somehow in a weird way be a blessing in disguise. You know not every single circumstance that you don't understand is a conspiracy, LD. Have you ever heard the phrase; things are happening for you NOT to you?"

"Yeah, maybe you're right but…."

"No buts, actually I'll allow two butts. And that's your butt and mine getting into your car so that we can get these bags out to the homeless before New Year's. And yes, you're driving because I've had three cups of my holiday fav-, cognac and eggnog and I'm feeling gooood."

"Fine. Let's go. I'll put on some holiday cheer so we can finish out this god-awful year." I fell out laughing at my ridiculous attempt to rhyme.

"Oh sis, that was bad." Sasha said as she put on her red pea coat.

"Whatever, at least I'm trying."

"And I appreciate your efforts, just stick to your day job. C'mon."

As we drove out of Sasha's driveway, the streets were bright with lights from all of the neighbors' outdoor Christmas decorations. Everyone's houses and yards were so unique and beautifully put together. Candy Cane Lane was a place that people would walk for blocks every year to see the Christmas decorations, Sasha's neighborhood resembled Candy Cane Lane to the tee. And the crowd had already started. It was hard getting out of Sasha's neighborhood. Sightseers filled both sides of the sidewalks with their families, baby strollers--eager and excited people filled with joy and happiness. Christmas spirit filled the air.

We arrived in downtown LA in no time and as we drove around looking for the people to bless with the gift of giving, gratitude began to sink in.

"You know what, Sasha, I'm so thankful for Mom and Dad. The choices they made dictated the entire trajectory of our lives and we're truly blessed."

"Oh damn, LD, what the hell are you talking about now? You always trying to go deep and trust me the only time I want to go deep is when there's a tall dark and handsome man on top of me. So, can you spare the heart to heart right now and turn up the music?"

"Ummm no, nasty. They need to create an entire Christmas slogan just for you that says, "Santa, I've been Naughty and Nasty all year."

"Ha, that's not a bad idea. We all got a little freak in us. I'm just open with mine."

"That's not all that's open about you."

"Oh whatever, hurry up with your little speech so I can replay my favorite song."

"Like I was saying, we literally have everything we want and need. And I'm so grateful for our parents because one of the only differences between these homeless people that we're helping and us is a support system."

"You know what? That's really enlightening and gives me something to think about. Are you done?"

Sasha reached for the knob on the radio, and I smacked her hand.

"No, I'm not. Seriously, Sasha, no matter what happens in my life, even if Devin and I don't rekindle things."

"Rekindle things, am I missing something? You're divorced, LD."

"I know but I had this crazy idea that maybe just maybe there could still be a chance for us; couples get back together all the time."

"What the hell is with the back and forth? I thought you were happy with Jason."

"I am but then I realized that maybe I went about my marriage the wrong way, maybe I wasn't the wife I should have been."

"LD, these types of things happen all the time when people get divorced. You start to think back and wonder about what you could have done differently but you use that information to move forward, not contemplate going backwards."

"I hear and understand you, which is why I was also saying, I know that Jason could never really take his place, not that I expect him to, but the bottom line is I think I'm going to be okay. As a matter of fact, we both are. Whether I get remarried or whether you ever get married, we will be okay."

"You're damn right, because I'm always going to keep one in my back pocket to help keep me warm at night. It may not be that steady love that India Arie talks about but there won't be any cobwebs in this coochie mama."

"My God, why do I even bother?"

"I don't know, why do you?"

"I'm not like you though, I struggled getting back into the dating scene. I didn't know exactly what to look for or what to ask. But Jason helped me out big time to discover those things. Devin set the bar so high."

"Well, I'll tell you, from what I've seen lately based on the couple of guys I've attempted to date, it's pretty slim pickings. Rule number one, LD, you have to stop being so picky, there's only one Devin. And no one is perfect. I always tell you that you were truly blessed being married to Devin. Now Jason has done a great job so far, you haven't had to mold him into learning how to love you, he has been doing a good job all on his own. When two people get together, sis, they are never on the same page, but they eventually learn how to grow together. We come up with these expectations in the beginning of relationships, sometimes even before there is a relationship and expect our mates to follow them. But expectations lead to complete and utter disappointments. I'm not saying don't have standards. Learning to love someone for who they are is all a learning process in itself and an adjustment."

"For someone who doesn't do relationships, you sure do have a lot of advice to give about them, Sasha."

"I'm just saying, we put so many stipulations on a relationship before it even gets started and before we've even learned the other person. 'If you're forty you should act this way,' 'if you've been married before you should know this or that,' when really you should tailor your relationship to what works best for the both of you. Take time to learn your partner. A person going into the situation with a list of expectations seems counterproductive. What if some of the other person's personality traits go against some of the expectations you have? So now what you've done is ended your relationship way before it even started."

"Not necessarily."

"I mean, think about it LD, just because that person doesn't meet all your expectations, does that mean that she or he is the wrong person? NO. It just means adjust and come to some type of common ground."

"Are you saying people should settle in their relationships?"

"No, what I'm saying is accept people for who they are. Sometimes allowing things to flow naturally will automatically allow you to have an influence on the other person and they may change on their own merit. You have to be willing to take yourself solely out of the equation because it's no longer about self. You become selfless. Things stop being a "me thing" and becomes a "we thing". And if people in relationships could just realize these things there would be a lot less resistance when it comes to considering your mate and how they feel and desire to do things.

Take the time to learn their love language and how they express themselves. You know what I mean."

"Well, damn, you said a whole mouthful. I still don't understand why you're single."

"We've had this conversation; we've went over this when I told you that entire spill about how I felt about my biological mother."

"Oh, my bad, I forgot. You're right. It's just that I see you and I see so much potential in you as a wife."

"Girl, it would take an act of God himself to come down here, lead the man to me, look me square in the face and say to me, 'My child, this is the man for you, I ordained him specifically for you so let him in', I have my own vices that I'm dealing with when it comes to men but that doesn't mean I'm not hopeful for you. Besides I'm too free spirited. Now I hope we're done because even if we are not, I'm turning up the music anyway. Oh, and listen to the words of this song because you might be able to relate."

I smiled at Sasha and just shook my head. She was confident within herself and was completely worry free. I only dreamed to one day be as free spirited as she was.

"LD, can you stop at that Starbucks, I'm in the mood for a hot chocolate."

I pulled into the parking lot and the drive thru had cars lined up for what seemed like miles, as usual.

"Hey sis, do you want to get out? The drive thru is ridiculous," I said.

"Yeah, I can do that, I want to stretch my legs anyhow."

We had drove to the Inland Empire and the ride home would take us over an hour and a half. So, Sasha asking me to stop at Starbucks was not a bad idea. She got out of the car, and I took my phone out hoping to see a text from Devin. A text from Devin would be my opening–a chance to try and redeem myself. Or maybe a text from him suggesting that we get back together would indicate that God had answered my prayers. But nothing.

I let the idea go for the moment and decided to get into the holiday spirit. Sasha was right. Maybe some things are better off left alone. It just seemed like there was this strong hold on me that was telling me there was more I could have done.

Jason and I had planned on getting together that night when I got home. Fifteen-minutes after I walked in the door, I started to prepare the take-out I prepared for us. It had gotten a little cold, so I popped it in the oven.

The food was almost done warming up when Jason called.

"Hey you," I answered.

"Hey gorgeous, I'm sorry but I have to cancel dinner tonight. I've have to go into the hospital. Looks like one of my patients has been admitted and has taken a drastic turn for the worst, so I'll be there for the rest of the night."

"Oh no. I completely understand, Jason. Maybe if you're up to it you can come over for breakfast and sleep here."

"I'll call you and let you know; I have to go."

"Okay."

Before we hung up, Jason began speaking again.

"Hey LD, I need to tell you something. No matter what, understand that things are not always what they seem to be. Know that I am here for you no matter what happens in life. I cherish you so much."

"Okay, I don't know where that is coming from but thank you."

"You're welcome, have a good night, gorgeous."

Thrown off by Jason's comment, once I hung up, I grabbed two plates, forgetting just that quick that he was not coming.

As I was putting the second plate back, I thought to myself, "Maybe I'll make it for Jesus and eat his plate." I chuckled and started eating.

After dinner, I sat at the kitchen table for a moment, contemplating everything Sasha said. She made a lot of sense, and I was going to take her advice into account, stop comparing Jason to Devin and get over the obstacles of being a divorcee. The housekeeper was coming early in the morning, so I made no attempt to clean the kitchen. Besides soap and water was calling my body.

In the shower I could hear my phone ringing off the hook. I turned off the water from the shower, grabbed my towel and wrapped myself in it. Picking up my phone before it vibrated off the dresser, I saw that it was Sage.

What on earth could she have been calling about and where was the fire?

"Sage, girl what's up? I was in the shower."

I could hear her crying on the other end of the phone.

"Sage, are you okay, what's going on?"

"Devin, he-he oh my God, please," she started crying hysterically.

What about Devin? Why was she calling me in tears mentioning his name? My heart started racing fast and I was not prepared for what came next.

"What about Devin, Sage? Please calm down so I can understand you."

"He's not going to make it, Elle, one minute we were laughing, watching a movie, then he just collapsed. There's all these tubes and I—"

"Collapsed, tubes, Sage what are you talking about? I'm not sure that I follow you."

"Devin, Devin–the guy I've been seeing. Remember him. He's in the ICU and they don't think he's going to make it."

I was at a complete loss for words. Devin was in the ICU. What was going on, had he had a heart attack from all of our drama? Was I to blame? I should have just listened to him that night he tried to call me. I then realized that I had jumped off the deep end. The Devin I knew appeared healthy as a horse and maybe Sage was just overreacting. I could still hear Sage crying on the other end of the phone and the cries grew louder and more intense.

"Where are you, Sage? When did this happen?" I was trying to remain calm but the more she cried the more my breathing grew heavy, it was like I had a fifty-pound weight on my chest.

"We're at Cedar Sinai, I'm trying to call his family but the only person I really know is his friend, Tony. The nurse said they tried to call the person on his emergency contact list, but they aren't answering. I don't know who that person is and because of HIPPA, they won't tell me."

"I'm on my way," I told Sage as I rushed to find some clothes to put on.

When I hung up, I could see I had missed calls from Jason and some number I didn't recognize, but I couldn't deal with Jason or that number. I had to get to the hospital. But then it dawned on me that I was probably the emergency contact number that they could not get a hold of. I called the number back and sure enough it was Cedar Sinai's automated system.

Racing to the hospital, I knew I was probably in no position to drive. Before leaving the house, I called Sasha and told her what was going on; she agreed to pick me up and take me to the hospital, but I felt like that would delay me getting to Devin, so I told her to meet me instead. Not being able to think straight, I was almost in two car accidents.

At this point I was over hiding who I really was from Sage. I no longer cared about her feelings. I needed to be there for Devin. He needed me by his side, he needed me to help him pull through whatever this was.

Sasha and I pulled up to the hospital at the same time.

Coincidentally we parked right next to each other in the underground parking. Sasha got out of her car and took one look at me; she could tell that I was frantic and distraught. At that moment, no words were spoken, she just pulled me into her arms and held me tight.

"Sasha, I don't know what's going on. I'm so scared," I said crying uncontrollably.

"La'Dai, calm down, you're shaking. Everything will be okay, let's not jump to conclusions."

"I wonder if this has anything to do with the text, he sent me earlier?" I asked rhetorically.

"What text?"

"Devin sent me a text that said, 'I wish I could have told you sooner, but I promise everything has been for your own good.' I assumed he was still talking the same talk about our divorce. So, I didn't respond to the message."

"Now is not the time to speculate when we can just go up there and see for ourselves. And again, like I told you on the phone, don't worry about her. We aren't here for her. We're here for Devin and he's all that matters right now."

When we got upstairs to the ICU, Sage met us at the elevator. Her eyes were puffy, and her hair was a mess. She was wearing a Nike sweatsuit with Gucci flip flops. The state of panic was written all over her face.

"Elle, thank God you're here." She gave me a big hug and started crying over my shoulder. I knew she thought my presence was for her, but she would soon find out otherwise.

Not wanting to seem insensitive, I embraced her for about thirty seconds before I gently pulled her away, still holding both her shoulders in my hands.

"Sage, where's Devin?" I asked her, getting straight to the point.

"He's right there in ICU, she replied still crying. "They won't let anyone in except for family."

Right then and there I let the cat out the bag.

"Sage, I am family."

She looked up at me confused and started to stutter. "Wha— what are you talking about?"

"I'll explain it to you later, right now I need to check on Devin." Sasha and I walked past her and headed over to the nurse's station. Sasha was on my heels, right behind me.

"Nurse, I need to see my husband, Devin Roswell."

Sage yelled from where she was standing, "Your husband. Did you just say your husband? What the hell is going on?"

I could see from the corner of my eye that she was walking toward me. The nurse responded to Sage's reaction.

"Ma'am, I need you to lower your voice, or you'll be asked to leave."

"I'm not going anywhere until she tells me what's going on."

Before I could say anything, Sasha lashed out at Sage, "Devin is her husband and right now her main concern, so be quiet so we can figure out what the hell we're here for."

Sage tried a rebuttal, but Sasha stopped her mid-sentence and told her, "Sage, right now is not the time or the place, you need to relax."

"Don't talk to me as if you know me, you don't know me."

Sasha being Sasha responded, "Oh, but I do."

"Look," I said trying to put an end to the madness, "Sage, I'm not here for you. I'm here for Devin. I understand that you may be confused but like my sister said, right now is not the time or place."

Sage started going off, cuss words were flying everywhere, and she was completely belligerent. Sasha was ready to let her have it, but I tapped Sasha's shoulder and nodded my head no, as in do not go there.

The nurse typed into the computer then asked for my identification. I handed it to her.

"Mrs. Roswell, we tried calling you. Right this way, please. And are you Sasha Bell, she asked.

Bell was my maiden name.

"Yes," Sasha answered.

By this time the hospital security had come over to rectify the chaos going on.

"You're welcome to come with her," the nurse informed Sasha. "Mr. Roswell made it clear in his advance directives that you were to come back with her."

"Advance directives," I asked in shock. "How serious is this?"

"Just try to remain calm, I'll page the doctor to come and talk to you," the nurse responded picking up the hospital phone.

"Okay, thank you."

"In the meantime, he's in room 1216, right down the hall and to your right." She pointed, trying to get us moving in the right direction.

Once we got into Devin's hospital room, I could still hear Sage yelling and what sounded like security trying to calm her down. But all of that subsided when I saw Devin.

There he was lying in the hospital bed, barely hanging on to life. Tubes were coming from everywhere. His nose, his mouth. The breathing machine let out a noise as he tried to talk when he saw me.

I walked over to the hospital bed with my hand covering my mouth and Devin could barely move.

"Devin, honey, what's happening to you?" I said with my tears starting to block my sight.

Barely able to catch his breath, he answered, "I'm dying LD, cancer has won this battle."

"Devin, what are you talking about? You don't have cancer.

Does the medicine they have you on make you hallucinate? I need you to tell me what's really going on. I'm here to help you D, and this time I'm not leaving."

"LD, I have stage four lung cancer and it has metastasized into my brain, I'm not getting out of here. You have to ac-." Before Devin could finish talking, he started coughing up blood. Sasha handed me some paper towels and I tried to help Devin sit up. My eyes weren't playing tricks on me and the blood on the paper towel told me that Devin was seriously sick even if I didn't believe it.

"Devin, why didn't you tell me? You've been battling this by yourself the entire time?" I again wiped blood from his mouth. I had so many questions, I was so confused. Was death really knocking on Devin's door? This was so sudden.

"Devin Roswell, you're one of the strongest men I know. You are not dying. I know things look bad now, but you are going to get better. I'm going to find you the best oncologist there is. You will beat this. Now let me call the nurse so she can tell me what we need to do to get you home."

"LD honey, I have a good doctor, one of the best. There's nothing more that they can do."

"Like hell they can't. Where is your doctor because I have some questions?" Just as I said that the nurse walked in. "Oh nurse, hi I'm Mrs. Roswell, can you please call the doctor in here. I need to know exactly what's going on so that I can take my husband home."

The nurse looked at me as if I was speaking a foreign language. Then at Devin. He nodded his head to give her permission to call in the doctor. Just then she started fluffing his pillows and checking his temperature.

"Nurse, he was just coughing up blood, what can we do about that?"

"Nurse, give us a minute please," Devin asked. The nurse stopped taking Devin's temperature and walked out of the room. Sasha was still sitting in the corner bearing witness to everything going on.

"LD come here. I need to explain some things to you."

"Yes, baby you do. But right now, we need to focus on getting you better. You can explain later."

"LD listen to me! You have to stop talking and start listening. There won't be a later." Devin's voice got stern, and he had the look of desperation in his eyes.

I walked closer to Devin with a surprised and scared look on my face. Surprised by him raising his voice and scared because he was serious.

"Okay honey, I'm listening but please stop…"

Just then Jason walked through the doorway. I knew he worked there but I don't know how he knew I was there.

"Hello, La'Dai," he said as he walked in with a chart in his hands.

"Jason umm right now is not a good time. I'll call you later."

"LD, this is not a social call. I'm Devin's doctor."

"You're Devin's doctor?" I repeated, anxious for one of them to explain what I had walked into when I stepped foot onto the hospital floor.

I looked at Jason, back at Devin and again to Jason. I sat back down next to Devin on the hospital bed.

"What is going on? No more cover ups, Devin. What is going on? You tell me right now."

Jason started speaking, "LD, please try to remember that Devin is in a very fragile state, and we don't want to raise his blood pressure or put any stress on him. I understand why you're upset, but let's try to remain calm."

"Jason, stop. My husband, who seems to be on his death bed

is trying to tell me that he has cancer and is not coming home. Cancer, Jason that I never knew he had but you did. You've known all along and haven't mentioned a word. Why didn't you tell me that you were his doctor?" I was demanding answers. "And just so you know, I'm far from calm."

"Sis, I think Jason is right; let's try to remain calm and give Devin a chance to speak."

"Okay, okay," I said shaking my head and trying to regain my composure.

"LD honey come closer. I want to give you a kiss." Devin motioned me to come closer with his finger, still very weak. I leaned into him and he turned my face and gave me the gentlest kiss he had ever given me. Tears began to roll down my cheeks and his.

I could tell that Devin was in pain. Seeing him that way hurt to my core. I wanted so badly to do something. But I was too late, he was slipping away right through my fingers.

"Sit down, LD, I want to explain everything to you."

"Okay, Devin."

"Jason, I got this, man. Let me handle it."

Jason left the room, and I was so furious with him. He knew this entire time that Devin was dying. Why didn't he tell me? And what kind of doctor pushes up on his dying patient's wife. What kind of sick man was he? I could have been taking care of Devin but instead I was wasting time with his ass.

"I'm going to talk, and I need you to listen, okay?"

"Yes."

"La'Dai, you know that I love you more than anything in this world. Anything. But this is the end of the road for me, that's just the reality of it. I've known about the cancer. I didn't tell you about it because I knew that you would spend every waking moment you had trying to save my life and I couldn't do that to you."

"Devin baby why didn't you just let me be there? I was your wife my love, for better or worse, in sickness and health. Devin that's what we vowed."

"When they told me that I had stage four lung cancer, with only eight months or less to live, I knew it was over. I could have decided to fight the inevitable and waste the last months of my life in and out of the hospital or I could have taken charge and get my affairs in order. I chose to get my affairs in order. I know the divorce was sudden, but if I did not initiate the divorce, you would have found out about the cancer and tried to stop me. Which you would have been well within reason to do but you would have just been racing against time which would have been a waste of time. So, the divorce was my only way of forcing you to move on. I wanted you to get into the groove of moving on before I left this earth because I needed to make sure that you were going to be in the hands of the right man. I couldn't leave this earth until I knew that you were going to be well taken care of. And Jason told me that things are going well between you two."

"Devin…"

"Just listen, La'Dai. Jason has been my doctor since this entire thing started. But it wasn't until a few months ago, when I purchased the new property that I realized that he would be the perfect match for you. I'll get to the property later. You see honey, Jason is already established, he's successful, has a good heart and he's going to help you with what I'm going to ask you to do. You may not be in love with him just yet but that will come once I'm out the picture and he's willing to wait. He's perfect. You have a lot to lose and because he has his own and then some. I know for sure that he won't take advantage of you. He expressed to me that he's already in love with you and I know when a man is being sincere. I mean look at you, you're great. You will be in good hands with Jason. I've groomed him well."

"Groomed him well?"

"Yes, it's funny because when I asked him if he was seeing anyone. At first, he was apprehensive to answer but then he went on telling me about how he was seeing this beautiful woman, how she was not like any other woman that he had met. Then finally he tells me about his experience in Zen City, once he mentioned the garden at our house, I knew right there that he was talking about you. And I knew right there that I was making the right decision to make sure that he continued to pursue you and with seriousness. I told him everything that he needed to do to keep your attention and everything he needed to do to impress you."

"Yeah, but did you tell him not to tell me about your cancer," I asked with some anger.

"Yes, I did, and because of the HIPPA laws he had no choice but to comply. Plus, he takes his job seriously. There's no way he was going to violate those laws, not even for you. Anyway, I told him not to tell anyone that he was my doctor. LD, I know you and because you don't understand the nature of this situation, you would have tried to take matters into your own hands, and I had to make sure everything went smoothly."

"And the property?" I asked feeling sick to my stomach.

"The property that I purchased is for you and Jason to start a Cancer Treatment Center in memory of me. I have to leave my legacy behind by giving people hope, and there's not an affordable cancer treatment center in Los Angeles that's accessible to cancer patients who are less fortunate. You see LD, you know how to run businesses and Jason is an Oncologist, so you two are the perfect ones for the job. Plus, you're a couple. I'm not trying to replace what you and I had. But this is the road to a new beginning for you, to do something meaningful. LD, you have to marry Jason, he's the man for you. I don't want you grieving over me for too long."

"Devin, this is all too much, too fast."

"LD, this is when I need you to be very strong. I need you to see the bigger picture. There's more to life than the little every-day nuances. You are going to be a part of something great. And you're going to do it with a man that knows what he's doing and who has your best interest at heart. Jason wanted to start his own practice anyhow. He too lost his wife to cancer so he's going to see you through this. Do you see now why I picked him?"

"And your little girlfriend that's still out there yelling."

"She's not my girlfriend. She introduced me to the mayor, I needed him to approve the Cancer Treatment Center. She works in finance, so he also helped me purchase the property, she asked what I was going to use it for. I told her, and she let me know that her uncle was the mayor, and she could help me with getting him to approve the building. One day she invited me to lunch. I figured it was for business, but she had something else in mind."

Yup, from what Devin was explaining, that definitely was Sage thirsty self. I continued to listen to Devin talk, not wanting him to strain himself, I didn't interrupt.

"This girl has been relentless, but I had to stay focused LD, so I entertained her, but I kept it at a minimum. I never slept with her, I'm not a dog. And I never had a conversation about us being a couple either, she made those assumptions all on her own. We went out a couple of times and she took that to mean that it was something other than what it was. Getting everything in order and having the Treatment center signed off was my main priority so I paid no attention to her delusions. I kept my eye on the prize. I made no sexual advances toward her whatsoever. Please believe that."

"I believe you," I said with my deepest sincerity. There was no way that I was going to break his heart and tell him about the bull crap that I had been up to and all the things that I thought he was doing.

All this time searching for answers, I had become the bitter wife that I despised. I spent so much of my time trying to make my theory about Devin definitively proven that I'd convinced myself he was this bad man, full of lies and deceit. When in all reality, he was clinging to dear life by a wing and a prayer.

"Devin, my love I'm so sorry. Please forgive me."

When did I lose faith in him as a person? When did I stop giving him the benefit of doubt? I completely misjudged everything. Everything in my head was twisted. I wanted a reasonable explanation besides what he told me; I should have just been open to the evolving discussions.

"LD don't be sorry. I know that these last few months have been hard on you, but I had to do what I had to do to secure your future and my legacy. When you go into the office at DannyLane's you'll find all the business plans for the cancer treatment center."

"Is that the office you used to put all of this together?"

"Yes, I knew I could conduct business there and didn't have to worry about you snooping around. You haven't stepped foot into Danny Lane's in about a year, besides that incident that happened with the mafia. Do me a favor, make sure you do better at showing your face around there. I know we have bigger businesses, but that business was the steppingstone to where we are now, and those guys need to feel the owner's presence. Keep things in order, get it?"

"Yes, Devin. You always have things so figured out. Always five steps ahead."

"The day that I married you, I vowed to love, honor and cherish you. And I've worked hard every day of my life to make sure that I kept those vows. And no disease, not even cancer was going to stop me from fulfilling my promise. I love you, LD."

"I love you too, Devin. Just get some rest."

I was so engaged with Devin that I forgot that Sasha was in the room. For the first time she was quiet as a church mouse with nothing to say. Just then she broke her silence and said, "Sis, I'm going to be right outside if you need me, okay?"

"Sasha, you're not off the hook. Come here, girl," Devin called out to her. Sasha walked over to Devin's bedside trying to stop her tears. But they just kept streaming down.

"You've been a great sister. Take care of LD, Sash. Make sure she doesn't drive herself crazy trying to be a perfectionist. Stay patient with her. Don't let her wallow for too long. I need you to continue to be her backbone times two, you're taking my place now in that area, okay?" He waited for Sasha to answer.

"I got you, big bro. You know I will do everything in my power to make sure she swims and doesn't sink. I love you." Sasha turned around and walked out of the room. I could hear her crying in the hallway.

Sitting on the chair next to Devin's bed, I moved closer and folded my arms over his stomach and we both fell asleep.

I woke up from what felt like an hour's nap, to the medical machines going off. Sasha and two nurses came running in. I jumped up and tried to wake up Devin, but he was unresponsive.

"Devin, Devin, wake up baby. Come on, you can do this. Wake up, please." I was crying out to him, but he wouldn't wake up.

One nurse tapped me on my shoulder and asked me to move to the side.

I continued yelling, "Help him please, wake him up! He can't go yet. Dear God, he can't go."

"Sis, it's okay. Come here," Sasha said trying to pull me out of the way.

"Nurse, do you hear me? He can't go."

One nurse looked at the other as she checked Devin's pulse

and shook her head side to side.

"What does that mean, what does that mean?" I yelled, stomping my foot.

"I'm sorry, ma'am, but he's gone," the Asian nurse replied to me.

Devin was dead.

"Sasha noooooooo." I looked at Sasha, pushed past the nurse and laid my upper body on top of his.

"Devin, please, please. I know you can beat this. Baby for Christ's sake don't leave me, not now!" The tears from my eyes were landing on his face.

"You have to do something, use your machine and bring him back. Hurry up!" I yelled grabbing the defibrillator.

"Ma'am, I'm sorry but he asked not to be resuscitated."

"I'm going to get the doctor," the other nurse said heading to the door.

"Yeah, you go get the doctor, because clearly you don't know what you're talking about. My husband is not dead. You just don't know what you're doing. Go get the doctor!"

Jason came in and looked at me, then walked over to Devin and checked his pulse, then his watch and said to me, "I'm sorry, LD, I have to do this." He looked over at the Asian nurse who was holding a pen and clipboard in her hand and said the words that I wouldn't want my worst enemy to hear, "Time of death, thirteen-forty-five."

I collapsed onto the floor, Jason and Sasha both ran over to me to try and console me, but I was completely inconsolable.

Chapter Fourteen

"He tried to prepare me for this day, but I wasn't prepared to let him go then just like I'm not prepared to let him go now." I stood up at the podium in the church, where over two hundred people had gathered to celebrate Devin's life. Putting the funeral together was like reliving the day he died all over again. "He was so unselfish, loving and kind. Devin spent the last days of his life trying to fulfill mine. He gave back what cancer took from him: hope. His legacy will forever be found in the Roswell Cancer Center of Los Angeles. Devin, honey, I love you, I miss you and I'm sorry." I said, grief-stricken looking down at his casket.

I walked down to the casket and kissed him on his cheek. His face was cold and stiff. He didn't look like himself and just then I finally broke all the way down. I clung to his casket as I felt myself losing balance and my knees buckling.

I heard Dad's voice coming from behind me saying, "I got you, honey; it's going to be alright. C'mon." But I couldn't move, I couldn't let go, I didn't want to let go.

"God, please give him back, please. I'll do anything. You can have it all, just give him back to me. Plllleeease!" I cried out.

I wanted to just lay right there with him. I had never felt this kind of pain. The kind of pain that couldn't be cured with any drug. The type of pain that no matter how many times I'd fall asleep hoping to wake up and see his face next to me, he wasn't coming back. This was it, the end. All I had left of him was the memories we shared. My heart felt like it was being weighed down by stone, it was heavy. How was I ever going to be whole again?

Devin died and took a piece of me with him. This just couldn't be real.

I don't remember anything else after that. I was completely numb. I guess I blacked out, because the next I knew we were back at my parents' house. Everyone there came up to me to offer their condolences, but I wasn't receptive to any of it. Their mouths were moving but I couldn't hear anything. Just my heart beating. I just sat there, waiting for Devin to walk through the door.

Sasha over to me trying to get me out of the trance, she snapped her fingers twice in my face. But even still, I gave her a deer in the head lights stare while the tears were streaming down my face.

She looked at me, sat down and pulled me into her like a mother would her child. More cries of sorrow filled the room as I cried out.

"Sshhh, baby girl, I promise you it's going to be okay."

"No, it's not, Sasha, he isn't coming back, the love of my life isn't coming back."

"No honey he's not, but we're going to get through this."

"How? I can't do this without him. He was my partner; he was my everything Sash. The air in my lungs. I don't understand why God took him from me. Why? And like that? Cancer Sasha. Cancer?"

"Baby, this is going to take some time. We didn't see this one coming. I see how hard this is for you right now. But I promise you as being my sister's keeper, I'm going to make sure that you get through this. One day at a time boo, you're going to get through this. As God is my witness."

"Mphh, God. Yeah, well. If he's planning on being there, then I'll get through this shit myself."

"Sis, I know you're grieving but watch your tongue. Don't talk like that. Let's get you something to eat."

"Nah, I'm not hungry. I'm going to go upstairs and lie down."

I went into the kitchen poured a glass of wine, again more people talking to me, but I was in full zombie mode totally zoned out and drunk with grief.

The spare bedroom at my parents' house felt like pure solitude. I was clear on the other side of the house, away from everyone. I slipped into the covers, took a Xanax, one sleeping pill and closed my eyes, wanting to forget everything and everybody. I thought maybe, just maybe if I stayed asleep long enough Devin would come back to me in my dreams. And if that was going to be the case, I didn't want anyone waking me up.

There was something cold on my forehead. I opened my eyes to Ma's face.

"Hey baby, you were starting to make us nervous."

I put my hand on my head and lifted the cold towel she must have put there.

"You were having night sweats, tossing and turning so I thought it might be best to try and keep you comfortable with cold towels."

"Thanks, Ma. How long have I been asleep?"

"Almost forty hours."

"Forty hours?"

"Yes, Sasha tried to wake you up, but you were totally out of it. She was able to get you to the bathroom, then into the bath but you slept on and off the entire time. All you did was cry. La'Dai, we understand how hard this is for you. We're here for you, your dad and I want you to stay here for a while. Your sister is even going to stay for a couple of weeks, okay?"

"Thank you, Ma, but I think I'll be alright."

"And any other time I would have agreed with you but LD honey you took Xanax and Ambien with a full glass of wine. We're your family, we know this isn't normal behavior for you and we can't risk you trying to self-medicate again. We're already dealing with one tragic situation, honey I can't handle two. I'll feel better if you stay here."

"I just wanted to numb the pain, Ma. I wasn't trying to take my life. I just wanted to sleep and wake up to what I was hoping would only be a really bad nightmare."

"I know baby, the wine you can have—one glass at a time but the pills I'm taking away. Understood?"

"Yes ma'am."

"Now let's get you into the shower. I'm making you some vegetable soup. Please just try and take a few bites."

I nodded my head in agreement.

Sasha walked into the room as Ma walked out.

"Hey little-big Sis, how you are doing?"

"I don't know, Sasha, I don't know where to go from here."

"Well, the good thing is you don't have to figure it all out today. On another note, Jason is here, and he would like to see you."

"Not right now, Sis, I'm a mess and I can't look him in the eye. I know that he was only doing what Devin asked of him and I know that he never had intentions on deceiving me, but it still hurts."

"I get it, it's a lot. These last several months have been hell for you but, listen, he's here and he's trying to make an effort. Who knows, he may be able to bring you some comfort. Don't send him away LD without hearing what he has to say."

"Okay sis, I have no fight in me left. So, whatever you say." Jason came into the room, and when he looked at me there was adoration in his eyes. He sat down on the bed next to me and hugged me, but I put no effort in to hug him back.

"Hey, gorgeous," he said, that was his name for me since the day we met. "I just wanted to come and check on you. I know you're probably still upset with me, but I can handle the pressure. How are you feeling today? You have your family here, but can I get you anything?"

My silence continued; I had no idea what to say. Jason moved my hair out of my face as he waited for me to respond.

I looked him deep into his eyes and asked him, "Does this feel right to you? I mean, you were my husband's oncologist, and dating me at the same time and now he's dead. I'm not blaming you but the circumstances of our 'arranged marriage' doesn't exactly make for your typical love story."

"No, you're right there's nothing typical about this. Nothing. But one day you will be able to see the bigger picture."

"Aren't you optimistic?" I responded sarcastically.

"Yeah, gorgeous I am. I'll admit, when Devin first brought this subject to my attention, along with his intentions, I was hesitant. I told him that I was going to stop seeing you because I knew that if you found out you might be resentful and not be willing to understand. He told me that you can be a bit stubborn but if I am patient with you, you will come around. I mean in your defense, you did not have the same amount of time that he and I did to digest everything, so know that I'm willing to be as patient as you need me to be. Do you remember the night I was supposed to come over, but I had to cancelled because of a patient I had to monitor? Well, now you know Devin was that patient. Do you remember what I said?"

"Refresh my memory, Jason."

"I told you things aren't always what they seem; know that I am here for you no matter what happens in life, and I cherish you so much."

"Yes, I remember that."

"Everything I said that night was genuine and sincere. When we met at Jazzy's I had no idea that Devin was your husband. I knew nothing about you except that I wanted to get to know you. There was just something about you that drew me near to you. It was magnetic. And I haven't been able to let go since. I'm telling you this, so you understand that the time we've spent together was not in vain and everything I've done and said thus far has been with great sincerity and has come from a genuine place, my heart."

"I hear you Jason, but I just need some time right now. I'm in no rush to do anything."

"I get it, I'm going to be here no matter what, and we still have a promise to fulfill for Devin regardless of how things turn out with us."

Jason had always been outspoken and straightforward, so I didn't take offense to him being so direct. I guess that came with being an oncologist. You can't sugar coat telling someone they have cancer, and only have eight months to live.

When Jason left, I ate some of Ma's soup and went to bed. When I awoke it was three o'clock in the morning, I grabbed a blanket and went to sit outside on the balcony. Somehow the motion sensor went off and lit up the entire backyard. Ten minutes later Dad came onto the balcony asking me if everything was okay.

"Hey Dad, yes I'm okay. Just getting some fresh air and admiring the stars."

"Okay honey." Dad turned around to go back into the house, but I didn't want to be alone, so I struck up a conversation.

"Dad?"

"Yes, LD," he answered as he turned around.

"Do you think Devin is up there, you know–heaven? Looking at the sky, I can't help but wonder if he's in heaven looking down on me now."

"Yes, baby girl, I believe he's up there."

I shook my head in agreement.

"Can I ask you another question?"

"Sure, anything."

"When I came to the house that time, crying because Devin wanted a divorce, you told me that you and Devin had a talk, and you respect what he had to say about his reasons for wanting a divorce. What did you guys talk about?"

"Well, I swore Devin to secrecy then, but I see how heartbroken you are now, so I'll tell you. Devin called me and asked me to meet him at the hospital. So, I did. He assured me that in that moment he was fine, but he needed an older male figure to talk to. He confided in me and told me that since his father passed, I was the only male figure he felt like he could really trust."

"Okay, go on."

"I met him in the cafeteria of the hospital, and he was in full blown tears, his hands were shaking, and he said 'Dad, I'm scared'."

"I asked him what was going on and that's when he told me that he had cancer. He asked me to keep it between the two of us. He told me what his plans were. He explained how he wanted to ensure you were able to move forward when he was gone."

"Dad, how come he didn't fight harder?"

"La'Dai, that man fought harder than anyone I know. Once he told me how severe the cancer was and that it was spreading, it became my obligation to be his right-hand man. Devin was the son I never had, when he married you, he became family, there was no biological bias. I was the one taking him to his appointments. I watched him vomit, there were times when he could not make it to the restroom to relieve himself, he was so sick. He never wanted you to see him that way. You were his Queen."

"Dad it just seems like I should have been there, you know?"

"I get it honey, and I sympathize with you, but I saw the weight loss, the nose bleeds, he was in great pain, I saved you the trouble of having that to bare. Devin lost his strength, so I gave him mine. There are some things that only a father can do."

"Oh Dad, I probably couldn't have dealt with seeing him that way. Devin was so strong, so resilient."

"If you didn't put him out, he was going to eventually have to move out or you would have caught on to him. There were many nights that I spent at his condo."

"Did Ma know?"

"No, I told her that he was having a hard time with the divorce, and I was going over to help him through it. I mean one time or another she had a few suspicions as time went on and me running to his aid became more frequent, but I told her to trust her husband and she did."

"Dad, why did he hide it from me?"

"LD, Devin knows that you would have tried to save his life. Devin accepted his reality, but he knew that you would not have been able to. He wanted to spend his last days making sure that the loved ones he left behind were well taken care of, especially you. He wanted you taken care of in every area of your life."

"Yeah, Dad but I could have at least been there for him. He spent a lot of his last days with that broad instead."

"See that's the problem, you think you want to know the truth and when the truth is revealed, you can't handle it. This man tried his best to hide a terminal illness from you for your benefit and all you can think about is why he spent his dying days with her instead of you. La'Dai, get your shit together. Quite frankly I think we've spoiled you a little too much and so did Devin."

"Dad?"

"I'm sorry, honey, I didn't mean for that to come out so harsh, but I need you to open your eyes. This man found you a man to take his place, a suitable man, you've been blessed with another stand-up guy and more."

"Yeah Dad, I mean Jason and I may be compatible and complement each other. And we may even have the potential to be that power couple that Devin envisioned us to be. But Devin and I belonged together, we had history, he was my soul mate. There's a difference. He can't be replaced."

"La'Dai, Devin isn't coming back, ever. And you're right, he can't be replaced but you owe it to him to see to it that his legacy lives and you owe it to him not to let his efforts go in vain in his attempts to look out for you. Give Jason a chance; he might just be able to help you heal."

I stayed at Ma and Dad's for the time being. I decided to try and make amends with Jason, because Dad was right. I couldn't let Devin's efforts go in vain. Jason reached out to me again, and this time I took him up on his offer to pick me up and get a change of scenery at his place.

Sitting on Jason's couch I began being transparent with him, "Let's be honest with each other. I understand that Devin set us up and I know that we tried dating at one point but let's face facts. I'm damaged goods. I don't even know what's best for me anymore. I spent the last months of Devin's life dragging him through the dirt because I couldn't see past my own rationale."

Jason paused for a moment before responding.

"Listen, I'm not worried about your past mistakes. What I do know is that we have a very bright future together. You're beautiful, talented, and don't take No for an answer. I can help you move past all negativity and doubt, but you have to be willing to start somewhere. I was once just like you. I had the whole cake but if one piece was missing, that's all I could focus on. You have to start counting your blessings. We're going to get through this together. It's what Devin wanted and it's what I want. But I want you to want it too."

Jason kissed me on my forehead and led me into his guest bedroom. It was spacious, with only a bed, lounge chaise, a TV stand that held a 50" flatscreen TV. There were a few pictures on the wall that seemed to be fine art. Every time I had stepped foot in this room, I was impressed with his sense of decor as a man.

"You can sleep in here. This way you can be comfortable with your own privacy and that door there," he said pointing to a door that I thought was the closet. Leads to the bathroom and walk-in closet. Please let me know if you need anything, baby girl." I never slept in that room, so I was happy when he pointed me in the right direction.

"Okay, I will. Thank you."

"Would you like me to blow out this candle?" he asked as he walked out the door.

"No, you can leave it burning for now. I love the smell of eucalyptus."

"Alright, have a good night. I'm headed to the hospital. Again, call me if you need me."

Jason walked out the room and I felt a sense of peace. I felt secure again. I felt like I did when I was with Devin. I felt safe and cared for.

Chapter Fifteen

I was sitting in Dr. Monroe's Office; physically I was there, but mentally I was somewhere else. I felt numb and out of place. My heart was still heavy, and I definitely did not want to talk about my past. I was no longer that person. The old La'Dai was buried right along with Devin. But Dr. Monroe insisted we get to the root of my issues. I guess she was right and there was no use wasting time, I was paying her one-hundred and fifty dollars an hour. And my sessions were running two hours or longer nowadays.

I began telling her about the incident in college that I believe changed my entire outlook on life.

"Well, Dr. Monroe, here we go," I said staring her in the face as I sat upright on her brown leather sofa. "I was only nineteen years old when I started see my philosophy instructor, Professor Van Newman. The professor didn't want to take the chance of getting fired, so I would have to meet him after class only. I know what we were doing went against school policy and was considered misconduct, but I was in college. I was supposed to have fun, right? Plus, growing up I went through a lot of years not being that cute attractive girl that got all the guys' attention. But that changed my senior year and well into college. I will admit that I didn't know how to handle the attention. Let alone, the attention from a professor that every college girl in school thought was so fine, myself included. The first time Professor Van Newman told me to meet him after class, I was clueless. But it didn't take me long to catch on."

"La'Dai, I'm going to stop you right there because you've said a lot that I want to address. What it sounds like is you were a young insecure college student without any direction."

"I wouldn't say I lacked direction; my parents provided a good moral upbringing, but I still had a mind of my own."

"Would you say that you were easily influenced?"

"Maybe." I shrugged my shoulders.

"What do you mean by maybe?"

"Well, I had convinced myself that if I could gain control over the situation, I wasn't being influenced at all. It was my way of making sure that I didn't become a victim in any circumstance."

"Okay, can you give me an example?"

"Yup, I'll continue. When Professor Van Newman and I were together after class he made a pass at me by rubbing my thigh as he said, 'You have some pretty strong legs.' I didn't correct him, although I knew damn well he was wrong. And I knew damn well that I was being sexually harassed but instead I responded, 'Yes, I do, they're strong enough to wrap around your waist while you're holding me up.' Right there I was taking control. I mean I had to. I couldn't switch classes in the middle of the school year and risk failing in my first year of college. And I couldn't report him, I've seen how that story could end up, plus it was just the two of us. It would have been his word against mine. Of course, I could have said no, but you don't tell a man like Professor Van Newman "No." He was used to getting what he wanted at any cost. So, I went along with it."

"La'Dai, as a professional he was held to a much higher standard and regard."

"Yeah, but I was of legal age and I knew right from wrong too."

"Do you know when you're being taken advantage of? I want to be sure that you're able to say 'No, stop right now. I don't agree with this or that and we aren't moving forward.' And that's in any situation."

I thought about her question for a moment before answering. Truth I never had to use my voice in that manner, being assertive was not something I had to worry about demonstrating. I always had my family to protect me. I never learned how to handle saying no properly.

I started sobbing as I answered the question, "Yes, I do but I don't know how to communicate in a way that it believable. The night the professor and I had sex for the first time, I knew I could get expelled from school, but he kept inviting me back afterwards, and I felt compelled to go, although I had free will. The very last time we had sex, he asked to take off the condom, I told him hell no. But when we were done, I noticed that he wasn't wearing one. And when I asked him about it, he said that it broke while I was on top of him, so he took it off."

"Without telling you?"

"Yes. Eight weeks later I found out that I was pregnant. When I told him, he grew angry and said that I had no choice but to have an abortion. If I had the baby his entire life would be ruined, and I would be a college drop out. I didn't tell a soul what was going on. I was ashamed, embarrassed and I felt lower than low. He made me an appointment at an outside clinic. When the procedure was over, I woke up crying hysterically demanding my baby. All I remember saying is, 'Where's my baby? I want my baby.' When it was time to release me, he picked me up. We drove five miles, he pulled over at a bus station and told me to catch the bus the rest of the way because we couldn't be seen arriving back on campus together."

"It's okay to cry, La'Dai. Let it out, honey."

"That experience left me broken, hurt, lost and confused. The next year I transferred to Grambling and toward the end of the year is when I met Devin. He was opposite of every other guy I'd met in high school or college. He was gentle with me and never played on my weaknesses. He allowed me to take my time, there was never a rush. I was a priority, Devin was God-sent. Oh Devin!" I cried out his name and fell into the fetal position right there on Dr. Monroe's couch. "Devin is the only person I talked about that experience with. Before we got married, I had to tell him. I had to tell him because I was unable to have children."

"What do you mean?" Dr. Monroe asked.

"A few days after the abortion, I had a fever, and I was passing large blood clots like there was no tomorrow. I called the professor since he was the only one who knew what was going on and I asked him to take me to the ER. His response to me was, 'I'm not taking you to the ER because you got your period.' I convinced my roommate to take me, although I didn't explain to her what was going on. Come to find out, the clinic left some of the fetus inside of me and I developed pelvic inflammatory disease. My uterus was scarred, and I was told by the doctor that I may never be able to have children. I guess in a sense it was God's way of punishing me."

"Oh La'Dai, I'm no pastor but I'm a believer and off the record let me tell you that is not the way God works. He is a merciful, forgiving God. He sent his only Son here to die for your sins do not punish you for them. Now there is such a thing called polarity. Where there's good, there's evil. And the only thing that comes to steal, kill, and destroy is Satan. And it sounds like he's trying to steal your hope. This isn't church but as your therapist, I felt the need for you to understand those important facts."

I wasn't at all offended. In fact, I was enlightened and had been thinking maybe I should try going back to church.

"You know, Dr. Monroe, I thank you for that. Because this entire time since Devin's death, I've been blaming God and myself."

"The fact that you've been blaming yourself is another topic for another session. Let's get back to you feeling broken after your relationship with the professor ended and having the abortion."

"Actually, Doctor Monroe, I think I've had enough for today. Can we pick up next time?"

"Absolutely. Make yourself an appointment with my secretary. And in the meantime, I'm not going to give you any exercises to do at home but try to focus on gaining some mental balance. Listen to the meditation series I sent you via email. And begin using the techniques I've told you about so that you can start self-healing in addition to coming to these sessions. We're going to get you through this, La'Dai. I know it's been tough, but you're tougher."

"Thank you, doctor, I'll see you next time."

I thought about what Dr. Monroe said about never dealing with the abortion. She mentioned to me that I suffered with abandonment issues which stemmed from my relationship with the Professor. I contemplated my life and concluded that she may have been right. During that time, my experience with the professor, left me feeling alone and confused. I always had my parents or Sasha to look out for me. And when I went through that whole ordeal, I didn't tell a soul. Apparently, that did more harm than good.

I left Doctor Monroe's office and headed straight for the cemetery. I missed Devin so much. I would have done anything just to feel a single touch from him. To hear the deepness in his voice. Smell his scent. Anything just to see him in the flesh.

I pulled up to the cemetery, pulled a blanket out of the truck, wrapped it around me and headed to his grave site. Standing there looking at his headstone, I saw a picture of my handsome husband staring back at me. His headstone read: If tears could build a gateway, and memories a stairway, I'd run right up to Heaven's gates and bring you back home.

I could not stop the tears from falling. At first, I was crying, then I was filled with anger, then sorrow again. It's like his presence was there with me.

And if his presence was there, I thought for sure he could hear me, so I began to speak out loud, "Devin, it seems so unreal. This feels so unreal, this emptiness won't go away. Baby, I would give anything to have you back even as friends. I love you so much. I'm so sorry that in my own selfishness I didn't take the time to really sit back and try to understand better. I'm so sorry that I never listened when you tried to tell me. I just didn't understand what was happening at the time. Do you know there are times that I just sleep in your shirts or spray your favorite cologne all over? It doesn't change the fact that you're gone but I'm doing everything I can to try and get through this, everything I can, just to feel some type of normalcy again. I have to admit you were right, had I known what was going on with you I would have done everything in my power to try and force you to get better. But that's me being selfish again. I know that you would not have wanted to live that way. In and out of hospitals, not able to care for yourself. And I know you don't like me talking this way but F cancer. Devin, I love you, always have and always will. Do me a favor and keep watching over me until I get there. And this time when we meet again, it will be forever."

I kissed his headstone and started walking back to my car. As I was walking back to my car, I noticed a man crying hysterically over two graves that were side by side. I knew exactly how he felt, call me bold but I walked over to him to see if there was anything that I could do.

"Excuse me, can I offer you some Kleenex. I see that you're having a tough time; do you mind if I offer my condolences?"

He looked up at me. The rims of his eyes were crimson, and he thought a moment before answering.

"I apologize, I don't mean to intrude but I just lost my husband and I completely understand the feeling of grief."

"You don't have to apologize. This is hard for me; I can't believe that I'm having to even come to a cemetery. Not only that but coming here to visit the gravesites of my wife and daughter."

I felt sorry for this man. I couldn't imagine what he was going through. Well, maybe partly but I hadn't lost a child. This man's heartache was doubled.

"I'm so sorry for your loss. You lost them both at the same time?"

I looked down at the headstone and noticing the dates, I realized that it had been several years since they passed, and his daughter was only seven when they did. Seeing him like that after so much time had passed, I wondered if this grief was ever going to get easier.

"Yes," he responded sniffling and wiping his nose with the Kleenex. Their deaths have been hard on me, and this is the first time that I have been out here to visit."

"I understand," I said, nodding.

I felt compelled to sit down next to him, so I did.

"Do you mind if I sit with you for a moment, I would feel really bad if I just walked away. Besides, I could use a distraction right now anyway. And I mean that with all due respect."

He looked me up and down and extended his hand to give me a handshake."

"No, I don't mind. I'm Valentino. Thank you for your empathy."

We shook hands.

"Hi Valentino, I'm LD. It's unfortunate that we are meeting on these terms but who else better to talk to than someone who has been through the same thing."

"Yeah. Lily, my daughter…would have been fourteen. Fourteen, starting high school and maturing into a beautiful young lady just like her mother."

Valentino started crying again. Feeling so sorry for him, I put my hand on his shoulder and tried to console him by telling him it was going to be okay.

Immediately he put his head on my shoulder, catching me completely off guard. Once he was done crying, he lifted his head up and began apologizing.

"You don't have to apologize. I understand."

"No, I do, you probably think that I'm a complete weirdo," he said.

"Don't be silly, like I said, I completely understand."

"You said you recently lost your husband?"

"Yes, to cancer."

"Oh man, I'm sorry. How long were you married?"

"Ten years, we almost made it to eleven."

"Wow. You know we hear about and see death every day. But when it hits close to home it comes down on you like a ton of bricks."

"Yeah, tell me about it," I responded.

He pulled out a flask from inside of his black jacket. Valentino was of Spanish descent. He had a head full of curly black hair, and light brown eyes. I could tell underneath his scruffy five o clock shadow that he was somewhat attractive. His smile was there but faint.

He took a quick drink from the flask then offered me a drink.

"Do you drink tequila?"

"Normally, I don't but considering the circumstances, don't mind if I do today."

Trying not to let the flask touch my lips, I took a long gulp and handed it back to him.

"Oh man, that was smooth. Don Julio 1942?" I asked as I felt the warmth of the alcohol running through my veins.

"You know your liquor, huh?"

"I know a little something."

We both laughed. He began to stand up and so did I.

"I appreciate you showing some concern. This is the first time I've been able to smile in a while."

"Not a problem, you never know who you'll run into at a cemetery."

He gave me a strange look.

"I'm really bad at telling jokes," I said in slight embarrassment.

He nodded his head as he grabbed his motorcycle helmet.

"You're all good in my book; what you just did by sitting here with me was better than any joke."

"You're welcome. Well, Valentino. Take care of yourself and I hope that you find peace and healing soon."

"Thank you, you as well."

We began walking in separate directions. As I opened my car door, I could hear his motorcycle revving. When I got into the car, I began checking my cell phone, a few moments later, I was startled by a knock on my window. Valentino was standing outside of my car with his helmet half on his head. I rolled down my window.

"Hey, you scared me."

"I'm sorry I didn't mean to. But I thought to myself that I couldn't let you leave without repaying the favor."

"What do you mean?"

"Every other Wednesday, I attend grief counseling, it's in a group setting but I find them to be really helpful. If you want to give me your number, I can forward you the information. And no, I'm not trying to make a pass at you." Valentino assured me.

"Oh, I didn't...."

"A woman as beautiful as you are, I'm sure you get passes thrown at you all the time. Okay, wait that was a pass. But the invite was not. I promise you my only intention is to let you know about the grief counseling."

"Umm, I'm usually not into that sort of thing but I guess I can try to have an open mind. My number is three one zero, three, three, six, zero, eight, eight zero.

Typing my phone number into his phone he responded, "Okay, I will forward you the information."

Chapter Sixteen

started to reach a point of forgiving Jason and myself. Visiting Devin's gravesite gave me some clarity. I cannot say that I was back to normal, but I can say the grief was starting to subside, I was starting to heal. Of course, I thought about Devin every single day, and of course the seemingly what ifs crossed my mind too. The truth of the matter was, I had a lot of support. Everyone around me was wishing me well and offering lending hands in any way that they could, so it was only right for me to try my best and move forward the best way that I knew how.

Although I was not in love with Jason, I cared deeply for him. I spent time thinking about the potential of our relationship and where it could go. But then my past would come back to haunt me. What if he wanted kids? That's one thing I wouldn't be able to give him, my insecurities began to sink in. Then there was the great void that I did not think could be filled. Like I said, when Devin died, he took a piece of me with him. In my heart I felt like I could never love like that again.

Four weeks passed, and Valentino was insistent at extending the invitation to the grief counseling. I kept coming up with every excuse in the book but still he tried.

Finally, I decided what could it hurt? I'll give it a try.

Wednesdays were usually the day Jason and I would make it a

point no matter what to put everything else aside and spend some quality time with each other.

"Sasha, hold on, that's Jason on the other line," I said as I put the phone on speaker and clicked over.

"Hey, you, what's going on? I should be ready in an hour," I answered.

"I'm sorry, gorgeous, but I have to stay here at the hospital. We have new residents that just started and I'm in charge of getting them acclimated," Jason responded.

"Okay, no problem. It's still early so I'm sure I can find something to do. Have a good night. Are you coming by in the morning when you get off or should I come over there?"

"Come to my place, and to make it up to you, I'll cook you breakfast in bed. Or maybe I can be your breakfast in bed," Jason replied jokingly.

"I like the second option better."

I clicked back over, hoping that Sasha had not hung up yet.

"You still there?"

"Yes, but I was just about to hang up, I have to go. I have to prepare for court tomorrow. I've procrastinated enough."

"I must admit, this is the most focus I've seen from you in a long time. I love your passion." I could hear her moving around in the background.

"Let's just say more money, a lot more problems. There's a lot of pressure on this case I'm working. It's of high notoriety so I have to dot my I's and cross my T's."

"Yup, that's why they pay you the big bucks, love you, Sis. Chat with ya later."

"Mmmm-kay bye."

Sasha hung up and I sat on my chaise, staring out of my bedroom window, trying to figure out what to do with myself. I thought about going to visit Devin at the cemetery. But decided against that when I realized I hadn't looked at the business proposal for the Cancer Treatment Center, not even once.

I started to scan through it, just when my phone went off. It was a text from Valentino that read: *Hey counseling is tonight; I hope you'll come. There's a couple of ladies that started last week and I think they could use another female presence. Let me know if you can make it.*

"This guy puts the P in persisent," I said out loud, heading over to my closet to get dressed.

I arrived at the meeting a little early and Valentino was already there. I wanted to scope out the scene and see for myself what the group was about. Valentino walked up to me with open arms and a smile on his face.

"Hi, LD, what's up? I see you decided to come, you haven't texted me back, so I figured I'd try again next week but now I don't have to. Welcome."

"Yeah, life has been really busy," I responded looking around and scanning the room.

"Well, you're here so let me introduce you to some people."

"Miguel, this is LD. She's going to be joining us tonight. LD, this is our sponsor, Miguel."

Miguel was an older Hispanic guy, he aged well. Had it not been for the grey beard or the salt and pepper hair you would not have guessed that he was a day over forty. He stuck out his hand to shake mine, but I was still trying to process where I was.

"Oh, I'm sorry," I said, finally acknowledging his notion.

"Welcome LD, we are a fairly mixed group of men and women. This place is a safe zone."

"Miguel, let me tell you about this woman. I was at the cemetery. I was having a tough time to say the least and she willingly came over to me and sat there with me as I was grieving."

"I remember you telling me," Miguel responded. "I'm happy

to know that there are still some unselfish people out there."

"Yeah, I understood what he was going through. I lost my husband not too long ago."

Miguel and Valentino both nodded their heads in agreeance.

The sponsor looked down at his watch. "Excuse me, LD, I have to get class started."

Miguel walked past Valentino and me as he went to the front of the room.

"We aren't going to have to go up there, are we?" I asked nervously.

"No, he leads us from up there and we chime in from our seats."

"Oh okay, when you said group setting, I pictured everyone sitting in a circle."

Valentino let out a chuckle, "Like an AA meeting or something?"

"Yeah, kind of."

"No, this is an entirely different setting. Come on, let's sit over here."

Valentino led us to the second row from the front, we sat on the two outside seats.

Other people were starting to trickle in; there must have been about forty people. I thought to myself, all of these poor people. Heavy hearts, feelings of hopelessness, I'm not alone. Just then I became interested enough to get a little comfortable in my chair.

"Hello everyone," Miguel began, "Welcome. And for those of you who are new, my name is Miguel. I'm your sponsor and would like you to know that I'm happy you decided to join us. Before we get started, Monica would like to share a poem with everyone to set the tone for tonight's meeting."

A beautiful black woman came to the front of the room and stood behind the podium.

"Hello everyone, I'm going to read a poem by an unknown author: 'Don't cry for me, I'm not gone, my heart is at rest, my spirit lives on, Light a candle for me to see and hold on to my memory, but save your tears for I'm still here, by your side through the years.' She came to the end of the poem and I could feel the tears starting to begin.

Sitting there, I realized that I didn't want to go down that road. The road of sadness, confusion, and shame. I had finally got to a place where I could say Devin's name without bursting out in tears. I was finally looking toward a better day.

Leaning over to Valentino and whispering in his ear, I said, "I'm sorry, but this was a big mistake. I have to go."

I got up and practically ran to the restroom. I grabbed some tissue and looked myself in the mirror trying to hold back the tears. When I came out the restroom, Valentino was standing there waiting for me.

"LD, are you okay?"

"Yes," I said sniffling, "this group meeting isn't for me. I appreciate you inviting me, but I'd much rather move forward in the grieving process on a more personal level."

"I understand," Valentino said trailing behind me.

"Look," he continued, "let me at least buy you a cup of coffee. I can see that you aren't okay, and I would feel bad just walking away from you."

He made me laugh trying to impersonate me the day that I saw him crying by his wife and daughter's gravesite.

"A smile, that's a start. There's a coffee shop up the street. Follow me in your car." He motioned, leading us to the door.

Against my better judgment I agreed. Call me crazy but I just couldn't resist. There was something mysterious about Valentino. It's like there was this bad boy demeanor hiding behind the black framed prescription glasses on his face. His eyes told me he had a story to tell. And a part of me wanted to find out what it was.

As we pulled up to the coffee shop, Valentino was already off his bike and at my car door. He opened it and I got out.

"Thank you."

"Not a problem, again no funny business. It's in my nature to be a gentleman."

"I'm sorry but did I at some point insinuate that you were trying to hit on me?"

"No, I just want you to know that I'm not some creep trying to take advantage of your vulnerability."

"Well, just so you know, that thought never crossed my mind."

As we sat down, Valentino began texting on his phone. One moment later, he was fully engaged. I could tell he was lying about our interaction being strictly about the grief session, his eyes said otherwise. But hey I'm a responsible woman who knows how to behave around the opposite sex, so what was the harm?

"So, I must admit that it was a pleasant surprise seeing you tonight. What changed your mind?" Valentino asked while putting his cellphone back into his pocket.

"Well, you don't give up easily and I told you that I would have an open mind and come."

"A woman of her word, I like that."

Trying to appear modest, I looked away slightly and smiled. Valentino continued.

"What do you do in your spare time? I can imagine that you probably try to stay busy all things considered, I know I do. His death was recent, right? No dating for you either huh?"

He stopped himself before becoming apologetic.

"I'm sorry I'm asking you questions and answering them for you, jumping to conclusions, that's one of my character flaws."

"A man who knows himself well and isn't afraid to admit when he's wrong, now I like that."

Yes, I was being flirtatious and I'm not going to lie, there was definitely chemistry between Valentino and me. I didn't mention the relationship between Jason and I because the fact still remained that I didn't know this guy well enough to open up to him about my business—the story of how my relationship with Jason's unfolded was on a need-to-know basis and he did not need to know. On the flip side, maybe I wasn't so forthcoming because there was something mysterious and captivating about him. I wanted in.

"I'll be right back; I have to go to the restroom." He got up and headed to the back of the café.

Just then my phone rang, and it was Jason. I looked back over my shoulder before answering just to be sure Valentino was still on his way to the bathroom.

"Hello, hey you," I answered.

"Hey gorgeous, turns out the residents are only working half a shift tonight; they have to make up some hours in Med-Surge tomorrow. I'm on my way to your house. Let's go out to dinner."

Just as I was getting ready to reply, the clumsy waitress walked by me dropping a full tray of dishes, exposing the fact that I was not home.

"What's all that noise, are you out with your sister?"

"Ummm yes, Sasha and I came to this Asian restaurant one of her coworkers recommended," I lied.

"Oh cool, I'll just meet you there. What's the name of the restaurant so I can get the address?"

Becoming nervous, I began to stutter. I had never lied to Jason before.

"Oh umm, umm actually I would rather us be alone, that way we can unwind and have a few drinks too. This place doesn't really have good drink selection."

"Okay, whatever you want, gorgeous. Meet me at my place

and I'll drive us to our favorite spot."

"Okay, bye-bye, see you soon," I said trying to rush Jason off the phone as I noticed Valentino heading back to the table.

"Hey, I'm sorry but I have to go, something came up." Gathering my things, I wasted no time getting up.

"You good?"

"Yes. Thank you for the tea, but I really have to get going."

"Not a problem, but I wasn't finished getting to know you. Listen you seem like a real down-to-earth woman, and I like your style. Let me cut to the chase, sitting here with you got me to thinking that we should hang out sometime, nothing serious," Valentino said.

"Ummm…"

"C'mon, we can talk as I walk you to your car. I know you have to go."

He dropped thirty dollars on the table, and we headed for the door.

"Look Valentino, to be honest with you…"

"I said nothing too serious," he interrupted me, "which means there's no need to be honest about anything. Don't tell me that you don't feel the chemistry between us."

He was right, I did feel it. It was strong and tantalizing.

Just then he took off his glasses looking me deep into my eyes and for a moment I was mesmerized. He was so smooth, confi-dent– and the complete opposite of anyone I had ever thought of dating.

As I was getting ready to answer, he pulled me into him, com-ing close to my lips but stopping just before his were about to touch mine. Grabbing me tighter, standing body to body, he whispered in my ear, "Think about it."

I was thrown off but completely turned on.

He opened my car door and I got in, still at a loss for words.

He closed the door and winked at me as he walked away.

Jason and I reached the restaurant, but I couldn't get the interaction between Valentino and me off my mind.

Jason could tell I was somewhat distracted, "LD, you good?"

"Yeah, I'm fine."

"You sure, do you need to talk about anything?"

"No-no I'm good," I responded with a forced smile.

"Okay, well let me know if you do. On another note, I wanted to talk to you about something."

"Sure, what is it?"

"I would like for you to meet my mother. We can either go to Nigeria where she is, or I can fly her here."

Suddenly Valentino was no longer on my mind and I was starting to see clearly again. In that moment I realized how serious Jason and I were and how much respect I owed him to be committed to what we started, the relationship I said I would give a try.

"Well," I said with an excited pause, "I've never been to Nigeria before. So why don't we go to her? Wow, I would love to meet your mother, you think that highly of me, huh?"

"Seriously gorgeous, do you have to ask?"

"It's just sometimes, Jason, I look at you and I'm waiting for you to change. Sometimes it feels like you're too good to be true."

"I've already told you; I've been waiting for a woman like you for a very long time."

"You're so sweet. Can I bring Sasha with us?"

"Of course, you can."

When Jason and I got back to his place, I blocked Valentino's number and deleted it. I needed to stop this situation before it got started.

I spent the next couple of weeks looking at the business proposals for the Cancer Treatment Center. Jason and I spent the next several weeks meeting with contractors, getting the blueprints approved, and working with the interior design team. Jason and I single handedly picked the oncologists, aside from the doctors everyone else was hired on through online agencies or word of mouth. The mayor loved Devin, giving us his blessing.

It was Thursday evening, and Sasha called earlier that day wanting to meet at Ma and Dad's. When I got to my parent's house a quarter after six, I was drained from all the work we were putting in the Center. Sasha and I were meeting up to discuss our trip to Nigeria and catch up.

I walked into the house, everyone was sitting in the living room, Ma, Dad and Sasha all welcomed me with a warm embrace. They had these peculiar looks on their faces as if they were up to something.

"Hey, ya'll, what's up?"

"Come sit over here by your momma, chile, I need to hear all the juicy details," Ma said tapping on a spot of the sofa next to her.

"Details of what, Ma?"

"Well, your sister told me that two weeks ago Jason asked to take you to Nigeria to meet his mother."

"Okay and…?"

"Chile, are you blind? Keep up or take notes, a man doesn't invite you halfway across the world to meet his momma unless he's proposed or is planning on proposing."

"Oh, my word, is this why you guys have those silly grins on your faces because you think I'm getting married? No, we're just going on a trip and I invited Sasha because Nigeria is a beautiful place. I don't know when we'll ever go back, and I didn't want her to miss out on the opportunity to travel there and for free. Jason insisted on paying for everything." I was shaking my head at their preconceived notions.

"I told you guys that it wasn't going down like that," Dad said. "Jason doesn't seem like the type of guy that would consider marriage without first having a man-to-man conversation with the woman's father first. The man has morals."

"Oh, be quiet, Phillip," Ma said, playfully throwing one of the accent pillows in Dad's direction.

"Besides, you guys, I'm still adjusting to being a widow."

"Oh no need to adjust to that, just go with the ebb and flow of life. See where the tides take you," Sasha said getting up from the couch.

"Come on LD, let's go to Dad's office and use his computer. I want to do some cybershopping."

There was Sasha being free spirited as usual and there I was playing it safe like always. Except for when it came to Valentino. Although I deleted his number and had not been in contact with him, thoughts of him still penetrated my mind and sometimes those thoughts lead to penetrating my body.

Ma came into Dad's office and told me that one of the stores at the Lot was going out of business and the space would be vacant. I went into panic mode. She was handling majority of my business affairs since Devin's death, helping me until I got my mind right. This was until recently when I felt the need to transition back into doing business and gaining a sense of normality. I will say, Tony also stepped up and was a big help. Although he was our contractor, him working closely with Devin while he was alive, helped to bridge the gap on a lot of our projects. When it came to business, Tony thought a lot like Devin.

"Ahhh." I let a long sigh and began tapping my foot and biting my bottom lip in nervousness. I knew that I needed to gather myself and not let my imagination go off the deep end assuming the worst. Therapy was helping but let's just say I still had a long way to go.

"You know, Ma, I really appreciate you helping. I really do. You're the best, but I will handle this. I'll meet with the tenant tomorrow and get all the details. This just gave me an instant headache, I don't understand why they didn't mention this sooner, hoe convenient being that rent is due." I headed toward Ma and gave her a kiss on the cheek.

I went back to the desk where Sasha was and gave her a kiss too.

"I'm going to head out, Sasha, we can get together again another time."

"Leaving so soon?" Sasha asked rhetorically.

I left and went over to Jason's place. When I got there, he was on the couch, watching CNN and working on the website for the Center.

It felt awkward walking into his house as if it were my own but since he gave me a key, I thought why not use it?

"Hey gorgeous, what's going on? I didn't know you were coming over."

"I texted you and called but you didn't respond."

As I sat on the couch Jason leaned over and kissed me. I took off my shoes and got comfortable.

"Oh, my phone is still on silent from work, sorry I missed your call," Jason said putting his phone back on the end table.

"It's fine. I just need to relax right now."

"Well, relax." Jason said as he lifted my foot onto his lap giving me a massage to die for.

"Do you want to talk about it?"

"Not really but I probably should so I can figure out a solution."

"So, tell me what's up."

"Ma just informed me that one of my tenants has to vacate the suite they're leasing because they're going out of business. I mean I'm sure I can find another business to lease the space, but it's been a while since I've conducted business for the lot and quite frankly, I was hoping to ease back into things but now I have to hit the ground running to make sure that all budgets are met going forward."

"Well, I might be able to help."

"Really? How so?"

"There's a pediatrician at the hospital whose wife is a stay-at-home mom. She recently started an online boutique, selling women's clothing. Apparently, business is doing well online, and she wants to expand. Yesterday he mentioned her wanting to open a storefront."

"What? That's awesome!"

"I'll talk to him tomorrow. Send me pictures of the space and I'll talk to him and see if they'll be interested in renting it."

"Oh gosh Jason, this would take a big load off my shoulders. I swear, baby, you are always right on time."

I realized the words came out of my mouth as well as the way my heart fluttered said them.

"I love you too, LD, and don't you forget that. I'm always going to have your back."

Jason saying, I love you, pierced the hardened heartbreak cast around my heart. Layers of sadness, grief, guilt, and bitterness started to peel away and just like that I was open.

"I love you too, Jason."

My view of Jason was crystal clear, and we were in sync.

I had never said those words romantically to another man besides Devin. But when I said them to Jason, they were true, they had authenticity. I felt pure love.

I did not think it could happen. I literally could not see myself loving someone else. How could this be? Not that I was complaining but I mean; right under my nose Jason had entered my heart and made me whole again. I exhaled and let the spirit of love radiate throughout my body.

I spent the next month getting ready for our trip to Nigeria; we were set to leave in two weeks. I was slightly nervous and happy at the same time. I played the conversations that Jason's mom and I would have over and over in my mind. I went back and forth between her liking me and not liking me. What if she didn't think I measured up? What if she thought that I wasn't polite enough? I mean what if she thought my American ways were too laid back and mistake them as a form of disrespect? I was going crazy in my mind about the what- if's. One thing I didn't want to do is try to be overly nice and come off as fake.

I looked myself in the bathroom mirror and said, "LD, you got this."

Jason startled me as he walked in.

"Yes, LD you got this."

He came up behind me and kissed me on the neck.

"Babe, you scared me."

"I'm sorry, and what exactly am I agreeing that you've got?"

"To tell you the truth, I'm nervous about meeting your mother."

"Oh, well I can understand that. The good thing is my mother is very honest. If she doesn't like you, she will tell me right in front of your face, then ask us to stay at a hotel."

"What?!"

"I'm just kidding. She hasn't met another woman since my wife passed away. I didn't think she would meet another woman ever again. Until I met you and trust me, she knows everything about you already."

That Friday I went to Danny Lane's to check out the shop and pay some of its bills. For some reason maintaining the shop was always easier for Devin. Maybe it was all the testosterone that got in my way. Liam was another head barber, besides Daniel, who also helped run the shop when Devin and I were away. He did pretty good at keeping things in order.

"Hey Liam." I walked over to his booth as he was giving a haircut.

"Oh, Hi La'Dai, I didn't know you were stopping by today. I would have made the deposit for this month's booth rent. I'm almost done collecting from everyone."

"Thank you, but I was in the neighborhood. And the real reason why I'm here is because we're changing cleaning services again and I need to meet with them. Will you be available in about thirty so you can sit in with us?"

"Oh yeah, sure thing."

"Good, I want to make sure you're in the loop."

"Not a problem."

I walked over to the receptionist station and looked at the system to make sure it was still running properly. I planned on changing out the computers in the shop, so it was a perfect time to take inventory. Liam walked over and began telling me about an issue they were having with the phone system. As he was talking, he paused and said, "Hey Valentino man, have a seat and I'll be right with you."

I looked up and as sure as my name is La'Dai Roswell, Valentino was standing right there in the lobby of Danny Lane's.

For a second, I paused, not knowing what to think.

"Hi LD," Valentino said. He had a smile on his face, and you could tell he was happy to see me.

"Ummm, hi Valentino," I stuttered back in surprise.

"How have you been? I've been trying to reach you."

"Oh, I ummmm, I ummm." I couldn't think of a lie fast enough. What was I supposed to say right there in that moment? I blocked you to keep myself from cheating on my boyfriend.

Lord knows the chemistry between Valentino and me was strong and electrifying.

"You two know each other?" Liam asked. I was saved by inquiring minds.

"Yes, but not very well," I responded.

"I was hoping we could change that," Valentino said in a flirtatious tone.

I cleared my throat and asked him what he was doing there.

"I've come to get my haircut; Liam has been cutting my hair for a while. We played football together in high school."

"Small world," I said trying to sound interested. Truth was I was nervous as hell. I never mixed my personal life with my work life. Liam was one of my employees, and there I was unfolding right in front of him. Business all in the street. Liam knew that I was dating Jason. And yes, my reputation mattered.

Cutting the conversation short, I said, "Excuse me I have some work to take care of. Nice seeing you."

Before I could walk away, Valentino asked if he could talk to me in private. I looked at Liam, he could tell I was uneasy talking in front of him, so he walked away.

"I apologize for going MIA on you but right now is not a good time for us to talk. I can call you later tonight to clear the air."

"Okay, I'll be waiting," he said as he kissed me on the cheek before walking away.

What was it about this man that secretly drove me wild? They say curiosity killed the cat, but satisfaction brought it back. I pondered on letting Valentino make this kitty cat purr. Whether it was curiosity or satisfaction, it didn't matter. I wanted him to take me and take all of me, I wanted to be sure that I wasn't missing out on anything.

I don't know why I was suddenly craving guilty pleasures but giving into temptation was only going to be a giant wrecking ball that would have come crashing down. My morals and values were starting to be compromised, and life was to blame for it. Subconsciously, the pain and hurt was still poising my mind, and Valentino was beginning to seem like the antidote.

Was I willing to say to hell with everything, and dive into the deep end for momentary pleasure? I just wanted to feel whole again. I was struggling again to find my center. I knew Jason was what I needed but my body wanted Valentino. My priorities were nonexistent, my selfish wants were taking over.

Sadly, being careless was the least of my worries, I was careful my whole life and look where that had gotten me: brokenhearted, confused and picking up the pieces after my husband's death. So, there I was getting ready to open Pandora's box and I didn't think twice about it.

Was I making the right choice? No. Life had become full of twists and turns. And I was done walking the straight line. The life I knew no longer existed and neither did the woman who once lived it.

I did not want to hurt Jason. I knew I should have let Valentino go but seeing him was gratifying. Motorcycle rides, late night walks on the beach, and last-minute turn around trips to Vegas made me feel so free. I feared that Jason would catch on to my games, but I was going to cross that bridge when I got there. Spending the last two months sneaking around with Valentino made me feel young again, nonetheless had revisiting my youth caused a good girl to go bad? Maybe I was like a penny with a hole in it, hopeless. But what me and Valentino did, nobody needed to know.

"What are you doing here? Now is not a good time, it's a private affair with my family." I asked Valentino as I tried to pull him to the side and out of view.

"I know but live a little and come with me."

It was my parents fiftieth wedding anniversary and Valentino was not on the guest list. Luckily, Jason was called into work and had to leave early, or it would have been hell to pay. I told Valentino I would be busy and could not see him this weekend, apparently, he did not care. Things were getting messy with him, and I need to put him in check just not tonight.

"What, are you crazy? I can't leave right now."

"Your problem is you think too much, everything always has to be planned out. It looks like you guys are wrapping up anyway."

He hit the nail right on the head. My wheels were always turning. I dared to seize the moment. I wanted so bad to go with him, everything he was saying and doing was making me want to say yes but I knew everyone would grow suspicious of where I went. But that didn't stop me, I decided to let my hair down.

"Hold on, I'll be right back." I said looking around, hoping no one saw us together.

Walking over to Sasha, I asked, "Hey, can you finish wrapping up without me, there's a problem at one of the sites and the property manager can't be reached."

"What? Right now, La'Dai? Well, do you need me to come with you? Who's that guy?"

"No, I don't need you to come. He's one of the contractors."

"Is he new? I've never seen him and why is he working so late?"

"Can you cover for me or not? You and your damn twenty-one questions."

"Yeah sis, I got you."

"Thank you. I'll call you later."

I grabbed my jacket and he followed behind me. When I looked back to see if I had forgotten anything, I could see Sasha looking at us while we walked out the door.

When we arrived at Valentino's house, he handed me his flask and told me to relax. He got out of the car, came to the passenger side, opened my door, and picked me up off my feet. "I missed you," he said as our lips touched. He stuck his pulsating tongue into my mouth, overpowering all of my senses, sending my clitoris into a tailspin.

"I can't wait to get you inside," he whispered, momentarily stopping our passionate moment.

Valentino's house was clean and well kept. Everything was in its proper place. The atmosphere was romantic, and I had the profound desire of wanting to get to know him completely.

His kisses were intense as he swept his tongue across my neck and down to my navel. He began undressing me. Then the doorbell rang.

"Forget the doorbell, I'm all you need right now," I said not wanting him to stop. The way he handled my body made me cling to him not ever wanting to let go. Every touch he made evoked vibrations in my body that I didn't know was there.

The doorbell rang again and again.

"Hold on, baby, I have no idea who that could be."

I could hear him open the door.

"Where is she?"

"I'm sorry, do I know you?"

"I said, where is she? Don't play dumb with me."

"You can't just barge into my house like that."

"Oh, I can, and I will, step to the side."

"Where is my sister?"

I tried to hurry up and put my clothes on to see what all the commotion was about. Just as I was pulling down my dress, Sasha came busting around the corner.

"Sasha, what the hell are you doing here?"

"I followed you. I needed to make sure you were safe. Your

little story wasn't making sense. If I know you, and I do, you're too smart to go to one of the sites this late and alone."

"Girl, I can't believe you."

"Believe me?" she said with her hand in her chest. "You're the one who ditched Mom and Dad's party for Mister Rico Suave' and his mini me that's not so mini."

Sash was looking down at Valentino's prize possession that was peeking through the hole in his boxers.

"Sasha focus," I yelled trying to get her to look back at me and not Valentino.

"You might want to put that away." I pointed down to make him aware that it was out.

And man was it out, still fully erect and calling my name.

Valentino hurried up, closed his boxers, and zipped up his pants.

"Oh, don't be shy now, I saw the entire thing. Ya'll up in here giving the entire neighborhood a show."

"You did."

"Yup, right through that window."

"You didn't close the curtains." I let out a long sigh.

"C'mon La'Dai, let's go."

"No, Sasha, what do you think this is?"

"Let's go, sis, I need to make sure that this man is not taking advantage of your emotions. You're still vulnerable."

"Oh, trust me he's not." I responded taking my index finger and running it down his chest.

"Well, I'm not leaving then. Do you have any liquor in here?" Sasha asked as she opened his refrigerator "I'm going to need a drink if I'm going to be up all night. Judging from his one-eyed willy he's far from being done with you, La'Dai, and we might be here for a while."

"You have to be kidding me. I'm fine—you can go."

"I don't think so. I'm not leaving you alone with some strange man."

"You'll have to excuse my sister, she's a little overprotective. Look, let's finish this later. I'll call you." I said kissing Valentino on the cheek.

I grabbed my things and headed for the door.

"Sasha, let's go." I was annoyed.

"Coming Sis," she said in a playful tone as if she was happy, she had won.

As we were one foot out the door, Sasha stopped and turned toward Valentino.

"I just have one question, Mr. Suave'."

"Of course, you do, go ahead," he said with a half-smile on his face.

"Do you have a brother?"

He put the palm of his hand to his forehead and shook it as he laughed.

"Sasha, let's go now!"

"Okay, okay."

Sasha and I went back to my place, I slipped into my night gown and climbed into bed. Sasha came in yawning, "Oh, you're calling it a night–me too. But can you make me some chamomile tea while I'm in the shower. My job has me with a bad case of insomnia."

"Sure sis. And thank you for staying."

As soon as Sasha was sound asleep, I took the first opportunity I to find my way back to Valentino's place.

I showed up at Valentino's wearing nothing but my black trench coat and a pair of black, red bottoms. I knocked twice before he answered. When he did, I proceeded to open my trench coat, exposing my naked body, and said, should we finish what we started? He pulled me in and said," Oh, hell yeah."

We kissed passionately, he led me into the kitchen, bent me over the sink, gently pushing my head down as he leaned into me softly biting the side of my neck. His man' hood was rising and had my full attention.

Just then my phone rang, I prayed that it was not Jason. I felt guilty that I succumbed to allowing my lust for Valentino get the best of me, but my body still wanted what it wanted, and it was him. I promised myself I would satisfy my craving one time and would move on. So, I planned on making the best out of this one time.

"I have to get that" I said, heading to my jacket to grab my phone out of the pocket.

"No, you don't." Valentino tried to pull me back, but I knew better.

"Just give me a minute."

Valentino slapped my ass as I continued to walk over to my jacket.

"Do you mind if I take this upstairs?"

He gestured for me to go ahead.

"Hello." I rolled my eyes at the caller ID.

"Hey Sasha. I thought you were sleeping."

"I was but never mind that, where the hell are you?"

"Ummmm, I'm at Jason's. I couldn't sleep so I decided to come here."

"Oh, good. I'm glad you've come to your senses and decided to forget about the other guy. But listen, the detectives at the 3rd precinct have been working on this high-profile case with me and they just got a lead on this guy's whereabouts. I'm headed in, okay. I'll call you in the morning when all the madness is over. Tell Jason I said hi. Oh, hold on."

I could hear Sasha pick up her work phone.

"This is Sasha. No, you tell them to wait until I get there, and I am briefed on what's going on. I'm the DA and nobody moves until I know that this case is going to be sealed shut, you understand?"

I thought to myself I do not want to be on the other end of that line, I know that person's ears were bleeding. Sasha did not play.

"Okay," Sasha came back to the phone, "like I was saying I'll call you in the morning."

As I hung up, I got the bright idea to turn on the water to the bathtub. I took off my shoes and climbed in as I heard him coming up the stairs.

"I think we should have some fun right here tonight. Come join me," I said to Valentino, looking at him as if he was good enough to eat.

He put the two drinks down on the sink, took off his sweats and climbed in.

No words were spoken, he just picked up where we left off. Spreading my thighs apart, he put my legs over his shoulders. His head went underneath the water as his lips met mine, he let his tongue play with my kitty kat until she started to purr. Coming up for air, he flipped me over on top of him. Water went splashing everywhere.

I slipped my head down into the water to return the favor, just before I went to put him into my mouth, his hands grabbed the knap of my neck, pulling me back up.

He kissed me before he stood me up in the water, turning on the shower, water was pouring over our bodies as he kissed me from head to toe, covering every inch of me.

He took both of my arms and placed them above my head, holding both of my wrists with a firm grip in one of his hands. Valentino was aggressive and I liked it. Our eyes met, my hands were still above my head, he took my right nipple into his mouth, gently biting it.

When he turned me around, the cold marble kissed my cheek. I couldn't tell if it was the water dripping between my thighs or the warmth of my juices flowing from how much he turned me on. Either way, I was wet. He gently pressed his chest into my back pushing me more against the bathtub wall. Holding his manhood in place, Valentino was ready to enter me from behind. Just as I felt the tip going in, a loud boom came from downstairs.

Scared shitless, I screamed.

Valentino jumped out the shower, asshole naked he pulled a 9mm from the top of his toilet.

By this time a swarm of police and what appeared to be a few FBI agents were upstairs joining our private party in the bathroom.

"Drop the gun, drop the fucking gun or we'll shoot, get your ass down on the ground," one of the officers yelled, pointing his gun directly at Valentino.

LA County Sheriff was storming this man's condo. Immediately I froze, standing there naked, with my hands in the air, I had no clue what to do.

"You, too, get your pretty little ass on the ground," one of the officers said demanding for me to lie down on the ground next to Valentino. I did exactly as they said, still dripping wet from the shower. Again, I couldn't tell if my face was wet from the shower or from my tears.

I was terrified. Just then I heard a familiar voice, saying, "Move over, let me through."

I turned my head to look, and I couldn't believe it was Sasha.

"What the hell are you doing here?"

Sasha ran over to me. "Someone get her a damn towel," she demanded one of the officers. "I knew his damn face looked familiar to me. Damn LD, you told me that you were at Jason's.

Damn you." Sasha's voice was enraged but the look on her face was more of concern. I could tell my sister was deeply worried about me.

She pulled me off the floor, leading me over to Valentino's bed. She turned back to him giving him the look of death and said to one of the officers. "Make sure his ass stays down. Motherfucka," Sasha said still looking at Valentino.

Hugging me she asked, "Sis, are you okay? You told me that you were at Jason's."

"Sasha, what's going on?" I asked, beginning to cry.

"Don't worry, sis, you're good."

Walking toward Valentino's living room soaking wet, wearing nothing but a towel, I glanced back at him upset and as my eyes met his, the look of sorrow came over his face as he put his head down, embarrassed to look me in the eye.

Chapter Seventeen

One month later, I found myself back at Dr. Monroe's office. This time things were more complicated than before. This time, I was not just dealing with Devin's death AND my past. I was dealing with a new relationship I almost threw away for a guy I'd known for only five minutes--a guy that my sister arrested on attempted murder charges. Feeling overwhelmed, I did nothing to get myself ready that morning. I put on a hat without brushing my hair, strands of my hair stuck out from underneath the hat. I had not one care in the world that I was walking around with bed head, I threw on a pair of sweats, a white tank top and a pair of flip flops. Every part of me said mess.

Dr. Monroe sat across from me waiting for me to speak. She sat patiently writing down notes and occasionally looking up at me to see if my position had changed. Moments of awkward silence passed before I said anything.

"I don't understand why I'm in this vicious cycle of bad luck. Why do I feel stuck?" I said, turning my attention to Dr. Monroe.

Before answering, she put down her pen and removed her reading glasses, making sure to make direct eye contact.

"What do you mean by that, La'Dai?"

"I mean just thinking about everything from the college professor on, is this really supposed to be how my life turns out. Why have I been blindsided? When do I get to move on with my life?"

"Elaborate on that for me."

"I mean, I met the professor and although I knew the situation would not end well, I went there with him anyway. Despite that God-awful situation, Devin comes along and rescues me from that mess and mental turmoil, only for me to lose Devin. Then here comes Jason again. Perfect man for me, he too saves me. Then Valentino comes along and AGAIN, just like with the professor; I was willing to throw everything away for a man I barely knew and to satisfy my own needs. I put my priorities on hold for irrelevant acts of temporary self-gratification."

"Okay, interesting self-evaluation. No one is perfect. First, I would like you to stop beating yourself up. What I believe the issue is, and it's completely fixable; is your lack of gratitude. Hear me out, and please don't take offense to what I'm about to say. You are on the road to recovery and I'm going to get you there, but you have to allow me to be honest as your therapist."

"By all means," I said, gesturing her to continue.

"For some reason it seems as though it's easy for you to take things for granted. This could be because of your upbringing where things came easily and were easily replaced. Now I'm not saying that your parents didn't raise you right but often when things come to us too easily, we overlook their value and devalue them. This applies to all other instances except the professor and Devin's death. Both of those situations were not initiated by you."

Dr. Monroe was right. We continued the session for another twenty minutes. She had yet again given me something to think about. I left her office and headed straight to the hospital where Jason worked, I dreaded going there in hopes that I wasn't triggered by Devin's death since that was the hospital in which he died. But if I was going to move forward in life, I was going to have to take the necessary steps to do so.

I stepped off the elevator and took a deep breath in. The oncology floor of the hospital was one that I could not avoid even if I wanted to, the smell and the atmosphere was familiar, and I felt the hairs on the back of my neck starting to stand up. Devin spent his last dying days mapping out a business plan for the Cancer Treatment Center, so this is where the girl was going to have to meet woman. I was going to put on my big girl panties and start dealing with shit head on. His legacy was going to be kept alive no matter what demons I had to face. As I got off the elevator and headed over to the nurses' station, I felt a tap on my shoulder.

"Excuse me, Mrs. Roswell."

I turned around to an unfamiliar face.

"I know you don't know me, but I was one of your husband's nurses and I recognize you from all the pictures he had up of you in his home. As the cancer became more aggressive, he hired me to make house calls four days a week."

"Wow, you spent a lot of time with him during his last days."

"Yes, Miss, I did. He told me that if I ever saw you on this floor after his death that I was to give you a message. I hope I'm not overstepping boundaries. It's just that your husband was a phenomenal man, which I'm sure you already know, and I want to respect his wishes."

"Okay."

Devin was a very calculated individual. Always forward thinking, making sure to cover all bases. That is exactly why all of our business remained successful over the years. If you ask me, he was a genius.

"Well, he told me that if I ever saw you on this floor, that you would be coming to visit Dr. Maxon and would need some reassurance. He also said to let you know that whatever doubts you have about the two of you, let go of them, forgive yourself for whatever mistakes you've made because they were to be expected as you tried to deal with his death and move on. Don't worry about Dr. Maxon being upset; he's committed to the process of you guys coming together and holds nothing against you but will steer you in the right direction."

"Is this what he told you to say?"

"Verbatim. He would make me rehearse it and I didn't mind because what he did with you and Jason, I mean Doctor Maxon, is truly Godsent. He said that he knew you better than you knew yourself, and when you have second thoughts about something you shut down and do away with it altogether: fear of the unknown."

I smiled. "He was right."

"Well, these words are my own," the nurse continued..." he loved you very much. He talked about you all the time; he would talk about this plan he put together for your life after his death. He spoke about how perfect things were going to work out between you and Dr. Maxon. I think the thought of it all is what kept him going for as long as he did--he was happy with the thought of your happiness. Once he found out that you and Dr. Maxon were serious and finally moving along in the direction that you were, he told me that he could go home now and let his body rest."

I stood there in awe taking in everything she had to say. "Devin coached Dr. Maxon until his dying day on how to treat you, how to care for you, how to handle you even when you were going to find out that he was his doctor. He wanted to make sure Dr. Maxon was well prepared to be your husband one day. When he found out that you and Dr. Maxon had already met, he said that's when he knew Dr. Maxon was the one. I only wish to have a man love me that much one day."

"Thank you, thank you for your time, Karine," I read her

name tag. "Do you happen to know where Dr. Maxon is?"

"I will have the charge nurse page him for you."

"Thank you."

Jason showed up ten minutes later, stepping into the doctors' quarters, I started to plead my case. Apologizing for my behavior and wanting badly for Jason to understand my sincerity, I did not tell him the lengths to which I was ready to go with Valentino. But I knew I had to be honest with him as far as some of my dealings. In the middle of my little speech, Jason cut me off mid-sentence.

"LD, listen to me and listen to me good." It had been a long time since I heard Jason refer to me as LD, so I knew he meant business. "I love you. All of you, the good and the not-so-good. I knew that there would be some tough days for us to get through. But I want to know that we are in this relationship together. I want to know that you are fully vested in us." Jason rubbed my shoulders.

He continued, "I need to know and feel like I'm one of your priorities. I understand that we will have challenges and adjustments. But I need to know that us being together is worth the fight. I do not want to second guess what we are building because your actions suggest otherwise. It's important for me to know and see that you have left your past behind and are looking forward to a future with me in it. It seems like you have been using Devin's death as an all-access pass to not give a damn. There need to be boundaries set that are clear and understood. You are in a committed relationship and if you want this to work, you truly need to make sure that I am the man you want to be with and no one else. I feel unappreciated and taken for granted. The woman I fell in love with is not the woman I am dealing with right now. Our relationship needs to be one where there's mutual love and respect, trust and honesty."

"Well, I guess you set me straight, huh?" I responded with a smirk.

"LD, I'm not joking."

"I know, Jason, and I truly do apologize. I apologize for the way acted. I had to work through some stuff. But I am ready to move forward if you are." I kissed him on the lips, trying to make up. "And besides, we have work to do. We have a treatment center to start."

Jason had a way of making me back down without seemingly bruising my ego. Now that he and I were going in the right direction again. I was completely ready to get to work. There was another relationship I had to rectify if I was going to do things right.

I was completely ready to implicate myself and give Sage an explanation of everything in an attempt to mend fences. Roswell Cancer Center of Los Angeles was getting ready to come to life, and I was going to need to maintain my relationship with the mayor. I didn't want any bad blood lingering around. I was sure Sage filled him in on how I conned her. I had no choice but to make the call and try to bury the hatchet with her.

Ready to turn over a new leaf, I picked up the phone with the positive attitude that Sage would answer. I mean my attitude was positive but clearly hers was not, which was to be expected—one of the main reasons why I approached the conversation with serious caution. I came at her with a sound mind, and a tone that could sweet talk anyone into a state of surrender. I had the intent to let bygones be bygones. Needless to say, she was not the least bit excited to hear from me.

"You have some damn nerve calling me. And I do mean damn nerve," she said.

"I'm calling you to take responsibility for myself. I would like you to know that I'm aware of my actions. I took things too far and I am so sorry," I responded, swallowing my pride.

I knew this conversation was not going to be easy, but it was going to be well worth it. Besides, after thinking about how everything went down; I was holding onto a lot of guilt.

"You're sorry?" She chuckled. "Do you know that after that night in the hospital leading up to the repast and two months after Devin's death, I went through the most agonizing three months of my life. I built up anxiety, resentment, and anger. You name it, I felt it."

"Sage, I am really sorry; things weren't supposed to get that out of hand."

"They shouldn't have started to begin with. You set out with an agenda to manipulate me. So why in the hell are you calling me? You know that I have nothing to say to you, let alone any motivation to trust you."

"I understand, and you have every right to feel the way you do."

"Oh, I know I do. I don't need you to validate my feelings. Now what do you want? Because of you, I now have to see a therapist. My life was perfectly fine before you came along. And I know damn well Devin would not have approved of your actions either."

"Wait a minute, I know you're mad, but you need to leave him out of this."

"Look, you called me, and now not only are you wasting my time but my free minutes too. Please do not aggravate me. I really do not think you want to see me aggravated LD. That is your real name, right?"

"I'm not trying to aggravate you," I said easing up on my tone, remembering that I had an agenda. "All I'm saying is you shouldn't bring up people who aren't here to defend themselves."

"Yeah well, I'm two seconds from hanging up so what do you want?"

Pissed off, Sage was becoming a real liability; her mouth was moving at lightning speed with anger and wrath. I think at one point I felt the steam coming out of her ears full throttle through the other end of the phone.

Again, I did not want today's words to be tomorrow's regret, so I proceeded with caution. I did not know if my asking for her help was going to make her flock or flee. But hell, I was not about to let her scare me away from the one thing I was certain about since Devin's death and that was starting the cancer treatment center.

"Sage, I want nothing more than to take back everything that happened. But we both know that I cannot do that. Now Devin spent a significant amount of time during his dying days putting together a plan for his dream of leaving his legacy behind, the Roswell Cancer Treatment Center. My reason for calling is because I want to bring his dream into fruition. I was hoping that we could smooth things over for business sake?"

"Are you deaf or just dumb? I want nothing to do with your trifling ass. You're a snake in the grass."

"Okay, you know what, I've taken enough of your insults. I get you being upset with me but what I am asking you for goes well beyond me and you. It serves a bigger purpose than you dare to even think about. So, forget it, I will find another way. Thanks for nothing."

The was an awkward silence.

"La'Dai, wait, don't hang up. Snake in the grass is just an expression." she chuckled. I thought to myself now this heffa is trying to back pedal. She continued, "You have to cut me some slack. You had all that coming for doing what you did. Although what you did was ass backwards and wrong, I would like nothing more than to help you with getting the Cancer Treatment Center up and going. Devin was a great man. I will talk with my uncle and let him know there's no hard feelings between us."

"Thank you," I said, letting out a quiet sigh of relief on the other end of the phone. "I'll be waiting for his call."

Sage and I hung up and I wanted to jump for joy, the hard part was done, and the best was yet to come. I called Sasha and told her our entire conversation. I could tell she was disappointed to learn that I reached out to Sage, but I don't think she understood the dynamics of what needed to be done.

I responded to her frustration on the other end of the phone. "Well, what do you recommend that I should have said to her, Sasha?"

"Why are you being sarcastic?" she said.

"I'm not, so why are you receiving it that way? Look I'm going through yet another pivotal moment in my life and right now I'm counting on the support of my sister."

"I do support you; I'm just saying that you should not have let her talk to you that way, you should have just told her like it is. I need your help; either you are going to help me or not. But with or without your help, the show will go on."

"Sasha shoulda, coulda, woulda. You know, I aspire to be as domineering as you one day," I said, rolling my eyes.

"Don't get sarcastic with me, you should have directed that energy in her direction."

"For what, Sasha, what did she do to me?"

"First off I don't like the way she showed her ass at the hospital. Once she found out that he was your husband, considering the circumstances, she should have shown some damn respect and demanded answers later."

"I hear everything you're saying. I'm heading out the door to meet Jason and fill him on what's going on. So, let's chat later."

"Not a problem, I'm heading out myself. Really quick before I let you go, when do you propose the Treatment Center will be ready?" Sasha asked.

"I'm not sure. Devin had everything mapped out, the business plan, the buildings, everything. All Jason and I need to do is pick up where he left off, dive right in, ya know? Which reminds me, I need to call Tony too."

"Sounds like you have your hands full."

"Yes, I do."

"Well, don't let me hold you up any longer."

"Hold on, Sasha, you've been busy and quieter than usual. What is going on with you? And be honest but brief because I really do need to go."

"Umph, the nerve of you. Not only are you all in my business but you are rushing me too. Do you remember when you and I stopped at Starbucks the night we passed out the Christmas care packages?"

"Ummm," I responded, trying to remember.

"You know LD, when we drove out to the IE."

"Oh yeah, I remember. The night my entire world changed," I said, trying not to think about the God-awful phone call I got from Sage and stay focused on what Sasha was saying.

"Well, that night I met Christian, you know that fine football player that we went to high school with."

"How can anyone forget Christian?"

"Yeah well, let's just say he still looks good even with the grown man weight he has put on. So anyway, we exchanged numbers and we haven't stopped seeing each other since that night."

"What?!" I shouted, overjoyed. "My sister in a committed re-lationship? What did you do—pull out your special lingerie and handcuffs, now homeboy don't want to leave?"

"No, that's the thing, LD. We haven't had sex at all. He says that being the star football player came with its perks but also with some curses too. He talks about learning some hard lessons about life and women in general. He's on a spiritual journey now."

"And you're okay with that?"

"At first I was not. But after a few dates and meaningful conversations, I changed my mind."

"Wow, Sasha. Why didn't you tell me?"

"LD, really? What was I supposed to say, 'hey sis I'm sorry you lost your husband, but I think I might have found mine?' You were grieving and things just took off between us anyway."

"I guess you're right. Well, I'm excited and I can't wait to meet him. As a matter of fact, I'll make time this week. Let's double date."

"Okay, I would like that. And I think he would too. He's heard so much about you, he's already your number one fan."

"Cool, text me and tell me which day and which restaurant; Jason and I will be there. Dinner on us."

"Gotcha, see you then."

"Bye sis, love you."

"Love you too, LD."

Chapter Eighteen

"Jason, c'mon babe, I want us to be on time for this meeting. It's with the mayor. Can you zip up my dress please?" I asked him, lifting up my hair and turning around so he could zip up my dress, giving him a sneak peek at my laced thong.

"Yes, but what's this meeting about? I feel like I can't even keep up nowadays. The last seven months have been a blur. Six meetings or so a week; it's starting to seem excessive."

"I know, babe. I'm tired too but we are almost at the finish line. In fact, tonight's meeting is to discuss the grand opening of the Center."

"Well, good. Speaking of which, we have two more oncologists to interview and then I think we'll be fully staffed. And get this, one of them used to work at Cancer Treatment Center of USA."

"Oh really, how did you find him?"

"He comes highly recommended. Apparently, he has healing hands."

"What?"

"Yes, I've heard all the testimonials."

"Jason, that's great. I'm going to let you and your team handle those last two, I trust your judgment."

"My God, woman, I love you and I can't wait until you're my wife," Jason said kissing the side of my neck.

"C'mon, Jason, not right now, you know that's a sensitive subject for me. Besides, you would have to propose first."

"Don't you worry your brilliant mind about that."

"I'm not, right now I'm worried about getting to dinner and meeting with the mayor on time. Now chop-chop." I playfully slapped him on his butt as he walked away.

I could not help but briefly revisit Jason's comment about becoming his wife. Was I opposed to it? No. I just didn't want to live in that moment right then and there. Of course, if the opportunity presented itself, I would say yes in a heartbeat. I had deep feelings for Jason. He was holding true to his word of taking care of me.

I took a quick glance at Jason and thought out loud, "No, they don't." Jason was the full package and then some. A man that came with bonus features, what was there to say no to?

On the way to the restaurant, we discussed Sasha and her new relationship, it was pleasing to know Jason cared about Sasha just as much as I did.

"Okay, gorgeous, we're here, on time just like you wanted and with ten minutes to spare. Why don't we get a glass of champagne while we wait?" Jason said as we pulled up to valet parking.

"Babe, you know I usually don't like to drink when we're conducting business, so I'll just have one glass."

"Loosen up a bit, it's dinner so I think a glass of champagne is appropriate. That and the fact that we're meeting with the mayor about the grand opening of the Center, one would say a glass of champagne is well deserved considering all of our hard work."

"Let's just remember that our hard work isn't done yet, okay, babe?"

"Yes, gorgeous I hear you."

The mayor showed up twenty minutes after we did. The conversation was light but serious. He expressed a couple concerns and like a boss Jason tackled them with confidence and reassurance that everything would go as planned. The mayor gave us his blessing to open the Center within a month's time and from there, it seemed as though he and Jason were having dinner on their own. Their conversations ranged from sports to fishing to Nigeria, none of which I was an expert in. I think at one point I heard Jason invite the mayor to Nigeria, letting him know that he would be happy to show him around. I was fine with that as long as he knew that Sage was not invited. I did not need any triggers. Being around her for business purposes was one thing but casually was another. I was not harboring any old feelings; I just did not want to send any mixed signals. Or, like I said, risk being triggered.

There wasn't a cloud in the sky on this twentieth day of June. The sun was high in the sky illuminating the earth with a graceful warm atmosphere. Birds were chirping and cars were filled with families ready to venture into summer. Smooth jazz played through the speakers of Roswell Cancer Treatment Center, as staff hung the large sized photo of the wonderful, brilliant late Devin Roswell in the lobby; the moment was surreal. Here we were, the big day had come. And yet I felt unworthy of being at the center of what should have been his moment. And as quickly as that thought came, I felt a swirl of wind overcome me and a voice in my head that whispered, I still love you. It's like Devin was standing right there to utter those very words himself. I shook my head in disbelief and as I came back to what was my current reality, Jason came up from behind me, rubbing my shoulders and for a moment I said nothing, just breathed deeply and took everything in.

"Just remember, gorgeous, we're in this together and even though the day may get crazy, all you have to do is give me one look and I'll step in wherever you need me to," Jason said, breaking the silence.

"Okay, but I think I'm going to be fine. We've done so well. And I want you to know that I could not have done this without you. Look at our staff working so diligently to help us bring this day together. Their actions aren't going unnoticed, look at them putting last minute touches on cleaning the floors and watering the plants. I'm so grateful. My God, I'm so grateful."

"I know you are. As I promised everything is going to go according to plan."

"Honestly, what did I do to deserve you?" Grabbing Jason's face, I gave him an innocent kiss on the lips. I could hear Sasha's voice as she walked up behind me.

"My gosh sis, ya'll really did it. Not that I doubted you one bit, but this is far beyond what I could have ever imagined. Look how intricate every detail is. And look at my brother on the wall, still overlooking everything. That's right, bro, but we got you now."

"Thank you, Sasha," I responded.

"But what I really like is the shrine that you guys put together of all the doctors' awards and accolades, along with their pictures. If I were a patient, I would be able to rest easy knowing that I had some of the top oncologists in the country responsible for my care. Man, pure genius." Sasha exclaimed.

"Hi Christian," I said, embracing him with a hug.

"Hi LD, I must admit I'm blown away myself; this place is phenomenal. I know I didn't get a chance to meet Devin, but I've heard nothing but great things and I'm sure if he were here, he would be proud of you and Jason," Christian said, looking around the Center as he spoke.

When Christian and Jason met on the double date, they hit it off pretty well. Christian owned his own gym, had a master's degree in kinesiology and was a well-known dietician. He and

Jason had become gym rats together and trust me, with Jason's new physique I was not complaining about all the time the two of there were spending together.

Jason greeted Sasha and gave her a hug as well, whispering the words "Congratulations" in her ear. His failed attempt at whispering allowed me to hear exactly what he said.

"Congratulations for what?" I asked, confused.

"Babe, you told him?" Sasha said, turning to Christian.

"No, no I didn't," Christian answered, motioning Jason to be quiet.

But typical Jason, when he was excited about something, he could not help himself; that's just who he was.

"Come on, Sash, I'm a doctor. There's just certain things you can't keep from me," Jason said with a big smile on his face.

"Hello, is anyone going to tell me what we're talking about here," I demanded.

"Not right now, sis, this is your day, your moment. But I promise we will catch you up to speed when all of this is over."

"Sasha, you know the suspense is going to kill me."

"Well, you can't die just yet because here comes the mayor."

Opening the Center was gratifying and humbling. Devin's unprecedented actions touched not only me, and Jason's lives but now the world-renowned Roswell Cancer Treatment Center was open and going to provide an extraordinary level of care to so many people with needs and hopes of beating cancer, without the worry about how they were going to afford it.

I spent the entire evening shaking hands and taking pictures. Smiling from ear to ear, I couldn't be happier. Truth be told, giving the speech of how Roswell Cancer Treatment was founded and letting Devin's legacy live by telling of the man he was, healed me in more ways than one. For once, I was actually able to remember him and talk about him without tears streaming down my face but with a smile and a sense of honor. I felt honored to be his wife and honored that he entrusted me with a dream so prevalent in the Los Angeles community.

The past was gone, and I was moving forward into the new life that Devin built for me. Being lost in acute nostalgia of my marriage with Devin was no longer serving me. I was ascending into higher levels on my new life journey.

As much as I loved walking down memory lane, Jason was waiting, and it was time for me to grab hold of life and embrace the new beginnings. I was qualified and certified to officially be the woman I was meant to be the bold, courageous, strong La'Dai Roswell. The Center was going to need me and so was everyone else in my life who had been carrying me all this time. It was time for reciprocity in all of my relationships.

It was around one-thirty in the morning once Jason and I returned to his place. I went over the success of the night in my head. As soon as Jason's head hit the pillow, he began snoring. I lightly rubbed the side of his face and looked at him with a smile as he slept. I felt so privileged to be the woman lying next to him. Jason was right there by my side the entire night and I knew without him none of what was would have been possible. Jason really was my right-hand man. I got up from the bed and decided to pray, hoping God would hear my prayer. I started with:

"Heavenly Father, It's me, your child, La'Dai. I don't know what I've done to receive such mercy and grace. I know that I have not been perfect. But I thank you anyway. I pray that as I continue on in the blessings that you have brought my way, help me to stay humble, patient, and give me strength on the days when I feel weak. Tonight, could not have been a better night and I have my angel in heaven, Devin, and my angel on earth, Jason; to thank for that. Lord, I pray for peace

and health for all the patients that walk through the doors of Roswell Cancer Treatment Center, and I pray for healing and comfort for the families of patients who do not win their fight against Cancer. Help me to lead the entire team in a way that prioritizes exactly what the Center stands for. In Jesus mighty and powerful name, I pray. Amen."

It had been a while since I literally got on my knees to pray but it was well-needed. As I climbed back into bed, my phone lit up. It was text message from Sasha that read: Great job tonight, Sis. I'm so proud of you.

Just then I remembered that Jason congratulated Sasha right before the opening ceremony started. I replied: Thanks. Oh, and don't think that I forgot about you needing to let me in on the little secret.

She replied with a happy face emoji and said: Brunch at my place tomorrow, bring Jason with.

I agreed, put my phone on silent, and was fast asleep.

Jason woke me the next morning with a phone call from the mayor. He saw that I'd awakened and kissed me on the forehead while finishing his conversation. Then he closed the bedroom door behind him before going down to the living room to continue his conversation. I laid in bed for a moment before grabbing my cellphone.

Once I did, I noticed I had five text messages. Two from Sasha, making sure we were still coming over for brunch, letting me know that I had better not have her in the kitchen cooking for nothing. One from Ma, telling me how great the night turned out, along with a picture that she and I had taken. And the last one caught me by surprise, it was from Sage. She told me congratulations on such an amazing night, and she hoped that one day we could truly put the past behind us and move forward into a real friendship. For a moment I dwelled on the thought of that--at least until Jason walked back into the room and distracted me.

"So, I just got off the phone with the mayor."

"I know, what did he say?"

"You know? How do you know?"

"Ummm- 'Okay, Mister Mayor, I will get back to you on that… gave it away."

Jason laughed at my sarcasm and continued telling me about his conversation.

"He let me know that he was pleased with the way the night went. He also mentioned how impressed he was with the Center itself. He said he didn't have a doubt in his mind that the center would be successful and a great resource for the community. He personally wants to meet all the doctors himself on Wednesday."

"Jason, that's awesome."

"You say that like you're surprised. La'Dai, we're a dynamic duo, a real powerhouse. Together you and I can move mountains."

"You're so confident, what a real turn on."

"C'mon now, have you known me to be any other way?"

"No, not really."

Jason came closer to me, and I could tell from the way he started to caress me that he wanted to go further than just kissing me on my neck. Truth was, I still was not ready. So, I stalled him with the excuse that we needed to get ready to go over to Sasha's place.

On the way to Sasha's, I could tell that brushing Jason off left him in wondering. I sensed a little irritation in his demeanor, but being the man he was, he would never verbalize it. He knew when to hold 'em, fold 'em, and walk away.

"Sasha, we're here," I said as we found her and Christian in the kitchen.

"Finally," Sasha said jokingly.

"Don't I know it. But enough small talk, I'm gonna jump right to it. Let me know what's up, what's going on in your world? I was on pins and needles the entire ride over here."

"Geez, so nosy." Sasha laughed.

"Christian baby, I'm going to take Sasha out onto the lanai for a little girl talk. Can you keep Jason busy and let him help you finish up with brunch?"

"The man is a guest in our home. I'll finish up brunch and you go do your thing. I got it covered in here."

Sasha gave Christian a big puppy-in-love smile and led me onto the lanai.

"Well, aren't I proud of you, it went from raining men to you finding the one. Sis, I'm so happy for you."

"I know. I'm pretty surprised myself. He is so amazing; he loves my cooking, and can you believe he has me going to church every Sunday?"

"Cooking? Church? Okay, who the hell are you and where is Sasha?"

"I know right? He's helping me transform into a different woman. I feel like I'm actually starting to find out who I am and what my life purpose is. Before I felt like I was just going through the motions of life but now I'm more conscious and aware of what's going on."

"You're even talking different, Sasha. I've never heard you speak like this. Excuse me if I kiss him, I'm just happy to see the change. Who says you can't teach an old dog new tricks?"

"Who are you calling old, heffa?"

With us both laughing, Sasha moved closer to me. "I haven't told you the best part. There's more--he proposed."

"Well, with the ring on your finger and Jason telling you congratulations at the grand opening, I figured as much."

"No, sis, much more. Let me see your hand."

Sasha took my hand and placed it on her stomach.

"You're going to be an auntie."

"What?" I yelled. "Oh my gosh, Sasha, congratulations. I wasn't expecting that one. We have to toast. Oh, shit you can't. I'm so excited I don't know what to do. Okay, we have to pick the colors for the nursery. Do you have a name picked out? I have to start planning the shower."

"Slow down, sis. But I'm happy to see you're excited."

"Girl, excited? I'm overjoyed."

"LD, I'm learning how to let love, love. I mean he's been so patient with me. He holds me accountable but he's so gentle and loving. I'm still waiting for him to change."

"Well, stop. Stop waiting for him to change and receive the blessing of love that God has given you. Love is a beautiful encounter and you have someone to share it with, embrace it with arms open wide. That makes it so much more enjoyable. Let go of yourself and embrace your new life. I'm proud of you for not chasing him off."

"Don't be fooled. I tried but he said he wants me to be his wife and he's not going to let me go. He told me that he would do whatever it takes for us to get to the next level. And he has, LD. He has, I'm so in love with him."

Sasha started to let tears of joy stream down her face, and I could not help but follow suit.

"It must be my hormones that have me all emotional like this."

"No baby girl, it's the happiness, the peace, the love, and the joy that has you all emotional like that."

Sasha smiled, leaned over to give me a hug and said, "I love you, big-little sis."

"I love you more."

When we got back into the kitchen, brunch was ready. Both

Jason and Christian could tell I had gotten all the scope because I could not stop smiling.

I looked right at Christian and said with my deepest sincerity, "Thank you for coming into my sister's life and being that ray of sunshine. I know that sounds corny, but you are exactly who she needed. Thank you for staying grounded and staying true."

Christian gave me a wink and a nod and walked over to Sasha kissed her on the cheek, rubbed her belly and pulled out her chair at the table. He was so gentle with her, just like she said.

"So, Sasha, I'm sure Mama was the first to know. How did you get her to keep your secret for so long?"

"We both agreed that it was your moment and when the time was right that I would tell you. It was pretty simple. She knew how excited you'd be, so just know she is waiting for your phone call so you two can be in excitement together."

"My gosh, the first grand baby."

"So, LD with your new beginnings, why not keep the blessings going and join the club. You know, have a couple of your own. Jason, you want kids, don't you?" Christian asked.

Jason damn near spit out his food trying to shut Christian up.

"It's okay, baby." I tapped Jason so he would ease up on Christian.

"Well, I'm not able to have children. But I'm sure that Jason and I will make great babysitters. You know married life can get pretty busy so you guys will need that alone time from time to time."

"Oh, I'm sorry, LD, I didn't know."

"Honestly, it's okay, how would you have known? Plus, I have come to terms with the situation. You know adoption is always an option."

"Yup, adaption is always an option. Either way it's all good. I want whatever you want, gorgeous," Jason said, coming to my rescue, insinuating that he was right by my side.

Reality sank in, and the truth was Christian's question about kids got me to thinking. I was a little concerned by the baby conversation. Not by the fact that Christian brought up the subject, but it made me wonder if Jason did in fact want kids.

Of course, he was saying it's fine now, but what happened once the honeymoon phase started to fade, and he realized that he did want kids. That's the one thing I couldn't give him, the one thing that actually may have been able to stand in our way—being able to expand our family. My insecurities were starting to rear their ugly heads.

When we made it to Jason's house, he sat down at the end of the bed and began to take his shoes off. I climbed onto the bed behind him and began to massage his shoulders.

"Aw, man, gorgeous that feels good. A little to the left."

"How's that?" I asked following his directions.

"Perfect. Just like you."

I stopped instantly and started a conversation that I knew was going to be hard for me to have.

"That's just it, Jason. I'm not perfect."

"LD, what are you talking about?"

"Jason, I'm not fully functional as a woman. I can't give you babies. I can't help your legacy live. We won't have generations after us or kids to help us in our old age or grandkids to spoil."

"Hey, hey slow down. I need to stop you right there. I already told you that if you wanted kids there's other alternatives. Baby, I know that you might feel some type of way after the conversation at your sister's, but I already made myself clear that I was on board either way. I'm okay with it being just the two of us. Which allows more time for me to walk around naked." Jason laughed.

"Jason, c'mon, this is serious."

"Okay look, I apologize. I was just trying to lighten the mood.

Besides I'd rather you walk around naked. Matter of fact can you do so right now?"

"Jason!" I exclaimed.

"LD, you already know my stance. But if this is that important to you and you feel the need to have the conversation, then I'm all ears."

"Well, I was hoping to be all ears as you tell me how you 'really' feel about the matter."

"I'm not sure I follow you. Why are you under the impression that I haven't been honest with you?"

"It's not that I don't think you've been honest." I paused for a second and realized that it was me in that moment who wasn't being honest.

"Jason, I love you. I know that you support me either way. I just want to know that later down the line you won't change your mind. I mean what if it becomes too much to bear and you decide to leave me for a younger girl who can help your legacy stay alive."

"What?! Don't ever talk like that. I am not that type of man. I get you being insecure but putting the label of being a selfish-disrespectful cheating two-timing man is an entirely different subject. I would never do that to you. I know what I signed up for and like I said before, I'm here to stay and I accept you as you are. It's me and you baby, Me AND You, together, as one."

Once Jason gave me reassurance, I left the subject alone. And that night we made love for the very first time. It was passionate, better than anything I could have imagined. He took his time and handled me with such care, making sure his tongue touched every part of my body. I felt his love with every stroke, the caress of his hands gently grabbing my ass. He made sure pleasure was the only sound coming from my lips. Jason was incredible.

The next morning on my way to the Center I called Ma. Yes, Jason made me feel very good the night before. Yes, I enjoyed every minute of it, all three times, including this morning but again, being honest with myself, sleeping with him and not being married was weighing heavily on me. There I was again, over-thinking and giving into my negative thoughts.

"Hey Ma, it's LD."

"Hey baby, how are you?"

"I'm good. I'm great now that I know I'm going to be an auntie and he proposed. I'm so happy for Sasha, Ma. We are going to have so much fun planning her baby shower and wedding."

"Don't I know it, sweetie. I've been waiting for both of my girls to settle down and enjoy the bliss of marriage and being fruitful and multiplying."

"Yes, well about that, the topic came up as to me and Jason having kids. I had a serious talk with Jason, Ma. I will admit my insecurities sunk in and I let my feelings show on how I truly felt, I expressed to him that my fear is he would later realize that he does want kids and possibly leave me for someone younger to keep his legacy alive."

"Oh, my child, you're so dramatic. Jason does not come off as that type. And please tell me that you did not insinuate to him that you believed him to be a cheater."

"Ma, I did. But I felt it necessary to be honest."

"Baby, that was too honest."

"You're right but the thing about it is, he was so patient with me. He didn't get upset. We discussed the subject, and he was so reassuring. His gentleness just made me feel secure and so wanted. I made love to him for the first-time last night and now I feel bad about it because we're not married."

"Well, you are human and so is he. And I understand your morals not letting you live that down. You were raised in the church. But you will have to decide which approach you want to take. Now that you've opened pandora's box, he's going to want more. You're beautiful and he's attracted to you in more ways than one. Decide if you're going to continue or wait until marriage. Either way, don't play with the man's emotions."

"Ma, I love you so much. I love that I can talk to you about anything and you're going to give it to me straight. How did I get so lucky to have a loving and supporting Mom like you?"

"Anything for my girls, even if it does make me uncomfortable thinking about you having sex. And because I'm a little uncomfortable, I'm going to switch lanes on you. Your dad and I are moving to the vacation home for about a year."

"What? Why? What's in Malibu that's not in View Park?"

Ma laughed. "Is that a trick question? The water for one. Dad and I are looking for a change of scenery and it makes no sense that we have that beautiful home, overlooking the beach and we only go for weekends at a time. So, we've decided to change it up a bit."

"Okay, so in the meantime, you're just going to leave the house in View Park idle?"

"LD, Malibu isn't Bora Bora. We aren't that far and besides we have two daughters to help us out and stop by the place to check on it."

"Yes, sure Ma whatever you need. I guess you guys getting away isn't such a bad idea. Heck, as a matter of fact it's a great idea. Please have my room ready, I could use a vacation."

"Speaking of which did you get everything squared away with your vacation home?" Ma asked.

"Yes, it's set to close next Thursday. We battled a little with the asking price but in the end, I got what I asked for and some."

"Well, that's good honey. Now I have to make breakfast. I love you and we'll chat later."

When I got to the Center, I could tell that everything was copacetic. I walked in as I normally do, looked at Devin's picture in the lobby, smiled at it and said thank you as I walked by. This was a ritual I performed to make sure I stayed humble, and it also reminded me of why I was doing what I was doing.

Forty-five minutes after arriving and preparing for a meeting with the oncologists, Jason walked in all smiles and of course, I knew why.

"Hey gorgeous." He greeted me with a kiss.

"Good morning. How are you?"

"I'm great, you know that. You hurried out the door fast this morning. I was hoping that we could pick up where we left off."

"Jason, here? Now? You're at work and so am I."

"C'mon now, gorgeous, in a lab coat or out of a lab coat, making you feel good I still reign supreme."

"Oh, is that right? We're sure of ourselves, aren't we?"

"Oh yeah, I definitely earned bragging rights. I made your body quiver this morning. You loved every minute of it."

"You're right, I did. But to keep it real, Jason, we can't continue on."

"What? No, you can't take that back; I waited so long to get there. What's up with the sudden change of heart?"

"Jason, I really don't want us having sex before marriage. I take our relationship seriously and if I want what we have to be blessed then we have to wait until marriage."

Jason took a deep breath and a long pause before responding.

"Okay, I mean you know that we're getting married and it's not like we're sleeping around. But if that is what you want then I have no choice but to respect your wishes. Damn, just turn around for me really quick, I want to get a good look at…" Jason bit his fist as I modeled for him one last time. "Are you sure we can't just have one last rendezvous right here in our office?"

"Jason, no. We have patients fighting for their lives coming in and out of this Center. This is our place of business, now come on before we're late for our first meeting."

I knew I was probably driving a hard bargain after making love to Jason then reneging on the love-making his body craved. But playing my cards right and getting my life back on track the right way was really important to me. Yes, Jason was a man's man who had needs so I knew that I could not put that type of expectation out there for long before he was back in between our sheets begging for more. So, this meant I had to be willing and able to satisfy his needs in other ways. I was going to have to step my game up and rely highly on my feminine energy to get me through. There's power in the femininity of a woman if she knows how to use it right. And I for one sure as hell did.

That night when I got home, I was sure to clean the house and get it smelling just right. The aroma of lavender and jasmine essential oils dominated the air and the sound of jazz played from the ceiling speakers. I was sure to order Jason's favorite--hell he deserved some lobster and steak after being so patient. When I left the Center, I told him to be at my place by 7:00 p.m. and it was 6:30.

Time was ticking and I was almost ready. In my mind, the night was planned perfectly, and I was psyched up. I left the lingerie in the drawer, and his favorite scent of perfume in the bottle, I was careful not to come off as a tease. I slipped into an all-black silk dress, threw my hair up into a messy bun and put on some lightly scented perfume.

The doorbell rang and I was ready to show Jason just how much I appreciated him.

"Hi baby, come in," I said as I opened the door. Jason was six feet one inch tall, as he leaned down to hug me, I could tell by his warm embrace that he was happy to see me.

"Hey gorgeous," he responded walking into the house. "Man, it smells good in here, and it feels so relaxing. What's up? Are we celebrating something?"

"Shush with the twenty-one questions; you'll soon find out." I put my finger over his lips and then his lips met mine. His kisses were sweet like honey, they gave off pleasure that just stuck with you.

"Come here, I have something for you." Taking him by the hand I led him to the kitchen, where his lobster, steak, mashed potatoes, and asparagus were waiting for him.

The element of surprise drove the message home, I wanted him to know our intimacy went well beyond the bedroom and I planned to keep him intrigued.

"Is all of this for me?" Jason asked sitting down at the table.

"Yes baby, all this and more," I said while pouring Jason a glass of Pinot Noir we picked up from Napa while wine-tasting a few weeks prior.

While Jason indulged in one of the best meals, he had all week, I began to express with deepest sincerity my appreciation of the man he was.

"Jason," I began, "I love you. Not just because you helped me get through one of the toughest times of my life and not because you decided to come along the new journey of running the Cancer Treatment Center alongside me. I mean those are a couple reasons why, but my love for you goes deeper than that. I love you because through it all you've been gentle and patient. Your unwavering love and respect for me had me wanting to show you my boundless gratitude in more ways than one. And since passionate lovemaking can't be one of them yet, I've decided to make it one of my priorities to be intimate with you in other ways."

Jason began to speak but I wanted to finish.

"Hold on, baby, I'm not done yet. I know that men have needs and I know how attracted you are to me. So, I feel like it's my duty as your woman to help you through this season of celibacy. I understand it's not going to be easy, so during this time I want to be there for you like you've been there for me. If that's okay with you."

"Wow, I was not expecting that. But yes, you have just let me know that we're in this together. I admire the fact that you care enough to even consider my feelings to such a magnitude. You know most women would just expect you to understand and not give it a second thought but you, you're so graceful about it. Damn, La'Dai, I know where you've been. But I'm going to say it anyway. Where have you been all my life?"

I smiled and told Jason to finish his dinner. Once he was done, we went into the garden and talked about some visions he had for the center. Each one of his ideas were so detailed and well thought out. I saw them coming alive so vividly in my mind.

"You know, babe, I was honestly a little nervous about taking on such a huge responsibility when it came to becoming your partner and opening the Center. I mean who wouldn't be? You're telling a community of people who are fighting for their lives and looking to you as their only hope, to trust you wholeheartedly, that there is in fact light at the end of the tunnel. Being an on-cologist at a hospital is one thing. But taking on an entire Center, becoming the head oncologist, and setting the standards for how their treatments will take place, Jason cared on an entirely different level."

"Well, what made you say yes beyond the shadow of doubt? Because hearing you speak right now tells me that your decision came along with a promise to yourself."

"And you're right. I told myself that if I was going to do this, that I would try with every fiber of my being to not let any patient suffer the way my wife suffered."

"Oh, Jason baby, come here." Jason began to cry uncontrollably; I laid his head on my shoulder and allowed him to be as vulnerable as he wanted to. One part of me knew exactly how he felt due to losing Devin, but another part of me felt like I was unworthy to relate since Devin spared me from watching him suffer. That moment was my time to be there for Jason just as he had been for me. I knew that he loved his wife and he'd expressed to me before how hard that time was for him.

An hour later when Jason was out of the shower, I gave him an hour-long back massage before he fell asleep. Seeing him cry the way he did touched me in a completely different way. I went downstairs and began to think about how I wanted to handle the rest of my life. I vowed not to spend any more time mourning or reliving the past, not even for a moment. I wanted to once and for all come to terms with the way my life unfolded, I learned to fully step into the woman I had become. I was finally in love with her. I was READY. This entire life experience had pushed me into purpose.

Chapter Nineteen

Three months into celibacy and I was feeling good. Jason and I were in the rhythm of our relationship. Conversations came up about moving in together which I knew could not be avoided for long. But for the time being, I put the conversations on pause. Things were going so well at the Center, and I didn't want to lose focus.

"Good morning, everyone," I greeted the team as I walked into our ten-a.m. meeting. "I would like us to focus our attention on Ms. Hunter-Greene. Ms. Hunter-Greene came to Roswell Cancer Center with stage four cancer. In my hand I am holding her latest test results as recent as this morning." I signaled for my assistant to put the results up on the projector.

"Monica, can you please display the copy of Mrs. Hunter-Greene's results for everyone to see."

"Now can anyone tell me what they notice about the results on the left which is when Mrs. Hunter-Greene first began treatment here. How different are the results on the right which were taken earlier this morning? Anyone." I encouraged the team of doctors to speak up.

"From the looks of it she is starting to go into full remission," one of the doctors said.

"That is correct, given the two pictures side by side, it's a no brainer, right?" Everyone in the room began to speak at once in awe and excitement, some even began clapping. We were all very happy for Mrs. Hunter-Greene but my reason for holding the meeting went far beyond relaying the great news. Our team needed to know exactly how we were affecting our patients with their hard work and consistent efforts.

"Okay, everyone simmer down for a moment," I said gaining back control of the overjoyed crowd. "Now due to the fact that Mrs. Hunter-Greene was literally diagnosed with only a month to live when she first started here, I needed to know what changed between then and now. I personally sat down with her, and I asked if I could record her testimony, yes testimony, I use this word because what has happened to her is a true testament to what healing one's mind can do for the rest of the body, even with stage four cancer."

Monica turned the interview with Mrs. Hunter-Greene and me, on the projector. I grabbed my cup of tea and took a seat in the back of the meeting room with Jason. He squeezed my hand as he sat next to me, gave me a wink and a smile before he turned his attention to the video.

The video played for about seven minutes with a Q&A between me and Mrs. Hunter-Greene. The seven minutes mostly consisted of her giving us some background knowledge of who she was, where she came from and how she learned about her cancer diagnosis. Then suddenly the momentum in the room started to change when witnessed Mrs. Hunter-Greene get up out of her seat right in the middle of the interview and start to jump up and down, shouting 'Glory, Glory, Glory, Glory be to God', when I asked her how things were going."

Everyone started to sit upright in their chairs and were completely tuned in. Mrs. Hunter-Greene went on to say, "You know I want to thank this Center for bringing me into remission but

I don't think that God gave you guys the idea for the "Room of Hope" so you can take the glory. So again, I say, "To God be the glory. That room is miraculous, I feel like angels are standing by just ready to help anyone who walks through the doors." She shouted again, "Glory!".

"Trust me, Mrs. Hunter-Greene, there's nothing wrong with that." I said waiting to continue on with the interview.

"Honey let me tell you when I first stepped foot onto these premises, I could already feel a supernatural presence. The atmosphere of this Center has the Holy Spirit up and down these halls. This place is anointed. Now I usually don't speak that way but after everything I've experienced here, I know it to be truth."

"Well, can you tell me what you mean by that, Mrs. Hunter-Greene?"

"Most certainly. Now I remember it being my second time here. I was hopeless and had given up all possibilities of me beating this thing. But then Dr. Jason Maxon changed it all, I guess he knew I needed a change of pace after having just gone through chemo. Chemo just takes so much out of you. He asked me if I would be interested in visiting the "Room of Hope" while I waited for my family. At the time I didn't care where I waited; I just wanted it all to be over. But something happened to me when I stepped foot into that room. The walls were covered with biblical scriptures about healing. The piano worship music playing in the background took hold of me and as I looked around, I began to weep, and I no longer felt like I was in a hospital type setting. I felt like I was in a healing sanctuary. I sat down in one of the most comfortable chairs yet. One lady brought me over a glass of water, told me to put my feet up, while she gave me a head massage."

The team was still deeply engaged in watching the interview, the room was still and quiet as the interview continued on.

"The pain, anxiety, and stress I felt seemed to subside. I was completely relaxed. Then another lady came over to me when that was done and asked me if she could entertain me for about thirty-minutes. I was a bit apprehensive as to what that meant but I said yes anyway. We went into another room, where she and I played a couple games of connect four and we laughed the entire time. You see what that room did was put me in a relaxed state of mind, let me forget all about my trouble and the fact that I was sick. And then laughter was used as another form of medicine which kept me on a natural high for the rest of the evening. Doing this four times a week at your center, and then practicing it at home helped me to heal. I eventually stopped telling myself I was going to die, and I started to tell myself and even feel as though I was going to live. The 'Room of Hope is miraculous, and I believe that's what helped change my life."

When the interview finished, a standing ovation was in order. Jason got up and took his rightful place in front of the room. Thinking back to the night when he wept on my shoulder and told me about his idea of the "Room of Hope", I had no idea that his explanation of it would do the room no justice once it was fully functional.

Jason began speaking, telling everyone in the meeting of where the idea for the Room of Hope came from and how he wished his first wife could have experience holistic treatment at some point in her battle with cancer. Jason was standing proud.

As he spoke, I got the urge to stand up, so I did. I glanced out the floor-to-ceiling window overlooking the 10 freeway. Santa Monica was not too far from the Center. I looked at all the cars going east and west on the freeway, and I couldn't help but think about how Devin managed to think about a plan so great, Devin's legacy was touching lives, the Cancer Treatment Center was functioning exactly how Devin intended for it to.

Looking over my shoulder, I focused my attention back onto

Jason. I thought about the trajectory of my life up until this point. I felt nothing but pure gratitude. I was healthy, happy, and healing.

Once the meeting was over, I went back to my office to plan for the quarterly "Way to Remissions Ball" we decided to incorporate onto the event's calendar. After all, life was worth celebrating. I sat down at my desk and thought about giving the party planner a call but called to check on Sasha instead.

"Hello lovely," she answered.

"Well, hello there, aren't we in a good mood."

"Yes, I would say today is a good day."

"I'm happy to hear that. And how's auntie's baby doing."

"You mean besides driving me to eat pickles and vanilla ice cream all day or draining all of my energy causing me to sleep all day? Oh, auntie's baby is happy and satisfied, it's me that needs some TLC."

I laughed at Sasha trying to complain. I knew damn well she was ecstatic about becoming a mother and everything that came along with it.

"Oh, girl give it a rest. I know better than that. I know Christian is not over there letting you go through it. You're probably lying on the couch with him fanning you with a giant leaf in one hand and feeding you with the other," I teased.

Sasha laughed. "Go ahead, kick me when I'm down. But you're right, the man hasn't let me lift a finger. In fact, he made me take leave early. With good intentions, you know. He says that with the type of work I do he doesn't want the baby experiencing any type of stress. He wants me to be emotionally stable and stress free, he wants a happy baby. Girl, he has me doing meditation and yoga. Eating all these different vegetables. Beets and celery."

"I mean, can you blame him? He's on his J-O-B, as he should be. I really like him Sis, he's a good man."

"I know. I just wonder what took him so long."

"Oh, please Sasha, It's not like you were exactly open. I mean you couldn't keep dating men that were no good for you; something had to give. So, God sent you Christian. God sure does have a funny sense of humor."

"What do you mean?"

"Well, in your single days when I would lecture you about settling down you would always say how it would take God himself to come down here and pair you up with someone. So not only did he send you a Christian man, but his name is Christian."

"Yes, girl sometimes he's too Christian."

"I don't follow you, Sasha."

"So, the man has cut me off until we get married."

"Cut you off?"

"Yes LD, cut me off from sex. Even with this pregnancy, my hormones are raging out of control, and I want him more than ever. He says that he backslid and has since repented to God. He told me that he wants us to be on the right path. I told him it's a little too late; we're pregnant. His rebuttal was 'it's never too late to get right with God.'"

Was Christian reading my mind?

Sasha kept talking, "He gave me some speech about how God's mercy and grace is new every day, and how the important thing is once you realize your wrongdoing and ask for forgiveness, you don't continue on the same path. So, although he had a moment of weakness, he can't allow us both to continue having sex before marriage. Can you believe that?"

"Actually, yes I can."

"You can?"

"I mean, yeah, it's funny that you bring this up. Jason and I have been celibate for the last three months."

"What?!" Sasha exclaimed. "Please explain how any of this makes sense."

"I mean for me, it's something that God put on my heart to do. I personally feel like our situation will be blessed if we choose to walk the right way."

"LD, you're already blessed; look at your life,"

"I hear you, Sis, and you're right, I am. I want those blessings to continue to come and I don't want to take God's mercy and grace for granted, so I'm continuing to try and do things the right way."

"When did you get religious?"

"You remember when Ma would always tell us, "You girls will thank me later, the Bible always says train a child up in the way that he should go, and he will never part.""

"Yeah, how can I forget?" Sasha laughed.

"Let's just say her lectures about fornication have stuck with me, even if I have had a few moments of poor judgment."

"Oh girl, you can't be serious."

"Oh, but I am. Anyway, I think Christian is perfect for you, I love how he's helping you to see things from a different perspective."

"What's wrong with my perspective?"

"Oh nothing, let's just say sometimes seeing things with a fresh pair of eyes helps to shine light on some things that were once overshadowed with darkness."

"My gosh, I can see you and Christian now trying to form some type of alliance. Well, let me say this, Batman, I hope you and Robin are just as supportive at three a.m. when this baby decides to wake up crying, and I need some sleep."

"What? I'm sorry. All of sudden my phone is breaking up."

"So how are things at the Center?" Sasha asked.

"Things are great which is why I called you. We are having our first semi-annual Way to Remission Ball to celebrate our patients who are showing an active road to recovery. We want to honor these patients and allow their friends and family to come together to celebrate their lives and the long journey they are overcoming."

"That's awesome, LD."

"Thank you, so it will be on the 16th, three weeks from now, at the Center in the Events hall that we have here. You and Christian be sure to wear the colors lavender, pink, orange, or blue. Those colors represent the fight against the cancer, each color is specific to the type of cancer the patients' are being set free from. Lavender symbolizes the fight against all cancers so that's the color I'll be in, just FYI."

"LD, I have to admit. I never thought I would see this side of you. This side of you is totally different from the real estate side of you."

"Thank you, Sis."

"But look, I have to go, so remember the 16th. And let Christian know asap just in case you get pregnancy brain and forget," I teased.

"Oh, shut up heffa and goodbye. And by the way, maybe you should send me an invite so I can put it on my calendar, that's what phones are for."

I hung up from Sasha and immediately called the event planner. This one came highly recommended by the mayor's assistant. She told me that she used this company for all major events that the mayor's office hosted.

Three weeks flew by, in between getting ready for the event and checking in on Sasha every other day--who recently had a pregnancy scare by falling down the stairs--I was one busy chick.

The day was here, from checking the tablecloths and centerpieces to adding last minute names to the guest list, I was beginning to sweat. Lucky for me, I was not dressed just yet.

"Monica, do me a favor. When the press gets here, show them exactly where to set up," I directed my assistant. "Also make sure that the videographer knows where she should set up as well. Oh, one more thing, please be sure to put an extra pitcher of water at Sasha's table. I need to make sure she stays hydrated. Thank you, doll."

Jason walked in from his last-minute briefing with the on-cologists who were being recognized for their excellence. I could not have been happier to see him.

"How it is going in here, gorgeous?" he asked.

"Good baby, I'm happy to see you. I need your help."

"Of course, let me say good job picking the event planner. Everything in here is set up nicely. We did it."

"It's a little too early for a victory lap; the night is still young. But I do agree they've set up the place nicely. They definitely exceeded my expectations."

Midway through the ceremony everything was going as expected. Smiles on faces, cameras flashing, and music that made you get up out of your seat. Patients enjoy the company of their family and staff alike. Jason worked the room engaging with everyone. I even saw Sasha take a few photos with patients while letting them rub her belly for good luck.

I was starting to feel a little light-headed, I grabbed a chair next to Ma and Dad and sat down to try and eat something.

"Well, hello, Super Woman. I believe this is the first time that I've seen you sit down all night. And might I add that everything is put together so nicely. Honey, your Dad and I couldn't be prouder."

"Yes, and I know for a fact that Devin is smiling down on you now, baby girl," Dad added.

"Thank you, I want nothing more than for his legacy to live on." I stood up ready to bring the ceremony to an end.

"LD, are you okay? You don't look so good all of a sudden."

"Yes Ma, I'm fine. I think I just stood up too fast. I got a little

light-headed. I'll be fine. I'm going to go up on stage and announce the end of the ceremony."

"Okay honey, are you sure that you don't want to take a drink
of water first?" Dad asked, sounding concerned.

"No Dad, I'll be fine."

Jason was over talking with Sasha and Christian, I signaled
him to start heading over to the stage.

Just as I took the last step at the top of the stairs leading to the
stage, my vision went blurred, then black and I could no longer
hold myself up. I could hear Sasha's voice call out my name in the
distance, as my body hit the floor.

Before I opened my eyes, I could hear chatter and I felt a
strong presence on the right side of me. My head was throbbing,
and I realized I was no longer at the ceremony. My vision was still
a little blurred as I opened my eyes. I saw Ma and Dad standing
next to me and Jason was sitting on my left. I was laying in one of
the vacant outpatient rooms at the Center.

Rubbing the side of my head, I looked over to Jason and asked
what happened. He immediately stood up and came closer to my
bedside.

"Hey gorgeous, you scared the shit out of me. Excuse my language, I just…" Jason began to explain to my parents.

"No need to explain. We're all adults here and we were thinking the same thing, you just said it." Dad gave Jason a smile of
reassurance.

"Baby, you fainted," Ma said.

"I did?"

"Yes, you did, I knew you didn't look too good when you
stood up." Ma grabbed my hand.

"I must have over-exerted myself; I was fine all day long. I
mean I know I probably waited too long to eat but not to the
point where I would become faint."

"You hit the ground pretty hard, Sasha was one of the first ones to run to your rescue besides me," Jason informed me.

"Sasha, where is she?" I asked.

"We sent her home; she was too shaken up. We wanted to be sure she did not stress herself out or the baby. So, I told her to go home and try to relax. We would call her when you came to. I couldn't risk both of my babies in here falling out," Ma said, grabbing my hand even tighter.

"I'm going to have Dr. Lumbardie come in and check you out. I checked your vitals earlier and they seemed fine, but I want him to do blood work on you STAT." Jason headed towards the door.

"Jason, no. I know that by nature you feel a need to try and diagnose me, but I will decide which doctor I want to see. Yes, I fainted, but you said my vitals are fine. So, I'm just going to take it easy until I'm able to see my primary care doctor."

"Okay, that's your choice and I respect it, but I'm worried about you so please let's make that appointment as soon as possible."

"You have my word," I said promising Jason that I would take care of it.

I chose to take a week and a half off. I spent the first couple of days contemplating what happened and searching google trying to self-diagnose. That was only driving me crazy, so I went over to Sasha and spent a couple days with her. Eating ice cream, preparing the nursery, and putting our ideas together for the baby shower got me back to feeling normal. I knew it made no sense to try and figure out why I fainted without seeking professional help first so I stopped searching for answers. The leisure time spent with Sasha definitely helped me to calm my nerves.

The following Tuesday I returned to the Center, and it felt amazing to be back. I walked in refreshed and ready to go.

"Hi Mrs. Roswell. I'm glad to see you," David yelled out from the security station.

"Likewise, how are you this morning?"

"As good as can be expected," he responded with a huge smile on his face.

"Good, enjoy your day and thank you for keeping us safe."

"Not a problem."

As I entered into my office, the aroma of fresh flowers filled the air. There were several dozen bouquets of flowers spread out in different areas of my office—ranging from roses to tulips to lilies. Balloons that read "Welcome back" floated around and I was in awe.

About three minutes later a host of my team came busting in the door with donuts, coffee, and orange juice.

"Hey, welcome back," they all began to say at once.

"Thank you, thank you. What is all of this?"

"We missed you while you were out, so we decided to do something nice upon your return," one of the nurses responded.

"Well, I truly appreciate it."

"This isn't all, we have lunch being catered today at twelve-thirty."

"That's wonderful. Can we do an early lunch and make it eleven? I have a doctor's appointment at one."

"Sure thing, whatever you want, your wish is our command."

"You're too kind, and again. Thank you all."

I spent another fifteen minutes catching up with everyone before I was alone in my office checking my emails.

Reading the host of get-well emails came with a sense of gratitude and appreciation. I was overjoyed to learn that I had so many people wishing me well and praying for me. It was another confirmation that I was doing something right.

After eating lunch and being surrounding by such positivity

with my staff, I was on an emotional high. I wore a smile on my face that said I didn't have a care in the world, until my calendar alarm went off reminding me that my doctor's appointment was in fifteen minutes.

The last fifteen minutes of my drive to the appointment felt like thirty. I went back and forth in my head from thinking I was going to be okay to thinking the worst-case scenario. I played the conversation in my head of what the doctor would tell me and how I would react if it was bad news. Then I came to my senses and realized that I was healthy as a horse and talked myself off the ledge but not before I talked myself back to reality and reminded myself that sickness and disease are not prejudiced. Trying to calm myself down I turned on some smooth jazz and spent the last five minutes of my drive slowly counting to one-hundred and fifty, desperately trying to quite my mind.

The doctor's office was surprising slow, only two other patients were in the lobby besides me.

"Good morning, Mrs. Roswell. I'm already checking you in, you can have a seat," the receptionist informed me.

"Thank you, Janice, you're always on it."

I picked up a magazine in a continued effort to remain calm. Not wanting my blood pressure reading to be high. I wasn't in the lobby for more than five minutes before my name was called by the LVN.

"Mrs. Roswell, we're ready for you."

This is exactly why I loved coming to Dr. Salvache's office, although I knew him on a personal level from graduating high school together. He was definitely doing his thing. He graduated med school and was brave enough to start his own private practice. Judging from the celebrities that I'd seen in here on occasion, the man wasn't doing too bad, and neither was his practice. Organized, clean, and they took confidentiality to a whole new level.

After the nurse did the routine intake, my weight, blood pressure, temperature and all that good stuff, she took me into the evaluation room where I was given a nice cold bottle of water. I turned down the tea, not wanting the caffeine to give me the jitters. Sitting down in the lounge chair next to the evaluation table, I patiently waited. I guess I had fallen asleep because I didn't hear Dr. Salvache come into the room.

"Good morning, getting a little nap in, are we?"

"I guess so, you know it's not hard to do. You have it set up so nicely in here you almost forget that you're in a doctor's office."

"Well, LD, that's the point, I don't want you guys to be on edge while you're here. I'm here to maintain your health not to disrupt it."

"And that's exactly why I love you."

He laughed before asking me what brought me in.

"A week and a half ago, I fainted. I hit the ground face first at our first event, in a room full of people."

"I get that you may have been embarrassed but I'm happy you didn't get a concussion or crack your front teeth—only that lingering bruise. Now let me take a look at you."

He put his stethoscope in the middle of my back and told me to take three deep breaths. He then examined my eyes and ears.

"So, looking at your vitals and evaluating you, you seem to be okay, but I don't want to stop there. I'm going to ask you a few questions about how you've been feeling lately. Then I'm going to put in a couple for blood. I don't want to miss anything. Now besides the obvious stress of managing a new Cancer Treatment Center, what else has been going on in your world?"

I spent another forty-five minutes at the doctor's office. I never liked needles so having my blood drawn almost sent me over the top. When I was done with my appointment, the range of emotions I felt throughout the day had me feeling exhausted. I decided to take the rest of the day off and head home.

Walking through the doorway, taking off my heels and laying on the couch, I grabbed the remote but T.V. wasn't on my mind, it was wine-thirty. I got up, went into the kitchen, and poured myself a glass of Robert Mondavi Cabernet Sauvignon. I thought, hell it's five o' clock somewhere.

I sat back down on the couch and took a big gulp of wine, let out a long sigh of relief and threw my head back. It wasn't long before my phone rang; it was Jason probably wondering what happened at the doctor's office.

"Hey gorgeous, how are you?"

"I'm doing better now that I'm home."

"Oh, good you decided to take the rest of the day off. Well, what did the doctor say?"

"On the surface he says that everything looks normal, he's tying the fainting spell to stress and anxiety along with my recent poor eating habits."

"Stress? What are you stressed and anxious about?"

"I mean we did just have that big event. Jason, I know these emotions are temporary. I believe they came from the pressure of wanting everything to turn out perfectly, but the good thing is the event is over and I can move forward so I don't anticipate kissing the ground anymore."

"I hear you, but I mean is that it?"

"What more should there be? I'm young and healthy. Always have been, I don't think me fainting was anything more than just a moment of being overwhelmed. Dr. Salvache did order a few tests just to be sure but I'm confident that they will come back normal."

"You're holding out on me, girl. That's what I wanted to hear— that he went the extra mile to be sure. Well, that's good news; you should have the results back in a couple of days if not sooner?"

"Yes, but like I said, I'm sure they will come back normal."

"Good, because I couldn't imagine running this Center without you by my side, I couldn't imagine going through life without you by my side."

"Lucky for you, you don't have to imagine either."

"I'm going to wrap up here around six, what would you like for dinner? Do you want me to pick something up or did you want me to make us a nice meal at home?"

"Let's go out and eat, I feel like being social."

"Alright, be ready about seven, I'll pick you up."

Finishing my glass of wine, I thought about what I was going to put on. I knew I wanted to get dolled up but still be casual too. I put on some mood music and hopped into the shower. My goal was to refresh, revitalize, and renew. Clearing my head and allowing my imagination to run wild as the warm drops of water hit my body, relaxing my mind and muscles. Just then I thought that it would be a good idea for us to just go to a nice tavern in Santa Monica, then walk the beach.

I put my head up in a cute ponytail, and painted my face with a light coat of make up... I always loved a nice natural look. I pulled out a cute Nike number, me in leggings was one of Jason's favorites.

As I finished putting on my shoes, I could hear my phone vibrating across the room. I knew it either had to be Jason or Sasha. Most likely Sasha because it was too early for Jason to be on his way. To my surprise it was Dr. Salvache.

"Hello," I answered somewhat perplexed.

"Hello LaDai, it's Dr. Salvache."

"Hey, what's going on? Did I miss doing one of the labs you ordered?"

"Actually, that's why I'm calling, concerning one of your labs. I got one of your tests back and I want to go over the results with you. Can you come to the office first thing tomorrow morning?"

"Doctor, you're making me nervous. There's no way I can stay in suspense until tomorrow morning. Can I just come now?"

"You know what, for you, yes. I'll be finishing up with my last patient so you may have to wait a moment before I call you to the back."

"Not a problem, I'm on my way."

When I hung up, I could not move. In a daze I stared at the wall in front of me. Should I call Jason and let him know what was going on, I was trembling. Not knowing what to expect I got in my car and headed for the doctor's office.

"Hello, LD, my apologies for keeping you waiting." Dr. Salvache said walking into the room. "I called you back because one of your labs came back positive. Now I have a better explanation as to why you may have fainted. I know that what I'm about to tell you may come as a surprise to you bu…".

"But what?" I interjected. "Doctor Salvache, please just give it to me straight. I went through enough mental torment on the way here."

"Well, the reason why you fainted is because you…"

As the words came rolling off of Dr. Salvache's tongue, I was in complete and utter shock. Every word he spoke from that point forward was falling on deaf ears. I just stared at him like he was an alien from out of space.

"LD, are you with me?"

"Yeah, yeah. How did this happen?" I looked up at him trying to keep my cool. "I mean how could I not have known sooner?"

"LD, you are not the first to experience this and you will not be the last. I know you're in shock right now, but I want you to keep an open mind."

"Open mind? I don't think you understand how this news is going to change my entire life. I mean how exactly am I supposed to move forward when all this time I thought that something like this could never happen to me."

"I need you to stay calm, let me get you a drink of water. I will be right back."

When he left the room, I began to cry. I began to cry uncontrollably. Just when everything was on track and going right, just when I had my emotions in check.

"Here you go." He handed me the cup of water with a look of compassion in his eyes. "Listen this is not the end of the world so please stop crying. I will be here to help you every step of the way. Now you understand I have to get you over to a different doctor, but I will still be here for you. I know you may have some reservations. But I also know you will work through those."

"I'm sorry, but can you do the test again? Just to be sure. I can't believe this."

"Sure, we can do another test if that will help ease your mind."

"Yes, it will."

"Okay, I'm putting in the order for the test now. I want you to go down to the lab and when I get the results back, I will call you. In the meantime, I want you to go home, try to calm yourself down and relax. From this point on your health is priority number one, even your mental health."

I looked up at Dr. Salvache, wiped my tears away, and with great seriousness said, "I can trust that you will be discreet with this, right? Not a word to anyone, not even the nursing staff."

"Done, not a problem," he responded.

Leaving Dr. Salvache's office, I was coming upon Kenneth Hahn Park. I decided to pull over and try to compose myself. I thought that a little fresh air could not hurt.

As I parked, Jason was calling. I totally forgot about our dinner date. I could not stop crying. There was no way I was going to be able to see him, looking or feeling the way I was. I thought about maintaining distance from Jason to resist divulgence, but I knew damn well he would not go for that.

"Hi babe," I answered trying to sound unbothered.

"Hey, I'm headed your way. I'm leaving the center now."

"Umm, I was just getting ready to call you. I'm not feeling so hot. I think I drank too much wine. I am going to sleep it off. I won't be of any good company so I was thinking that you should sleep at your place tonight."

"Okay," he responded sounding suspicious. "Are you sure you're okay? I'll be happy when they come back with those test results."

"Oh, the doctor called earlier, he told me that all the results came back normal, they're still waiting on one, but he said he's confident that it will come out to be the same." I lied straight through my teeth.

"That's good to hear, why didn't you call me and tell me? I've been sitting on pins and needles."

"Since he didn't give me any significant news, I was just going to tell you at dinner."

"Makes sense. Well, I'm going to head home. I want you to get some rest and call me if you need anything, I don't care what time it is."

"Okay, I'm going to let you go now."

Getting out of the car, I felt like I was having an outer body experience. I kept replaying Dr. Salvache's words over in my mind. The sun was out and there was a slight breeze. Kenneth Hahn Park wasn't too far from Mom and Dad's. Mom would be the only person that I could trust with this information, and she would be the only person I was going to tell.

I knew I could trust Sasha, but I didn't want to overwhelm her--preparing to be a first-time mom was doing that already.

Sitting on the nicely cut grass, I crossed my legs Indian style, put my hands together and looked up to the sky before I began to pray.

Inhaling and exhaling deeply, I let whatever came to my mind flow off my tongue. Emotions were running high; my feelings were ardent and I was desperate for my prayer to be heard.

I started singing We the Kingdom's lyrics to Holy Water. God, I'm on knees again, God begging please again I need you, Oh God, I need you. I don't want to abuse your grace, God, I need it every day, it's the only thing that makes me really want to change. Praying out loud, I said:

> *"Dear God,*
> *I hope you can hear me right now. I need your guidance, I need your wisdom and understanding because what I'm facing right now isn't making any sense to me. I know that I'm supposed to trust in you and lean not on my own understanding, but I'm scared. Lord, please give me the strength to get through this. I know you have your reasons for everything but this one has thrown me completely off guard. And I know I'm blessed to have a man like Jason who's going to be right there every step of the way but that doesn't mean that the uncertainties don't cloud my judgment just a little. Right now, I'm asking for peace of mind, and courage because I know that if you are with me, I will not fail. In Jesus name. Amen."*

I sat there for a moment wiping my tears away. I observed everyone walking by and I couldn't help but think for a moment how lucky they were in that moment to be at perfect peace, at least those were the images being portrayed. Fifty feet to my right there were two teenage girls taking turns taking pictures of themselves. And rightfully so, they were pretty girls. Ahh, to be young again and worry free. I envied their innocence.

One-hundred feet to my left was a couple who seemed to be so in love. I didn't envy them, I was blessed to have found love twice. It was at this moment that my guilty conscience was starting to catch up to me. I knew that I was wrong for trying to avoid Jason. I knew that I could not jeopardize the trust in our relationship by withholding this important information. It was time for me to pull myself together and head to View Park to get some sound advice from Ma.

Walking into the kitchen, I could smell Dad's famous chicken casserole cooking.

"Hey Dad," I said, greeting him with a kiss.

"Hey baby girl, what you up to? Where's Jason?"

"I had a few errands to run, so he's finishing up at the office then heading home."

"Oh good, so does that mean you're staying for dinner? It would be nice, you know."

"That's not a bad idea, yes Dad I'm going to stay for dinner."

It had been a while since I had dinner at my parents' home, quite frankly I missed Dad's cooking.

Ma walked into the kitchen took one look at me and as much as I tried to hide it, she knew something was wrong. I knew exactly what she would say if I tried to deny it. Her words would be, "Baby, when you share a body for nine months and spend every day of your life raising that little person, there isn't anything that they can get past you."

And Mama was right, she knew me better than I knew myself.

"LD, hi honey. It's good to see you."

"You too, Mama." I embraced her with a hug and held her tight.

"Are you up for a cocktail while we wait for Dad to finish dinner?"

"I'll take some tea, Ma, I need to calm my nerves a little."

"Baby, you have to slow down, stress is not good for you."

"I know, Ma."

"I'm going to pour myself a cocktail and I'll make you some tea, go and have a seat in the den, baby girl. Put your feet up and relax. I'll be right there with our drinks."

"Dinner will be ready in twenty," Dad yelled out.

The atmosphere at my parents' house was serene. As soon as I sat down on the recliner, I closed my eyes in an attempt to get a quick meditation session in, but I fell asleep instead. Ten minutes of sleep felt like an hour, that quick snooze was exactly what I needed. If it wasn't for Ma waking me up, I could have slept for the rest of the evening.

"Here you go, baby, be careful it's hot."

"Thank you, Ma." I said grabbing the cup of tea and sitting up in the recliner.

She sat on the couch next to me. "Now, we aren't going to waste time with small talk. Tell me what's going on, baby girl,"

"Well, I went to see Dr. Salvache. He did a few blood tests to try and figure out why I fainted. He called me back to his office to tell me about one of the tests that came back positive."

"Positive for what?"

When I told Ma the news, she couldn't hold back the tears. She pulled me into her embrace and kissed me on the forehead.

"Oh honey, God is in control, and everything happens for a reason. I know you may fear the unknown but just like we've been here for your sister, we will always be here for you. Have you told Jason what's going on yet?"

"No, I just found out before I came here. I'm a mess right now and I don't want to alarm him. It's all about deliverance and timing, you know."

"Right, I will help you tell him. Give me a couple of days, let's get through planning Sasha's shower and then we will take care of putting Jason in the loop."

"Okay Ma."

"I'm just speechless, but I will tell you that although this is unexpected, and I know you had your own beliefs about this, apparently God had other plans. Trust him, baby."

"That's all I can do."

"LD, it's not the end of the world. Now come on and let's go eat dinner."

As good as Dad's casserole was, I did not have much of an appetite. After we ate, I headed home and climbed into bed. Waking up the next morning, I was happy Saturday was here. I looked over onto the nightstand where my cellphone was, I had three missed calls. Two from Jason and one from Sasha. I knew my conversation with Sasha would be brief, she was probably just wondering what time I would be over. So, I called her back first. Once I was done, I called Jason.

"Good morning, babe."

"Good morning, gorgeous. You must have really been tired, I called you twice."

"I know; I saw that. How are you?"

"I'm good now that I'm talking to you. So, what's on the agenda today? I talked to Sasha, and I told her that we will be over about noon to plan the shower. Christian is going to put some meat on the grill, and she said they'll have the game on."

"Okay, sounds good, I'm going to go and get a haircut, then I'll head to your place. I'm just going to shower and get dressed there."

"Right, I'll see you soon."

I hung up the phone and tried not to feel guilty about not telling Jason what was going on with me. About an hour and a half later Jason was at my place and we were off to Sasha's.

When we got there, Christian was on the grill as promised,

Jason grabbed a beer and joined him outside where the TV was on.

Back in the house Sasha had her feet kicked up on the couch, rubbing her belly.

"Look at you, all barefoot and pregnant."

"I know, right? So, Ma called, and she told us to get started without her."

"Okay, so since we know it's going to be a boy, that narrows down the color scheme."

"Yes, I was thinking that we could…"

Just then Sasha's phone rang, and before she answered it on speaker, she said, "Give me a second, Sis."

"Hello."

"Hello Sasha." The voice on the other end spoke.

"Who is this?"

Sasha's voice became serious, and her tone was stern. Although the call caught her off guard, she took full control of the situation.

"Who this is isn't important, what I'm about to say is. You're going to give the word for the cops to stop looking for the missing evidence on your dad's case. And you're going to tell the cops to back off the Mexican Mafia. And you're going to have the prosecution take the death penalty off the table. I would hate for anything to happen to that new addition of yours. Besides we could use him to keep your father's lineage alive."

"Look, you son of a bitch, I may be on maternity leave but that doesn't mean that I won't come looking for your ass. Did you forget the power that I have with my father's blood running through my veins? I can be just as heartless as he is. Now this is your only warning Jackass. Don't call my phone threatening me again. Or I will come find you, rip your heart out, and send it to your mother as a Valentine's Day gift. You got me?"

Sasha hung up the phone and I couldn't believe what I had

just heard from her and the guy on the other end of the phone. Sasha let out a loud scream of frustration and made a phone call.

"Hey Brian, it's me. Please tell me I kept him on long enough for you to trace the call."

"Good, I know what the boss said but keep me in the loop anyway. I want these bastards bad, along with the leak."

"Sasha, what is going on? I thought you washed your hands of your father's case." I asked.

"Well, I did, it turns out that no one was as passionate as I was in their efforts to make sure he paid for what he did. Since I've been off the case, evidence has come up missing, prison guards have changed their minds on testifying and the prosecution's case has weakened while the defense's case has strengthened."

"Sasha, that guy didn't sound like he was making idle threats."

"And he wasn't, which is why we have to catch him and the leak within the LAPD who's been helping the Mexican Mafia. They're paying off cops and judges and we are close to shutting that shit down for good."

"Sasha, I don't know how you do it."

"Yeah, there are some days I ask myself that same question. But enough of that, let's get back to planning this shower."

I ended up at the first praise and worship service at Church the next morning. I needed a renewed mind and softened heart for what I was up against. I needed God to speak to me.

Times like this I missed Devin. It was something about having that familiar voice to talk with that made me wonder what he would say at a time like this.

I went back over to Ma and Dad's after Church and laid poolside. Dad came out with some sandwiches and joined me.

"Hey baby girl, Mom told me what's going on with you. How are you feeling?"

"Church was refreshing and I'm coming around. Dad, it's times like this that I miss Devin. May I be honest with you?"

"Yes."

"Dad, I know Devin was trying to protect me from what he thought the burden of his illness would cause but I just wished it didn't not have to end the way it did. And for the life of me I feel like we could have gotten through things together if he hadn't spent his last dying days with Sage. I wish that…."

"LD let me stop you right there. Stop wishing and let things be. Honey, you have started life all over, don't waste your second chance by living in the past trying to get answers to questions that you already have the answers to. Just because you can't accept the truth doesn't mean there's another explanation. Keep moving forward, LD."

My feelings were a little hurt by Dad's attitude, but he was right. I needed to keep pushing forward.

Chapter Twenty

*A*nswering my phone with an overjoyed tone, it was months since I'd talked to Devin's mother.

I had not spoken to her since a couple of weeks after the funeral. She lived in Texas and had a life of her own. Devin's mom was young at heart, aging pretty well, vibrant and full of life.

"Hi, Mama Roswell," I answered.

"Hi baby, how are you holding up?"

"I have my days."

"Chile, don't I know it. Well listen, I'm standing on your doorstep and I've been ringing the doorbell for quite some time, do you mind coming to open the door?"

"You're at my house, right now?"

"Yes, chile, that's what I just said."

"Why didn't you tell me that you were coming?"

"Well, it would not have been a surprise had I done that."

"I'm not home butttt since you're at my house I'll be on my way. There is a keypad on the door, the code is Devin's birthdate with the number 7 at the end. Make yourself comfortable and I'll be there shortly. I am so happy you are here. I can't wait to see you."

Although Mama Roswell lived in another state, we would always make it a point to go and see her or bring her out to see us when Devin was alive. After Devin's father passed away, she never remarried. It was now thirteen years since his father's death.

Arriving at home, I could smell the aroma of chili beans coming from the kitchen. Mama Roswell's Southern homecooked meals made my taste buds sing. During my drive home, I contemplated telling Mama Roswell about Jason and me. I decided against it; I just wanted to enjoy her company.

"Mama!" I ran into the kitchen and gave her a big hug.

"Hey baby."

"You got it smelling so good in here," I said, peeking in on the pot of chili beans.

"Well, I know my chili beans is your favorite and was Devin's favorite too, so I thought that we would sit down and catch up over a pot."

"No argument here."

"Let me fix us some of my favorite tea; I want to have a chat with you," Mama Roswell said walking over to the kitchen cabinet.

She and I had not had a deep conversation since Devin's death. Even before his death, she and I did not have a chance to talk. I never pondered whether or not she knew what was going on with us. She was out of state, by herself and the last thing I wanted was for Devin and me to stress her out with news of the divorce, having her all worried with our nonsense. So, I never mentioned a word of it when she would call but I wondered had Devin.

"So," she said sitting down at the dining room table handing me a cup of tea.

"So," I replied.

"How are you really holding up, suga?"

"Mama, it's hard. I miss him every single, moment of every single day. Devin was all I knew. He was my world. And I regret not spending the last months of his life expressing that to him; will I ever feel whole again?" I said beginning to cry.

"Yes, you will, honey. Because I am going to help you. Remember I too lost my husband and not only that, but Devin would have wanted you to. You continuously wanted to make him happy so why stop now? You're going to keep pressing forward with Jason and the two of you are going to run the Cancer Treatment Center in your husbands' honor."

A peculiar look came over my face. I had no idea that she knew about Jason.

"Mama Roswell, you know about Jason?" I asked in amazement.

"Of course, dear. Devin was my only child; you know he never kept anything from me."

"The Cancer Treatment Center–I get you knowing everything about it but knowing about Jason and knowing that we're running the Center together. How?"

"Yes, that's what I wanted to talk to you about. When Devin was diagnosed with cancer, he called me from his car while he was still parked at the hospital. I could hear the fear in his voice. He explained to me that he did not have much time to live. He said that for quite some time he had not been feeling right but was living in denial. Not only that, but he also loved you and did not want anything slowing you down. I did not know the severity of the situation until he flew me out the next day and I saw the test results."

"You came out here? When?"

"Yes, my dear. Devin put me up in the penthouse suite of a hotel and I stayed for a week. We did not tell you because Devin said he needed to carefully plan out how you would be taken care of after he was gone. He knew that I would be against not telling you, he knew that one look into your eyes, and I would sing like a canary. That's why he put me up in a hotel. So…he would come to the hotel every day while I stayed there. We would have dinner and go over the arrangements. LD, it wasn't easy for me but it's what my son wanted and with the state of his health hanging on by a wing and a prayer, I had no choice but to go along with whatever he wanted."

"Mama, please don't feel a need to explain. I know Devin was your baby. And I know that you would have done anything for him. Please understand that I don't take it personal."

"Well, I'll go on. He let me know that he was going to ask you for a divorce. He also knew that once he did, you would not have been interested in finding love and starting over. The result of heartbreak would have kept you stuck. The idea of finding you a match that he approved of came from him wanting you to move on with the perfect man. A man that was not going to take advantage of your vulnerability. Not only that, but he also explained the man had to be someone who was well established and not easily taken back by your beauty. Devin said, in order for you to be able to move on and fulfill bringing the cancer treatment center to life, the man had to be a real standup guy, someone he knew could handle you."

"Since his death, you're the second person to tell this."

"Yes, we planned it together. Devin mentioned you need constant reminders and validation. La'Dai honey stop second guessing yourself so much. He was hell bent on making sure you were taken care of from every angle, it's okay to live happy again. Devin had no idea that you and Jason had already met when he set out to put his plan into motion. It wasn't until after a couple of Devin's visits with Jason as his oncologist that he learned about you two."

"I don't understand."

"Well, let me explain. When Devin was diagnosed, he asked to be assigned to a black doctor. He felt like a doctor of his peers would understand his approach to the situation—his approach of wanting to die with dignity and self-respect. He said that he worked his entire life to be a man of strength and honor; he didn't want to spend his dying days in and out of the hospital, clinging to machines and not living his life as he wanted. He felt like only a black man could relate to that. Devin was assigned to Jason as his doctor. After a few visits with Jason, Devin finally asked him about his life story; he wanted background information. When Devin learned that Jason lost his wife to cancer and wanted to eventually own his own practice in honor of her, Devin said he knew Jason was the one. Not only had he gone through what you were about to go through BUT he was already established financially AND he was on the same train of thought as Devin. They were on the same wavelength. I remember that day vividly because Devin came to my hotel room, excited. I did not know anyone who would have been that excited after a chemo visit. But he explained that he thought he had met the perfect match for you. And he told me that he was going to propose his plan to Jason. Devin asked my advice on how he should approach the situation because he did not want Jason to think he was psychotic. Devin and I prayed about it and I told him to leave it in God's hands–he would make a way."

"Mama, I'm speechless. Every time I hear how he planned everything out for me, I fall in love with him all over again."

"Honey, don't I know it; he was exceptional. But I'm not finished. Apparently, the day Devin was going to propose his plan to Jason, during his visit, Jason wanted to pick Devin's brain about a woman he had met."

"What?!"

"Yes, Devin called me that night and said Mama, our prayer worked. God is working everything out. I said 'son, slow down; tell me what you're talking about.' I could tell that he was pacing back and forth in excitement on the other end of the phone.

He was breathing heavy and there was a lot of movement. Devin went on to say, "Today during my visit, just before I was getting ready to bring up my plan to Dr. Maxon, he said to me, 'I don't mean to be all in your business, but can I ask you a question?' Devin explained that Jason wanted his advice on a woman that he had taken to dinner. He said that Jason was embarrassed at first to come out and ask him because he usually did not engage with his patients in that manner." Mama Roswell gabbed my hand as she finished telling the story.

"But he felt compelled to ask Devin his opinion. Jason explained that he met this beautiful woman who was also intelligent and ambitious and had taken her on a date. The only issue was she was going through a divorce, and he felt like he wasn't able to get through to her. Devin asked what she did for a living and Jason responded real estate--one conversation led to another and Devin found out that the woman Jason was talking about was you. Devin told Jason all about the plan he had and why he was going about it the way that he was. He said at first Jason was apprehensive because he didn't want to mislead you or start your relationship off in dishonesty. But Devin explained to him that he knew you better than anyone on earth and to trust him, this was the best way to go about it."

I was crying tears of joy. I still had nothing to say. Nothing. Even after his death, Devin never ceased to amaze me.

"Oh my gosh, I was completely wrong about Devin. I'm finding out more of the truth after his death than when he was alive. Had I known all of this I would have approached things completely different."

"Honey, it was meant to be how it was. Devin knew you would try to stop him, and that would have only been a distraction. You know your husband, my son was a forward thinker, focused, and determined. He wanted nothing standing in the way of making sure you continued on with your life. He said to me, 'Mama, I made a vow to love, honor, cherish, and protect her. Even if that means protecting her in her time of grief long after I'm in my grave."

"Mama Roswell, this is all too much. I loved Devin with every fiber of my being. What am I supposed to do now?"

"Live honey, live! You're going to get it together and LIVE ON. Don't let everything Devin did for you on his deathbed go in vain because you're still holding on to what was. It's okay to grieve. I'm here to help you with that. But I can't make you want to live; you have to find the strength to push forward yourself."

"Thank you for raising such a beautiful, loving, sensitive, and caring man."

"His father was the same way; that's why it was hard for me to move on after his death. No man could fill his shoes. Until recently when I met Stanley."

"Stanley?" I asked.

"Yes, Stanley. He was pursuing me for some time but I'm a prize, darling, and I have too much going for myself to be out here trying to teach a grown man how to be a ladies' man. He's never been married so I had to whip him into shape. Now he's the head pastor at our church."

"That's right, Mama," I said giving her a high five.

Mama Roswell was no joke. A true gem. Both her husband and son preceded her in death, and she still managed to keep it together. Besides Ma, she was one of the strongest women I knew. Truth be told between her, Ma and Sasha, I was surrounded by beautiful, strong black women. They knew how to ride the tides of life one wave at a time, coming out on top every step of the way. I hoped to one day develop that type of strength.

Thirty minutes into Mama Roswell giving me all the juicy details about her and Mr. Stanley. My doorbell rang.

I looked at Mama Roswell, "I'm not expecting any company, are you?"

"No, I'm not, I just got here. But I'll get the door."

I could hear Mama Roswell opening the door, whoever was at the door was familiar because I could hear her saying hello in a calm tone, oddly I didn't hear them responding. Soon after the moment of silence, Jason, Sasha, Ma and Dad all came walking into the kitchen.

"This is another surprise; what are you guys all doing here. What's up?"

Sasha responded, "We were in the neighborhood and saw Mama Roswell's rental car as we were driving by, so we decided to join the party."

"Oh, whatever Sasha." I assumed Mama Roswell invited them over since she was in town, which was no surprise, we were all close knit. Mine and Devin's marriage really brought us all together.

I got up and embraced everyone with a hug. When I got to Ma, she held me a little tighter and a little longer. I guess she could tell I had been crying. We all spent the next hour eating chili beans and having casual conversation over a few drinks. As I walked over to the refrigerator to fill Jason's cup with more ice, I could hear the distinctive chat coming to complete silence. Everything seemed to be normal until I turned from the refrigerator and heard Sasha, Ma, and Mama Roswell scream—looking down I saw Jason on one knee, my heart melted, and I was completely flabbergasted! I admit, I didn't see this coming.

It was clear that on this day Jason had his very own plan in place. The way Sasha, Ma, and Mama Roswell started screaming, I could tell that they were just as shocked as I was. As Jason was on one knee, they all appeared around us right there in my kitchen. Trying to take in the moment, I watched Dad hand Jason a small box. Jason proceeded to open the box with an engagement ring in it. I was in such disbelief that I didn't hear him the first time he asked me to marry him. Jason asked again and I was so happy, I looked at Mama Roswell. She nodded her head to me with a smile on her face, as if she were telling me what my answer should be. I cried for about a minute before answering. Jason said, "So...?" to which I excitedly answered, "Yes!"

After the proposal, Jason give a heartfelt story of how he fell in love with me. He stated he knew the first time he saw me that he wanted to marry me, he went on to say that although the circumstances of Devin's request for him to take his place in my life was unusual, it solidified everything for him. Jason said he knew right then and there that God answered his prayers.

Here I was, engaged to be married for a second time. I was not going to mess this up. This was the exact gesture that would force me to completely close the door on my past, both good and bad, but there was one last thing I had to do.

When I arrived at the visiting area at the California Institution for Men, I knew I had no business there. Maybe I should have just written Valentino a letter. But there was no turning back now, he was already sitting at the table waiting for me, dressed in all blues, with the words "CDCR PRISONER" on the back of his shirt. Valentino's back was turned to me, the corrections officer pointed me to him. I don't know if he could sense my presence because as soon as I started to head in his direction, he turned around.

"Hey," I said, sitting down. I wanted to hug him, but I could tell they were strict on enforcing the no touch policy. As I walked in, I heard an old lady get reprimanded for moving a girl's hair out of her face—a girl most likely her granddaughter.

"Hey," he responded. I knew he was curious as to why I was there, and he was about to find out. "I have to admit, I was pretty surprised when my counselor called me into his office for a consent to visiting with you. I started to write you a letter, but I didn't have your address. Then I was going to call but wasn't sure if you'd accept the call. So, I decided to just wait for this day."

"Well, I'm happy you decided to see me although I feel completely manipulated. I want answers, Valentino. Why would you portray yourself to be someone you're not?"

"We can have this conversation, but I will not be judged by you. Especially when you're the one who wouldn't even talk to me after your sister busted down my door. Furthermore, you're lucky I'm here sitting with you. How do I know that you didn't set me up? Coming out of the blue and shit, with tissue at the cemetery. And why didn't you tell me that your sister was the DA?"

"The nerve of you, set you up? You are a convicted felon who was on the run for attempted murder after being out on a manslaughter charge. I felt sorry for you, I allowed myself to connect with you emotionally, only to find out that your wife and daughter died at your hands?"

"You watch your filthy mouth; never talk about them, ever."

The conversation between Valentino and me was getting heated. The guard walked over and asked if everything was okay. Once we both conceded that it was, he walked away, reminding us to keep it down.

"I know you're upset and without question, but obviously you came here for answers you said, right? And I'm willing to answer them but like I said I won't be judged by you, especially when you don't know the truth. You have to be willing to forget what you think you know and hear the truth from the horse's mouth. Otherwise, if you're here to give me some lecture based on your own personal conclusions, then you can get up and leave now because I don't need to hear it."

I sat there in silence for a moment. He was right. I didn't give him a chance to explain. Hell, I didn't have a chance to. One minute he was getting ready to bring to life every lewd sexual fantasy

I had, completely exposing my salacious side. And the next minute he was buck naked, gun in hand, ready to go to war with the cops. Complete and utter mayhem. Up until now every thought I had about this situation had derived from the story I heard from Sasha--a story that was God awful. Apparently, Valentino is the person who killed his wife and daughter, the same wife and daughter he was crying uncontrollably over in the cemetery the day we met. And if that's not enough, the attempted murder he was arrested on was for attempting to murder his wife's brother. I asked myself, was this guy some type of psychopath? We were about to find out how crazy psycho-Michael really was once he spilled his guts. Because I was definitely about to be all up in his business.

"I'm all ears, Valentino, go ahead."

"I have one question before I do: how do I know that I can trust you? What if you're here working for your sister trying to help her build a better case."

"Seriously, stop it with that. First of all, I had no idea about you, your past or your present. I sure as hell didn't know that I would eventually become a part of your future. Valentino, I trusted you. I poured out my heart to you. I was ready to throw away the relationship I was in just to see where you and I could end up. Only to find out that I could have ended up behind bars too for aiding a fugitive. Let's not forget the fact that you pursued me. So, don't ever again question my loyalty because whether I like how things ended or not, I'm still here trying to end things on a better note."

"I can respect that. I get it that you thought we had some type of connection, and I take part ownership in that, but we barely know each other. You can't be so quick to paint people into your picture."

"Now who's giving the lecture?"

Valentino put his head down with slight embarrassment. When he lifted it back up there was a grin on his face which helped to clear the air.

"Look," he began, "what I'm about to tell you is not easy for me. You're asking me to re-live one of the most detrimental events of my life. But I'm not a complete asshole and I think you deserve to know the truth."

"Thank you, and like I said I'm all ears."

"The night my wife and daughter died, is the same night I found out that my wife's brother tried to take our daughter's innocence. The bastard tried to molest my baby girl. I wanted to rip his head off his body. I was angry and filled with rage. A part of me felt like I failed to protect my family, my daughter. I had an obligation to her as her father, and I failed. My wife wanted to file a police report and handle things the "right" way--it was so like her. Every time I looked at my daughter while we were waiting for the police to show up and take the report, all I could think about was how that bastard violated her. I felt compelled to take matters into my own hands, what father wouldn't? My wife tried calming me down. I made myself a drink and once I started drinking, I didn't stop. I went on a binge. It took the cops eight hours, eight fucking hours to get to our house. When they asked to do a rape kit on my baby girl, violating her all over again, it was a wrap. I grabbed my keys and told my wife I was just going to go and talk to him. She didn't believe me and insisted on going with me, to make sure I didn't do anything stupid and so she could drive, because clearly I was drunk."

I was dumfounded and stammering. "Valentino, I'm so sorry, you don't have to explain anymore."

"No, I do, you came all this way and since I've already started, I have to finish. Closure, right?"

"Go ahead."

"It was late, and my wife always had a problem falling asleep while driving. We were ten minutes from her brother's place. And because she started falling asleep, we switched seats, I felt okay to drive at that point. It was a while since I drank my last drink, and I felt like my high was coming down. Five minutes into me driving there was some type of hazard in the road, I swerved, lost control of the car and went off the side of the freeway. When cops and first responders arrived on the scene, I was passed out. They took me to the hospital, and when they tested my blood alcohol level, it was twice the legal limit. Once I came to, my hands were handcuffed to the bed and read my Miranda rights. The charges were vehicular manslaughter while intoxicated. I was charged twice for killing my wife and daughter."

"Oh my God."

"Sad part is the cop who was at the hospital waiting for me to come to, was the same cop who was at my house earlier and took the report for our daughter. He tried to testify on my behalf but obviously it didn't work. That's not a story you just go around telling and having drinks over you know. And it's definitely not a story that you want to keep reliving, so I didn't feel like I needed to disclose everything to you."

"Why didn't you ask the judge for leniency?"

"I woke up in the hospital, handcuffed to the bed, and the first face I saw was a cop who was there to tell me that my wife and daughter were dead, and I killed them. I went to a very dark place after that. I was never going to see them again, ever. Not even at their funerals. I did not speak to anyone for months, not even my lawyer. I had nothing left to live for. I failed my family not once but twice. I took the cards that were handed to me and let guilt and shame eat me alive for seven years. It was not until my eighth year of being in this place that I started attending self-help groups, trying to rehabilitate. I mean there I was ready to kill her brother for trying to take her innocence and I took her life; the weight fell heavier on me."

"Valentino, it was not your fault, you didn't intend on taking their lives."

"I thought about it the entire time that I was locked up. I knew that when I got out, I was going to pay him a visit. I promised myself that he and I were going to have a real man-to-man conversation—while I beat the living daylights out of him."

I could see the rage in Valentino's eyes, it's as if he was right there in the moment all over again. The veins in his neck were starting to pop out.

He continued, "A month after I got out, I went to see him, initially I only went to talk to him. I felt like I was really rehabilitated and strong enough to face him without harming him. I just wanted to know what his logic was, why he would do something like that, and to his niece. When I arrived at the house, my mother-in-law let me in, the last time she saw me was in court where I was completely torn apart in handcuffs and shackles. She embraced me with a hug. You know she never blamed me for my wife and daughter's death. She wrote me every single week. Made sure I had money on my books and sent a pastor here monthly to pray with me and make sure I stayed sane. I asked myself if it was her guilty conscience for raising a child molester for a son. But eventually I let the thought go because it served me no real purpose and I accepted the better fact that maybe she was doing right by her daughter and caring for her husband in her absence. I learned the power of living in light instead of darkness."

"What do you mean by that?" I asked.

"I'll explain more about that later but let me finish. There I was in the house; within five minutes I could feel my adrenaline starting to rise. When I walked into the bedroom where he was, it was if he had seen a ghost. I tried to tell him that I was just there to talk to him, but I guess he was scared shitless because he pulled out a gun on me. I told him to put the gun away and stop pointing it at me, but he didn't. He started yelling, I tried taking the gun away from him, we struggled, and it went off. I ran because I knew I was coming back here; I was on parole and I had just shot a man. I didn't even stay to see if he was alive or dead."

"Valentino, it could have been self-defense, you shouldn't have run."

"You don't get it; I should have never stepped foot into that house. I knew five minutes after being there that I should not have stepped foot into that house. I knew one wrong move and I would end up right back here with these bracelets back on me," Valentino said, lifting up his wrist.

I could tell that nothing I said was going to get through to Valentino.

"You see LD, a man like me is not someone you need in your life. This is my reality; you still have a chance to change yours. So, stop blaming yourself for your husband's death and move on."

"You think you know me so well, Valentino? I am moving on."

"Then why are you here? You do not survive prison by not learning how to read people. This place keeps you on your toes. You have to stay woke, or someone will have you taking a dirt nap. Get me?"

"I just came here for closure. I wanted to know the truth of who you really are."

"Does it matter? Look where I am at and think about where you are going? We were just two people who met during a time that we needed each other's shoulder to lean on. We did not share a connection, we shared similar experiences. And everything else we engaged in just helped us both fill those voids. Why do you need validation on everything anyway?" he asked. "The only person that will ever have my heart is my wife. I think about her and our daughter every day. Even if I was not in here, we live two totally different lifestyles."

Valentino was colder than ice, I guess if I lived his life the space where my heart was meant to be, would be hallow too.

"Valentino don't flatter yourself. I was never looking to start a life with you. Nor had I ever thought about taking your wife's place, so I don't know where that comment came from about her being the only woman for you. I told you, I just wanted closure."

"Do me a favor and never come back here again," Valentino said, standing up. "It was fun while it lasted but every good thing comes to an end. I got to go; it's almost count time."

Valentino walked away and I knew that I would never see or talk to him again.

Relief was not the only thing I felt when I closed the door between Valentino and me. Initially I felt uneasy at the thought of keeping something like me going to visit Valentino in prison, from Jason. But on the flip side of things, it was for the best.

Chapter Twenty-One

*I*f time is the father of truth, then patience must be his son. That is something I never possessed, patience. Patience forces you to keep your eyes open and your mouth shut. Dominating the very existence of strength and focus. You see, with strength comes the will power to focus on what really matters. Because the truth was, well my truth at least, was no matter what I said to Devin or what I did with Sage; the truth was always going to be revealed in the end.

I thought that if I paid attention to everything, observed, and drew my own conclusions, that the truth would reveal itself but paying attention to everything just revealed who I was. And to what lengths I was willing to go, to get what I wanted. My reaction to the things I thought I had found out, exposed my true colors like darkness to light. Yes, darkness to light, I did some things I wasn't proud of. The irony is, this is where my true healing process started. Living my life, driven by chasing assumption after assumption, making bad decisions after revealing circumstances, only to be led down the road to where my true destiny waited for me. This occurred right before I almost made the wrong turn onto Self-destruction Lane.

Although Devin's death and how we spent his final dying days will always be a chain of events that will forever speak to my soul, the fact would still remain that everything he did was a true testament to how much he really loved me. The love we shared while he was alive made him the love of my life, the man he found for me preceding his death, Jason; was my soul mate.

If I'm being honest, and, again, these days I am and you were to tell me that the love of my life and my soul mate were two different people, I would have judged you and argued you down on how they were one and the same. But there is this thing called experience, and damn it's the best teacher. It makes you wise and sets you straight at the same time.

Pulling up to Living Waters Church in Christ, I was nervous. I was about to sit down with Pastor Sheila Sagway. Pastor Sheila was known for her healing capabilities: mental and emotional being her areas of expertise. I needed help in both areas. There are just some things that call for an entirely different level of help. Pastor Sheila's techniques were unlike anything I had ever experienced before.

Usually when I went to church in my desperate times of need, the pastor would pray over me and tell me to continue to pray and trust God.

Pastor Sheila was hands-on and in the trenches with you. She fasted and prayed with you, you had acts of faith that you need to exercise and show God just how serious you were on your journey to victory and breakthrough. With Pastor Sheila, it was not a one-day thing.

She showed me how to pray in the Spirit and how to seclude myself in order to really hear God's voice. She completely helped me to turn my religious relationship with God into a spiritual one.

This was our last day together, when we would discuss everything that had transpired and, together with new divine knowledge and wisdom, all truths laid out on the front line, and with my renewed mind and pure heart, we were going to finally lay to rest my past, coming to divine mental and emotional healing.

I was truly ready to fully welcome my rebirth. But there was one thing I had not shared with her yet. The one secret that I told no one but Ma. The secret I was carrying around for the last five months since the doctor's office.

My pregnancy.

Finding out that I was pregnant in Dr. Salvache's office that day, transformed me. The news changed my entire existence. Initially I was in denial, I didn't know if I was crying tears of joy or tears of shame for having a child out of wedlock. The one-time Jason and I had sex, was all it took. This baby was meant to be here. I was meant to be a mother.

But during this entire time, I couldn't help but ask why it never happened with Devin. Devin and I tried so many times to have a baby. My OB/GYN at the time confirmed what the doctors in the earlier years told me, that I would never be able to conceive.

I believed what I was told, I just knew that I was being punished for having an abortion. I had even convinced myself that I did not deserve to be a mother because of my selfishness. I mean I made a mistake and because of that mistake I deemed my baby a mistake and got rid of it. I felt truly unworthy.

"I'm happy that you decided to tell me; I'm not here to judge you. There's nothing to judge, God has performed a miracle in your life. Congratulations!"

I gave a peculiar look, "Miracle, but I'm not..."

"You're not what, married? Chile, our God works in mysterious ways, and he is limitless. He isn't bound by the rules that religion sets forth. Our God is the alpha and the omega. His word is truth. Now his word says in Ephesians 3:20, he is able to do exceedingly abundant above all that we ask or think, according to the power that works in us. You imagined a new life with Jason, you got that and *then* some, a new baby. This baby will help your legacy live, that is where the abundance comes in. LD, your latter days are becoming better than your former days; that's one of God's promises. So, forget about everything in your past, God is doing a new thing. Receive it.

"I never looked at it like that before."

"Yes honey, your setback, was a set-up for your comeback. Now stand tall and let's kick the enemy in the face for trying to steal your joy about this baby. This baby goes deeper than just being a miracle. This baby is going to set the tone for generations to come, your family lineage. Your parents paved the way and it's only right for you to keep it going. Your family blood line deserves abundance, prosperity, the gift of divine love. Yes, you faced some difficult times, but you were never alone. God has been with you every step of the way, guiding your footsteps."

Everything that Pastor Sagway was putting into perspective was making sense. I'd let fear, anxiety, and worry set in and cloud my judgment about what was really going on.

"Pastor Sagway, I just knew that God was punishing me. I had an abortion in college, I knew it was wrong, but I was trying to cover up..."

"LD, stop. Listen, God sent his only begotten Son so that you can have life and have it more abundantly, he came so none shall perish. Which means you are redeemed from the curse of the law. You are forgiven and set free. God's mercy, forgiveness, and grace is new every day. The moment you ask for forgiveness, not only are you forgiven, but it's also forgotten. We weren't meant to be perfect; if we were perfect beings, what room would that leave the Almighty God to work in our lives? Jesus Christ does not walk the earth anymore, that's where the Holy Spirit comes in. Those who choose to follow God and allow him to use them with his Spirit are filled with the Holy Spirit and become ministering spirits. Whether it be by financial service, emotional support, counseling, and I can go on, assignments are given, and people are chosen to do the work of the Lord. Problem is that many people haven't discovered that they are co-creators with the man himself. And the purpose for co-creating with God is for his kingdom."

"Pastor Sagway, I'm speechless. I have never ever had things explained to me this way. I mean all this time I thought we were just supposed to go to church, do good in our daily lives and help where we could, and be good citizens; but what it sounds like you're saying is that it goes deeper than that."

"LD, you think Roswell Cancer Center was just a dream Devin came up with because he was dying and wanted to do something good? No. That Center is God-sent. You are changing lives, you and Jason. God knew exactly who to put together to bring that Center into fruition. You and Jason both lost the love of your lives to cancer, which means your passion for that Center will be driven by love, one of the most powerful energetic forces on Earth."

"I just thought that Devin didn't want me to be alone and wanted to make sure that I was with a stand-up guy."

"Nothing is a coincidence in this life. Nothing happens by chance. Yes, you lost Devin and not that he's irreplaceable, but, honey, God never takes something away without replacing it. You lost Devin and the life you built together at the time, but you gained Jason and ascended into an entirely different level of life. You went from selling commercial real estate to running a lifesaving, hope-giving, world-renowned Cancer Treatment Center. You are going from widow to wife of one of the top oncologists in the state of California, and now you're having his firstborn child, and judging from the shape of your belly that you've been trying to hide, it's a girl. LD, you have truly been given beauty for ashes. God has made you whole again."

My soul had been set free. I no longer felt bound by unworthiness, guilt, shame, or hopelessness. God knew the plan he had for me this entire time. His plan was never to hurt me or punish me. But his plan was to prosper me, his plan was to give me hope and a future. And now with the birth of the new baby coming, our future would go on for generations to come. I was literally walking in the truth of God's Word, Jeremiah 29:11 was centered around my new life.

I left Pastor Sagway feeling electrified. I literally felt like my life had an entirely new meaning. God had a bigger plan for my life. That was the TRUTH all along. I experienced a revelation when my life took an unexpected turn of enduring a divorce or what I thought was a divorce, good was really redirecting my steps for something better. I was taken from ordinary to extraordinary.

Sasha's baby shower was set to start in three hours. I headed to Ma and Dad's to finish helping with last minute set-ups. I knew I needed to tell Jason about the baby, I did not know how he would take being left in the dark but what I did know beyond a shadow of a doubt was that we could get through anything. One thing I knew about my man was that he was understanding.

"Hey Ma," I said walking out onto the patio. Jason was standing over by the pool. When he saw me his eyes and smile lit up like fireworks on the 4th of July. My smile back to him had a sense of relief behind it. Today was also the day that I was going to let him in on the fact that he was going to be a father. I was more excited than nervous.

"Hey honey, all we need to do is finish setting up the dessert table, put out a few more chairs and then get ready and we are all done." Ma informed me.

"Ma, thank you."

"Thank you for what, honey? I would do anything for you and Sasha. You know that."

"No, thank you for helping me get through this. I was apprehensive about being a mother before but I'm all in now and I'm ready to be the best mother I can be. Will you teach me everything you know?"

"Of course, but I think you're not the only one who's ready to set out to be all that you can be as a parent."

"I know, Sasha will be a great mother too."

"No honey, I'm talking about Jason. Judging by the way he's looking at you, he knows."

I turned around to see what Ma was talking about and Jason wouldn't stop staring at me.

He yelled from across the patio, "Are you going to keep checking me out or are you going to come over here and greet me the right way; with a kiss and hug?"

I smiled and headed in his direction.

When I got over to him, I kissed him passionately and this time I embraced him fully without trying to hide my baby bump.

Jason let me go and looked into my eyes and said, "LD, I'm so in love with you, you're going to be a great mother."

"Wait, what, how did you know?"

"Your fiancé' is one of the top oncologists in the state, I know when a woman is with child, especially my woman."

"You're not mad at me for hiding it from you?"

"You mean trying to hide it. No, I knew that you needed time to process what was happening. You spent your entire adult life thinking you were unable to bear children. LD, you've been through a lot, I'm patient, gorgeous. I know that things take time. But promise me from this moment forward you won't try and hide anything else from me. Let's start with a clean slate."

"Agreed."

As I hugged Jason, I looked up at the clear skies filled with beautiful clouds. I smiled, feeling Devin's presence surrounding me. Devin was my angel in disguise and my angel on earth while we were married. He was the love of my life who slowed me down enough to meet my soul mate. I mouthed, "Thank you, Devin, I love you," as I looked up to the sky.

In four months, Jason and I would welcome our baby girl. And we will call her Devin.

Glory be to God.

-Jeremiah 29:11

CPSIA information can be obtained
at www.ICGtesting.com
Printed in the USA
LVHW081310011221
PP17045000009B/36